CREMONA HOUSE

An Italian Migration Journey: 1905-1950

Laura Di Martino

First published 2024 by KLMN Publications
Email: lauradimartino.author@gmail.com
Socials: https://linktr.ee/lauradimartino
ISBN: 978-0-975 6214-0-0 (paperback)
ISBN: 978-0-975 6214-1-7 (ebook)

Cover Illustration: Mariel Kempt
Text typesetting: David Bradbury (www.dbtype.com.au)
Printed and bound in Australia by Griffin Press

To Nick and Mariel

For giving me the space to dream

Table of Contents

Ossolaro, Provincia di Cremona, Lombardia, Italia

"Sit still Carlino, or you'll be leaving without your ears," whines Nonna as she trims my hair in our warm kitchen. I've just emerged from my bath in the old tin tub. Clothed only in an old nightshirt, I hug my knees and resign myself to this next torture. From outside, I can hear my younger siblings and my cousins frolicking in the new snowfall, but mamma insists I remain by her side so she can 'fix my face into her memory' on my last day in her home. She's being brisk and overly happy for me, but when she thinks I'm not looking, her eyes are downcast and chin trembles. I should be sad too, I suppose, but I can't help my jubilation. After all, my boyhood dreams are about to come true.

As soon as Nonna finishes, I jump up and launch into an energetic sea shanty. Grabbing Nonna's waist, I waltz her around the table, reach out for mamma's apron along the way, and pull her and my little sister Maria into a joyous dance. The baby, Nino, perched in his wooden cot, gurgles with glee, holding up his hands to be included in the parade.

Finally, I'm released to go upstairs to get dressed. On the way, I hear Nonna doling out advice.

"It's no use crying Leonilda, it is what it is. Your brother will do right by him."

Life in our little farm complex outside of Cremona is changing. Our centuries-old way of life is disappearing. The noble family who owns our *cascina*, the house and land complex which we and nine other families have leased as a co-operative for generations, are no longer interested in investing in outdated agricultural practices. There's better money to be made in train networks and industrial factories.

Last week, Zio Carlo, mamma's older brother, captain of an Italian Merchant Marine cargo ship, left his ship at the port of Genova and travelled by train to Cremona, as he has done many times before to celebrate Christmas with us. This time, he had also come to offer me the position of Assistant Purser aboard his ship. I am only fourteen, but the right age for this opportunity. Given my youth, my parents are naturally hesitant. My eldest brother, Federico, left when he was eighteen to do his obligatory four-year military service and Giuseppe was sent off to Australia, last year, just after his own eighteenth birthday.

"We'd been hoping to hold on to this one a little longer," said my mother. Even if he doesn't have a future on the farm, Padre Rodolfo says he has the intelligence to continue his studies at the Monastery. He doesn't have to choose whether he'll enter the priesthood until he's eighteen."

"And what then?" my uncle replies. "You won't be able to afford to send him to university, so knowing his Greek and Latin will be pointless if he doesn't enter the priesthood."

"Trust me Leonilda," he insists, "the boy is quick on his feet, he has an agile mind with a strong mechanical bent. He's calm and observant – just the right sort of lad for life on a ship. Once he passes his Purser's Exams, he'll be able to get a position on the long-haul cargo ships or the passenger liners making the transatlantic crossing, where he'll earn wages unheard of in this village."

With my chin cupped in my hands, my elbows resting on the edge of the table, I look from one to the other, waiting for them to make the final decision. I know better than to disrespect my elders by interrupting the discussion with my own opinions, but eventually, after many nights of similar discussions, my father turns his intense eyes on me.

"Well son, what's your choice? Stay here and continue your studies, and maybe become a priest, or go off with your Zio Carlo, to make your life at sea?"

Sitting up straight, with my hands gripping my seat, I look squarely at my mother, because she's the one who needs convincing. I make my choice known very clearly.

"I'm not interested one bit in becoming a priest."

My father winks at me and extends his hand to my uncle.

"I only have one more question," says my father. "What about this Purser's Examination you want him to take? How much do we need to put aside for that?"

"He can't sit for that until he's twenty-two, so there's plenty of time ahead," reassures Zio Carlo. "And you don't need to worry Giovanni, I'll see to putting funds away for when the time is right."

* * *

"Ciao, Ciao" I yell, swaying my woollen beret in wide arcs above my head from my perch on papà's cart.

Mamma, Nonna, my siblings, my cousins and their parents are all crowded at the gate, waving Zio Carlo and I off.

"Don't forget to write," yells Mamma, her big white handkerchief held up to her eyes.

"Remember your prayers," adds Nonna, juggling the wriggling Nino in her arms.

I turn to my uncle. "What are they so worried about, we'll be back at Christmas, won't we?"

He reassures me with a wink. We both make our last wave as the cart turns onto the main road to Cremona.

Once we are finally on the train, rattling towards Milano, I let my uncle snooze as the flat landscape of fields and the river valley pass by. This is my first time on a train, and the speed is exhilarating even though my stomach hasn't made up its mind yet. We are in an enclosed second-class cabin that seats six, with gleaming wooden benches, but are alone for the moment. I pull the canvas rucksack down from the overhead shelf, into which Mamma has arranged a spare set of underwear and the parting gifts I received last night. As soon as I open the drawstring bag, I smell the peppery odour of the soft linen sachet filled with lavender soap made by Zia Teresina. Tied into Zia Matilda's handkerchief, embroidered with swooping swallows, are a good fistful of almonds. I count out five to nibble on. There's also a precious orange, come all the way from sunny Sicily. I'll save that to share with Zio Carlo when he wakes. The thick slice of Provolone cheese wrapped in vine leaves will keep for longer, especially if I tuck it into the beaten copper bowl and spoon, with my initials stamped on them, received from Zia Olivia and Zio Angelo, my godparents.

Zio Luigi, papà's brother, repaired and polished a pair of sturdy leather boots that I am currently wearing. They are a little big, but he stuffed the toes with some soft woollen wadding. In my trouser pocket, I feel for the pen knife papà bought me. My younger brother Armando was quite jealous when he saw it, though he pretended not to care. Last of all, from my shirt pocket, I pull out the soft linen frame Nonna has sewn for me with the picture and prayer of Saint Nicholas, protector of sailors. I give the saintly image a firm kiss, for insurance, before slipping it back into my shirt pocket.

My rituals completed, I stuff the bag between my head and the window, finally ready for my own snooze. My dreams take me far away, into swashbuckling adventures, pirate ships and deserted coves. Even though I've had years of listening to my uncle's stories, and I know that his life aboard ship is probably more boring than in my imagination, I can't help my excitement. Zio Carlo has promised that if I work hard, I'll be able to see the world. I can't believe the adventure has finally begun.

Once in Milano, we stop at the railway station dining room for a sustaining bowl of creamy, fragrant risotto studded with bitter wild greens. We finish our meal with a small tumbler of sweet wine and an aniseed biscuit before Zio Carlo hurries me to the Genova train for the final leg of our journey to the port.

Ship ahoy!

Staring up at the enormous funnel painted in large bands of black, red and white poking high into the clouds, I feel my chest tighten. Zio Carlo leaps onto the swaying gangplank, and in a few quick steps, lands on the main deck.

I brazenly attempt to mimic him, but a gust of wind shakes the rickety, wooden gangplank violently, threatening to topple me into the murky chasm between the side of the ship and the edge of the dock. With Zio Carlo's throaty laugh ringing in my ears, a surge of adrenalin propels me forward, and tightening my hold on the wobbly handrails, I clumsily clamber to the main deck. A slap on the shoulder from Zio Carlo confirms I've done the right thing.

Inhaling deeply to steady my breathing, I glimpse a man dressed in a navy suit with a neat short barrel cap descending from the bridge above us, and three more arrive from the hold, wearing navy trousers and navy knitted sweaters with pom-pom berets on their heads.

"*Capitano*," salutes the one with the barrel cap.

Both men quickly lean into each other for a handshake and then a kiss on each cheek. Zio Carlo turns towards the men and accepts their salutes, before signalling them to stand at ease.

He beckons for me to come closer to him.

"Men, this is my nephew and my namesake."

The three men from the hold, slip off their berets and welcome me aboard, energetically pumping my hand while giving me their names, or rather their nicknames – *Bubo*, for the one whose big, half-shuttered, round eyes, really do give him an owlish appearance, *Matton*, for the stocky, square fellow built like a brick and *Francese*, who's throaty rrrrs immediately mark him out as a foreigner. Then Zio turns me around to face the other man.

"This is Gianni, our Engineer, and my friend since we were your age."

I take off my felt cap and shake the hand extended to me, my gaze transfixed by the shiny metal buttons of his double-breasted jacket.

"I've heard so much about you," he says in a rounded, melodic voice, quite different to the accent of my region.

I look up into a pair of warm hazel eyes winking mischievously at me.

"I've a ton of stories to tell you about this one," he rasps, jerking his thumb in my uncle's direction.

"Don't believe a word that comes out of his mouth, all exaggerations, I can guarantee that. But, on the other hand, Gianni handles a flute very well, so you and your fiddle should get on famously with this rogue.'

Gianni's eyes move to my back where my kitbag and violin are firmly held via thick straps criss-crossed against my chest.

"We'll have plenty of time for music and getting to know each other once we leave port," confides Gianni, flinging his arm around my shoulder and drawing me in for a welcoming hug. My uncle assigns

Bubo to take me on a tour of the ship.

On the bottom deck, there is a hold filled with the coal needed to power the steam engine next to it. Another hold is lined with an intricate zig zag of metal tubes and packed with six large, steel-lidded vats. Bubo proudly explains that the steam engine also powers a generator which keeps this room refrigerated, for the transport of perishable goods.

"I don't know what your uncle has told you, but the SS Duchessa di Genova plies the route between Genova and Liverpool, offloading cheese and grains from the Lombardy plains at the British colony of Gibraltar, in exchange for Mediterranean Tuna for the Liverpool canneries."

The deck above this has more space for other cargo and also quarters and messes at either end for the crew, which are nothing more than slim little cubby holes. Each sailor has a lockable metal box in which to keep his kit bag and a few personal effects. The mess has a long metal table and at the end, a narrow steel ladder leads to the galley on the deck above. I'd always been embarrassed by my short, thin frame, but here I can see that it will be an asset for me when moving around the confined spaces.

The next level up has more substantial cabins, four along each side of a narrow corridor, with room at either end for two larger cabins, one for the first mate, and the other one for the chief engineer. The eight single cabins in the middle are for the passengers. I can't help stepping inside to get a closer look at the wall-mounted electric lamp over the little desk in one of the cabins, amusing myself with turning the switch on and off. The only place I've seen electricity before is in the Cremona Town Hall. Bubo chuckles when I flick it on and off several more times.

At the very top of the ship, in front of the enormous funnel, is a substantial hut-like structure. Here, Bubo leads me through a passenger's saloon and dining area, which open up to a narrow balcony.

The saloon is set out like a railway car, with plush, green velvet-covered cushions attached to ornately carved wooden benches arranged either side of narrow tables. I glimpse a bar with liquor bottles secured behind a key-bolted cage.

We make our way from the saloon into a dining room. A simple affair with a long, beautifully polished table and ten tall-backed upholstered chairs.

"Why are there so many hooks on the wall?" I ask Bubo.

"They're so we can store the chairs safely during rough weather."

"*Toh*," I exclaim, impressed by the simple ingenuity of this solution.

Above this is the captain's cabin, and next to it, the navigation room with its wide windows looking out to sea, from which I can peer down onto the top deck, where the crane-like derricks, used to winch cargo from the docks and drop it into the hatches sit waiting like stick insects. There is all manner of rigging and ropes, including sails, in case the steam-powered generator fails. Readjusting my backpack and violin case, I sigh:

"It's so much bigger than I ever imagined."

"Don't you worry lad, we'll look after you," says Bubo, giving me a friendly pat on the back. "By the end of the year, you'll be as knowledgeable as anyone else on board. Anyway, you'll be mostly confined to working in the saloon and dining room to start with. All you need to know is how to get from those spaces to the kitchen and back in the first few weeks."

Over the next couple of days, I accompany my uncle from early morning to late at night. First, a visit to the offices of Credito Italiano, to open an account into which my monthly pay will be deposited, and which my father can access. Next, a visit to the head office of the shipping company, Navigazione Generale Italiana, to arrange for travel papers and to give them the details of my new bank account.

I am also scheduled for a medical examination by a local doctor. My eyes start twitching when the doctor asks if he can proceed with the mandatory venereal disease talk. My uncle gallantly offers to wait for me at the café across the road.

I can't make my escape quickly enough, nodding vigorously when Zio Carlo suggests that surviving the Dr. Barberini lecture deserves a hot chocolate and a taste of Genova's famous chocolate and nuts *pandolce*, typical of the festive season. After seeing me wolf those down, Zio Carlo orders me a *farinata* from a street vendor, which I discover is a thin dough of toasted chickpea flour, slowly roasted in a pan set on an open fire, tangy from the herbaceous Ligurian olive oil. The vendor shows me how to roll up the thin rectangular slices into little cigars for easier consumption. There's no need for my uncle's proffered handkerchief, I do a neat job of licking my fingers clean.

We also visit company warehouses where Zio Carlo inspects the merchandise allocated to his ship and arranges to have various bundles delivered.

"Our passengers are mostly British and German merchants. If the weather is good, I invite them to dine at the captain's table in the dining room, rather than in their own rooms or the saloon, as I've found that it's a good way to practise my English and German, and also learn important information about which trade goods are in demand. This way, I can continue to make good profits for the company and keep my position on this relatively safe route."

Once we are back on the streets outside the warehouse, Zio Carlo whisperingly admits that he has learned to keep his ears open during these dinner conversations for opportunities to do a little trading of his own.

"Usually small amounts," he whispers, "nothing too noticeable, just enough to bring in some extra coinage. Learn to keep your wits about you Carlino, and in time, I'll teach you to speculate some of your earnings for a little extra profit. But be wary, because many a sailor has lost all his money on foolish purchases, because he hadn't understood the market well enough, or had followed the advice of some braggart in a tavern, skilled at fleecing the witless."

I was firmly advised that conversations about this topic were to be kept strictly between the two of us.

"I try to discourage the crew from speculating, as it makes for desperate men who are easily distracted on the job," he said. "To do this, I use some of my personal profits to provide them good food on board, with a dose of fine *grappa* on Sunday nights. Plus I slip them a few extra coins for their families when they take their annual leave. In this way," he said, tapping his index finger to the side of his nose, "I maintain a regular and loyal crew."

One of my favourite days in that first week away from home was a visit to a mariner's outfitter to procure a uniform, a pair of gumboots with good, gripping soles, and a long oilskin jacket and broad-brimmed hat to protect my clothes against wet weather. Zio Carlo also ordered me a black suit, with two white shirts with collars, which I am to wear when serving dinner at the captain's table or for accompanying him to important meetings.

Next we stopped at a stationer for some paper, ink and a pen with a few spare nibs so that I can keep my promise to write to my mother. Finally, there is a visit to a compounding pharmacy for some lemon-honey balls on which to suck should anyone develop a sore throat, compounded clove pellets for toothache and liquorice bark sticks to relieve stomach pains. Zio Carlo bought himself tooth powders and spare toothbrushes, some soaps and razor blades and some lemony scented eau de toilette.

At the end of the day, I found a paper bag on my bunk with my name inscribed in a flowing script. It contained some tooth powder, a toothbrush, a comb, a razor, some soap, and a hand towel. I felt so grown up at the sight of these little luxuries and was even more eager to do my best to repay Zio's kindness in the months and years ahead.

I had not really had time to miss my family yet, but the sight of the writing paper reminded me of them, and I wished I could have shared my good fortune. I promised myself that this very evening, I would begin a letter to send off before we set sail at the end of the week. I puffed out my chest, imagining the look of jealousy on my cousins' faces when they heard my news, but I was swift to remind myself that I was luckier than most to have such good connections through my mother's family. I imagined myself returning as an older man, dressed in the finest Milanese suit, with pockets full of money and stories of adventures across the world with which to regale them all. It was at this point, even before we had set sail that I promised myself I would make my parents proud and do my utmost to help them get ahead in these uncertain times. I hoped that one day soon, I would have the ability to offer opportunities to my younger siblings, and anyone else in my family who needed help.

Dreams re-routed

Sitting at a desk in the room I now share with my twenty-four-year-old brother Giuseppe, whom I've always called Beppe, I need to write a letter to my parents to let them know I've arrived safely in Australia. The last letter I'd written, more than six months ago, had been from London. I had to let them know that our beloved Zio Carlo had succumbed to a massive heart attack en route. Our Engineer, Gianni, had insisted I come to stay with his family in London while funeral arrangements were made, and they had been very kind, sympathetic to my shock.

Gianni took great pains to discuss my future with me. In the last couple of years, Navigazione Generale Italiana had been moving away from the transport of perishable cargo over relatively short distances to concentrate on the long-haul passenger ships, especially those making the transatlantic crossing, filled with migrants for the growing American factories.

My uncle had set aside money for my Purser's exams with the Genova Marine Authority, but at nineteen, I was still too young to sit for them. Gianni had done his best to find me another position, but without my uncle's connections, my prospects were limited. Approaching his sixties, and with a wife and grown up children, Gianni had decided it was time to give up the sea, especially since the newspapers reported endlessly about the recent developments between Italy and Turkey over territorial claims in Libya. It was hard to determine the truth of the matter, though all aboard La Duchessa were alarmed at the thought the Italian Government was planning to go to war again.

"Surely, the defeat in Abyssinia in ninety-six taught the Italian Government that another African War would be futile," fumed Gianni.

"I'm worried for you Carlino. You may be recruited if you return to Italy. There's been talk that the Merchant Marine's ships could be commandeered for the war effort."

Then a letter had arrived from my parents, echoing these thoughts. They insisted that my best option would be to join my brother, Giuseppe, in Melbourne, Australia. Beppe's postcard with the single word *'vieni'*, exhorting me to come, hadn't filled me with much confidence. However, from Liverpool, it wasn't too hard to secure a steward's assistant position aboard a British passenger ship, so I resigned myself to making my way to Australia. After all, I'd said I wanted to see the world.

In the last two years, my parents' letters had been full of despair at the loss of their old life. All the cheap American grain and rice imports had destroyed all hope they could make any more than just subsistence living off the land. When I went home last year for Christmas, half of the families in the *cascina* had already left for better opportunities elsewhere.

I was relieved to hear that my oldest brother, Federico, had made some good contacts from his military service days and had already secured a position in a Milanese factory. His wife and son, and my parents and younger siblings were hoping to join him soon.

My brother Armando, at the age of fifteen, had been whisked off a few months earlier, to Mexico, by my father's cousin Camillo. My parents were worried that he might be forcibly conscripted into the projected war. Camillo, who had established a rope factory and a young family in Mexico City, had come back briefly to collect and resettle his own parents.

Even my sister Maria, now fourteen years of age, had been placed in service with the Bianchi family in Cremona. It was probably a good thing that darling Nonna had passed away last winter, she would have been so disappointed that Maria had been denied a glorious, traditional wedding. I finished my letter, promising that I would send money to Maria so that she could purchase writing paper and stamps to keep in touch with us all.

Beppe had been working in a factory run by my mother's cousin, whom we called Zio Roberto. I arrived in Melbourne at the height of summer, so Zio Roberto's Ice and Ice cream factory were in full operation to meet the needs of this busy, crowded city. Many of the workers were family members or locals, and nearly all were recent immigrants, almost all Italians. I was very surprised to have found another of my mother's relatives, Martino Bonetti, from Castelgrande, living a few doors down. Martino had a little cart for shoe repairs that he walked around the city, doing repairs in the alleys or on the footpaths. He was married with two rosy-cheeked children who attended the local school and who called me *zio* too, as a sign of respect.

Zio Roberto was very pleased that my English was of such a high standard. I silently thanked Roger, the British Chief Steward from my six years aboard *La Duchessa* who had trained me for meal service and spent his spare time schooling me. He was from London and had insisted that I learn both to read and write the language, as well as speak it.

From the beginning, Zio Roberto decided to send me out with his eldest son Bobby on his rounds to the various ice cream retailers. I watched and listened carefully. Bobby was a great salesman. He had an easy manner, and he rarely left an establishment without convincing the shop or restaurant owner to raise the quantity of their next order.

As well as selling to other retailers, Zio Roberto had a stall managed by his younger son Frank, in the eastern market on nearby Bourke Street, in addition to a fleet of hawkers to whom he leased wooden ice cream carts with jolly red and white awnings. The hawkers bought the ice cream from him and kept the money from whatever sales they made. I was impressed, understanding that there was little risk for Zio Roberto. It was the vendor who risked all if his ice cream didn't sell before it spoiled.

"By Australian law, ice cream must contain added cream in order to achieve a minimum of ten percent fat content," explained Bobby. I found that it sat heavier on the stomach than the fruit ices I had occasionally tasted in the summer in Italy, but this Australian ice cream was very smooth and creamy on the tongue.

The hawkers scooped out their ice cream into little wax coated cardboard cones, barely the size of a closed fist, which avoided the use of the glass penny-licks I'd seen in London, a sure source of disease if not properly washed. The inspectors of the Melbourne Municipal Authorities were always sniffing about making sure that the production facilities were clean and that the correct quantities of cream, milk and sugar were added to each batch. This was not such an easy feat because of the heavily populated zone in which the factory was situated, where some of the houses were rather dilapidated and there were still open sewers in the street.

Zio Roberto had admitted that a year ago, he'd been shut down for two weeks when mouse droppings had been found in the storage room where sugar was held. While he lost money on his ice cream enterprise for a couple of days, the ice making business which was on the other side of the road, was still able to function.

I shared some of the drawings I had made of the refrigeration system aboard ship and was rewarded with a great smile as Zio Roberto congratulated me on my fine technical drawings and my obvious interest in engineering. He suggested I talk to the engineers at the tram parts factory at the end of our street. They had been most helpful, encouraging me to sit in at lectures at the Mechanics Institute in Collins Street, which I could attend for a small annual fee. Beppe, who'd been working on the factory floor since his arrival seven years ago, teased me for my earnestness.

"Why don't you get out of that head of yours and join me for some fun?"

Beppe's idea of fun was the Gun Club, the Busy Bees Hotel after work, and to my alarm, Madam Dora's brothel once a month. I had not forgotten Dr. Barberini's venereal disease talk, or my Zio Carlo's warnings too, as there had been many times when the crew would arrive in port and some of them wanted to take me for an 'initiation'.

The other thing that shocked me, and that I carefully left out of letters to my parents, were the copious number of opium dens in our enclave of 'Little Lon'. These establishments were frequented by rich and poor, and the patrons who stumbled out of there, often in the early hours of the morning, frightened me to the core, especially the old men who looked like walking corpses. I chose to socialize within the family or at church-organised social functions where I could continue to practise my English.

Zio Roberto's second son, Frank, was my age and already a father himself. He hadn't married the mother of his child, as Zio Roberto did not approve of her, since she was not of Italian parentage. However, the family did support her and the child financially. She lived with her mother in the next street, so I had been introduced to her and her two-year-old boy who called Frank papa.

Beppe warned me off Frank, who seemed very carefree with his affections and was already keeping company with another girl.

"*Sentimi* Carlo, stay away from him. He likes to attract trouble, and since we're both foreigners here, we risk deportation if we're found to be involved in any unlawful matter."

I had noticed the heavy police presence around the city, especially in the zone where the National Parliament sat and where the headquarters of banks were situated. Over the next year, I established a routine for myself, starting work at 7.00 am and finishing around 3.00 pm, Monday to Saturday. After work, I sought out of some fresher air by strolling in one of the parks dotted around the city. On Sunday evenings, the extended family liked to gather in their little tree-studded back yards for shared meals, some card-playing and general gossip. I was always begged to play my violin, both the ancient folk tunes and the popular operatic arias and I happily obliged, letting the tedium of the work week fly away as I coaxed the music from my instrument.

The area was also very close to a number of theatres, and on Saturday nights, I hung about to watch the glamourous people come and go, occasionally catching a snatch of a tune to try to replicate on my violin. Melbourne had many Italian itinerant musicians whom I befriended, and Zia Mimi, my uncle's mother-in-law, with whom Beppe and I boarded, introduced me to one of her cousins who played in a respectable orchestra and who would let me know when they played in outdoor concerts. It seemed every park had its own bandstand, with elegant iron lacework decoration, and attendance was free.

In October 1911, when I received a letter from my mother, it was filled with political news. The Melbourne newspapers were right. Italy had declared war on the Ottoman Empire and the fighting had been very heavy in Libya in Northern Africa the previous October.

In Italy, the prospect of new colonies was welcomed by all those poor people who had been displaced off the land by changes in agricultural practices. Italy was bursting at the seams and desperately in need of new jobs to be created using modern industrial methods. Without these, emigration was the only solution. Other countries around her had managed to modernise their economies by having the good fortune of access to natural sources of coal. Many Italians had found themselves working in the coal mines of Wales, Belgium, France and Germany which provided fuel for the factories producing steel and textiles on an industrial scale. The British and French, with their colonies around the world, had access to raw materials and ready markets. But Italy, with its economic activity still entrenched in feudal agricultural practices, languished.

My parents were grateful that Federico, working at Pirelli, would be unlikely to be called to service, as the factory was considered an essential industry to support the war. My father confirmed that Beppe, Armando and I, had escaped in time. He explained how he walked past the Galleria Vittorio Emanuele where the daily newspapers were displayed under glass and watched the anguish on the mothers' faces as they searched the columns upon columns of names of the dead and wounded.

I was astounded to learn that while Italy, on the face of it, had outnumbered the Ottoman army by four to one, the Italian army had faced strong resistance. Italy had superior warfare technology in the form of modern, powerful armaments, armoured cars, heavily loaded warships with long-reaching guns, airplanes capable of dropping aerial bombs, and even the famous inventor, Guglielmo Marconi's telegraph, for communication between headquarters and the front line.

Still, because of a sustained guerrilla war, the Italian Army had been held not far from the shoreline, unable to make any real progress into the interior. In November 1911, an Italian brigade had been caught defenceless on the outskirts of Tripoli and five hundred troops were massacred. In retaliation, the Italian leaders had ordered the massacre of an equal number of local civilians innocently caught up in the skirmish. This news had turned both the Italians at home, and the international community, against the Italian government and military, creating a no-win situation.

The Socialists had managed to unite the other left leaning parties in a call for a cessation of support for the Nationalist Giolitti Government by declaring a National Strike in the same week that an attempt was made on the life of the King, Vittorio Emmanuelle II, who was celebrating fifty years of Italian Unification. Soon after, Italian troops were withdrawn. Instead of a gloriously triumphant return, the Italian military had been forced to limp home to lick its wounds, having managed to capture barely a few districts beyond the Libyan coast. The only news which aroused some pride in me was the news of the superiority of the Italian Navy in all its skirmishes, defending the Libyan coastline and also capturing twelve islands in the Aegean Sea, including the Ottoman stronghold of Rhodes. However, I was to learn later that in the Ouchy Treaty signed in Lausanne the following October, Italy was forced to surrender these islands.

What a waste of lives. I was naive about politics, but even I could see the futility of the war and the puffed-up, irrational dreams of the military and political leaders who had endorsed it.

"*Porca miseria*, our parents made the right decision sending us away." I told Beppe.

Beppe talked about the situation endlessly, mostly because it was his passion. He had loved hunting as a boy and was still fascinated by all manner of guns. He had joined a gun club in Melbourne and sometimes went out for what he called 'roo shooting'. A couple of the members of his club were ex-soldiers who had participated under the British flag in the Boer War in South Africa about ten years previously.

Politics, both at home and abroad, bored me. I kept up with the news in the newspapers and was often called upon to read out articles during our Sunday night gatherings for those who hadn't had my good fortune of an education, but I didn't really engage in it. I was just grateful that I had escaped being called up for military service and possibly had my life terminated in a senseless massacre.

After a year in Melbourne, Italy and Europe seemed so far away from me. I was nostalgic for the regularity of the old way of life on the farm, but I had left that behind eight years ago and I was a very different person to that fourteen-year-old boy who had only fanciful dreams to sustain him.

While I was very grateful to Zio Roberto for sponsoring me and teaching Beppe and I, the ins and outs of his operation, I soon realised, that as a hired hand, it would be difficult to accumulate any real wealth. During some general chit chat with Beppe one night, I raised my concerns, and much to my surprise, found he had been thinking about the possibility of branching out on his own in Geelong, an area he had often visited with his gun club. We agreed that the following Sunday, we would catch the ferry for the ninety minute journey, to have a good look around the port city, southwest of Melbourne.

Taking a leap

The summer season had been particularly hot and humid and the call for ice and ice cream in Melbourne had never been stronger. The supply of ice to households and businesses was firmly entrenched, and each sector of the city and suburbs had their own supplier. The pubs, butchers and dairies were now producing their own ice and installing cool rooms, and even the smallest corner grocers had introduced the use of ice chests in which to keep perishable goods. The newspapers, with their constant reporting of the dangers of harmful bacterium multiplying in the heat and haphazard storage conditions, fuelled the demand for cold storage.

But, at the Melbourne Institute, there was an exciting wind hinting at changing conditions. Cool rooms in ships had been able to successfully provide frozen shipment of meat and dairy to the UK for several decades. The word amongst engineering circles would be that soon, households would be able to install a machine small enough to cool their larders using the ammonia driven refrigeration machines invented in Geelong by Scotsman, James Harrison. New machines had been refined and were becoming smaller, safer and more efficient.

An incident, half-way through February, led Beppe and I to speed up our decision to branch out on our own in Geelong. After a particularly scorching and sultry week, Zio Roberto's market stand was closed down by health inspectors who claimed that they were acting on a report of unsanitary practices. It didn't take much digging to discover that a rival ice cream producer, by the name of O'Grady, had encouraged a journalist to publish the defamatory article, prompting the raid. This harassment from the newspapers was not new. Italians, and most non-British were seen as fair game for the most outrageous, unsubstantiated claims.

The inspectors left after several hours without finding anything, and Zio Roberto immediately contacted a lawyer who advised suing the rival for defamation. That evening, a group of us from the factory had all been sitting around shirtless in the privacy of Zia Mimi's backyard, trying to cool down after a long, hot day. Frank was making us feel even hotter, spitting vile threats against the O'Grady's. Zio Roberto kept urging him to calm down, claiming that the law would get them.

"Wait and see, when they lose the court case, the damage will cripple their business too," suggested Zio Roberto.

Frank was inconsolable and left without any of us being able to calm him down. Zio Roberto sent Bobby after him but the mood was sombre and the few people remaining soon left, leaving just Beppe, me and the two other boarders. We took refuge in our newly erected backyard sleepout, completely enclosed with gauze mesh to protect us from mosquito bites. In this way, we managed to pass a pleasant evening, playing a few hands of our favourite card game *Briscola* and telling each other tall tales, completely unaware of the drama which was unfolding just a few streets away.

Somehow, all the pasteurized milk stored in steel vats in the

O'Grady's cool room had been tampered with. Employees had arrived the next day to the sour smell of festering milk and fly swarms. We didn't see Frank for several days, but when we did, Frank was no longer angry, instead, he strutted about like a self-satisfied rooster, crowing about people getting their just desserts and the value of good connections.

I stole a glance at Beppe. He didn't know where to look either. We were horrified that Frank would resort to such extreme methods of revenge. Zio Roberto and Bobby were devasted, worried now that they would be subjected to more retaliation and their loss of face in the community, as naturally, the event had made headlines in all the city papers. But worse, of course, were the suspicions of the police who had been to Zio Roberto's factory to question both management and employees. Zio Roberto suggested Frank take some time off to visit family acquaintances in Sydney for a few months, until the disgrace had been forgotten and the police had been placated. Feigning ignorance of the matter, Frank had refused to leave Melbourne, claiming friends in high places who would not let anything happen to him.

Beppe and I decided that we'd rather not get mixed up with these friends, having both been out with Frank, and well aware of the seedy nature of his connections. By the beginning of March, we had firmly settled on Geelong, a prosperous coastal town that had a few small ice cream manufacturers in cafés and confectionery shops, but no commercial factory. Transport connections through sail and train were excellent, it had recently opened a telephone exchange and industry was booming, so the population of around twenty thousand was increasing steadily. At forty miles distance from Melbourne, Beppe and I hoped that we would be far away from Frank's reach too.

We scoured newspaper advertisements and visited several times, and eventually secured the premises of a former brewery with offices upstairs, two large production rooms downstairs, a secure yard out the back, and even a shop front, all of which could be converted for our purposes.

Zio Roberto had been paying us both modest wages, but we had accumulated enough savings to purchase the stone building, which had stood abandoned for a few years. We would need to borrow money in order to fit out the premises and begin operations. To that end, Beppe had had the foresight to become a naturalised British subject. With Zio Roberto acting as guarantor for the loan, we were able to secure enough funds to be able to purchase materials for repair and machinery and other goods to get our own business started.

When Beppe had acquired his citizenship, he had urged me to write to our younger brother Armando in Mexico. The family had received only a single postcard from him since he had left Italy in 1911. We were hoping that he would be interested in joining us in Geelong, and Beppe had promised both to sponsor him and send him money for his travels, but as yet, we had not received any word from him.

We began our renovations by installing a bedroom, bathroom, small kitchen and dining area upstairs. There was nothing fancy to these living quarters, but it suited we two bachelors. Most of our efforts went into installing the necessary production equipment, securing clean town water and an electricity supply, establishing links with nearby dairies for supply of milk and cream, and contracting with other wholesalers for supply of sugar, eggs and salt, as well as essences for our flavourings. Six months passed before we could declare ourselves fully in operation.

I also made sure we introduced ourselves to the local community. We were very pleased to find a few other Italian shopkeepers who were friendly and helpful, eager to integrate us into their families. There was a jolly grocer, another gentleman who ran a small café where we could get our precious coffee, a confectioner who was eager to stock our ice cream, and a cobbler and a tailor. Most of these families were from the Veneto region, so we struggled at first to understand each other fully, but eventually with a lot of teasing, we found some common ground, throwing in words from our own dialects and some English, making a hybrid language we could all understand. There were a handful of young men of similar age to me and Beppe, sons of the shopkeepers, with excellent English, as they had all been born in Australia. A few friendly discussions with these young men led to the name which we decided to give our venture: the Bellarine Ice Cream Company.

I made myself known at the local Catholic Church which was located not far from our premises and had a parish school attached. I even managed to drag Beppe along to a few Sunday services, telling him it would be good for business if he showed his face and tried to impress the parents of the children who might eventually stop in our shop on the way home from school. On our previous visits to Geelong, we realised that there were already several well-established and quite large ice manufacturing businesses in existence, so it wasn't worth trying to compete with them. We would concentrate on selling our ice cream in bulk, to local confectionaries, tea rooms and hotel refreshment rooms, as well as make use of the proximity to the local railway terminal to ship our wares to outlying districts of the Bellarine Peninsula.

It was October by the time we had ironed out our technical problems, satisfied the local health authorities and been granted a licence to operate under the laws related to Confectionery Producers and Retailers. We made our first big batch, just in time to be able to offer some for free at the local Catholic Church's Spring Fête. Our ice cream was a hit, and we were just as generous benefactors to other church groups, regardless of denomination. In this way, by the time the warmer weather set in, we had a steady flow of customers to our little shop and a growing list of commercial clients.

We got up early in the mornings to produce the ice cream, which contracted drivers took to our trade customers in the early afternoon. We employed a couple of local women to serve in the shop front for the afterschool and after factory trade. There was a mill close by, with plenty of young female workers, who enjoyed dropping in after work. Very quickly we saw the sense in providing a wide verandah with seating so the mill workers and the children could sit for a while to enjoy their cardboard cones. We also sold 1-pint packages in little square tins lined with insulating cardboard, that I had convinced a local cardboard works company to make up for us, so families with ice chests could request a delivery on Saturday afternoons. There was also a well-frequented pub next door where men stopped in for a quick drink after work, and thanks to Beppe's friendship with the publican, drinkers were encouraged to stop at our place for a pint of ice cream to take home to the family.

We took out newspaper advertisements in the local paper, announcing we could provide delivered bulk packages for dances, socials, children's parties, fêtes, and other celebrations at special rates, which became very popular. For this, I developed a way of inserting our tins into thin plywood boxes with enough room on the sides to pack sawmill shavings combined with charcoal powder to form an insulation, so that they could be transported in refrigerated rail carts to the nearby towns of Portarlington, Drysdale, Queenscliff and even as far as Ballarat. By making use of local products, we also made connections with other local businesses who promoted us amongst their staff and customers. By the end of the following year, we had also imported an American machine for making a moulded waffle cone. It took some experimenting with the batter recipe – the suggested almond meal was too expensive – but we were able to use local cornflour and add vanilla extract and orange flour water to the eggs and sugar to create a firm, but light and crispy dough which held up to the high temperatures needed to create a sturdy enough cone. With the addition of this machine, we also had to add more employees, so that now, our factory staff had reached the magic dozen, including the two women in the shop for the afternoon rush, as well as two sub-contracted drivers with horse and cart, who delivered our bulk orders.

Beppe took care of production, and I took care of the machinery, sales and paperwork. We worked well as a team when we kept out of each other's way. Beppe was sensitive to criticism and had a chip on his shoulder about being older than me, and me not showing him enough deference. I tired easily of Beppe's brusque manner, not to mention the horse-racing, shooting and other athletic interests which I did not share, and of which he would talk about endlessly. Beppe had very quickly found people to go hunting with. He enjoyed the local football matches, which, as far as I was concerned, were just a senseless melee of surly men leaping onto each other with an occasional high kick. My interests were in mechanics, in enjoying intellectual discussions about new technology, in preparing and talking about food, in the music of the great masters. Unfortunately, I hadn't found many people in Geelong to whom I could connect intellectually in that busy first year.

From the beginning of production, sales were very good and grew quickly. The outbreak of hostilities in Europe which had started in July sounded grim, but newspaper reports were touting an end to the war by Christmas 1914. Many young men, eager for adventure, had already signed up to join in the defence of the Commonwealth. Geelong, being a port city, had immediately organised para-military groups to protect the harbour. Beppe, who was now calling himself Benny, had organised an Italian section with a dozen of our new young friends to join the Geelong National Defence Alliance, a patrol group who would take turns with other patrol groups to defend the foreshore and key businesses against any possible invasion.

Exactly who was going to invade, was never really made clear, but the local government initiative was well received by the Commonwealth War Department. Of course, the port became busier, and so did our business. As well as regular visits of troop ships, traffic included a much larger range of cargo ships carrying military supplies, on top of the usual holiday makers from Melbourne and the countryside looking to escape the summer heat. To our list of commercial customers, we added the numerous hotels and guest houses which were blossoming.

We built two insulated carts, contracting two local lads to hitch these carts to their own bicycles so that they could sell our ice cream, conveniently loaded into little cups with little wooden paddles. I had seen this idea in an advertisement from an American trade magazine to which the local Mechanic's Institute subscribed. I'd drawn a replica and taken the picture to a local paper and carboard mill, and it hadn't taken them long to come up with a conversion for their machine which already made longer cups for the confectionaries selling the new fad of soda drinks. The lads stocked their carts with the Bellarine Ice Cream Company's four most popular flavours: vanilla, chocolate, strawberry, and mint. A very favourable review in the local paper, about both our new machinery, with ultra-clean, sanitary premises, and our innovative flavoured ice cream, gained us many new customers too.

Christmas came and went, and summer screeched to a halt towards the end of March 1915, and still the citizens of Geelong were unmarked by war, except rather positively, as the local mill's wool production increased and many other industrial and agricultural concerns on the peninsula also contributed meat, dairy, and flour to the war effort on behalf of the Commonwealth. It was late July before the Australian public heard about the real carnage that had taken place at Gallipoli. It was around the same time that our little Italian community learned about Italy's entrance into the war in May 1915 and the attacks by the Austrians, particularly at Ancona and Venice. The news was good, with the Italians rallying to the defence of the nation and repelling the Austrians on all fronts.

Beppe and I discussed our own possible involvement. We were two relatively young men; I was twenty- four and Beppe four years older. I would have to return to Italy, as I was still considered an alien in this country. Beppe, on the other hand, as a naturalised British subject could enrol in the Australian Army. Unlike me, Beppe was keen to go, swept up in the euphoria of the recruitment campaigns, but I reminded him of papà's letters and after many nights discussing our options, we decided to adopt a wait and see attitude, since the newspapers kept promising a swift end to the war. Britain had introduced conscription, and much debate was occurring in Australia as to whether it would have to introduce such measures as well. It seemed that this move would require a referendum, so we reasoned that any such change was at least a year away. In any case, we decided that if Beppe were called to war, I should be okay to keep the factory running.

By the end of 1915, the economic situation had changed significantly. Inflation, especially on basic goods like our milk, cream, flour, and eggs, had hit us hard. We were forced to raise our prices and hope that customers would still be prepared to pay. However, customers were feeling the pinch too, and ice cream became a luxury product. Obliged to reduce our workforce, we were grateful that some of the younger men had decided to enlist, and were already down four men. We reduced our production quantities to match demand, but of course our profits declined. We had been wiring money to our parents at least once per year, usually around August to ensure they had enough money for heating over the winter months. This year, we agonised over whether we could still afford to do this, all too conscious of how much our financial help was vital to our family in Italy. We managed to honour our commitment by drastically trimming both our business and personal expenses.

In September, one of our friends, Virgilio, announced his engagement to the sister of another friend, with the wedding to take place at the end of November. He was the first one in our group to be taking on such a commitment, yet he was younger than me. This put the rest of our group into a bit of a tailspin. I started thinking about my own situation. I'd always imagined that I would be married and have children one day. Beppe, though, was categorically against shackling himself to anyone, let alone a brood of kids. He hoped that as soon as he had enough money to retire comfortably, he would be able to stop working and enjoy the fruits of his labour.

"Look at Zio Roberto," I argued, "approaching his sixties and still working."

"That's because he's got to support his wife and kids, and now their kids," Beppe countered.

There were very few girls of marrying age in our fledgling Italian community here in Geelong and I started to wonder if I could integrate into the wider Australian community. Like in Melbourne, society in Geelong was divided on religious lines – Catholics versus Protestants – and people very rarely mixed outside their own circles, let alone married someone from another faith.

Our small group of Italian families were still mostly socially shunned by the wider community. Even though I had not personally experienced any direct verbal or physical assault, I was still very conscious of the suspicious looks sent my way when I ventured out to the more affluent part of town.

Here in Geelong, my church was full of mostly Irish Catholics with a smattering of Italian, Dutch or Polish families in attendance, and I felt comfortable, with other young men welcoming me to the musical evenings. Normally, a reserved person, I decided I should make an effort to at least talk to some females my age when I attended the next church social. When I did, I found that most of the young ladies were carefully chaperoned by their relatives, but as my violin playing and the ice cream shop were well known in the area, some of those mammas were rather too keen to introduce their daughters. Their forwardness shocked me. In Italy, I would have had my mother, grandmother or other female relatives to advise me of the suitability of a young girl and to make the first advances to her family on my behalf. I was left feeling very much alone and uncertain here in Geelong, unsure of the protocols, making me miss our *cascina* and our extended family. I especially missed the easy company of my mates aboard ship and my Zio Carlo, to whom my thoughts often wandered. Although I had Beppe, our very different personalities and tastes meant we did little together outside of work. There were many days where I felt very much alone.

*   *   *

Beppe and I had imagined that by now, we would have had the funds to open a second ice cream factory on the other side of town, but given the downturn in the economy, we decided we would need a different strategy, one that didn't involve as much capital investment.

As the insulated boxes had been very successful, we discussed shipping them further. But in reality, we had explored all the short rail spurts in our region, transporting anything further afield would mean using Melbourne as a linking hub – not a logical solution.

Another alternative was making use of the intercoastal steamers which stopped at the Port of Geelong and travelled up the east coast all the way to Townsville and across the south coast to Adelaide and Perth. It was time to do some reconnaissance before the summer season set in.

I approached several captains who were able to provide the information we needed. Most steamers already had capacity for frozen storage, so the idea was quite sound, provided there were no other local producers. The only way to find out was to see for ourselves. I thought I could fit in a two-week round trip so that I would be back for Virgilio's wedding. Beppe was not that keen, trying to convince me to hold on, that the war would soon be over, and that production would increase again.

Beppe, significantly taller, with a more muscular build would strut around, yelling at the top of his lungs when he didn't agree with me. He could never just acquiesce to his younger brother's ideas without a fight. Inevitably though, I won the argument through logic and persistence.

Relishing a return to my sailing days, and a break from Beppe's aggression, it didn't take me long to convince my brother I could take a short trip to Adelaide and scout out the other harbour towns along the way as suggested by a Mr. Donaldson, the steamer captain of the SS Riverina, belonging to the Adelaide Steamship Company.

I quickly packed a few personal belongings and organised for ten gallons of ice cream to be sent to the harbour. I had eighty tins with which I could spruik our wares. Captain Donaldson had indicated that there would be five major stopping points where the steam ship would be unloading other cargo, allowing me at least a day in each port for exploration. We would be stopping in Warnambool, Portland, Robe, Goolwa and Port Adelaide.

I stood steady on deck, exhilarated as the ship departed the port, hoping that my sea legs had not deserted me. I was soon offering help and making friends with the crew, who could see I was quite nimble at getting around the ship. There were other passengers on board, and I was over the moon to discover a trio of Italian musicians, aged in their seventies, who were returning to their home of Adelaide after a performance in Melbourne. The musicians told me they were all originally from an Italian town called Viggiano in the southwest of the boot, near the regional capital of Potenza. Their accents and excellent English attested they had been young when they had arrived in Melbourne as child musicians in the 1870s. I immediately regretted not having thought to take my violin with me.

"Where did you learn to play the violin?" one of them asked.

"Oh, at home, the brothers from the Dominican Monastery in Cremona taught me. It's the burial place of Antonio Stradivarius, so I was part of a large violin ensemble, and I started learning to play from the age of three. But I haven't played much since I moved to Geelong."

At my revelation, Domenico immediately unclipped his case and handed over his violin after briefly tuning it. I played what I could remember, but my playing had most certainly become quite rusty. I apologised profusely at my lack of practice, but they were very kind and applauded my efforts enthusiastically. Nevertheless, I was relieved that I had displayed my fading talents before I had heard these professional musicians playing in the saloon that night.

I learnt later that Domenico and his brother Pasquale played for a highly reputable Adelaide symphonic orchestra, directed by another

Italian, and that their cousin Vincenzo played in a popular local dance band. The brothers offered for me to stay with them and attend their regular Saturday night concert. I couldn't believe my luck. I repaid their generous offer by treating them to some of my ice cream, of which they were also very complimentary.

But when Vincenzo started questioning me exhaustively about my business interests, I became a little more guarded.

"How do you know so much about the manufacture of ice cream, Vincenzo?"

"My daughter runs a Confectionery Store and all the Italians in Melbourne know your uncle Roberto. He's a good man, he's done a lot to help Italians to settle. When my wife was alive, we socialised with Roberto and his first wife's parents on many occasions."

My suspicions allayed, I felt like the enchanted boy by the time I arrived at Port Adelaide. Everywhere we had stopped, not only had I managed to sell some ice cream, but I had taken orders for more supplies, everyone complimenting me on the quality of the product.

I had conversed with Captain Donaldson to understand how shipments were accepted, checked on their refrigerated hold and seen for myself the process of unloading and dispatching of goods from the wharves. I was satisfied that the ice cream could travel unaccompanied and reach its intended destination quite safely. And I'd taken the precaution of sharing some of our product with the crew, especially the kitchen crew, whom I took pains to befriend.

The night before we reached Port Adelaide, Vincenzo approached me.

"How much of that ice cream do you have left, Carlo? I've been thinking that my daughter and son-in-law would be interested in it. I know Domenico wants you to attend the concert on Saturday night, but how about I pick you up Sunday morning and you spend the night at our place? We're less than two miles away from the port, so you won't have any trouble getting back on board on Monday morning."

I fired a barrage of questions back at him and was relieved to learn that they were still using a bucket inserted into an ice and salt bath to churn their ice cream. There was no way that they were making more than one gallon a day, and it would cost them a pretty penny to produce if they were still relying on ice to cool down their custard base mixture and using electricity to turn the converted hand crank. But I was very curious to meet Vincenzo's daughter and her husband, who sounded like enterprising, successful businesspeople.

I also made the acquaintance of other Adelaideans on board this 5-day journey, eager to learn more about the capital city. One such person was the fastidiously styled Mr. John Hobson, who turned out to be a rather prominent city grocer and aspiring politician.

"As far as I'm aware, there's only one large-scale commercial manufacturer. I'm sure that most ice cream sellers in Adelaide are small family concerns, usually producing ice cream as well as other goods, and nothing in the volume or quality that I've just sampled."

Conversations with John, Vincenzo and the others had my mind churning. By the time we disembarked, I wasn't just looking for people to offload my remaining pints of ice cream to, but I was determined to scout for our second factory location. I'd have to wait till I got back to Geelong to seriously contemplate the figures and whether the move was feasible, but in the meantime, I began viewing Adelaide with different eyes.

Domenico and Pasquale had offered me a couch for the night in their rooms in Hindley Street, and Johnnie, the use of his cool room at his tea shop near the Central Market. I was excited to go exploring. One thing I did do though, before heading to bed that night, was to thank my maker and ask him to protect me, lest I fall into the trap of the ingenue, and risk being fleeced blind. In the bathroom, I checked that I had properly concealed the money I had already earned in the hidden pocket sewn into the upper leg of my trousers.

After two days in Adelaide, I had met dozens of other Italian business owners, mostly in Hindley Street, who bought my remaining ice cream and placed orders for more. Johnnie introduced me to Bill, the young man who ran Johnnie's tea shop and who also sold ice cream sodas.

"These soda drinks have been slow to take off here," Bill explained, "probably because the quality of the ice cream we've been using is quite gritty compared to the one you make."

By the time Vincenzo came to pick me up on Sunday, I was buzzing from the milk of human kindness, as well as the endless possibilities that had been presented to me here, all floating around my brain to the strains of the Vivaldi concert I had watched from backstage at the Adelaide Town Hall on Saturday night. I had been tremendously impressed with the elegance of the buildings along the main city thoroughfares, and the calm and prosperous central business district. Immediately, I saw the opportunities that would be available at the Central Market, though there were already two established confectioners selling ice cream there.

On Sunday, Vincenzo took me on the train heading back to Port Adelaide, to meet his family, and stay the night. As I had already given Vincenzo a pint of my ice cream to share with his family, he reported that they were very eager to meet me.

I barely spoke as I sat by the window watching the beautiful golden fields of wheat, pastures where contented cows stood grazing and gorgeous little hamlets with flower festooned gardens in front of tidy little cottages. As we neared Port Adelaide, there was more evidence of industry, with factories and imposing storage sheds all along the busy docks. Alighting from the train, once the steam cleared, I saw a slim man, with an impressively full and waxed moustache, sitting on the bench seat of a strong, wooden cart and holding the reins of a muscular horse. Waving at us, in rolled up shirt sleeves, but with a silk tie and a buttoned up, pale blue damask vest, from which hung a gold pocket watch, Antonio Latorre stood to hoist us onboard.

By the end of the day, I understood that he was the shrewdest businessman I had ever met. What I didn't realise then, was how important this man and his family would become in my life.

New Horizons

When Antonio Latorre picked us up, we took the road from Port Adelaide which led to the commercial centre of Semaphore. The main street was quiet, as most shops and hotels were not open, given it was a Sunday. I was happy to see a number of motor cars parked nearby and a few motorised trucks parked in the alleyways beside more substantial businesses. Several churches we passed seemed well-frequented.

"Is there a Catholic Church nearby?" I asked.

"There's a beautiful one, recently dedicated, approximately a block away, with a school attached, and there's also one in Port Adelaide, that has been there from the earliest days of the colony," Vincenzo informed me.

As we neared the end of the street, I could see a sparkling bay filled with both pleasure craft and commercial shipping. Along an elegant esplanade, well-dressed ladies in wide hats and gentlemen in high collars, top hats and walking canes were strolling amiably, taking in the sea air. There were amusements for children and a double storey kiosk with restaurant and dance hall in the main square. Many guest houses and hotels faced the sea, and as we trotted alongside the square, I spied an open-air movie theatre and a coffee palace. From my enquiries in the preceding days, I discovered that Adelaide and its burgeoning suburbs had a population of just over three hundred thousand people, enormous compared to Geelong.

The Latorre home turned out to be a modern cottage complete with front and back garden, a lace-lined, bull-nosed front verandah, a large, richly appointed parlour and dining room with tall pressed-tin ceilings and marble fireplaces. It was located in Blackler Street, one of the side streets off the main Semaphore boulevard, opposite the railway company's water tower, positioned on a slight rise and able to catch the breezes off the water, which I was a told was a boon in the hot summers. While there were still a number of timber-built buildings, all the more recent ones seemed to be in brick with sandstone facades and were positioned on quite tall foundations.

"There's a substantial white ant problem in the area, so raising the floors onto cement plinths, and building the shells of houses in quarried stone, not only minimizes the termite problem, but also keeps the houses cool," explained Antonio.

The three of us sat in Antonio's generous back garden, riotously full of the last of the winter vegetables, with spring ones just peeping through the well-tilled garden beds. We were under the shade of a grape vine whose new shoots promised fruit aplenty during the late summer. There were citrus and plum trees and even a pear tree trained along a side fence.

Antonio gave me a bowl and directed me to a section of bamboo staked climbing plants on which I was delighted to find an abundance of pea pods. I eagerly filled the bowl and brought it back to the long, wooden trestle table and chairs set under the pergola near the back door, just as Antonio was arriving with a tray laden with a gleaming copper *Napoletana* coffee pot. Antonio overturned the pot, allowing the boiled water to fall into the chamber filled with finely ground coffee beans, the distinctive drip sound signifying the water was ambling its way through the densely packed grounds. Setting out some fine porcelain coffee cups and loading them each with two heaped teaspoons of sugar, Antonio completed the familiar ritual of first dropping in a few drops of hot coffee and vigorously stirring the sugar to both dissolve it and develop the beautiful crema that rises to the top when the cup is filled with more hot coffee. I closed my eyes, breathing in the toasty aroma and savouring the thick, sweet foam at the top. Then I quickly tilted the cup for the bitter, bracing liquid below. It was only two mouthfuls, but its ability to reanimate all of my senses, was unparalleled.

Over the peas we shelled and sampled, making sure to leave a couple of cups worth to be added to the Sunday lunch, we discussed business prospects.

Antonio described what they had already ventured into. Vincenzo had been recruited to play in Adelaide several times, and after his wife had died in Melbourne in the winter of 1896, he had taken up a permanent position here in an Adelaide dance band.

Antonio and Elena, with their baby daughter, had followed Vincenzo and Elena's two sisters, who were still in their mid-teens. Antonio had started in Adelaide city, in Waymouth Street, where he had leased a business operating a stable, renting out horses, carts and buggies to local businesses and private clients. His son was born there in 1905. Then, once the babe was weaned, he and his wife Elena took the opportunity to take over the lease of some refreshment rooms at Glenelg. It was a substantial business, opposite the last train stop on the Jetty Road, a building of two storeys, but the upper one had not been in use.

"The couple remodelled the building, making the upstairs an evening restaurant on Fridays and Saturdays, and the bottom, a tearoom which was open seven days. Glenelg was already established as a seaside holiday centre, popular both in summer and winter, so business had been brisk.

"I worked out a way to attach a small electric motor to the paddle of my ice cream churn, but demand was so great, I could barely keep up," explained Antonio.

"Elena ran the kitchens, and her sisters ran the tea rooms and the restaurant. Word of Elena's superior baking soon brought in the customers. Unfortunately, the premises could only be leased. The owner, the old codger, absolutely refused to sell to us, but he had no problem pumping up the rents every six months. Eventually, the relentlessness of the work tired us out and, as Elena's two sisters married, they became less available to oversee the public face of the business. So, we decided to try our luck in Semaphore, in less demanding businesses."

I was surprised to hear that they'd only been in this house just over two years, given the profusion of the garden.

"It's in my blood," said Antonio, with a wink. "I arrived in Australia as an 8-year-old boy, at the tail end of the gold rush. My parents settled in the port city of Williamstown, where they knew some other Italians from their village and worked in the market gardens already established by these *paesani*. By the time I was fourteen, I was eager to stretch my wings a little and made off to Melbourne, to another Viggiano *paesano* who was in the ice cream business and had a stall at the new Queen Victoria Markets in Flinders Street. I worked there, picked up odd jobs with other stall holders, and eventually saved enough to buy out a stall and ice cream making equipment over at the old Western Market on

Collins Street. One stall eventually became two, one at each entrance to the market. I was happy with the money I was making, but there was a lot of competition in Melbourne, especially from your Zio Roberto who had opened a factory and was able to produce a much greater volume and a better-quality product than I ever could."

"Wow, you know my Zio Roberto too? Did you not think about opening a factory yourself?"

"When the opportunity to come to Adelaide with my father-in-law was presented to us, I jumped at the chance, as I knew that Elena wouldn't have survived being separated from her sisters, but unfortunately, I didn't have the funds at the time to think about starting a factory."

While Antonio had made his mark in other businesses, he still had his finger on the pulse and was able to give me plenty of information about the ice cream factories that had already established themselves – two in the city centre, one in Goodwood, in the eastern suburbs and one in Thebarton, in the west. However, Antonio believed that there was still plenty of opportunity for another factory, especially in Port Adelaide where land was plentiful and there were a large number of old business premises for sale, as people were choosing to move closer to the city. I told him about our ability to transport our product further afield. Antonio reassured me that the rail network here was equally extensive and I would find it easy enough to replicate our Geelong success.

At this stage, I was thinking that Beppe and I could sell our Geelong business and move to Adelaide. I was asking about prices and locations of dairies and suppliers, when behind me, noise of talking broke through as the side gate opened and a very neatly attired young man in a grey wool, fitted jacket and soft cap came tumbling through to wrap his arms around Vincenzo's neck. Behind him, two women sauntered through: a strikingly handsome woman with deep, auburn hair who appeared to be in her late thirties and a younger one who simply took my breath away.

Another couple, in their mid-forties, arrived at the same time. Antonio stood to greet them all with kisses to each cheek. He turned to me and introduced me to the newcomers. I didn't hear a word, until Antonio pronounced the name of the most glorious apparition before me. She was called Luisa. She was around my height, slender with a long, slim face and intensely deep brown eyes. Her skin was slightly dusky, and unblemished, with a healthy glow to her cheeks and lips. She had removed her boater hat as she was walking in, and her luxuriously thick, long, black hair was pulled back off her forehead but left in loose curls hanging at her back, ornamented with a simple white ribbon to match the colour of her blouse. She held her hat loosely in front of her, slim fingers methodically brushing the rim. When her grandfather spoke to her, she lowered her gaze and an alluring blush spread across her cheeks.

I didn't hear a word of the conversation and was afraid I'd made a complete fool of myself, my mouth clamming up at this unexpected vision of loveliness. Eventually, the women went inside, and I was able to compose myself, re-joining as best I could, the conversation of the men.

The first woman was Antonio's wife and Vincenzo's daughter, Elena. The other gentleman and his wife were neighbours and ran a laundry and clothes-mending business next door to Elena's confectionery shop on the Semaphore commercial road. The lady, named Connie, seemed to have a more Mediterranean look about her, but her husband had the distinctive freckle-faced Irish colouring, so I was quite taken aback when Antonio introduced him as Alfredo Zorna, formerly of Torino.

"Call me Fred," he immediately said as he pumped my arm in his strong double handed grip. The man was so enthusiastic to have met another Lombardo, he broke out in his rusty dialect, as often as he could, and laughed heartily when the other two southerners gently teased us through the course of the afternoon.

Ten-year-old Bartolomeo, Antonio's son, had changed into some more comfortable knickerbockers held up by sharp leather braces and was swiftly sent to the cellar for some bottles of home-made wine. Connie appeared with some glasses and a plate of roasted pumpkin seeds, slices of a small dry sausage studded with fennel seeds and specks of chilli and some home-made rustic Italian-style bread.

"Enjoy these, gentlemen." Connie said as she placed the plate on the trestle table and patted her husband's shoulder. "Lunch will be served indoors in an hour."

Fred's elbow met mine as he joked, "When my beautiful Connie and Elena get together in the kitchen, the Sultan of Arabia would be jealous of the riches they bring forth!"

"We aim to please," replied Connie with an exaggerated wink before disappearing behind the back door from where the distinct noise of cluttering pans and brisk instructions, interspersed with twinkling laughter emanated.

Eventually, Elena called us in for lunch and we quickly abandoned the cards we had been using to help Bart pass the time. The northern facing back yard had become quite warm, but the September sea breeze, even in the middle of the day, still had a cold sting to it. I made use of a tiny outhouse at the bottom of the garden, then made my way to the laundry attached to the back of the house, opposite the pergola where we had been sitting, and where the others were washing their hands.

While away from the group, I gave myself a stern talking to, admonishing myself for my earlier childish behaviour towards the daughter of the house. I took my place more confidently at an imposing dining table, covered in a lace-fringed and delicately embroidered white tablecloth surrounded by eight, carved, rosewood chairs. In the middle of the table, a silver platter on a tall pedestal, circled by little cherubs and bunches of grapes, held a range of the fruit I had seen in the garden. In Italian tradition, the eldest male, Vincenzo, was seated at the head of the table with a place for his daughter to his left and his son-in law to his right. Next came the guests, with Connie sliding in next to Elena, and Fred next to Antonio. I was seated between Fred and Bart. Luisa, ought to take her place opposite me, but there was no sign of her yet.

When she appeared, she was carrying a large, steaming pot. I immediately leapt up to relieve her of the burden.

"I'm fine, I do this all the time," she announced, jutting out her chin, her eyes willing me out of the way.

"It's quite hot, please let me help you," was all I could muster, sure that I was blushing outrageously, as I could feel heat prickles creeping up to my face and dampness gathering under my armpits. I was wearing a woollen suit with a starched shirt and rigid collar and tie, feeling quite stiff and formal.

Luisa directed me to a sideboard where gleaming porcelain plates were stacked. I put the pot down on the nearby trivet and asked if I could hand out the plates she was about to fill. Apparently, that was Bart's job, so I returned awkwardly to my seat, retrieving the cloth napkin that had fallen to the floor. To gather my thoughts and hide my awkwardness, I addressed Elena with a compliment.

"*Signora*, my thanks for you and your husband's hospitality and my congratulations on such an elegant table, I'm truly honoured. It's been a long time since I've seen such a beautiful tablecloth."

"No need to be so formal, please call me Elena, and you'll have to thank Luisa for the tablecloth; the nuns taught her to embroider to perfection."

"You are indeed blessed then, to have both a talented and beautiful daughter." I sent a shy glance Luisa's way.

"That's only the beginning of her talent," piped up her grandfather, Vincenzo, from the head of the table.

"You wait till you hear her play." He motioned to the piano behind him.

"You p-p-play … the piano?" I stuttered.

Vincenzo continued, as Luisa took her seat at the table.

"Tell him about the piece you're working on now."

Her eyes lit up, and grinning widely, she answered,

"Nonno has adapted Vivaldi's 'La Follia' for the piano."

My brain scrambled to respond, my mouth opened and closed in vain. Thankfully, Luisa saved me from embarrassment by continuing the conversation.

"Nonno tells me you play the strings, violin isn't it?"

I nodded silently, grateful when Elena cut in and suggested Vincenzo say a prayer over the food. He finished with a *Buon Appetito*, signalling it was time to partake.

The rich aroma of a smoky pork sausage broth rose from my plate. In the dark liquid, along with the peas we had shelled earlier, I also saw long, dried, red peppers, strands of a long green leaf and short pasta shapes. I used my spoon to explore the elements in the bowl.

"Hot peppers," I ventured.

"*Cruschi*" answered Elena. "From the seeds my mother brought with her from Viggiano nearly sixty years ago. Don't worry, they're sweet, and dried in the sun to intensify their flavour."

"*Cicoria*, I assume." I picked up a long, green strand imagining it's bitterness in contrast to the sweetness promised by the peppers. "And the pasta?" I enquired, looking curiously at the little flattened disks.

"In our dialect, we call them *recchie*," she answered. I jerked my head up, puzzled by this new word, but this time Fred saved me.

"*Non ti preoccupare*, I'd never seen them either before eating at this table. Apparently, they're a specialty of their region of Basilicata, but trust me, they're the most delicious ears you'll ever nibble."

Ignoring Fred's winks, I redirected my gaze around the fruit display to Elena.

"You make them yourself?"

"The broth is my handiwork," she said, tapping her chest in a show of pride. "But the pasta was made by Luisa this morning before we went to church, so that it could dry out a little."

This time, I couldn't help it, my jaw dropped, and my mouth opened in astonishment for what felt like a full ten minutes. I heard everyone at the table laughing and saw Luisa's eyes lower modestly.

"I've been making pasta with mamma since I was five," she explained, "I should well be an expert by now, but it only tastes good because of mamma's pork broth."

The others had already started eating and so I dipped my spoon in and could only reply with a sigh, as I felt my heart explode.

"*Paradiso*," I proclaimed, taking in a long, sweet breath, before plunging my spoon straight back in. "At home, I didn't really have the opportunity to cook – none of us boys were allowed in the kitchen. But once I started on the steam ship, I was required to help the cook in the galley to prepare vegetables and watch the saucepans, as well as serve dinner to the passengers. But, I've never made pasta," I confessed.

"Our ship's cook was French."

At my admission, many more questions were directed at me, mostly by Elena, asking about my family and my life at sea, how I had come to Australia and how the business was going in Geelong.

"Have you been convinced that Adelaide is the place to be?" Antonio chuckled. "And do you think you could convince your brother to move here?"

I had a sudden vision of Beppe, with his coarse humour, strident voice, and rough manners, sitting at the table with us, embarrassing me as usual.

"We'll see," I shrugged. "I can definitely see myself here, though. I'm very grateful for your introductions Vincenzo, I'm sure this trip wouldn't have been as eye-opening without them, and I hope to return as soon as possible, but I will keep in touch."

Leaning over to meet Antonio's gaze, I added, "if you'll permit me to write to you, *signore*?"

The response which spilled from Antonio's lips sent my heart thumping again.

"Write to my daughter," Antonio winked. "I can speak and read English well enough, but I'm not much of a writer and don't have the time. Luisa takes care of all my correspondence."

My heart somersaulted and an energy passed between the shyly smiling Luisa and me. My fate was sealed. Not only could I imagine making my life in Adelaide, but I was adamant that I would return alone.

Brothers Asunder

Back in Geelong, I did make a creditable attempt to convince Beppe, with comparisons of population size, information about what I had learned of already established ice cream and other businesses, and descriptions of the city centre, Port Adelaide and Semaphore. But as I hoped, Beppe wasn't convinced. He couldn't see the value of upping sticks and starting again, especially since it had taken us six months just to establish the Geelong business not that long ago. After many nights of discussion, guiltily without me ever revealing anything about the Latorre family, Beppe eventually announced,

"Well, if you're really determined to pursue this folly, I can buy you out. I can probably give you a half of what you've already invested now, and if we have a good summer, I may have enough to give you the rest. But I need you here for the summer season. If you're still determined to abandon me, you can go next year, after March."

We had never drawn wages for ourselves, so I had very little left in the bank, but the mortgage was in Beppe's name alone, so withdrawing from our arrangement would not pose a legal problem. I desperately wanted to take the first ship back to Adelaide, but I saw the merit of Beppe's proposal.

Anyway, I couldn't possibly turn up empty handed. I contented myself with writing to Luisa, at first, limiting myself to asking her for mundane assistance: names and addresses of dairies and other local suppliers, which I dutifully followed up. I was the one who collected the mail, so Beppe had no inkling, though I worried that my more consistent day dreaming might alert him to something being awry.

At Virgilio's wedding, I danced several numbers with the bride's friends, knowing that I needed the practice. I also danced with quite a few of the older ladies, even Virgilio's grandmother got a twirl out of me. The whole time, I barely registered the faces of my partners, dreaming only of Luisa's face before me. Beppe noticed my vigorous activity and couldn't stopped teasing me.

Of course, Beppe didn't dance at all, preferring to indulge in the freely flowing wine and the attendant carry-on at the end of the night as the drinkers spilled their revelry into the street. I had a difficult time hoisting my brother onto our cart, sure that he would roll off at the first bend. There was nothing on the open tray I could use to box him in. The anxiety of always being Beppe's keeper, soured my enjoyment of the evening.

As my correspondence with Luisa continued, I took the liberty of describing what I was doing, understanding that Antonio would need to know that I was working hard at the business and what my intentions were. I slowly dared to ask Luisa more personal questions and learned that she played the organ for her local church, conducted Sunday school classes, assisted with several local charities, helped to bake supplies for her mother's confectionery shop, occasionally relieved her father at his grocery store in Birkenhead, just on the other side of the Port River, and took care of his correspondence. I was astounded at the depths of her energy and talent and asked her if she had considered a musical career like her grandfather. She explained that she had attended school in the city in Pirie Street, with the Australian order of the Sisters of St. Joseph, and while they had acknowledged her talent, proud of her superior achievements in the exams organised by the University of Adelaide Board of Music, they had encouraged her to consider other careers, as there were very few safe places a decent woman could make a career in music in Adelaide. Her parents had agreed, happy to keep her in school and continuing her musical education, but also encouraging her to learn bookkeeping so that she could be of real assistance with the family businesses. She acknowledged how lucky she was, as most girls left school at twelve to work in factories or similar environments. She had lost many study companions whose parents didn't see the value of keeping their girls in education beyond the mandatory primary years.

I explained how I had learned to play the violin, but regretted I was quite rusty now. However, in secret, I had taken up playing again after work, while Beppe usually hung out at the pub or with his shooting mates. I started at the beginning again with scales and simple melodies.

Foolishly, I sent away to a music shop in Melbourne for the score of Vivaldi's La Follia which Vincenzo and Luisa had mentioned and been instantly mortified when I realised that I could no longer fluently read the music, let alone attempt to play it. I put it away, hoping that one day, I would be able to regain my prowess, though I was sure it would never be anywhere near as good as Luisa's. Nevertheless, I had many happy dreams about accompanying her at a local concert or evening soiree. So, I unearthed my old music notation sheets, the few half-dozen I had carried with me from Ossolaro and forced myself to learn how to read them all over again.

I worked hard with Beppe, to help increase sales, following up by mail with the contacts I had made on my recent trip, as well as approaching the guest houses and hotels where we were not already selling our ice cream. As word of mouth spread about that nice young fellow 'Charlie,' as one of my customers had christened me, and as the superior quality of our ice cream, compared to the watery or gritty ones produced by other local confectionaries spoke for itself, business improved steadily, much to Beppe's delight, so he wasn't as angry about my decision.

At our church fête, I bought a Christmas postcard, which had been embellished by some embroidery along with a small, lacquered wooden brooch in the shape of a sun. I also bought a palm-sized wooden puzzle, which I thought Bart might like. In early December, I addressed the postcard to all the family, but wrapped up the two gifts separately, into a small box, hiding a little personal note for Luisa in the silk crocheted pouch with the brooch. I confessed my deep admiration for her and my longing to see her again. For the next ten days, I was the proverbial cat on a hot tin roof, scared I'd done the wrong thing, scared that Luisa would be shocked by my forwardness, scared that her parents would disapprove and my chances of seeing her again would disappear.

Until I finally received a reply. Sitting inside a bundle of our regular mail was a small cream envelope with Luisa's familiar neat and pretty script. My heart was pounding as I plucked it out and eventually managed to open it with trembling hands. There was no family news, no chatty recount of her days, just a few brief words, thanking me for my thoughtful and beautiful gift, reassuring me that I was always on her mind and that she couldn't wait to see me again either. A little Red Cross lapel pin was attached to the notecard, explaining that she had bought it for the war effort and was thankful though, that I wouldn't be called up in the madness of this new war.

In a previous letter, she had asked my opinion of the war and the debate about conscription. I had told her the news I had gleaned about Italy's participation, but also the knowledge of the atrocities which had occurred in the Italo-Turkish war four years earlier. I was glad I was not in Italy and not yet an Australian citizen, so unlikely to be involved in any fighting. However, as we both had younger brothers, I also hoped that the war would soon be over before they reached their maturity.

In her next letter, Luisa said that her parents were too busy with summer trade, so she didn't bother reading out my letters, just summarised the news they would be interested in. I realised that this was a hint that I could be much more personal with my letters, addressing them directly to her, rather than her father, and I didn't waste the opportunity.

Nor was I disappointed with her replies. I spent the summer of 1915-16 floating on air, observing what was happening around me, but completely ambivalent towards any event, even the news from the war fronts, which consumed everyone around me.

*   *   *

Word of my planned departure had gotten around and, one day, I was approached by one of our friends, Henry Carretti, the tailor's son, who was thoroughly bored with his father's work.

Henry had been born and raised in Geelong, and whenever I took him to a client, the young man was able to find a connection to them in some way and make them confident about a handover of responsibilities. I was relieved, even a little jealous of his apparent ease, but overall thankful that I wouldn't be leaving Beppe in the lurch.

On top of training Henry about sales, I had to ensure that there was someone who was able to handle the maintenance of the refrigeration, packing and cone machines. Beppe had a good knowledge of these, but he would get frustrated if he couldn't fix things quickly, not taking the time to carefully analyse the problem. Jack, whom we'd taken on as a young sixteen-year-old, had shown great interest and was fascinated by the machines. I had already encouraged the young man to join me at meetings at the Geelong Mechanics Institute, paying for his subscription, and was pleased to see him turn up at every meeting over the last eighteen months, after which we discussed our engines and their operations at great length.

The incredulous grin on his face when Beppe and I had called him to our office upstairs and offered him a pay rise along with this new responsibility was priceless. Jack was approaching his eighteenth birthday, and with the expectation for young men to sign up to the armed forces growing, we asked him about his plans. He reminded us that he was a Catholic, and his Irish parents were very much against him supporting this British cause. We were satisfied for the moment, but I did ask Jack if he knew anyone else already in our employ that he could train and encourage to attend Institute meetings with him, given that there was much talk about the possibility of conscription being enforced.

Jack mentioned his mate Nathanial, another Irish employee. He was the same age as Jack, but had a distinctive limp, which hadn't been an issue for us, but meant he was unlikely to be drafted, so I proposed to sponsor Nat's enrolment at the Mechanics Institute too. By the end of the week, we had another delighted and loyal employee and an equally delighted and grateful set of parents, as I found out at church the following Sunday.

A few days before I was due to leave, I took the time to speak to Beppe, to acknowledge the excellent job he had done on the factory floor. It it was clear that the employees had great respect for him, and actually enjoyed sharing a joke with him, and even an afterwork beer at the pub. He was deemed a good bloke, not only by his workers, but by a number of important people in the town, especially since he had joined the Harbour Board and had organised a watch party of his Italian friends who patrolled the naval yards one night a week.

After Easter, we went to the bank where Beppe transferred the money owed to me for my half of the building and the split of profits earnt over the last two years. It was a triumphant day, as neither of us had fully realised how far we had come in such a short time, but sad too, that this now represented an official parting of ways.

"We made a good team, hey Carlino," said Beppe using my childhood nickname. "I still don't understand why you want to leave, but you know, you can always come back, no questions asked?"

"*Grazie* Beppe, you know I'm very grateful you took me under your wing. I just need a chance to test myself."

Beppe too conveyed his thanks for my efforts in getting the factory up and running, recalling all the missteps we had made and how 'Mr Brains' had always come to the rescue. He couldn't help adding that he was also thankful that he didn't have to come home drunk and get 'papà's look' from his younger brother anymore. I tried not to take offence to the jibing, but it confirmed that I was making the right decision. This wasn't how I wanted my life to look, and if I stayed in Geelong, even managed to convince Luisa to come to me, I would always have to contend with Beppe on my back.

A new life

By mid-April, I was ready to move to Adelaide. Antonio, true to his word, had already paid the first month's lease on premises in Port Adelaide because he said it was too good an opportunity to pass up, and reassured me that if my plans didn't work, he'd find another tenant to sub-let it. To confirm my intentions, I wired him the money to cover three month's rent and decided to be bold as well, letting Antonio know that I had serious feelings for his daughter and asked his permission to officially court her once I arrived in Adelaide.

This time, I received a short note in Antonio's own handwriting inserted at the bottom of Luisa's letter. In his note, he expressed his happiness to learn that I would soon be arriving to occupy the premises he had selected and that he and Elena would be honoured to welcome me at the family table upon my arrival.

I had been in contact with the mechanical engine company Whitfield and Sons, situated in Port Adelaide, who had started with the manufacture of steam engines but had evolved to the production of electric motors and were resellers for the German brand Linde who made compact vertical refrigerators, using ammonia gas to freeze water in coiling pipes. As Germany was currently out of favour, they had found they were carrying pricey stock, which they had been unable to sell. Antonio had inspected the machine for me, and negotiated a good price, provided I could get to the factory and pay for the machine before June 30th.

They also suggested a foundry where I would be able to source the metal vats and other steel equipment. It would require a serious injection of cash to obtain all of these supplies, but Antonio had reassured me that he belonged to a local entrepreneur's club, and they were prepared to invest in my venture. I wasn't overly keen on this idea, fearing loss of control of my business, but Antonio, through Luisa's letters, continued to reassure me that, as a group, they had backed many new ventures.

I had no choice really, if I were going to get this business up and running. It would be several more years before I could apply to become a naturalized British subject of the Commonwealth of Australia, therefore, a bank was unlikely to lend me the money I needed.

Before agreeing to anything, I wrote to Johnnie, the friend I had met on the steamer on my way to Adelaide, sensing he was a wily character with fingers in many business pies. Johnnie said he had done some nosing around and that Antonio's reputation was solid, and previous beneficiaries of the investment club he belonged to, all praised the help and guidance they received from them.

This reassured me enormously, as I was beginning to feel very indebted to Antonio and was concerned about my future should my relationship with Luisa not work out as I hoped. I was nervous but confident, sure I had the know-how and the strength to carry this off. But that didn't stop me from reciting many prayers. I recalled Zio Carlo's words so clearly, from when I first joined him on the steamer:

"Don't expect God to read your mind, he has too many people to take care of; you get on your knees, and you pray. Pray not for things, but for courage to make the right decisions, so that you can obtain the things you desire with your own hard work and enterprise."

From my little writing desk in Geelong, I had also made contact with Simpson's tin manufactory to find out the dimensions of their tin sheets to line my packing boxes and the time needed for an order to be delivered. A sawmill at Alberton was prepared to supply thin wooden sheets at whatever dimensions I needed so I could make my packing boxes in the right size to optimise the use of the tin.

In addition, Antonio had mentioned my name at his dairy suppliers in nearby Kilkenny and I had written to them announcing my imminent arrival to the area, explaining the quantity of milk and cream I estimated I would need to purchase on a weekly basis. They replied with an assurance that they could meet my needs and a price list with a discount for bulk orders. Local sugar, and essence suppliers, already used by Elena, had also been approached in the same way. Sugarcane from Queensland was processed at a branch of the Commonwealth Sugar Refinery factory right on the Port Adelaide wharf.

Naturally, the most exciting event I was anticipating was my reunion with Luisa and being truly able to start a proper courtship. I couldn't help being awed at how things had worked out, as in reality, I'd only spent around five hours in her company on that one Sunday the previous September. Our relationship had grown through our letters. I had been totally honest with her about my thoughts and feelings on every subject we had discussed and hoped she had done the same.

Finally, Port Adelaide with its massive storage sheds and dockside rigging came into view. I had already brought my case and violin up to the foredeck. As the tug guided the steamer into the pier, I could see a cluster of people waiting by the dock. It was early evening, with the light about to fade and quite cool and breezy. The ladies' skirts and hats were threatening to lift off. Being a little short-sighted, when I finally recognised the Latorre family, I nearly burst into tears. They were all there, Bart energetically waving his home-made Italian *tricolore*, Vincenzo, Antonio, Elena, Fred, Connie, and heading the pack, my Luisa. I wasn't sure how to greet them, but Luisa picked up her long skirts and ran to me, flinging her arms around my shoulders for a fierce hug and a kiss on each cheek. We returned to the Latorre house, where the ladies had once again prepared a celebratory meal. I distributed some gifts I had carefully selected before my departure from Geelong and was relieved by the broad smiles and hugs I received. Luisa and Vincenzo played for us, and I too, drew out my violin and played the few arias I had been practising. Vincenzo ribbed me good naturedly about my improved dexterity and rhythm, but I was too busy luxuriating in Luisa's delighted reaction to care.

Walking a few doors down to Connie and Fred's place, I found a comfortable little room at the back of the house with a simple bed, a wardrobe and a small table and chair, perfect for my needs. They had offered me this room at a very reasonable rate, for as long as I needed it. That night, I fell immediately into a long, dreamless sleep and woke the next morning raring to go.

Luisa and Vincenzo took the train with me to the Port Adelaide Railway station, and then we walked a short distance to the cottage Antonio had leased for me. It was a double block, with a small 4 room cottage that included the usual set up of a front parlour and a main bedroom at the front with an eat-in kitchen and another bedroom at the back. It was old and a bit musty smelling, but with a good clean and a new coat of paint inside and out, it would do very nicely as a starting point. The cottage faced the road, in fact it was on the main commercial strip of Port Adelaide, where there were other shops and businesses, so, if I wanted to, I could set up shop in the parlour, as many other people did.

Behind the house was a new, double height metal shed with concrete floor where I could set up the factory, and an adjoining animal barn to keep a horse and cart. I was still examining the sheds and stables when a whistle drifted past, and I heard someone calling out for Vincenzo.

"That'll be Vittorio," said Vincenzo.

Vittorio was a short, bandy-legged man wearing a hand-knitted jumper tucked into a pair of paint-stained loose trousers, all held together by a thick rope. His face could have been a leather saddlebag of many years, the wrinkles hiding his button-black, smiling eyes. He was accompanied by a similarly attired but taller man in his thirties, whom he introduced to us as his son Graziano.

"We're here to start on the repair work and painting of the house" Graziano said. "We just need to confirm terms."

Within an hour, they had their tools and plaster mix ready to start patching of the interior walls, where chunks of plaster had dropped off.

"You need to fix the channels outside, so water drains away properly from the foundations and moisture doesn't have a chance to get into these walls," explained Vittorio, taking me outside to show me what he meant.

I had dressed for work, so with a borrowed pickaxe, prepared to set myself to the task. Vincenzo and Luisa took their leave, once I convinced them I remembered where to catch the train and walk back to their place later in the day. It was hard physical labour, more than I had done for quite a while, but I found it exhilarating, knowing that I was doing this for me and my future.

By the end of the first fortnight, my refrigeration machine had been paid for and was ready to be delivered the following Monday. I had visited my suppliers for the metal vats I needed and arranged for delivery the week after that. I had borrowed tools and a cart to go pick up my tin and wood, so I could prepare my transport boxes. I was allowed to take Luisa with me and spend time with her, but only if we were chaperoned, which usually meant waiting for Bart to return from school or hope Vincenzo was free.

Luisa was enterprising though and arranged to visit some local second-hand furniture dealers who delivered a simple bed, a wardrobe and small corner table I could use as a desk, as well as a sturdy table with four chairs for my kitchen.

She cleaned and polished all the wood till it smelled and gleamed new again, and then filled my kitchen cupboard with some cups and glasses, plates and cutlery. She even managed to run up some cheerful curtains, thanks to a donation of offcuts from Fred and Connie's store.

One evening, Elena presented me with a copper *Napoletana* and a lidded terracotta pot containing some ground coffee, "To ensure you start your days happy," she'd announced. I had to choke back tears at the smell of real coffee, rather than the much cheaper roasted barley orzo we produced ourselves back in Italy.

In late June, a newspaper advertisement I inserted, looking for a second-hand small, horse-drawn covered van proved fruitful. Now that I was able to move around independently, I could start to build up some clientele outside of my immediate area, though the large number of pubs and refreshment rooms, groceries, and confectioneries around me meant there were plenty of customers already, as Antonio had promised.

I put all of my equipment together and did three test runs with my first order of milk. I had started with twenty gallons but had enough equipment to triple that if things went well. I sectioned off a part of the factory to create a cool room where I could store my 1-pint ice cream bricks. I decided that I would only work with wholesale customers, as there were plenty of places which sold ice cream along the shopping strip, it didn't make sense to add another.

I hired Jerry, a young man of nineteen, also of Italian heritage to help me on the factory floor so I wouldn't need to stop production in order to make sales rounds. He had joined his father and his uncles on the wharves, loading and unloading cargo, but was eager to try something new, with more prospects. Antonio, who had known the family for many years, had sent him to me, telling me the young man was too bright to waste his life on the wharves. He was exactly the person I needed, eager to learn, forward thinking, and responsible enough to be left on his own.

His younger, ten-year-old brother, Tino, took to dropping in after school, and armed with a pencil, proved useful in writing up our labels so that we could do the deliveries more quickly the next day. Jerry would turn up around 6.00 am and together we would start the production. Then, around 11.00 am, as he handled the boxing and storing, I was able to go out on rounds, delivering and trying to make new clients. Around 4.00 pm, I would return with orders for the next day.

The quality of my ice cream was well received, but I was barely covering my costs because my clients weren't prepared to pay enough. The only solution was to expand my output and extend my sales significantly beyond my immediate area. As Beppe and I had done in Geelong, I took out advertisements in all the South Australian newspapers, promoting bulk deliveries for social occasions and for anyone able to access a railway station.

The responses were a little slow, but they did start coming in, and I was able to increase production. The only snag was that we were still working to demand, as my storage facilities were just not able to handle the quantity I needed to produce, and a few times, my refrigeration capacity in the storeroom had been just on the borderline of acceptable, presenting a huge risk, both to the health of my customers, my reputation, and my profits.

"Why don't you make enquiries at the Port Ice Works over in Fisher Street," suggested Jerry. "It's only a couple of blocks behind us and they might be willing to hire out some cold storage space."

It was a brilliant idea, and I set out immediately to investigate the possibilities, thankfully with success. While this was one more expense, I took the risk that my increased production and sales would cover the cost.

Over discussions at dinner one evening shortly after my arrival, I floated some name ideas with the Latorre family. My thoughts were leaning towards 'Superior Ice cream' or 'Continental Ice Cream', but it was Bart who proposed the winning title. He had come up with the name 'Imperial Ice Cream Company'. It had a familiar ring to it, with many other industries using the word 'Imperial' in their title as it tapped into the intense feelings of patriotism circulating at the time, since more and more young men were signing up to the war effort, even though there was vigorous protest against compulsory military service in Australia. I had some sturdy carboard signs made up for my premises and clients' windows, so that their customers could ask for me by name, and hopefully remember to ask for me to be stocked at other premises.

I dined every evening with the Latorre family, and on Sundays, I was permitted to walk Luisa to and from mass at the Sacred Heart Church on Military Road, but always accompanied, usually by a family member. Luckily, they were quite discreet and let us wander arm in arm a little ahead of them, so we could talk in private.

Most of the chat was nonsense during these times, just two young people getting to know each other. Occasionally, Luisa's Irish friend from school, Dorothy, or Dot as she liked to be called, came to sing at church functions. Dot was usually chaperoned by her recently married older brother and his wife, and so the five of us became a happy set, attending Church socials in our own parish or in Glenelg, where Dot lived with her widowed mother and younger sister.

Luisa had suggested I invite Jerry along with us when we attended a dance at the Largs Pier Hotel. Jerry was closer in age to Dot and Luisa, but unfortunately, he and Dot seemed to have no affinity for each other. At work, Jerry confessed that it would break his mother's heart if he came home with a non-Italian girl, and besides, he didn't really appreciate Dot's loud, opinionated views and her tendency to drink a little too much.

I understood how he felt, remembering my battles with my brother Beppe, and hoped I hadn't offended him. I was firm with Luisa when she suggested we invite Jerry again, telling her that Dot's single status was her brother's problem, not ours. As a banker, I was sure he had access to many more single men than we did.

As it turned out, Michael, Dot's brother had solved Dot's employment problems by finding her a secretarial job, but with many young men in office jobs flocking to the recruiting stations in search of adventure, the sweetheart problem was more difficult to resolve. I didn't mind Dot at all, she was a great storyteller and a keen observer of human nature. She was very enthusiastic about my business and consistently sent me new clients in her area. I joked I would have to put her on the payroll soon. When we were out at large, noisy gatherings, which both Luisa and I found intimidating, Dot could be relied upon to animate the table and draw us all out of ourselves, including her sometimes severe banker brother.

The rhythm of my life in my new home of South Australia began to take on familiar and comforting patterns. As the summer progressed, my sales increased steadily. The feedback about the quality of my product was good and even the Health Inspectors could find no irregularities, granting me a licence without any issues.

On Saturdays, Jerry and I only worked half days and treated ourselves to a session at Salvatore the Barber, who filled us in on all the local gossip, but also proved to be a good place to meet others, which was useful when I was looking for new employees or someone local to help me with a problem. On his advice, in early November, I found a manufacturing jeweller, who was prepared to melt down the gold ingot the crew of the Duchessa di Genova, had pitched in to buy me to mark my eighteenth birthday. I ordered a ring to be made for Luisa, hoping I would be able to propose to her at Christmas.

Before I could take that step, I knew I needed to let Beppe know. Luisa and I had our first photo taken together at a seaside carnival booth the previous Sunday afternoon. I inserted a copy of the photo in a letter to Beppe in which I told him the state of my business and how I had made the acquaintance of Antonio's daughter, whom I hoped to propose to at Christmas.

Never much of a writer unless he wanted something, I had a reply back from Beppe within a fortnight. Of course, he had started his letter with a string of curse words. His first reaction was to take offence at not having been told about Luisa last year. He'd seen through my carefully worded ruse immediately, and had put two and two together, surmising quickly that Luisa had been my main motivation for going to Adelaide and that I wasn't to deny that anymore. He was disappointed I hadn't had the courage to confide in him, but he didn't blame me for keeping such a beauty a secret, especially since everyone knew that he, Beppe, was the better-looking brother. However, he wished me luck, and hoped to hear the good news about an official engagement soon.

I was so relieved. I hadn't really understood my motivation for keeping Luisa a secret, especially after our letters had intensified, but now I could put that behind me, and Beppe and I could be simple brothers once again. Beppe's news about his own business was good too, with Henry and Jack proving to be very competent, and Beppe keeping up with the accounts in my absence.

He was much more informed about the war and had received word from our older brother Federico in Milano about the situation in Italy. No one had heard from either my brother Armando or Zio Camillo in Mexico and were worried about the few snippets in the Italian papers reporting on a Mexican Revolution. There were many shortages of basic goods in Italy, especially coal for heating and flour for bread. They were worried about how they would keep warm this winter due to the spiralling inflation, and they were especially worried for my father who had become quite frail. Food imports, especially wheat and meat had stopped and, owing to the millions of men who had been taken from agricultural production and forcibly conscripted into the army, local production had ground to a halt.

Our sister Maria was still well but living in Milano now and working in one of the new factories that had sprung up, manufacturing uniforms, her wages being a huge help towards paying the rent. She and my parents, and my two younger brothers Nino and Nico, who were fifteen and thirteen respectively, were all lumped in together in a two-bedroom apartment. I couldn't imagine my father in that apartment, he'd been an outdoors man all his life. I worried for him and hoped that sending my good news might perk him up.

I had sent my parents a letter in September, inserting a bank slip for a transfer of as much money as I could spare and explaining my new situation, but I was unsure they had received it yet, as international mail had slowed considerably. I resolved to buy a pretty Christmas card that very day and send it with a copy of the photo of Luisa and me, hoping that it might arrive quicker than a letter.

I also sent cards to Zio Roberto and Zia Mimi in Melbourne, letting them know about my new connection to the Latorre family.

Luisa and Elena commented on my agitation that night and I told them about the situation in Italy, which had me very anxious. Two days later, Elena presented me with a box of warm, winter woollen undergarments, socks, hats, scarves and woollen mittens, something suitable to be shipped to each member of my family. I stared at her in amazement.

"Where did you find these? The shops only stock summer clothes?"

"These aren't from any shop, these are from my friends and now your friends too," she said as she urged me to take the box.

"This is too much, how will I ever repay you all?"

"You're a *buon christiano*," she continued, "you don't need to repay us. When you are in a position to do a good deed for someone else, then you do it, that will be your repayment."

Tears pricked my eyes and threatened to spill over, but I blinked vigorously, clenching my teeth to reign in my emotions. I could say no more, all I could do was grab these two wonderful women before me, Luisa and her mother, and envelope them in the biggest hug I could manage.

The only extra thing I placed in the box before I sealed it and prayed over it, hoping that it would get through to my family in Italy unscathed, was a little note – sent to you from Luisa, my intended, and her parents,

Elena and Antonio Latorre, my towers of strength.

For Christmas, I wanted to concoct a special ice cream dessert for the gathering at the Latorre residence. There would be thirty of us, as Elena had invited her two sisters and their husbands and children, the local friends we usually socialised with, and also Vincenzo's musician cousins. After hearing Sal, the Siciliano Barber, describe his traditional cassata to me, I had an idea.

His cake was essentially a sponge cake layered with a ricotta-based cream studded with candied fruits, chocolate chips and roasted almonds, covered in a pistachio marzipan. I described it to Luisa, and we put our heads together to design something similar made of ice cream. Thanks to Antonio's grocery, we had access to all manner of goods. We chose some plump local sultanas and dried apricots as our fruit element, which we planned to soak in some rum. There were plenty of nuts, all from further north in the Barossa Valley, and Elena always had marzipan imported for her confections.

Luisa took care of the sponges, making three large layers around two inches high. I folded the soaked dried fruit into two pints of vanilla ice cream, and the candied walnuts through another two pints of chocolate ice cream. We sandwiched the ice cream layers between the rum-soaked sponges which Luisa covered with a layer of marzipan, tinted pink. Then she used some white icing to create delicate lace patterns and studded the peaks with halved glacé cherries.

I fashioned a large round tin container with a lid, so I could store the cake in my cool room to be picked up frozen after church on Christmas morning. This would give it time to thaw slightly and be easy to portion for dessert.

For Christmas Day lunch, we started with a selection of pickled vegetables and cured meats which Elena had prepared during the winter. Connie had been called in to help make the pasta – *ferricelli* they called them, using a thin square-sided wire rod to roll the thin ropes of pasta dough, turning them into spirals. The tomatoes from the garden, perfumed with her special sausages, would make a delectable sauce. The mains would consist of roast duck and potatoes which Antonio and Vincenzo were charged with roasting over charcoal in a specially built oven in the back yard, and for which Elena would make a reduced bone broth sauce enriched with red wine, cloves and oranges. There would be the addition of a cooling salad and then my cold dessert, as Christmas day in Australia, occurred in the middle of summer and was inevitably swelteringly hot.

Elena insisted that there would be no gifts exchanged, but each guest would go home with a pot of her marmalade. Each guest though, did bring a small contribution to the feast, whether they were beautiful flowers, a bottle of wine, a round of cheese, a plate of biscuits, or in the case of the musicians, their instruments to entertain us between courses.

I picked up Luisa's ring a week before Christmas. Upon discussion with the jeweller, I had decided on a simple but wide band with an unbroken wreath of ivy carved all the way around the band and with nine tiny round dark sapphires, arranged in three clusters of three to represent the berries. The ivy was to symbolise eternal love, continuity and fidelity and the nine sapphires were the stone for the month of September, the month we had met.

Although the jeweller had marked up a drawing for me, the ring was far more beautiful in reality and brought a lump to my throat. Later in the day, I dropped off a couple of pints of ice cream, for the jeweller to enjoy with his family who lived upstairs from the workshop, as I'd seen a couple of his little kids scuttle behind his work bench when I entered the shop.

I was nervous about giving Luisa the ring, not because I thought she wouldn't accept it, but because I didn't quite know when the right moment would be. She had been extremely busy this month. Luisa spent many days at the council chambers in the Port area, where she volunteered with the Red Cross who were organising supplies for sick and wounded soldiers.

These last few days, she was rehearsing the carols she was to play at the Christmas services to accompany the schoolchildren's choir. She and Vincenzo were at the church now, and Elena and Antonio were in the garden. I squared my shoulders and called them over to the shade of the pergola and simply took the navy velvet ring box out, opening the lid to show them the ring carefully nestled in its white silk interior.

"Do I have your permission to ask for Luisa's hand in marriage this Christmas?" I blurted.

My shoulders were tense, and I was holding my breath, but Antonio simply slapped me on the back and uttered *"bravo"* and Elena told me the ring was *"bellissimo"* and Luisa was a lucky girl.

"When will you ask her?" She had pre-empted my most burning question.

"At Christmas lunch," I suggested.

"Yes, great idea, after lunch, and after we've sampled the sensational dessert you've both created. It's sure to melt everyone's hearts."

Antonio expelled a huge belly laugh as he pinched his wife's cheek.

"Sempre la romantica, 'Lena mia!"

I laughed in turn as they waddled back to their garden, Elena laughing and swatting away her husband's hand as he caressed her bottom.

Our cake was regaled with great cheers when we ceremoniously brought it to the table, but before Luisa began to slice it, I clasped her hands and turned her to face me.

Dropping down to one knee, I looked into her eyes and confidently announced,

"Luisa, you're the most magnificent woman I've ever met. Would you do me the honour of accepting my hand in marriage."

Eyes wide, Luisa gasped, bringing her hands to her mouth, looking up at the now silent company, seeking her mother's reaction. This gave me the chance to pull the ring box from my jacket pocket and open it for her to see.

"Oh, it's exquisite," she gasped. Then she dropped down to my level to envelope me in a hug. The family erupted in thunderous applause. Bart threw himself at the both of us, and Elena, Antonio and Vincenzo were the first in line to congratulate us, helping us to struggle back to our feet, allowing me to slide the ring onto Luisa's finger with a kiss to seal the deal.

Elena had insisted we invite our friends to the house on New Year's Eve for a light supper and drinks so they could all be told our news together. We dismantled the large dining table and rolled back the carpet to make room for dancing. Vincenzo and his musician friends were unavailable as they had their own musical engagements that night, but we had Bart to man the phonograph, and Luisa and I had chosen a couple of extra popular records to add to the collection as a Christmas gift to each other.

While discussions about the war dominated the early part of the evening, eventually we let the music transport us to a happier place. The year finished with our friends raising a toast and insisting I kiss my beautiful and much adored fiancée, and I was more than happy to oblige.

Elena very proudly showed us the brief engagement announcement which appeared in the newspaper on the 6th of January 1917.

War News

One Sunday morning, I was seated in the pew of the Sacred heart Church at Semaphore with the Latorre family, behind Luisa and Vincenzo who were perched on a narrow stool at the organ. The priest had been reeling off names of parishioners for whom the service was being dedicated this week. Then he moved on to the list of names for special prayers and a collective gasp arose when Mrs Black, Mr and Mrs Hodder and Mrs and Miss Torbey were named. They were well-known locals and had this week been afflicted with news of a lost relative. It had been the same, every Sunday, for the past month. The Battle of the Somme had been claiming many lives, and our little corner of the world was not exempt from the sacrifice.

The latest surprising news had been about the peasant uprising in Russia, an important member of the Entente powers. With Russia in disarray, the German Forces fighting there were able to be redirected and there was fear a new front would open up in Eastern France, or reinforcements would be sent to aid the Austrians, against whom the Italians were losing ground. Not even the arrival of several thousand

American forces had seemed to make a dent in the well-defended position of the German Army in Northern France, and more and more stories of atrocities against captured prisoners of war had everyone spooked.

Australian involvement in the war was still on a voluntary basis, as the conscription referendum had been defeated when put to the vote last October, and despite every spare wall emblazoned with posters urging young men to heed the call of their mates from the front, the rate Australians were joining the AIF was a mere trickle compared to the manpower that was actually needed.

Antonio examined the three local papers closely every day trying to make sense of what was happening. When Italy was mentioned, it was usually in a small paragraph, without enough detail to help us understand the real situation. News from my family in Milano, who were struggling along, but essentially fine, despite the grim circumstances, came very rarely, and spoke of massive numbers of dead and wounded and much shortage of basic goods.

One morning, Antonio read in the Port Adelaide News' shipping column that the SS Ormonde had docked. Nine months ago, he had placed some orders for fabrics and haberdashery notions as well as a range of copper tools and utensils which he sold through his shop. He had received a letter letting him know they were to be sent via the Ormonde. He also was expecting his usual bundle of Italian newspapers and journals, though they would be at least six months old by the time he received them.

"If you don't mind Antonio, could I join you when you go dockside to collect your order? I'm thinking that the captain might have a better perspective on what's happening in Europe."

The captain was busy, but he gladly accepted Antonio's invitation to dinner that evening, and I arranged to collect him later.

The following afternoon, I had a visit from two local constables, asking me if I had seen two Italian seamen.

"I've seen more than two," I answered light-heartedly, as whenever there was a large trans-continental ship in port, there were always gangs of sailors milling about the hotels and shops.

One constable drew his shoulders back and continued in a firm voice,

"Your horse and buggy were seen at the docks twice yesterday, once in the evening around 6.00 pm and again at night around 11.00 pm. Can you explain why you were there at those times?"

"Certainly officer," I replied a little more warily.

"My father-in-law is an importer of select Italian goods and he invited Capitano Raggianti of the Ormonde to dinner at his home last night. I picked him up and then dropped him back off after the meal."

The other policeman was taking notes and asked me again to specify times and with whom I'd been, as well as to spell out Antonio's full name and the address of his home and business. Then they showed me papers granting them permission to inspect the premises of any place where absconders might take refuge.

I had a good chuckle watching them overturn a pile of cardboard boxes and even look inside the brining tanks. The funniest was when they began throwing the pitchfork haphazardly into my poor old nag's hay. They left with a warning that it was an offence to harbour deserters and that if I should come across these fellows, I was to bring them to the station immediately.

"What will happen to them?" I asked out of general curiosity.

"They will be returned to their ship, but if the ship has sailed, they will need to register as aliens and then they would be released, provided they had some means of support."

The next day, another set of policemen came calling, asking the same questions and carrying out the same search to no avail. I had neither seen these men, nor been approached on their behalf by anyone else.

Two days after the policemen's last visit, I arrived at the factory earlier than usual to tackle some paperwork before production began. My normal routine was to enter via the side alley, tether my mare to her post and give her some fresh hay. Then I would come back up the alleyway to the main street and enter through my front door and head to the kitchen, where I would make myself a coffee before starting my day proper.

That morning, my *Napoletana* was in the sink, still full of coffee grounds, yet I was sure I had emptied and rinsed it out when I had used it the previous afternoon. I was finicky about not leaving wet coffee grounds in my coffee maker as that led to the development of mould which impacted on the taste of the coffee.

"Would Jerry have made himself a coffee," I wondered. "But hadn't I left after him?"

There were also a couple of tumblers in the sink. I stopped to rinse the items and left them to dry on the draining board. Then when I entered the bedroom, there was an odd, sour smell and the cover of the narrow bed had been lowered right to the floor so that it looked like someone had dragged it across the bed in a hurry. I decided to step through the bedroom and go to the bathroom opposite.

I turned on the tap but stood very still behind the slightly ajar door and watched two slim young men in sailor suits, noiselessly slide from under the bed. I opened the bathroom door and held my arms out in front, with my hands forming pincers – the universal Italian sign language for 'what's going on here?'

I spoke to them in Italian. "So you're the ones the police are looking for I guess?" The men looked at me sheepishly.

"*Santo cielo, you stink.*" I recoiled as I got closer to them. They still hadn't uttered a word but were looking back at me wide-eyed and scared.

"Okay, get yourselves into the bathroom here while I fetch some eggs and bread from next door, and I'll make you some omelettes."

I showed them where I kept towels and soap and then headed off to Mrs Marinoff's grocery next door. I wasn't sure whether they'd still be there when I got back. But, I was pleased to hear splashing noises, and by the time I'd made a few thick omelettes, buttered the bread, cut some cheese and apples and made another pot of coffee, Jerry had arrived, and I learned that he'd been complicit in sheltering these two until the ship had left. Jerry apologized for not having said anything, but he felt if I didn't know, then I wouldn't be forced to lie.

"But where were they when the police searched the premises?" I asked.

"Oh, they were only here at night. During the day, I kept them in my own back shed. Mamma got suspicious when the chickens started going a bit wild, but she never ventures down to the end of the garden."

Since the four other factory employees were due to arrive soon, along with the contracted drivers, I had to make a decision about what to do with them. In the end, I convinced myself and them, that it would be best if I took them to the police station to be registered, and then they could return here until I was able to think about jobs and accommodation for them, rather than risk the police turning up again and arresting them.

There was a manhole in the ceiling above the kitchen sink, I pointed to it and asked if they could get up there. They used the broom handle to shift the cover then hoisted themselves onto the sink and then into the roof space and covered over the manhole.

"*Va bene*, this is our story. You hid out here during the day and came down when everyone had gone."

I didn't want to risk involving Jerry or his family. We used the parlour and main bedroom for storage and the men sometimes had their lunch in the kitchen if it was wet outside. So, I began to concoct a plausible story.

"When the factory machinery gets going, we wouldn't have heard any noise. As I don't sleep here at night, once the factory is closed, it was safe for you to come down. You've been living on coffee and scraps from the men's lunches. This morning, I arrived earlier than usual and caught you out. I fed you and then accompanied you to the police station."

It was mostly truth, hopefully it would pass. They expressed their sincere gratitude as the three of us ambled down the street and around the corner to the police station, a cottage with a deep front verandah where a few native women and children sat gathered on the bare tiles. I sometimes saw them, dressed in mismatched cast-offs and bare feet, wandering around with babies tied to their backs. They mostly lived in the grasslands further out of the Port area, and once, when I was returning from a trip to the dairy in Kilkenny, a couple of children waived me down and I gave them one of my cans of milk and let them pat my horse.

"Gina, milk man," one of the children pointed me out to their mother.

They remembered my horse's name. Smiles spread across faces as we waved our hellos.

"Trouble mister?" One of the women winked as she pointed to the station door.

Not knowing their language, I shrugged and made a grimace of resignation as I shepherded the two sailors through the door.

We entered into a large room with tall ceilings which had been partitioned into a waiting area with wooden benches under the windows, separated by a tall counter running the width of the room. Behind the counter, was one of the constables who had questioned me two days ago. He was dealing with two elderly women making enquiries. The constable met my eyes and motioned me to the seats under the window, whispering something to another young policeman behind him, who moved out through a side door.

We took our seats and continued chatting. The two sailors were from Genova, so I understood them well enough, and I began reminiscing about my days aboard my uncle's steamer, and the places I would visit when we returned to home port. They were young and scared. They told me of German U-boats who had been threatening merchant vessels. The boys had been with their ship since they were twelve, both had come from the orphanage and had no-one else in Italy.

They had stopped in Fremantle and had spoken to some other Italians there and then made a pact to jump ship as soon as they could. They'd been assigned to scrubbing the foredeck when the ship had reached Port Adelaide, and they'd been able to slip away when Antonio and I had kept the captain distracted, and everybody else was busy unloading cargo. They'd heard me speaking Italian, so they thought they'd follow me. When I entered the factory, they had hidden behind a low front fence at the Newmarket Hotel opposite which hadn't opened yet. They only ventured to the factory lane once they saw me leave, but Jerry had spotted them and kept them hidden in the barn until lunchtime, at which point he usually went home for a quick lunch at his parents' place, which was located only a few minutes' walk away. Jerry had been very good to them, and had told them about the police visits, so they had begged him not to say anything to anyone until their ship had well and truly sailed away.

A side door opened and a uniformed man in his fifties stood staring down at us. I was only five foot six in my stockinged feet, the two boys about the same height, and this colossus who came to stand very intimidatingly in front of us, hands on hips, had me panicked, and leaning back into the wall behind me. I was expecting a bellow, but he was softly spoken.

"So, these are the two fugitives who've been wasting police time these last three days?"

Despite the dulcet tones, his regard felt ever more menacing. Then he turned to look pointedly at me.

"And who might you be, sir?"

I felt a tremor move through me, and my reply slipping out, almost as if a puppeteer had drawn it from me with a string: "Bodoni, Carlo, err, Ch-Charles, Charlie."

"Well Mr Bord-awny, you and your mates best come with me."

We followed him to a small windowless room with a narrow table and some simple wooden chairs. A younger policeman drew up three chairs at one side of the table and then stationed himself at the door. The interrogation was straightforward. I acted as interpreter as the young mariners spoke very little English. They were asked to give names, ages, places of birth, their work history, how long they'd sailed with the merchant ship they had just abandoned. Then they were asked to explain their escape from the ship and evasion from capture. When asked about their reason for jumping ship, they emphatically replied for themselves: *"torpedo."*

The Sergeant had been quite dispassionate till that point, but nodding, he replied with a sigh and a single word: "Lusitania." The whole world knew about the sinking of the British passenger liner by German U-boats as it left New York in May 1915.

The boys finished the interview by recounting the story we had settled on regarding their arrival at my factory. At the end, I caught the Sergeant lift his eyes and cock an eyebrow to the young policeman at the door who nodded ever so briefly. I had the distinct impression that this younger one was able to understand Italian and was confirming the accuracy of my translation.

Then the questioning turned to me. I was required to give my full name, my history of arrival in the country. I was questioned about why I had come to Adelaide, my business interests, and my residency status. I explained that I had worked my passage to Melbourne, but that I had travelled with all the appropriate British papers, including my uncle's sponsorship with a job waiting for me in Melbourne. The Sergeant turned to a ledger that he had brought with him and proceeded to look through a few pages of names.

"I see you're not registered here though."

I was puzzled, but soon found out that in 1916, as part of the War Precautions Act, all aliens in the country were required to present themselves to their local authorities to be registered. I apologised and said I had not been advised of that requirement. The Sergeant then proceeded to add our three names and residency details to the ledger. I had volunteered to let Marino and Gianfranco live at my factory and provide them with employment so that they did not have to be locked up for the night. An hour after we'd set off for the police station, we were back at the factory, a little shaken but unharmed. I explained to the boys what I had promised the Sergeant.

"You'll need to stay here at least for the next month, you can share the bed. I can't afford to pay you much, but enough to cover meals and you can help out in the factory during the day. Jerry will look after you."

Jerry, who'd been a little downcast, judging by the way he kept removing and resetting his cap, jumped up and volunteered,

"They can come to lunch with me, I'm sure mamma won't mind making a little extra pasta."

I left them with Jerry and made my way out to pick up orders for the next day. First stop was at Elena's shop, the confectionery at Semaphore. I knew I'd be able to rely on her and Connie in the shop next door to use their connections and help find them some suitable clothes.

"Don't you worry, you bring them home to dinner tonight and we'll sort them out."

True to her word, she'd found a couple of changes of clothes for each of them and after they'd tried them on, Connie whisked them away to shorten and lengthen seams as required.

"I'll leave them on the kitchen table, and you can take them with you tomorrow morning," she reassured, leaving us to enjoy one of Elena's simple but nonetheless satisfying meals. Luisa and Bart, who understood their parents' southern Italian dialect quite well, but were unfamiliar with the Genovese dialect spoken by these northern Italian boys, sat silently beside me, concentrating hard to understand the conversation, which naturally centred on what they had seen or heard of the war in Europe.

Two days later, another set of young constables turned up at my factory. Again, their reason for being there caught me completely off guard. I was served a summons to appear in a month's time at the local Magistrate's Court for having failed to register my status as an alien in accordance with the Commonwealth War Precautions Act of 1916.

"These young mariners are going to cost you a pretty penny,' Antonio advised, "you'd better engage the services of a lawyer to represent you too."

My appearance in court lasted no more than fifteen minutes. I was directed to the dock, had my identity confirmed, was sworn in and had the charge read out to me. My lawyer pleaded my innocence of the law, describing me as a successful and upright businessman, a pillar of the local community, someone who had taken all precautions to obtain the necessary trade licences and regularly passed the inspections by the Health Board with flying colours. He argued that had the requirement for registration been more widely announced, I would surely have done my duty by the prescriptions of the Act. The judge proclaimed that innocence of the law was no justification for pleading not guilty, but he accepted that I was of excellent character and fined me £5 with £1 for costs, in default of 3 months imprisonment.

Both Luisa and Antonio who had accompanied me, let out sighs of relief as we exited the court house. But I was incensed, adamant that I had been taken advantage of as a money-making exercise, in retaliation for not having let the police catch the two young sailors before the ship sailed, and therefore claim the reward the captain had posted, ironically set at £5, which was two week's wages for the local bobbies. I was convinced they thought I was lying.

At dinner that night, I tried to explain my disappointment.

"It's ..." I hesitated, unsure of what words to use. "In Italy, we expect that to get anything done, we'll have to grease the palm of some minor official, and his superior, and then literally bend a knee when we hand over the envelope to the one who puts the final stamp on things, otherwise, you can die waiting for the wheels of officialdom to turn in your favour. But here, well I just thought things were different here, I thought, for once, I could just get on with my life without always having to look for the knives ready to be plunged into my back for daring to pursue something perceived as being above my station."

Both Vincenzo and Antonio had been children when they'd arrived in Australia, so they were grappling with what I meant, but Vincenzo sympathised.

"*Sì, sì*, you've lost your *innocenza*. Welcome to adulthood. Did you really think you were going to be able to just walk through life without any obstacles or setbacks?"

"Just keep looking forward," advised Antonio, squeezing my shoulders. "Life has its ups and downs. The best thing you can do is to is not dwell on the disappointments and focus on your own dreams."

I sighed my understanding and resolved to take their advice. My business was humming along nicely, and Luisa and I had our wedding and our future together to look forward to.

Setback

Luisa and I had planned to have our wedding in early September, enough time for the women to get the right outfits made. In keeping with Italian tradition, Elena and Antonio would host the wedding banquet at a local eatery. We had our choice of musicians, and of course the service would be at our local church. Elena and Luisa had everything under control. Luisa had already asked her friend Dot to be her attendant. Her cousin, little four-year-old Anna, would be the flower girl and twelve-year old brother Bart would make a very responsible ring bearer. My only job was to get my suit made, organise a best man and the honeymoon.

I was spoiled for choice regarding tailors in Adelaide, Sal the barber would know the best place to go. As for a best man, I had written to Beppe and had received an enthusiastic reply. I had also written to Zio Roberto and his wife Gloria, hoping they might be able to come too.

My friend Johnnie, who had now sold his tea rooms and bought a licence to run a hotel in Gilbert Street which provided drinks, dining, and basic accommodation in the four rooms he had upstairs, would look after Beppe he said, and make sure he got to the wedding on time.

As for a honeymoon, I thought Luisa and I could spend the weekend at the Southern Cross Hotel on King William Street. The hotel was owned by a well-known Italian, Giovanni Raspo, and the head chef was Amadeo Rubino, and they had an excellent reputation for very refined dining and accommodation. I made sure that there was room for two days. Luisa had expressed a desire to return to her town of birth, Melbourne, to take in the music scene there. Now that Zio Roberto was living in more salubrious Fitzroy, he promised to host us, offering to pay for our trip as his wedding gift. I suggested I could book a passage for all of us on an intercoastal steamer, that way we could stop in at Geelong for a quick visit of Beppe's factory before disembarking in Melbourne.

I also had another surprise planned. Through Johnnie's connections, which had become substantial, as he had just been elected as the head of the West End Brewers Association, we had organised to hire me a motor car for the day, a move which would be considered quite bold and memorable.

However, I needed to spend a few afternoons remembering how to drive first. Bobby had taught me the rudimentaries in Melbourne, but I hadn't laid hands on a motor car in more than two years. My old nag Gina would soon have to be replaced. Even though I rarely used her to transport equipment or goods anymore and had switched to using a light buggy in which to get around, I could see she was beginning to struggle. I'd been pondering about whether I could afford a small motor car, maybe even a second hand one, they were becoming more popular, and more available, but a deposit on a house for Luisa and I seemed to be more sensible.

There was some land for sale not far from the Alberton Hotel which came with a decent house and a substantial block of land. It had the added benefit of providing enough space for me to potentially relocate the factory, which would mean the ability to expand and, more importantly, a shorter commute to work, which meant more time with my wife to be.

I would have to erect a large shed on the property, but it meant I could also have a purpose-built cool room and reduce the cost of storage and the inconvenience of having to shift the ice cream to the warehouse. The business had been growing steadily. I now had four employees and some sub-contracted carters to deliver my ice cream.

Last summer, I had employed three drivers with vans and had obtained licences to sell my ice cream on the esplanade at Semaphore, Largs Bay and Grange from early December to the end of January. I had used the trick we'd employed in Geelong of pre-filling mini paper cups with various flavours that were easier and less messy to sell compared to cones. They could also be stored in insulated boxes on a bed of ice, staying colder for longer.

I was proud of the sizeable turnover I'd made this summer, enough to pay off my debt to Antonio and his investors, saving myself three years of interest payments.

I was at my front door, about to set off to the property broker's office at the end of the street, when a young lad in a brown uniform approached me. He touched his cap, asked for a Mr Carlo *Baw-dough-knee*, and handed me a thin slip of pale pink coloured paper, folded into an envelope shape.

"Telegram for you sir."

Never having received such a thing before this moment, I stood on my doorstep, turning the envelope over several times before realising it had been sent from my brother in Geelong. I couldn't conjure up a scenario where Beppe would need to send a telegram.

My heart beating fast, I hurried back inside the little cottage, searching for my letter opener. The message was in an unfamiliar hand. It read:

> RECEIVED NEWS THIS MORNING FROM RICO. PAPA
> PASSED AWAY SUDDENLY TWO DAYS AGO. SICK FOR
> SOME TIME. MAMMA SAD BUT IN GOOD HEALTH.
> OTHERS FINE.

I sat at my desk, staring at the telegram for such a long time. I could hear the activity in the factory, but I couldn't move. I recalled my father, always with his sleeves rolled up, summer or winter. A man who commanded much respect, because as the miller, he was also the tax collector and the distributor of any largesse provided by the landowners. If there were decisions to be made in our compound, he would listen fairly to all arguments, but everyone knew he had the last word. He had been living in Milano now for two years, but I could never imagine him in that grey space.

My mother's last letter, written four months ago, in March, but received only a week ago had spoken about my father's heavy cold, but she said she was seeing signs of improvement as the weather was warming.

I was saddened for my younger siblings and my mother. I wished we could all be together to share our grief. Then I thought of my mother and her solid practicality. I had always been surrounded by death as I was growing up, it was simply part of the circle of life. I had to remember that and be practical. Prayers, patience, and hard work were her solution to everything. After some more time spent in reminiscing, it dawned on me that the family would need assistance for the funeral. I remembered the black framed glass wagons drawn by a pair of glossy black steeds that were the usual form of transportation for the important people in Cremona. I didn't know if that were possible in Milano, but I had seen the same thing in Genova, so I hoped that my father would be entitled to that importance.

I needed to get to the bank before they closed to wire them some money, and then to the Post Office to send a telegram acknowledging I had heard the news, and that some money was on its way. I would also reply to Beppe. Should I send one to Zio Roberto just in case Beppe hadn't thought to do that? No one had heard from Armando in Mexico. It was time to visit the Italian Consulate and see if they could make enquiries through diplomatic channels. I decided not to say anything to the workers, just yet. I would tell them in my own time, tomorrow, once I felt more in control of my emotions.

My mission completed, I headed home to Luisa, who gathered me in her arms and allowed me to shed the tears I had been holding back. By the end of the week, the news had spread, and as was customary, neighbours came by to give their condolences. Our priest organised a special mass on the Saturday afternoon for the repose of my father's soul and, at the end, when I stood at the front of the altar to tell the gathering some of my father's story, I was astounded to see the church was full. There was the extended Latorre family of course, the neighbours and local traders. I even recognised some of my customers. Sal was there with the local lads with whom I sometimes played friendly card games. My workers were there with their families. Antonio's investors were there, Luisa's friends were there, parishioners we often chatted with on Sundays were there. I was humbled by this unexpected outpouring of affection and hoped Beppe had this support too.

A week later, Elena broached a difficult subject. The wedding was three months away, but in Italian tradition, it was customary to observe a period of mourning. Usually, around a year, unless there were special circumstances.

"It would be unseemly," she said, "and not to mention bad luck, to have the wedding so soon after your father's death. Maybe we could postpone it till June next year," she suggested.

I looked at Luisa, she was trying to be brave. Her eyes were shadowed. Obviously, her mother had already spoken to her. She locked fingers with me, sighing and hunching her shoulders. Looking sadly at each other, we turned in unison and nodded to her mother. I still felt quite numb after the news of my father's passing, but sad to be putting our much-anticipated new life on hold. All I could do was clutch my sniffling fiancé to me and reassure her that six months would pass quickly.

"Don't forget to cancel your bookings," whispered Elena kindly as she gave me a hug.

Luisa walked me to her front gate where we had a little cuddle and stole a brief kiss.

"It won't be long, you'll see," she reassured me in turn.

Both of us sighed as I lifted the latch on the gate and headed a couple of doors down to my lonely bed.

In early August, all the newspapers could talk about was the third battle of Ypres, and the thirty-two thousand allied casualties lost in a single day. There was a renewed call from the British Government for more men. They were rumoured to be seeking to recruit another three million. I just couldn't get my head around that figure which was equivalent to the whole adult population of Australia.

I visited a Mr. Barrow, who was the Honorary Italian Vice-Consul. He was a businessman and a scholar who had spent twenty years in Italy and spoke the language remarkably well, and while he didn't report directly to Italy – that was the role of the official consul in Melbourne – he did receive the latest news. I went to him to ask about the possibility of sending a message to the Italian Embassy in Mexico, to see if official channels could locate my brother Armando and my uncle Camillo.

When I dropped into his office a month later, there was no news of my brother, but he offered me a coffee and we sat down for a chat. Mr. Barrow warned me that the Italians were also in dire straits, fighting a losing battle against the Austrians who held the upper hand, as they were positioned at the top of the Dolomite mountain ranges, and the Italians were in defensive positions below them, unable to move. The Germans who were no longer defending the Russian front had been sent to boost Austrian numbers. It didn't look good for Italy.

I shook my head in despair. Italy had been under an Austrian yoke for almost a century before fighting a twenty-year war of independence when the Italian Republic had been formed under King Vittorio Emanuele II. However, the promised prosperity of self-directed government had never really materialised. Even before the outbreak of war, Italy felt defeated morally, physically, and economically as other European nations powered ahead, reaping in the profits of industrialisation.

"Would being invaded by the Austrians really matter that much," I enquired of this earnest and gentle man.

"Well, you may soon find out for yourself," he sighed.

I could tell that the man wanted to say more but was hesitating, shuffling papers around his desk.

"Is there some more news," I coaxed, trying to read his behaviour for clues.

"Italy has requested the Australian Government forward lists of all the men of Italian nationality between the ages of eighteen and forty residing in Australia. I've been requested to write to the Police

Commissioner to obtain their lists of ..."

"Registers of Aliens," I jumped to my feet, "That damned register and those damned mariners. They've already cost me a hefty lump of money for the fine and the lawyer's fee, and I looked after them for a month, now my good deed is back to slap me in the face!"

I stopped to think through the consequences before I spoke again, my voice high pitched from the emotion and my legs needing to pace, to keep my wits about me.

"But it would take us at least three months to get to Italy, that's if we're not blasted out of the water by a German torpedo. And none of us would have had any military training. I haven't held a gun since I was thirteen, shooting hares on the farm."

Mr Barrow's forlorn eyes stared back at me. He was clearly distraught, caught between his need to perform his job, and the realisation that he could be sending hundreds of young men to their death. I reached out and took his shaking hand, as gently as I could.

"*Buon corraggio*," I whispered.

"*Altrettanto*." He replied, as I stepped into the corridor and firmly put on my hat.

I didn't say anything to anyone, I just didn't know what to say. I was in disbelief, and I kept hoping that something drastic would happen and the scheme would be scrapped. In my dreams every night, I saw myself floating face down staring at the ocean floor.

On Monday, the third of September, the day Luisa and I were meant to have been sailing to our honeymoon in Melbourne, the official letter arrived. I was required to present myself to my local Army Recruiting Office with this letter where I would receive further directions. Failure to comply within a month of receiving this missive would result in Police arrest. I had a month. I would let the family know tonight, but I would go to my lawyer first to see if there was anything that could be done.

It was Johnnie who suggested a medical exemption, and Luisa who suggested I should get a pair of glasses as soon as possible. My poor long-distance vison and my vanity at not wanting to wear glasses, had been a joke between us, but how ironic if now those glasses could mean the difference between life and death? I fronted up to the Recruitment Office in a pair of shiny round spectacles, only to find that the enrolling officer was sporting a similar pair. The official barely glanced at my letter, just confirmed that my personal particulars were correct and sent me through for a medical examination.

"We'll be in touch," was the only information I was given.

At the end of the following month, I still hadn't heard anything, but Johnnie drove down in his motor car one Sunday afternoon, bringing a flyer with him. On the following Thursday evening at the Adelaide Town Hall, an Italian academic, a certain Sergeant Leonardo Galli was scheduled to speak about his experiences of fighting in 1912 with the esteemed Italian General Luigi Cadorna, and then again in 1915 while wearing the uniform of the AIF in Gallipoli. Apparently, he'd been touring around the country, successfully drumming up around four thousand recruits, hoping to reach the magic number of five thousand before returning to Italy himself.

Johnnie said that word in the Italian quarters around the West End was that the Italian boys who'd been summoned with the same letter I had received would be turning up en masse to get the truth about the situation in Italy.

"Let's hope this man's genuine and not some propaganda tool who happens to be able to speak with an Italian accent," I said, tossing aside the flyer.

As I suspected, it had been a waste of time. Galli had been an elegant and stirring speaker, but it was clear he knew very little about what was really going on in Italy, beyond the fact that her defences were at the point of collapse. The young Italian men present at the meeting had all been shepherded into a side chamber with promises of a private meeting with Galli, but he only kept repeating what he'd already said. There were about fifty men, all Italian born, and registered as aliens. Those born in Australia or who had been granted naturalization were exempt. After animated discussion, we determined that we would hold out as long as possible, but that if we were going to be deported anyway, at least we could insist on going together, and in that way, hopefully would end up supporting each other on the battlefield.

News that my lawyer had come up with a possible solution brightened me and my supporters momentarily. He planned to claim that since I had travelled to Australia with British papers, I was de facto a British subject and no longer an alien. I felt I had nothing to lose by filing this lawsuit against the Commonwealth of Australia and hoped it would be a winning strategy.

By November, even the newspapers in Adelaide reported the terrible defeat of the Italians at the battle of Caporetto, the sacking of General Cadorno and the quarter of a million lives lost. Finally, in December, the Supreme Court handed down my judgement, with a non-judgement. They declared that only the Minister of Defence could rule in this situation, it was not a matter for the court. My lawyer suggested an appeal would be a waste of time, but he would write a letter to the minister.

Christmas was next week, what a difference a year makes. By late January, I received a letter informing me that I needed to be prepared to leave Australia in April 1918. No reply had come from the minister. I had serious decisions to make regarding my business and my planned nuptials.

Luisa wanted us to get married straight away, with no party, just a quiet ceremony at the church, but I wouldn't have it. It wouldn't be fair on her. What if when we consummated our marriage she became pregnant? I would be leaving her with a life-long burden and spoil her chances of ever finding love again. She was only eighteen years of age. No, prayer and patience I recommended, my mother's eternal words tumbling automatically from my lips. I told her how much I loved her and that I had every intention of coming back to her. But I was determined to extract a promise from her – that if she hadn't heard from me within two years, she should consider herself free of any obligation towards me and she was to promise me that she would move on with her life. There was a lot of crying from the both of us, but Antonio and Elena were grateful for my sensible decision, despite their daughter's heartbreak.

As for the business, I decided to keep trading until the end of the summer. I asked Jerry if he were interested in buying me out, but neither he nor his family had the sort of funds needed, and besides, he was considering joining up too. As he had been born in Adelaide, he would join the Australian Forces. He had several school mates who had made it through Gallipoli and were now in the Middle East. He felt he should do his duty. But he knew his parents would be furious. He and his cousin had decided they would enrol together, but he'd wait till the end of the summer.

Despite the war, the South Australian taste for ice cream rose unabated. Maybe it was because of the uncertainty of the future, people were determined to make the most of every day. At the end of February, I placed an advertisement in the local paper announcing I was soon leaving for the front as the reason my whole ice cream plant was for sale, I didn't want people to think my business had failed. I was angry

at being forced into this situation and terrified of the consequences.
I decided it would be best to sell everything so that it wouldn't be a
burden for the Latorre family. I would place the bulk of the money in
Luisa's name, for her to dispose of as she saw fit. The refrigeration unit
and all the metal vats sold quickly, as materials were in short supply. A
couple of weeks later, the cottage and the factory site were empty. A life
dismantled so easily. I was expected to be in Melbourne's Sturt Street
Barracks by the 27th of April.

I buried those traumatic final goodbyes deep inside my gut. In my
heart I left space only for the warmth of the love I had for Luisa and the
unconditional acceptance I'd found in Adelaide. They would have to
see me through. The other Italians were all leaving by train, but I had
asked permission to travel by steamboat to finalise my personal affairs.

I stopped in Geelong. Beppe, as a naturalized British subject, and
now as head of an important volunteer brigade protecting the Geelong
wharfs, had given up the idea of enlisting. He was full of plans for an
upgrade to his factory, looking to install new, more up to date equipment
and improve the safety features of the business. I wished him well, the
irony of the situation perplexed the both of us, but I was glad to have
been able to say my goodbyes in person.

In Melbourne, I did the rounds – Zia Mimi, still taking in lodgers,
Zio Roberto and Zia Gloria, Bobby and even Frank who had now taken
over their father's businesses. I met their little families. I was happy for
them but couldn't find the words to express those sentiments. I spent
my last day just lying on a little narrow bed in Zio Roberto's spare
room, counting down the hours to my departure for the training camp at
Broadmeadows, staring at the crack in the ceiling and playing with the
chain carrying a St. Christopher medal that Luisa had organised to have
blessed and had placed around my neck herself.

The only voice that came through loud and clear was Zio Carlo's. Onboard ship, my role had often required me to deliver food from the galley to the dining room, and if I forgot something it would mean another trip up and down the narrow stairs over two decks. My uncle would say, "If you don't use your head, you have to use your legs."

"Use your head, use your head, use your head …" were the only thoughts bouncing between my ears.

Unfortunately, my head felt like it was in a fog. I did the only thing I still had the power to do. I prayed for guidance and courage. I retrieved the St. Nicholas miniature I had received from my grandmother before leaving home way back in 1905 and tucked it into the upper pocket of my shirt.

"*Ritorniamo*," I whispered to it before I did up the button.

I'd be back for my Luisa.

Regimental Woes

The hundred or so Italian Nationals the Australian Army had gathered and paraded through the streets of Melbourne to the Flinders Street station with much cheering and flag waving by spectators were left rotting in the mud at the Broadmeadows racetracks for a whole month, waiting for the arrival of the reservists from Sydney and Brisbane. There was endless marching in formation, rifle practice without bullets, pretend attacking with blunt swords against stationary potato sacks filled with straw, and boot polishing. Interminable boot polishing. I couldn't understand the insistence on this last activity, given that we were tramping in mud again as soon as we put our boots back on.

The younger, more athletic men made sport of all the constant movement and found their fun teasing and egging each other on. I was just angry at the folly of all this pretence.

I became more and more disgruntled, complaining at every perceived injustice, until the Ruggeri brothers, whom I had known from the Adelaide Central Markets, and with whom I shared a tent, started mocking me, imitating, and even pre-empting my complaints. This had the effect of snapping me out of the shroud of misery I had spun for myself. The only positive aspect was that I could continue to write to Luisa. I didn't have much to say, but I could reassure her that she was always in my thoughts.

A rumour began circulating that the Australian Labour Party had organised a thirty thousand signature petition to the National Parliament, discrediting the legality of the Australian Government's action in our regard. But it was useless. As Italy had always had compulsory military service, all Italian men of serving age were technically reservists, and all liable to be called up for active service. France and Britain had enacted the same processes. There were no arguments to save us. If we didn't comply, we would be court-marshalled and imprisoned, and still eventually end up at the front. A visit from the Italian Consul in Melbourne, confirmed this information and gave us more accurate ideas about our impending journey.

We were all put aboard a converted cargo ship, with a huge shipment of Australian wheat as ballast, destined for bakers at the front. First stop Fremantle, where another lot of reservists came on board. We travelled up along the western coast of Australia into the Indian ocean with a stop at Colombo. Then across to the Red Sea, landing in Egypt, where we were processed depending on our region of origin and from there, taken to Italy.

On board, I made a bit of a nuisance of myself, exploring the ship, especially going down to visit the engineers and trying to sneak up to the bridge, until First Lieutenant Gainsborough, who was accompanying us, understood my genuine interest, and realised that I had experience as a purser. He put me to work organizing the meal shifts and the onboard entertainments by ferreting out the musicians, dramatists, and jokesters amongst us willing to perform. It was better than just sitting around for two months.

Once in Egypt, we were given uniforms and further supplies. The Italian uniforms were a greenish-grey, a little lighter in colour than the deep olive of the Australian uniforms. The Melbourne boot maker brothers were not impressed with the lesser-quality leather being used for our boots or the thin soles, declaring they wouldn't last more than a month in the winter mud.

The hopes of all the Adelaide boys who thought they'd be fighting together were immediately dashed. The purpose of this separation was a purely practical one. While Italy had been a unified nation for fifty years, battalions were formed on regional lines, so orders could be made clear in one dialect and its members could communicate with each other. The standard Italian language based on the writings of the Tuscan poets, was only spoken by those fortunate to have received an education of substance.

Eventually, I found myself with a group of about twenty Lombardi, who were being dropped off in Genova and then transported by train to the headquarters of the 61st and 62nd Sicilia Infantry Division in Parma. Parma was only a half day away from Cremona and I became quite emotional to know that I would be so close to my old home. Parma was also a substantial city. I sent up a prayer, hoping that we would remain there long enough for me to be able to send a telegram to Luisa, letting her know I had arrived safely.

I managed to send my telegram, and then a week later I sent another more jubilant one, and to my mother in Milano as well. I wasn't being sent to the front, well not yet anyway! Instead of lounging around waiting to be assigned, I'd made myself known to an American Sergeant from the Red Cross Ambulance Corps. I could see that they were working with huge numbers of wounded Italian and American soldiers and were struggling to keep up with the paperwork necessary to follow through.

The American Red Cross had been working tirelessly to transport soldiers from field hospitals to Milano or Firenze, but a better equipped base hospital which was able to perform surgeries and deal with gas victims and the shell-shocked was desperately needed.

In July, a single American regiment, the 332nd, had been sent to assist the Italian Third Army, and along with it, a fully equipped and staffed medical corps, who were now manning a base hospital in Vicenza, just fifteen miles from the Italian front with Austria-Hungary. The American doctors and nurses at the hospital were having trouble communicating with their Italian counterparts. Upon request, I recommended my friends Umberto and Francesco Vitali, two brothers from Adelaide, who had worked in their father's stable and saddlery business in Port Adelaide. They were in their late twenties, husbands, and fathers of young children, and luckily, had received some education, both in Italy and in Australia. The three of us, along with some Italian Americans doing the same job, formed a little tribe translating for the medical staff and acting as general ward assistants.

The atrocities we saw were not easy to deal with. My sleep was tormented by the screams of men looking for amputated limbs or writhing in an agony of burnt flesh, gassed lungs and sudden blindness. But the American Hospital canteen fed us well and we were safe, despite the terrifying noise of the bombs, and provided the front line didn't encroach upon us, which was a threat we lived with constantly.

After the disaster at the battle of Caporetto, the Italian forces had been regrouped under General Armando Diaz and finally, in October, at the town of Vittorio Veneto, just north of Treviso, they had achieved a rousing victory. This had been facilitated by the withdrawal of Hungarian Troops a week earlier, and the defeat of the Turks, in small part by a motorised division of the Australian Army. In this way, the Austro-Hungarian Empire collapsed and withdrew from the fighting, leaving the Germans open to attack from all sides.

Finally, in early November, the guns fell silent, and an armistice was negotiated.

Collectively, the world held its breath, hoping that it was truly the end of the war. At the Vicenza hospital, we kept on working though, inundated now with returned prisoners of war. As well as the physically wounded, there were the psychologically and morally wounded to deal with. The priests who worked with us organised masses to commemorate the end of the fighting but despaired at all those men and women who had lost their belief in God, and who turned their backs on the healing power of prayer and the institution of church.

I continued to pray every day, offering thanks to the God who had kept me safe. Watching the blank faces of the shell-shocked, the wounded learning to walk on crutches or make do with one arm or one eye, reminded me of the vagaries of fortune. Why me? Why had I been saved? I had no answers, but I was infinitely grateful.

By early December, I'd been at the Vicenza base hospital for four months and was granted three days of leave. Without wasting a moment, I headed to the train station and found a packed military train going to Milano. I jumped on board out of sight of any inspectors or military police and tried to make myself inconspicuous, in this way, arriving in Milano in mid-afternoon. I got some directions to the Pirelli factory, which was where my mother and my siblings lived. Once I arrived, I asked around the neighbourhood for anyone who knew their address. Just as night fell, I knocked on their apartment door.

My mother's beautiful blonde hair was now all grey, and her cheeks were sunken, but the spark in her eyes at my sudden arrival, brought back the animation to her face and her stumbling gait did not prevent her from leaping out of her chair to wrap her arms around my waist. Maria was a beautiful young woman in her early-twenties and my little brothers were teenagers, both of them taller than me. Rico was a greying middle-aged man, looking so much like my father, with children of his own – two handsome little boys of five and six and a kind and pretty wife, Anita. They lived on the floor above. I regretted not having packed some gifts for them, but they were happy enough with my presence.

My mother had me sit by her side and wouldn't let me out of her grasp, such that I could barely speak with only one hand able to gesture. They laughed at my accent, telling me it had changed so much, though I couldn't hear the difference. We spent the whole night talking non-stop. The next day, Mamma took me to the market so she could share me with her local friends, bragging about her handsome, successful son who had come from the other side of the world to defend his fatherland. I also had the chance to pay my respects at my father's grave.

I returned to my post the same way I had come, beaming with joy. I spent my last few hours of leave writing furiously to Luisa, anxious to get down all my tumbling thoughts.

By Christmas, the armistice had become official and peace negotiations were underway. The populace was rejoicing, but the problems didn't end. Winter had set in, and another harvest had been lost due to lack of manpower. Around me in Vicenza, the faces were less drawn, but the bodies still were gaunt and tired, weakened by four years of anxiety and near famine. Finally, some of the American grain and Argentinian beef, which hadn't been able to be transported during the war, began to arrive, and the bakers were set to work. However, much of the anticipated supplies ended up on the black market, and the imports fuelled inflation.

There was much political strife with blame for mismanagement being hurled left, right and centre. The old political parties were being destroyed and new, more radical ones were taking their place. Unlike in Australia, the newspapers here vomited the minutiae of political news and the devastating consequences of war. I was fed up, I just wanted to go home. The irony was not lost on me. In Australia, when I said the word 'home' of course I meant Italy, but not just any Italy. The notion of home here, was my little *cascina* community in Ossolaro, on the outskirts of Cremona, which sadly no longer existed.

My idea of home now was firmly fixed on my life with Luisa, and the home we would create together. I made discrete enquiries with my superiors about when we would be released but they simply said, "We'll be here as long as our government wants us to be here, and that may be a couple of years yet, judging by the volume of work we have," intimating that we Australians might be required to stay for that long as well. I was beside myself, so anxious to leave, but I couldn't just walk away, mostly because I had to wait to be assigned transport back to Australia. I was powerless to do anything except follow orders.

Imagine my glee when a few weeks later, the field hospital was given orders to dispatch all those still wounded to other more permanent hospitals. Bert, Frank and I were being sent to Parma with a warning. As well as dealing with the severely wounded, Parma was also dealing with an influenza outbreak. Dottore Bastogna called us into his tent to give us information about how best to protect ourselves from the influenza, which had been around for the last year, but had reached epidemic status now.

Finally, in August 1919, we received news that the Australians had not forgotten us and were sending the remaining Italian Australians first by train to France, from where there were more transport ships available, and then to Southampton. We eventually received our honourable discharges from the Italian Army in late August and were told we would be back in Fremantle by the end of November.

I had managed to return to Milano for a two week break. It gave me a chance to have long heart-to-hearts with my mother and my siblings, Maria and Rico, as well as the other two younger boys, who were babies when I had left for a mariner's life with Zio Carlo all those years ago.

Mamma and Maria surprised me on my last day by handing over a package for my Australian family. They had cut down one of Mamma's silk petticoats from her own wedding to fashion a pair of camisoles which Maria had delicately embroidered with fine silk ribbon and soft lace, for Luisa on her wedding day. I blushed when they showed me, which gave them all a good laugh, but sent my thoughts to places I had studiously avoided for the duration of my recruitment, fearful the melancholy might tempt me to find solace elsewhere.

The Italian economy was in ruins, the fields had been left untended for the duration of the war. Once again, this ancient land but still a young, fledgling nation was at the mercy of international forces. I made a vow to my mother to sponsor my younger brothers' emigration to Australia, once shipping resumed.

Getting Home

The spectre of the Spanish Influenza lurked all over Europe. In Parma, and again while waiting for embarkation at Southampton, we'd observed the proper hygiene practices insisted upon at the hospital in Vicenza. Bert, Frank, and I continued to replicate these on-board the ship, staying masked and washing hands well before we touched any food, and particularly, staying away from packed quarters. We were heading out in the European summer, so we chose to spend much of our time on deck, even sleeping there whenever we could get away with it.

Unlike the trip over to Europe, where I was desperate to escape my thoughts, by getting involved with ship activities, now I was dreaming with eyes open, making big plans for my future. I had only received two letters from Luisa, one that had arrived at Christmas in which I learned that her grandfather and my first real Adelaide friend, Vincenzo Nicoletti, had passed away at the age of seventy-eight. He had been instrumental in bringing me into the family, intending to introduce me to his granddaughter as soon as he'd perceived our shared love of music, for which I would be eternally grateful.

The second letter, which had been written in January but hadn't arrived till a few days before we were due to leave Vicenza, reassured me that she hadn't forgotten me, and she was eager for me to get home.

The ship I was on, the Marathon, was delayed in Port Aden on the Arabian Peninsula due to a dysentery outbreak aboard. An AIF infantryman, who had managed to survive two years of the atrocities at the French front, was struck down just weeks from home. After everything I'd experienced in the last year, I still found it hard to come to terms with the complete randomness of death. Bert and I often discussed this mystery, though Frank was more superstitious and insisted we were inviting calamity upon ourselves by harping on about it and would take himself off for a smoke until we dropped the subject.

We were on board with the remnants of the 50th Battalion, which had originally been raised from recruits who had enlisted in South Australia. Most of these men had been convalescing in British military hospitals for quite some time and were finally declared fit for travel, though some cases, especially those with lung and psychological illnesses, were still in terrible states. There were also families on board, mostly young English and French women who had married the Australian servicemen who were accompanying them, and had young children, either with them or about to be born. The doctors on board were swift to isolate and contain any diseases. We were stuck in Port Aden for a good two weeks without being able to go ashore due to the dysentery outbreak.

Having spent so much time together in Italy, the three of us found it easy to sit in companionable silence. Sometimes, we would listen to the AIF men as they recounted the push at Amiens, or Dernancourt and Villers-Bretonneux, names of battles we would hear over and over again in the ensuing years.

There was a further delay at Ceylon due to a monsoon.

Eventually, a month late, our ship whimpered into Fremantle on the 22nd of December. We were immediately shepherded to the Transcontinental Train reaching Adelaide Railway station on the 24th of December at 3.30pm. There was no need to organise further transport, all of our families were there. Very few Christmases, before or after, would compare to the elation of that day in 1919.

I couldn't take my eyes off my beloved's beautiful face, her dark, glossy hair matched only in brilliance by her twinkling eyes, followed by her gigantic smile and equally welcoming laughter, and reminding myself, all the way home that she was just perfect. I hadn't had any doubts before I left but was mesmerised now. Luisa was a girl when I'd first met her, and I had come back to a confident woman. Gone were the long curls, frilly ribbons, and puffy sleeves; her hair now was parted in the middle and fell softly on either side of her face and was gathered into a firm but fulsome coil at the nape of her neck, giving her a regal and statuesque air. Her skirts had lost their ruffles and were more fitted and shorter, with slim ankles and svelte hips on show. A small, neat collar peeked out under a fitted, almost military style jacket, emphasising her trim waist and the delicate curve of her bust. I wasn't sure whether I liked this new look, until she took a firm grasp of my lapels and planted those luscious lips possessively and hungrily on mine, holding me back on the verandah, once her family had traipsed through the front door and were well out of sight.

Luxuriating in Luisa's attentions and Elena's cooking, after the New Year celebrations, it was time to think about the future. I had received an honourable discharge and my full pay, along with an American bonus, so I had done rather well financially, even though it was only half of what I could have earned through my business. However, I had left two-thirds of it with Mamma and Maria, to help with family expenses. Luisa had faithfully taken care of the money I had left her, investing half of it in war bonds which were now coming to fruition. The Latorre parents were operating two shops in the Semaphore and Port Adelaide area, with assistants overseeing most of the day-to-day affairs and Elena and Antonio concentrating on making or sourcing supplies for the confectionery/tobacconists and grocery/hardware shops, and Luisa doing all the book–keeping, as well as teaching her half-dozen piano students.

Fourteen-year-old Bartolomeo, now in long pants, with some significant hair on his chin and a much deeper voice, but still preferring to be called Bart, was about to enter his final years of secondary school, aiming for his intermediate certificate. He very proudly showed me the certificate he'd received for a first place in Latin while I had been away. I congratulated him and joked that he'd make a good priest, suffering a quick one-two to my rib cage in reply, with the muscles he'd developed catching me off guard. He was still mad about sport, representing his school in tennis and cricket and had a formidable reputation in the local area.

He and his friends talked endlessly about the South Australian airmen, two brothers accompanied by two engineers, who had flown their Vickers Vimy plane from London to Darwin in under 30 days. He was going to work in motors he said, confident that the future would need many more motor engineers and mechanics.

I had tried to learn as much as I could during my time away, and one of the items I had been most curious about were motor cars. During my time off, I could be found at the depot where the Red Cross Ambulance cars, funded and supplied by donations from ordinary

American citizens, returned to be overhauled before they were needed again to ferry the desperately wounded between field hospitals near the front and our base hospital. I watched attentively as the mechanics pulled apart engines, wheel axles, steering shafts and body parts and talked me through what each piece served and where it went in the reassembly. I was determined to leave the horse and cart era firmly behind.

My visits around Port Adelaide and Semaphore confirmed that bulk deliveries were still carried out by teams of Clydesdale horses, though passenger motor cars seemed to have increased in number. With most of the roads within the area, and the ones leading to Adelaide, still dirt tracks which turned into mud at the first drop of rain and sent sand flying into your eyes in the dry, horses or trains were still the logical transport mainstay.

When I felt ready, Antonio and I returned to our evening business debates. I was glad to hear that no-one had really displaced me from the ice cream making business, at least in terms of quality. By mid-January, I set to work visiting property brokers both in the port area and in the city, telling them what I was looking for, as well as making enquiries about margarine manufacturing and the equipment and licensing needed. I hadn't had the opportunity to see Beppe in Geelong but had let him know via a long letter, once I had returned, about the family in Italy and my intentions to start over here in Adelaide.

Beppe had done very well for himself, and in his reply, he told me all about the new machinery he had installed in his new premises, the renovated building next door to his current factory. He also offered to ship me his old pasteuriser and refrigeration machines. It was a great offer and one which meant I could get started within the month. I said yes immediately and of course Antonio and his connections came through, finding me a suitable space in St. Vincent Street. It was a former butcher, with a large enough freezer room already on site.

The dirt floor would need cementing to meet modern regulatory standards, but it would do very nicely to begin with, especially as there were barely two months of summer left. The machinery from Geelong took about ten days to arrive and, in that time, I was able to renew my business contacts for raw materials. There was one interesting difference; the dairy where I once sourced my milk was now part of a co-operative that had been established right across the road from my new premises. All the small dairies in the district now sent their milk directly to the cooperative as soon as their cows were milked, eliminating the need for storage and the risk of milk spoiling, and having to do their own customer deliveries.

The cooperative had enormous cooling facilities, meaning the milk stayed fresher for longer. They also had mechanised cream separators which more effectively skimmed the cream off the top, reducing the risk of rancidity and contamination from farm debris, which had happened previously when milk was poured into large open bowls and set over gentle wood fires in order for the cream to rise to the top.

Bert and Frank had rejoined their father at the saddlery where business had continued, ably assisted by their wives in the absence of the menfolk. Their father was now more than ready to retire, and the brothers divided the duties amongst themselves based on their interests. Frank took over the horse stabling and hiring side of the business and Bert returned to the saddlery and other leather harness making. The good news was that they were only a few doors down from my new premises, so we could have a chat over a good coffee in the afternoons, before we returned to our various arenas of domestic bliss.

It took a little longer than I had planned for my premises to be re-established, pass the health inspection, have my trading licence renewed, get my machinery re-assembled and working and finally putting out a few test batches. I would need some help on the factory floor, especially someone I could train up to maintain the machines. I started in Butler Street, where my previous right hand man Jerry used to live with his parents.

I came away with a nasty shock. Once I had left Adelaide in April 1918, Jerry and his cousin Joe had secretly signed up to the AIF and were shipped out and fighting on the Western Front by September, facing the worst of the action. Both had been killed, just a couple of weeks after arriving. Both families were inconsolable, with Jerry's mother just repeating the fact that she hadn't been able to give her son a proper Christian burial and now his soul was destined to roam lost in Purgatory forever. Between the keening voice and the constant rocking of her body, I could barely make sense of what she was saying. The only person who still seemed sane was Tino, Jerry's younger brother who had once helped me with writing up my labels. He was thirteen and working on the docks. This time, I was the incredulous one. He was slight of frame and not particularly tall for his age.

"What are you earning a day?" I asked him. It was a pittance, as I knew it would be. "Would you come work for me? I can pay you two pounds a week."

The look of defeat on his face finally lifted and I hoped that over time, I could help him regain the joy for life I had seen in the ten-year-old Tino.

Another addition to my team was Luigi Carbone, one of the lads I sometimes played cards with. He had been just nineteen when we South Australians had been rounded up to be repatriated. As his family origins had been in Calabria, we had been separated in Egypt. He had seen action at the decisive battle of Vittorio-Veneto and had sustained a leg wound, for which he had ended up in one of the field hospitals once the armistice had been declared. From there, he had been moved to Genova and onto a ship to England quite promptly and had managed to get back to Australia by February 1919, almost a year earlier than I had.

However, the shrapnel had shredded the muscles in his right calf, and he found he hadn't been able to return to his previous labouring job. He'd been surviving by doing some single line fishing and peddling his catch to local housewives, as well as helping his father in a carpentry business, run from their home at Alberton.

"Well, we'll just have to invent a system that allows you to sit down on the job," I said, in all seriousness.

Between the three of us, and with input from Bart who was turning out to be an impressive engineering brain, we drew rudimentary plans, which I was able to take to the Halliday Brothers, a local mechanical engineering firm.

Luisa and I had reset a date for our wedding. Since Vincenzo had passed, I had been sharing a room with Bart. Connie and Fred were still a few doors down, but a young cousin of Fred's had arrived from Sydney, and they were training him up to take over their business, so the spare room there was gone. Enterprising Elena, who still had her finger on the pulse of the local gossip told us that Mrs McInerny, an elderly widow, in Coppin St. had decided she was going to join her sister, who had also been recently widowed and was living in rural Willunga. Therefore, her cottage was up for sale.

Elena had been to see the lady in question, armed with her famous afternoon tea almond shortbread biscuits, and had secured a private viewing for us. She told us to put on the charm, and if necessary, offer to help the lady with packing and moving, in order to get our foot in the door. After negotiating a suitable price with her formidable nephew, we managed to secure the cottage, our first new home together, only one street away from the Latorre house at Semaphore. Luisa and I had fun choosing colours and furniture styles. I really had no idea, deferring to her excellent taste most of the time, but still enjoying the opportunity to be together, making decisions for our future.

Elena had relaxed the chaperone rule when we were out shopping in the local area, so it was a precious time for us to talk and enjoy some physical closeness, even if it was only offering her my arm as we walked down the street.

Finally, our wedding was upon us. To be honest, I was so overcome, I don't really remember much of the details of the day. The week before the wedding date, Beppe had wired me to say he had broken his leg after a fall at a shooting outing, but Johnnie had immediately volunteered to take his place as best man. Johnnie, now a member of the state parliament, had even driven down in his new Model T Ford which he had painted gold for the occasion and offered to let me drive Luisa around in it for a few days. Antonio and Elena stood back, eyes like saucers, but Bart came for a spin around the block, and Luisa, couldn't stop laughing at the unfamiliar sensation.

We had a Saturday, mid-morning service at our familiar Sacred Heart Church at Semaphore. A half-dozen men from the newly formed Semaphore Returned Servicemen's League, of which I was now a member, came dressed in uniform and spontaneously formed an honour guard at the front of the church. One of Luisa's pupils played the wedding march on the church's organ. I clenched my hands and jaw so tightly, I thought I might faint when I saw my Luisa walk down the aisle in her sleek white satin dress, her face covered by a long tulle veil. She was accompanied by Antonio, sporting the widest smile I'd ever seen on this perennially cheerful man. Behind them, Bart, in his new grey pin-striped morning suit, gloves and spats, escorted Elena, decked out in a dove-grey, silk sheath dress and enormous matching hat, covered in sparkling bands of silver tulle.

The service was followed by a sumptuous three-course lunch at the very popular Wondergraph Café, next door to the open-air Wondergraph movie theatre on the Esplanade at Semaphore, opposite the jetty. The dining room had been decorated with miles of bunting in red, white and green and each table had artfully arranged vases of flowers. The coup of course was dessert – three flavours of ice cream served in tulip vases, accompanied by fresh wafer biscuits, strawberries, chocolate sauce and a dollop of fresh cream. We had a photographer take formal portraits of the both of us and with our wedding party and all the extended family.

Vincenzo's cousins, still important local musicians, had kept the festivities going, long after Luisa and I had left in our car, bedecked with streamers.

We had spent most of our money in starting the business and buying our home, so our honeymoon would only be a few days at the sumptuous Southern Cross Hotel in the city, where the celebrated Dorothy Daley's Jazz Band entertained guests in the mirror-lined dining room, and where we watched opened mouthed at some of the newfangled, rather energetic dancing, before daring to have a go ourselves.

When we returned at the end of the week, Elena proudly showed us a journalist's write-up that had appeared in both the local Port Adelaide News and the Adelaide Advertiser:

BODONI-LATORRE

On April 8, at the Church of the Sacred Heart, Semaphore, the marriage was celebrated between Luisa, only daughter of Mr. and Mrs. Latorre of Semaphore to Carlo (late R.E.I.), third son of Mrs. L. and the late Mr. G. Bodoni of Milan, Italy.

The Rev. Father O'Connor officiated. The altars of the church were decorated by friends of the bride. A string band played the bridal march as the bride entered the church with her father. She wore a frock of charmeuse and georgette, with court train of silver net and shell pink georgette, and she carried a sheaf of Easter lilies and roses. Cousin of the bride, Anna Hartford, who was train bearer, wore a dainty little georgette frock of shell pink and silver. The bride was attended by Miss Dorothy Sullivan, who wore a pale gold crepe de chine and georgette frock and a large black tulle hat. She also carried a posy of autumn tints. The Honorouble J. R. Hobson was best man. After the ceremony, the guests were entertained at the Wondergraph Café by Mr. and Mrs. Latorre. The tables were decorated with the bridegroom's regimental colours. The usual toasts were honoured. After the breakfast, Mr. P. Rossetto played violin solos. Mr. Gentile played some of his own compositions. Miss Sullivan also contributed to the programme. Mr. and Mrs Bodoni left by motor for their honeymoon amid showers of confetti and rose leaves.

"Finally, *mia bella*, I have you all to myself," I said, plonking myself down on the edge of the bed in our very own cottage.

"Here's to the rest of our lives," toasted Luisa, as she accepted the glass of champagne I poured, and slipped off her shoes.

Make-over

No sooner had we settled blissfully into our own little nest, than the opportunity I had never imagined presented itself. A sizeable plot of land on South Terrace in the city had been made available through the subdivision of the grounds of a more established mansion. The block was wide and deep and would allow for the construction of a new purpose-built factory. Luisa and I went to visit the site, drew up basic plans, consulted a reputable local builder, and did the sums, over and over and over. Of course, we consulted Antonio and Elena who helped us to talk through and clarify our ideas. We came to the conclusion that we could not afford it on our own, but if we got some backers, we could possibly make it work.

As well as continuing to produce ice cream, I was also hoping to expand my business by making the machinery serve a double purpose in order to produce ice. There were a number of ice companies in Adelaide, but none in the south-west corner where there were also a significant number of hotels and boarding houses. Refrigerated transport via smaller, easy to manoeuvre, motorised vans could provide some serious competition, especially to the more affluent homes on the southwest side of the parklands as the growth in population in the new suburbs represented more enticing opportunities.

The other avenue for development could be the margarine business which was becoming of greater interest to the baking fraternity for its lower cost and greater convenience. I had been introduced to margarine through the American canteen while I was doing my military service in Italy. There was no-one doing margarine on an industrial scale in Adelaide.

I had already taken the precaution of speaking to a couple of potential clients in the bakery trade who were currently relying on imports from New South Wales. The margarine recipe was one I had obtained from a British manufacturer using tallow from cattle fat, which once was prized for making candles, but since the introduction of electricity, was no longer in high demand. Abattoirs had plenty of surplus tallow, now available at a much-reduced price. I went to the Gepps Cross Government abattoirs myself to verify whether this were true or not.

While I had been waiting in Southampton for a ship home, I had asked around about Margarine manufacturers. The Australian government was offering returning AIF, who were stuck waiting for transport home, funds to undertake classes in a wide variety of industries. I wasn't eligible for the funds, but by asking around, I was able to learn that a newly established Margarine and Seed Oil production factory in Essex, around 30 miles from London, was offering tours to any interested servicemen. I took my chances and caught the train to London and another out to Essex. I had changed from my uniform to a suit. They were a little suspicious at first, but they accepted the story and gave me a tour, allowing me to take notes along the way. I was able to speak to engineers about the milling machines as well as to the resident chemist about the chemical reactions between the various ingredients used and the percentage of each ingredient needed.

I played around with the ingredients once I returned to Adelaide, producing small batches, until I was convinced that I had perfected a recipe that could be extrapolated to commercial quantities.

Antonio suggested I make a proposal to his fraternity investment club myself, with some of my produce, and examples of how it could be used in the baking industry. Elena tried out one of my sample pots of margarine on a tray of experimental biscuits and flaky mini fruit pies which she was prepared to replicate fresh for the meeting.

I produced detailed technical drawings and descriptions of the machinery and other equipment needed. Luisa and I put our heads together and came up with a cost outline and a five-year development plan for all three aspects of the proposed business. The sums were huge and so daunting, around £8,000, equivalent to around ten years of our current earnings. I was prepared to walk away. It was Luisa who suggested we sell our cottage in order to secure the land. She pointed out that since we would be building a factory, we could also build a substantial apartment above the factory for our accommodation.

"You want to sell our home? But we've only just moved in? Where will we live?"

"We could live with my parents, just for a short while, until the apartment is ready."

"But you've arranged everything so beautifully here for us. Won't you be heartbroken?"

"Don't be silly, this is just a house, it doesn't matter where we live, as long as we're together. And besides, we're building our future in the factory, that's more important isn't it?"

"Is it?" I replied, so confused. "Is the business more important than us?"

Luisa grabbed me by the shoulders and made me stand still and look into her eyes.

"Nothing is more important than us. If you don't want to do this, if you prefer to take things slowly, one step at a time, then I'll be right behind you. I trust you; I know you'll be a success at whatever you choose to do. But if you want to take a bold leap, then I'll be right behind you too. It may mean a couple of years of sacrifice, but that's fine with me. There's never any gain without sacrifice."

I continued to stare at her while my mind was doing cartwheels.

"My main reason for wanting to improve my business prospects was so that I can provide a comfortable life for you. It worries me to hear you talk about sacrifices. That's not what I want for you."

"A comfortable life. Do you want me to be some *bambola*, sitting in her little box, only coming alive when you get home? Darling, you've forgotten whose daughter I am. Do you think my mother ever wanted to sit at home waiting? You should try asking her that, see what answer she gives you?"

I didn't need an answer, I knew Elena was the driving force of the Latorre family. Antonio may have been its public face, but Elena was definitely the mastermind. As I looked into my wife's eyes, I saw that glint which I had assumed had been her joy at seeing me, but now I saw that it was also alight at the thought of a new challenge.

It destabilised me at first, dented my pride a little, I must confess. But the next night, when we were at her parent's house, the veil lifted. Yes, Antonio had all the smooth, reassuring words, but he was the male peacock, displaying his feathers, and Elena was the mother hen, smoothing the path before him, always a step ahead of him. A brief look passed between mother and daughter. They'd already worked everything out between them!

I sat back in my chair, arms crossed tightly across my chest and my right ankle sitting on my left knee staring at the both of them with squinted eyes. Luisa was a good head taller than her mother, slender where her mother was stocky and broad, but the looks they were throwing my way were identical. My own mother, my grandmother, even my younger sister, they all had the same look. They were the organisers; they paved the way for all the family successes.

"*Va bene – facciamolo*! Let's do this."

I lowered my foot, pulled my chair back to the table, rolled up my sleeves and opened my hand for the leather folder Luisa had brought with us. Spreading out all our information, the five of us, yes Bart too, talked over everything in minute detail.

By the end of the week, I was ready to face Antonio's investors committee. I pinned up our paperwork on a rolling corkboard which I placed at the front of the private room on the top floor of the Portland Hotel, where the committee of ten local, well-established businessmen usually gathered. Elena's delectable goodies were placed in the middle of the table. I had also added my invention of wooden transport boxes with tin-lined, 1-pint ice cream tubs. Antonio introduced me and spoke briefly about the previous investment I had received from this committee and how I had repaid it without any problems. Then I introduced my concept and invited the gentlemen to come to the board to view the drawings and the projections.

Quite a few of them were keen, so there were a lot of questions directed at me. The final deliberation yielded three serious investors. However, they suggested that I purchase the land and secure a loan for the building of the factory. Then they would be prepared to invest in the purchase of equipment and materials. They proposed a four-way profit sharing venture, with myself as the fourth partner. They assured me that we would have legal documents drawn up, so I would be sole managing director and they would be silent partners. As long as I was making satisfactory dividends, we would meet once per year, and I would be in charge of the rest. We would renew this arrangement after five years, at which point I had the option of buying them out by repaying their initial investment, or they could also sell their shares to other interested parties.

I was surprised by the terms, not having ever heard of this type of arrangement. The deal depended on me being able to secure the land and the bank loan to fund the building of the factory first. This meant I would have a substantial debt but only a quarter share of the profits with which to pay off my debt. It was still a huge gamble.

I felt I needed some legal advice, so made an appointment with the local lawyer I had previously used. He didn't feel comfortable giving me such advice and suggested a professional acquaintance of his in the city. I took Luisa with me, as by now, I had accepted her as my very necessary business partner. I was quaking in my boots at the very thought of the risk, but Luisa, calm as ever except for two bright pink rounds on her normally even toned skin, kept reassuring me that we could make it work. Our new lawyer agreed with her. He had an independent business accounting firm look over Luisa's projected figures and claimed that we could pay off our bank loan in under ten years, even with access to only a quarter of the profits, as well as live moderately comfortable lives.

He suggested drawing up a promissory contract, so that my three investors would be officially tied down to providing an agreed sum, before any purchase or building occurred on my part.

I'd also taken Luisa with me to the meeting with the loans manager at the Savings Bank of South Australia Building in Currie Street. I could see the bank manager's reservations when we'd first arrived, as he'd offered to have his secretary find Luisa a comfortable spot and a cup of tea in the outer office, and he was rather miffed when we both refused the offer. As soon as Luisa started talking numbers, I saw him hesitate, size her up, and thankfully, proceed with renewed respect.

"This is Adelaide," I thought. Hadn't Luisa proudly informed me in one of her letters when I was still in Geelong, that Adelaide was the first place in the country to give women the right to vote and the right to be represented in Parliament? Well, this Adelaide girl was going to be part of a manufacturing empire. I placed my hand over my shirt, feeling for the Saint Christopher medal she had given me, it had protected me well while I was overseas, how long could my luck last?

Factory forward

The start of our new enterprise began with the sale of our cottage. Antonio and Elena bought it from us and gave us free use of it until the factory was ready. That was a huge relief, one that I was very grateful for, and also allowed us to secure ownership of the land. This way, if we ran into financial difficulties, we retained title of the land and the building, which we could always sell.

We used Antonio's connections regarding builders for the factory and apartment complex. There would be two large adjoining spaces, one for ice cream and one for the ice works at the front. Then two more large spaces at the back for the margarine production and cold storage. Added on to the back of these spaces was a long, narrow shed for general storage like packaging equipment. The top floor would house our apartment consisting of a lounge room, dining room, kitchen, bathroom, three bedrooms and a separate office. The upper areas would have large windows to allow as much light as possible. There was ample room on site for two very wide driveways, one on either side of the building, which would allow deliveries of raw materials on one side and despatch of finished products from the other side. I had allowed for a bank of three-sided sheds at the back of the building to house the motorised vans I was envisioning, but for now would act as stables for the horse drawn vans I currently used.

Construction would require a minimum of six months and give me time to order appropriate machinery. The terms of the partnership agreement were finalised through my lawyer and the partners all kept their promise regarding the financing of the venture, so that I had a sum of £6,000 pounds from which to draw on for equipment and other necessary goods.

My first purchase was a 1915 black soft top Model T Ford, formerly owned by Mr Weston, one of the owners of the new Ozone Theatre at Semaphore, for the much-discounted price of £180 or less than half of what newly imported cars were retailing. For me, it was a comparable cost to owning a horse and buggy. For Bart, it was the chance of a lifetime, to explore his passion up close and personal. He loved going out with Luisa and I of an evening, both of them thrilled by their first driving lessons.

The factory building was being erected in the new fashion with a double wall of bricks to provide better sound and temperature control. On our last visit, we could see that both the first and second floors were complete and were awaiting the addition of a roof, the doors and windows, and a staircase to get us to the first-floor apartment and private office. It wouldn't be long now. I was excited, but nervous at the same time. This hadn't been part of my plans. But I couldn't help myself; it was like I could smell opportunity, and once I'd caught a whiff of a challenge, I couldn't let it go. Thankfully, I didn't need to explain myself to Luisa and her family, we were all built from the same mould.

One morning, Luisa was feeling unwell. She said she felt nauseous and a bit sweaty. Given the prevalence of infectious illnesses in the area, I wasn't taking any chances. I went straight to Elena and then called at Dr. North's on Semaphore Road to ask him to come see her. As it was early, and he hadn't opened his surgery yet, he hopped in the car with me, and we returned to find both women grinning foolishly.

"You can check her out doctor," smirked Elena, moving away from the side of the bed where she had been sitting, "but I think you'll find there's nothing wrong with her." Dr. North looked at the smug expressions on both of the women and extended his hand towards me.

"Ah, I see that congratulations are in order for the soon to be papa, if I'm not mistaken."

It took me a moment to fully understand his words, and as realization rose up my face to my bulging eyes, all three of them had a good laugh as I rushed to Luisa's side to wrap her up in an enormous hug.

"Are you sure you're well? You looked terrible only twenty minutes ago."

"Yes, but only after I managed to vomit. Mamma tells me we may have to bear this for a while."

"Don't worry, I was exactly the same. It will pass in a few weeks," reassured Elena. "You take the good doctor back to his surgery, and get off to work, I'll look after my daughter. But Carlo," she called, "best not share this news around just yet, we'll wait till she's showing, and that won't be for several months, I think."

Reassured that everything was perfectly normal, I did as I was told and whistled my way into the factory, to very curious looks from Luigi and Tino. I was about to blurt everything out, but remembered Elena's words, so just commented on the glorious sunshine.

That evening, Luisa and I couldn't stop talking and giggling idiotically. We wondered if it were a son or a daughter, we contemplated names; should we follow the traditional route or choose something modern? Would the names be in Italian or English?

I had been given three Christian names at birth, which I always felt was ridiculous. We talked about our personal best features and our worst ones, sending out a hope that the child would only inherit our better ones. One thought terrified me. My child would be born in Australia and would automatically be considered an Australian British subject, like his mother. I was still an Italian national after eight years in Australia. It was time to apply for citizenship. The spectre of that letter I had received summoning me back to Italy against my wishes loomed large. I was determined that this would not happen again.

By late January, I had submitted my paperwork, published my intention to seek Naturalisation in all the South Australian newspapers, and I had finally received an invitation to receive my Naturalisation Certificate, which was presented to me by the Port Adelaide City Mayor at a swish swearing-in ceremony at the Municipal Hall. Luisa's rounded belly was well and truly showing by this stage, but she was looking radiant and said she felt fantastic, though did need to take an extra nap in the middle of the day.

The factory building had been completed and I was working on the installation of all the machinery necessary as well as keeping an eye on the factory at Port Adelaide. I had decided I would keep the Port Adelaide factory open until Easter, which was at the end of March this year. Then we would move to the city.

Luisa and Elena had been to visit the private hospital, Narma, just a few doors down from our new factory and decided that the baby would be born there, as the two ex-war nurses, the Misses Braithwaite who ran it, and their staff, had very good reputations. According to Doctor North, the baby was due around the middle of May, so Elena would be coming to stay with us a week beforehand, to be on hand to help Luisa. Antonio and Bart were happy to fend for themselves for a couple of weeks, with Connie nearby reassuring Elena that she would feed them and sort out their laundry.

My intention with the factory at Port Adelaide had been to move the equipment and terminate the lease at the end of the summer. I had given my landlord three months' notice of my intention to have everything dismantled, ready to leave by mid-April. Of course, I had spoken to Luigi and Tino of my decision and reassured them there would be positions for them at the new factory.

In January, I had already begun to advertise for new workers, interviewing possible candidates. I was going to start in June with the margarine plant and the ice cream plant, then bring in the ice works in November, ready for the Christmas and summer rush. The margarine business was heavily regulated, with quotas imposed on production. I had obtained a licence to produce 300 gallons per year. With my equipment able to produce 20 gallons per week, that would give me work for four months a year, then I would switch to ice production for the other eight months. The ice cream would be at full production of 1,000 gallons per month in the peak months of November to April and then I would cut back to winter production of 4-500 gallons per month, depending on demand. I had also decided to hire a representative to drum up as much business as possible, freeing my time to manage the operations at the factory, and also allowing me to be on hand for Luisa's imminent delivery.

Babe in arms

The tensest twenty-eight hours of our lives resulted in a cherubic boy with a feisty set of lungs. We named him after our fathers, of course, but chose to use the English translation - Anthony John Bodoni, born 8th of May 1923.

I wasn't allowed in the delivery room, but Luisa had her mother to support her, and by all reports, my wife had displayed the strength of all three musketeers. I marvelled at her recovery, couldn't believe she was up and about within a week. I couldn't get enough of watching her feed the little guzzler either. When she'd pass him to me, his powdery smell and little milk burps would melt my heart. I never tired of singing him to sleep as I cradled him against my neck, remembering all the beautiful Italian lullabies my mother and grandmother used to sing.

In the last week of June, we had him baptised at the newly built St. Patrick's Church on Grote Street on a Friday afternoon and invited all the family and our closest friends to a sumptuous buffet supper at the church hall next door, ably arranged by Elena and her sister Beatrice.

We had chosen Bart to be his godfather and Luisa's friend Dot to be his godmother. I was finally able to introduce my brother Beppe to my family, who took the train to spend a week with us. I couldn't believe his transformation when he gingerly held little Anthony cradled along the length of his arm. The gruff, jokester who could never sit still, was suddenly calm, mesmerised by the little boy who had his mother's deep brown eyes.

"Fatherhood could suit you," I suggested.

"Nope, Carlino, not for me." He re-iterated his plans to retire early.

I had completed the setup of the factory, and we were well into production of ice and ice cream, though not yet up to our maximum capacity. I was still tinkering with the margarine making, finding reliable deliveries of tallow difficult to obtain. The Gepps Cross abattoirs assured me they had plenty of supplies in stock, but delivery drivers were self-employed, and they preferred to take supplies to reliable traders from whom they could get decent returns. I interpreted that to mean I wasn't paying them enough. One of my investors, George Preston, owned several franchises for the Samuel's Butchers chain in the Port Adelaide area, part of a huge state-wide network of butchers. I paid him a visit one evening, to determine whether I was paying the right fee.

He promised to make some enquiries. When I saw him again, the response I received made me see red. Mr. Preston had been in contact with the abattoirs and had received an interesting reply. Apparently, the cause of my lack of success with the delivery drivers had nothing to do with the rate I was paying them, which was the standard rate for deliveries, but had everything to do with the fact that I was a 'newcomer'. I shrewdly kept my temper in check, and nonchalantly asked Mr. Preston whether his contact meant newcomer to the business or newcomer to the country?

Mr. Preston looking at the floor, stammered, "I'm not sure what the fellow means, but if it helps, you're welcome to use my name on the order and that might resolve the problem."

I thanked Mr. Preston for his generous offer but said I would try to resolve the problem on my own before having to compromise his own business records.

I chose to detour via the Latorres in Semaphore to discuss my issue with Antonio and Elena. I was not surprised to hear that they had faced many similar circumstances with suppliers. In the early years of their business dealings, they had once made the decision to overpay, but found that it led to more extortion. Their best strategy had been to suggest that they would go elsewhere for their supplies, even if that meant they had to pay a little more for the goods. However, Antonio said that most often, he would collect his own goods directly from the supplier when possible. His suggestion had been that I go out myself to pick up my supplies. I agreed that this was probably the easiest strategy.

In discussing my dilemma with Luisa that night, she asked me a simple question.

"What name are you using on the order?"

"Well, my own of course," I replied, frowning at the question.

"Do you mean you use Bodoni, or do you use Imperial Ice Works?"

I had to think carefully. "I think I sometimes use the company name and sometimes my own surname," I replied.

"Go back over the invoices for the orders that did arrive. Go see if they had the company name on them," she ordered from the chair where she was nursing Anthony.

Damn, Luisa was right! The ones that had arrived promptly were the ones in the company name and would have been checked in by my goods clerk, young Patrick O'Leary, a fellow I had employed on the recommendation of our local priest. I rushed out of my office to Luisa, who had finished feeding and burping my son and was returning him to his cot in our room.

"You're right. They didn't have any problems when the orders were in the company name."

I was livid, pacing up and down and around our bed, getting in her way and risking waking the baby who had just dropped off to sleep.

"Alright then," said Luisa calmly. "You can stop with the Mad Milly impersonation. You know what to do."

"But this is totally unjust," I implored, still wounded by the racism I was facing.

"Unjust or not, do you want to run a business, or pretend you're a lawyer and take them to court in defence of the rights of migrants?"

I looked at her sternly, knowing that she was right and eminently sensible, as usual, but the situation did not sit well with me, and I slept very badly that night. Anthony's squalls kept me company and allowed me to pace out my anger as I rocked him back to sleep.

The next day, still smarting from the metaphorical slap in the face, I drove down to the Central Markets and looked around for an independent butcher, selecting a face that appeared English. I pointed to a side of lamb and asked him to divide it up for me. I got him chatting, asking how long he had been running his shop, where he got his meat from, who did his slaughtering and what happened to the excess fat. In my questioning, I discovered another smaller, independent slaughterer in the Adelaide hills.

A fortnight later, after a very polite reply to my letter, I received my weeks' worth of tallow, at an even better price than the one quoted by the government abattoir. My prize, apart from self-satisfaction, was a kiss from Luisa who held my cheeks in her hands and simply said, "I've married a genius."

The next time we saw Antonio and Elena, they agreed with their daughter, and we toasted our minor victory, but also a victory for all the injustices meted to our kind. This was not the beginning or the end of my troubles in my early years, but with this success, I developed the confidence I needed to believe that I had the necessary skills to conquer anything that came my way.

There was one more piece of surprising news to round out the year. I had finally heard from my brother Armando, whom we thought had gone to Mexico with our Uncle Camillo. In 1914, not long after his return from Italy, my uncle had decided that the revolutionary war which had started in the deep countryside the year before, looked like it was not going to end soon, so he chose to immediately move his business and the family to Venezuela. Fifteen-year-old Armando had moved with the family. However, in 1917, at the age of eighteen, the Venezuelan government agreed to repatriate Italian nationals to Italy, and Armando had been caught up in that scheme too, ending up fighting in Trieste, where he'd been made a prisoner of war by the Austrians after his first battle.

Upon being released from the prisoner of war camp, he and other South American Italian nationals had left Italy in early February 1919. He had written home but hadn't received a reply. Of course, he hadn't known that the family had moved to Milano. It wasn't until he got back to Venezuela that he found my letter which had been sent to him via the Italian Consulate in Mexico. He wrote telling me that the Venezuelan economy was very slow, and after his experience in Europe, he had found it very hard to settle down to working in the rope factory. He asked if my offer was still open and would I be prepared to sponsor him to come to Australia.

I wrote back immediately, after making enquiries about how to do that with Mr. Barrow, the Italian Vice-Consul, still at his job. I sent Armando all the necessary paperwork and a remittance for the transfer of money so he could obtain tickets for his journey. I wrote to Beppe and Mamma too; they would be thankful that he was safe and was returning to be with his brothers.

I was excited for his arrival. Although he was only thirteen when I had last seen him, he and I had always been the best of friends, often forming a team against Beppe and our cousin Angelo, who liked to tease us. I hoped we would make a good team again.

Family comes and goes

When Bart had finished his intermediate certificate, he had desperately wanted to pursue motor engineering. Elena's youngest sister, Violetta and her husband, Phillip Richardson, who lived just outside of Gawler, had found Bart an apprenticeship with a local mechanic. The Gawler Institute had an excellent reputation and had recently appointed a tutor for the practical motor engineering course they were offering in the evenings. Bart was overjoyed as he got to work on ordinary cars, trucks, and vans, but also on large farm equipment. Phillip was employed as a viticulturist in the area. Elena and Antonio had long ago invested in a plot of land where they grew grape vines for their own use which were tended by Phillip for a half-share of the wine they produced each year.

Since Luisa was happily settled, the Latorres decided to sell up their separate businesses in the Port area and open a new one in Gawler. They'd found a suitable location in Murray Street where there was a decent shop front with a house behind. It was in a rather dilapidated condition, but they had spent several months restoring the premises, installing electrical power to create a 'cool drinks saloon' where they sold the latest fashion in ice cream sodas, receiving the supply of my ice cream sent to them by train.

Elena ran this herself during the week, but Bart and Antonio were on hand to help during peak hours which were mostly late afternoons and evenings. Located just a few doors down from the new movie theatre, there was always a good crowd of young people, eager to stop by.

At Christmas this year, I had assumed Armando would be coming to Gawler with us as he always did, but now he was suggesting I could have extra time off and that he would keep the ice and ice cream deliveries going. We had produced enough surplus to store in our freezer room so that demand could still be met, and Armando promised he would make sure deliveries continued and take advantage of the shutdown to service the machines.

"But what about you? You'll miss out on Christmas, and you need a break too?" I was surprised by his offer. Then I saw him blush. "Spit it out then," I said, eyeballing him so he couldn't evade my scrutiny.

"You don't know her, her name's Agnes. She's invited me to Christmas lunch. I've met her parents before, her mum's Italian," he blurted, his face deepening to a beetroot red, hands nervously clutching an oily rag he had been using. He had turned away from me and was pretending to adjust a knob on one of the machines.

"And where did you meet this Agnes? How long have you known her?" I tried to keep my voice light, I didn't want to spook him.

"At a Euchre social at St. Patrick's. They have them on Monday nights."

The penny dropped.

"So that's where you've been going? I thought you were sneaking off to some illegal drinking hole."

"I don't mind a drink, but there are prettier girls at the social nights."

"Well, since they're going to look after you for Christmas, maybe we can invite them here for dinner one night next week, so we can meet them?"

Armando turned to glare at me.

"You don't have to act like my father."

"I'm just trying to support you. If she's from a decent family, I'm sure they're curious about your circumstances and whether they can trust you with her. Just trying to help you out. It's only a suggestion."

"Maybe. I'll have to ask," he replied, mollified for the moment.

"What time are the Euchre socials?"

"Seven till nine and then the ladies committee puts on supper afterwards and if there's someone to play music, we do a little dancing."

"Well, what do her parents do, would they be able to get here by six o'clock?"

"Her father runs the cycle shop on Hindley Street. It's called Jackson's."

"The chap with the long beard?"

"Yeah, that's him. He's quite friendly. Agnes works behind the counter and her brother and father do the repairs. They all live on top of the shop."

"Well, invite them over on a Monday night, then it will be a quick meal and you can go off to Euchre. They might even give you permission to walk her there," I chuckled, ruffling his hair like he really was a little boy and not a grown man of twenty-five. Wait till Luisa hears this one.

Agnes and her mother Daria, her brother Tom and father Stephen were ecstatic to receive our invitation. Apparently, Armando had told them all about the fabulous factory and the ingenious contraptions we had, and they were very curious to see it for themselves. We spent so long in the factory, that I was afraid there wouldn't be enough time for dinner. But Stephen declared that the young people could take a night off from Euchre for once. We spent a pleasant evening, sharing our experiences of settling in Adelaide, as we discovered that the Jacksons had originally lived in Queensland.

Agnes was twenty- two years old, and Tom was twenty-five, so the young people were eminently sensible, and we were able to have very interesting and stimulating discussions. After the meal, Luisa and the women went off to the kitchen and we fellows retired to the lounge room where Tom and Armando set up a Euchre spread, and Stephen and I allowed ourselves to be fleeced by the card sharps. It didn't take long. When the women eventually returned with tea and coffee, we let the young ones draw us into a variety of fun and fast card games, which resulted in a lot of laughter. I didn't even know Armando was capable of laughing.

The Jacksons had taken the West Terrace tram to get to us, so I suggested Armando run them home in the car. When they left, Luisa and I looked at each other and burst into more raucous laughter.

"I hope your brother's ready to wed, because those women aren't going to let him go without a fight," declared Luisa.

"Well, given that his personality has completely transformed around them, I'm guessing that my brother won't be objecting," I replied, absolutely sure of my assessment.

"They're happy for him to go live with them," revealed Luisa.

"We just need to get him a suit then," I finished, as we drifted off to our room arm in arm, like the young lovers we used to be not that long ago.

By the end of March, they were married at St. Patrick's in Grote

Street with a reception held in the festively decorated hall next door. Daria had organised for the lunch to be catered by a professional crew from one of the hotels nearby. Armando was beaming. He had invited some of the fellows from the factory and had asked Tino to be his best man. Tino seemed to be having a very good time chatting to Agnes' friend who was the bridesmaid, and an even better time once the three-piece orchestra they had hired started playing dance music.

Beppe had once again come across to Adelaide, but Zio Roberto in Melbourne said his wife, wasn't up to the travel anymore, but welcomed Armando to come visit anytime. My forthright mother-in-law, Elena, audaciously asked Beppe about his wedding plans, but he reassured her he was a confirmed bachelor and that as soon as he'd made enough money to retire on comfortably, he'd be selling up and living his real life, fancy free of any hangers on.

Always quite lean, I was taken aback by how much skinnier Beppe had become and I made time to have a good, long chat with him. His business was going well. He hadn't bothered to expand any further, happy with his new premises and steady production rate. He kept up his usual hobbies and had a firm circle of friends and seemed content.

Meeting the Jacksons had brought another blessing for us. Agnes' bridesmaid friend, Joyce, had a younger fourteen-year-old sister, Fiona, who had just finished her schooling and was looking for employment. She had a brood of younger siblings too, so was used to boisterous young boys, and great at inventing all sorts of games to keep them occupied. We employed her to come from 11.00 am to 4.00 pm, Monday to Friday, to give Luisa time to get her bookeeping sorted, organise dinner and even return to some of her charity work.

Now that we had found our fabulous Fiona, we also allowed ourselves a little time off to go to the cinema, a musical evening or even a dance some Saturday nights. Several times, we were invited by a new client, or even my investor George Preston and his wife Celia to join them in their private box at the newly built Palais de Danse on North Terrace. It was quite a sensational thing and it felt like at least half of Adelaide gathered there on Saturday nights.

Luisa had a new silky baby blue dress made that exposed her shoulders and throat and highlighted her still lovely, neat waist and slim ankles. The silver sequins forming eye-catching geometric patterns on the bodice, matched the jaunty little head band with a long, fluffy white feather she wore low on her brow to match the white feather boa she carried. She looked incredibly glamorous, and I wondered again at how lucky I was to have a beautiful, understanding, and intelligent partner by my side. I only hoped I was living up to her expectations too.

Since we had been at our South Terrace site for more than three years, we were becoming familiar with other businesses and families around us too. I had been approached to join the Finance Committee at our local church, which had introduced me to the joys of committee work. As a result, I found myself co-ordinating a few fundraising events, always donating ice cream, either as treats or raffle prizes.

I took advantage of this new outlet to also organise events to raise money for the Red Cross, at whose hospital I had worked in Italy and with whom Luisa had been involved since I had first known her. I put some announcements in the Italian newspapers which were printed in Melbourne, but widely distributed here, calling for all Italians to come to a ball I had organised. Luisa used her contacts with her great-uncles Domenico and Pasquale to organise for some musicians to play some modern dance music for the young ones, as well as traditional folk music for the older Italians to sing along to.

We organised for local Italian businesses to donate raffle prizes and drinks and snacks for the evening. I wasn't sure what kind of response I would get but was delighted when we sold nearly two hundred tickets for our first ball, to be held at the Cathedral Hall in Wakefield Street. I was overjoyed when I was able to present £100 to the local Red Cross organisation who would pass on my contribution to their Italian counterpart.

I also received a letter from the State Governor's wife thanking me for my efforts in support of this important organisation. Even more surprising had been the thanks received by those attending, who had longed to have opportunities for such reunions, as since the end of the war, the numbers of Italians migrating here had quadrupled the Italian population in the state. Before the war, there had been around three hundred families in the state, with two-thirds living in and around Adelaide and Port Adelaide and one-third spread in country areas, noticeably in the fishing industries of Port Pirie, or working in the smelters at Port Augusta.

After this success though, a shock to my sense of security came when Armando and Agnes announced that they would be leaving for Brisbane. Agnes' father, Stephen, had learnt that his father had fallen ill and there was no one able to carry on the family business, upon which his mother and two much younger unmarried sisters relied for income. Agnes was bereft at the thought of not having her mother nearby and had begged Armando to move with her parents. Entranced by the thought of a return to tropical weather, Armando hadn't hesitated to agree to his wife's request. It was a blow for me, as Armando had been a strong and reliable worker, and I had also enjoyed his calm company and his unquestioning loyalty. I had hoped that I might eventually be able to help him set up his own business, but somewhere here in Adelaide.

We would miss them terribly, as we had spent so much time with all the Jacksons who had brought good fun into our lives. My son Anthony would miss him the most as Armando had a special bond with him, instinctively able to listen to the toddler's babble and entertain him with ease, something I found hard to do. I wished Armando well and transferred as much money as I could to him, to help him get started. I urged Agnes to continue writing to us, knowing that Armando couldn't be relied upon to put pen to paper.

However, over the next couple of years, to balance the loss of one brother, I was to be joined by two more of my own siblings. Twenty-year-old Antonio (whom we always called Nino) arrived in 1925, sponsored by Beppe. He arrived on the ship Osterly, via Fremantle so had stopped briefly in Port Adelaide before continuing on to Geelong. He had been a slightly built, fifteen-year-old when I left Italy after the war, but he had a great sense of humour and was a natural mimic. He always had a joke up his sleeve and, having lived most of his life in Milano, was used to city life. Apparently, he found Geelong exceedingly boring and had ended up coming to me in Adelaide within three months of his arrival in Australia.

I was pleased to welcome him, though neither Luisa or I were quite sure what to make of him, or where on earth in my practical, stoic, family he had found such a lively personality. For the eighteen months he stayed with us, he was a whirlwind of activity, out every night, meeting new people, making friends so easily.

He made so much extra work for Luisa, yet he was so charming, she could never be mad at him for leaving his clothes and other personal items strewn all over the apartment. In the factory, he was a good worker, but easily distracted. He would break out into song and have half of the factory acting as his backing group in a heartbeat. He would have made a great sales representative, but with no real English skills on his arrival, he couldn't be sent out on the road just yet.

He was out till all hours every Saturday night, mostly at the Green Dragon Hotel further down our street which specialised in hosting boxing tournaments. One Sunday, when Luisa, Anthony and I returned from church and Nino was just stirring, we were shocked to see the purple bruises around his eyes. After several bouts where he found it took him several days to recover, he quickly learnt to ingratiate himself among the professional boxers as an assistant, rather than take to the ring himself. He worked his way into the circle of Mick Filleri, a much-touted Adelaide boxer, son from a very large family with Italian parents who had migrated to South Australia in the 1870s.

One weekend, we returned from a trip to Luisa's parents in Gawler to find Nino's room completely empty and a hastily scribbled note left on the dining table to tell us he had gone on tour with the Filleri Troupe and didn't know how long he would be away. No apologies for skipping out on work, no clue as to any sort of itinerary.

Apparently, it was obvious to everyone but me that he hated the factory work. Tino said we were better off without him, he caused too much disruption to the factory floor, but the other workers were going to miss his mischievousness. I asked what he meant. Unbeknown to me, Nino had begun a 'Hide the rabbit' competition where every Friday, he would take my son's old toy bunny and hide it somewhere in the factory. To spice up the game, he collected money from those workers who wanted to be in the competition. The money was minor – a penny, but it would all be pooled and then the person who found the rabbit, would win sixty percent of the prize pool, Nino keeping forty percent for his efforts at hiding the rabbit and organising the game. It turns out that he was so clever at finding ever more complex hiding sites that more and more of my factory staff and even my delivery drivers or the drivers from supply companies became involved, so that all Friday, my staff were preoccupied with finding Nino's hiding spot.

"How long has this been going on Tino," I asked incredulously, blanching at the thought of lost production time, or worse, distraction on the job which could have resulted in fatal accidents.

"About six months ... Sorry. It was funny and the chaps loved it. They may even want to keep it going."

"Are you serious," I blurted. "It's only funny until someone gets distracted and loses a hand in one of the machines."

Dammit! I was going to come across as a total ogre when I had to tell the men that the game must be stopped. Luisa and I spent several days discussing the dilemma, but we couldn't see a way forward. Until, on Wednesday afternoon, Tino approached me. He came as the spokesperson the men had chosen. They knew that the game was distracting, but they had come up with a solution. They suggested playing the game in their lunch break only and the rabbit could only be hidden in the storage shed at the back of the property, not in the factory where machines were running or in the cool room. I had visions of thirty men frantically tearing my storage shed apart. I made my decision and gathered the men together at the end of Thursday's lunch period. I told them that I understood they were only looking for a bit of fun to make their days less repetitive. However, I was worried about the collecting of money, as that was considered an illegal activity, except on Melbourne Cup Day, and I didn't fancy us all ending in jail for a bit of fun. The mention of the jail word both alarmed them and suppressed any anger or rebuttal. I told them I had another idea.

A handful of the younger workers had taken to kicking a football about in the park opposite the factory in good weather, which I thought was a great idea, but twenty-minutes break was not enough time. I proposed that on Fridays, we would extend lunch by half an hour, so that they would have ten minutes to eat their lunches and a good fifty minutes for some exercise; Football in the park opposite us or Bocce in the storage shed where the central aisle could easily be turned into a *pista* by rolling out a length of carpet. I would make sure to provide the necessary equipment and token prizes for the winners. The token prizes were Luisa's idea. She suggested we put into a lucky dip box, some small items such as cigarette papers, small pouches of tobacco, hair oil, some dice, a pack of cards, some chewing gum, some little bundles of sweets, glass marbles or pencils they could take home to their children or similar. I gave over that job to Luisa immediately.

The men were flabbergasted, they were getting extra free time, and I was not docking wages. They wanted to clarify that this would not affect their take home pays. I promised them that their wages would remain the same. In the end, the compromise was acceptable to all. I had a more contented workforce and the men had something to look forward to. I only hoped that production would not be too severely affected. I hoped Zio Carlo's and Beppe's examples of keeping their crews loyal would equally pay off in my gesture. I was proved right, with production actually increasing over the next month.

Still worried about Nino though, I visited the Filleri wood yard on the corner of West Terrace & Rose Street, round the corner from the Newmarket Hotel which my best man, Johnnie Hobson had bought and was in the process of renovating. They didn't set my mind at ease. As far as his older brother Arnold knew, Mickey was on a circuit around Australia where he had boxing matches lined up, reputedly from coast to coast. If I wanted to know what Mickey was up to, I'd have to read about it in the Sporting section of the local paper where his exploits were always reported.

"I went to see me *bruvver* off at the train station," Arnold Filleri drawled. "Didn't see yours hangin' about nowhere, though."

"Are you sure?" I puzzled.

"Yep, skinny lad, straight blonde hair, blue eyes, scar on 'is chin; new here, from the old country. Met 'im at the Green Dragon a few months back. Not a bad fighter."

My problem, according to Johnnie, who knew the Filleris well, was that I imagined my brother as an innocent lad, which was how he took great pains to present himself to me. Though, according to Johnnie, who'd had the dubious honour of watching him in operation at his own club, Nino was no innocent and had obviously learnt a thing or two during the war years in Milano.

"What do you mean?" I asked, more hesitatingly now.

"If he's made it look like he's left town, it's because he's been stirring up political trouble. The police have had an eye on him and his associates. I suggest you stop asking for him or you may cause him more grief."

I quickly finished my beer and grabbed for my coat replying very clearly to Johnnie: "Right, got you. There are some things it's best I don't know, otherwise I'll never sleep at night."

A few weeks later, I received a telegram from my sister. My mother had been taken to hospital but had not recovered from her bout of pleurisy and had passed away at the hospital. I felt a deep, sonorous bell clang in my head, stopping me in my tracks and making the air around me thin and hazy.

Luisa found me sitting on one of the steps of our staircase, slumped over, trying hard to breathe. Another one gone.

I shut my eyes, picturing my mother rising off the couch as I entered the apartment on my first trip to Milano during the war.

"It was such a shock to see how much she had aged," I told Luisa, "But there was such joy there too. It filled her eyes as she sat holding my hand, contemplating the whole of me."

I had grown up in a large, busy family, yet I had always felt absolutely loved. She had been a wonderful mother, not particularly physically affectionate, because that was not how our family operated, but I always knew I was cared for. She always took an interest in how I was doing, what I had seen or learnt, even as a young child. She took great pains and enormous pride in making sure we were all well turned out whenever we left the house, and always had a kind word for us when we were feeling down.

Not knowing if Maria had communicated with anyone else. I sent messages to Beppe, Armando and Zio Roberto, letting them know about Nino's disappearance too and requesting that they be on the lookout for him and the Filleri Troupe, in the hope that Nino had really run off with them. In the meantime, Beppe, Armando and I commiserated with each other. We had not even known our mother was ill, so her death was a profound shock. We were sad, but sadder for ourselves, that we had been forced by economic circumstances to have left her side at such young ages and to be obliged to live so far away from her.

I wired Maria some money to help with funeral expenses and I also wrote to my sister and confessed my failure to keep Nino out of trouble, explaining exactly what had happened. Maria's reply confirmed what I suspected. My mother knew of Nino's involvement with some fairly violent political groups that had sprung up after the war. He was bitter and unwilling to work, often accusing our older brother of being a capitalist slave, conditioned into submission. Maria admitted that our mother had hoped that sending him to Australia and getting him away from the thugs he associated with might have changed his attitude. Maria was sorry she had not explained the situation before, but she too had hoped he might change, away from the turmoil Italy was experiencing.

Even more surprising news was contained in my sister's letter. She had lost her job at the factory and was unsure she would ever find another as there had been so many labour strikes and factories shutting down. She didn't want to become a burden for Rico. Our youngest brother, Nicola, who was eighteen years old now had a much sweeter personality and looked up to Rico like a father. Rico had been able to find him a job in the Pirelli factory, so he was in a relatively good situation. Maria finished her letter with a bombshell. Would I consider sponsoring her to come to Australia? That way, they did not have to keep up rent payments on the apartment, as Nicola could go live with Rico. They had room for one more, but not two. Rico had been increasingly pressuring her to accept a marriage proposal from a widower of their acquaintance, but Maria just couldn't bring herself to say yes. He was twenty years her senior and while he was kind to her, she couldn't muster any feelings for him.

I went straight to Mr Barrow, the vice-consul, to set in motion the request for Maria to come. I sent all the necessary forms to her via post and wired her they were on the way with money for the trip. All she had to do was wait for permission and buy her ticket. I hoped Rico would be satisfied with that and keep supporting her for a while longer. I went to the Telephone Exchange and booked a call to Beppe, telling him only that Maria had lost her job and needed some money and that she wanted to come to Australia. He didn't hesitate, saying he'd wire her some money that very day.

On my return after visiting Mr Barrow, I was stricken with guilt. In my rush to save my sister, I'd completely forgotten about talking to Luisa about it. She'd been out collecting Anthony from school when the letter arrived. After Armando, then Nino, I was reticent about imposing on Luisa's generosity again.

"Don't be silly," she replied simply. "Of course, she'll come here, where else is she going to go? She can't go to Beppe, he wouldn't know what to do with her. She must come here."

That was how, nine months after Nino's disappearance, we had another Bodoni living with us. This time, things couldn't have been better. Luisa and Maria got on so well, it was as if they had known each other all their lives. Rather than being an extra burden, Maria lightened Luisa's load. She took it upon herself to take Anthony to school every morning, stop at the market for the day's groceries, and cook dinner which freed Luisa to do the accounts and sit with Anthony after school.

She even made wonderfully buttery *Bombonini* biscuits for the factory floor every Monday. Luisa rarely had time for home-made pasta these days, but with Maria's encouragement, they started making it again for Saturday's lunch when Tino often stayed to shut down the factory and do maintenance after the other workers had gone. I believe I might have actually been caught weeping the day Maria made a huge pot of polenta with roast quails in a wine rich onion sauce. She also undertook to help us polish our Italian language skills.

Since Luisa only spoke her parent's dialect, which I understood, but couldn't really speak myself, Luisa and I had always spoken to each other in English. We had been speaking to Anthony in English. We told Maria that the sooner she learnt English, the better she would integrate. But she was having none of that, she insisted on refreshing our Italian. She spoke to Anthony exclusively in Italian and the little tacker, only six years old, had no problem picking it up. Within a few months he was able to follow all her instructions and was even asking for things around the house in Italian. Maria had brought a couple of scrapbooks full of magazine and newspaper articles, recipes, and short stories with her. She had Luisa choose a snippet to read aloud every evening until her pronunciation and comprehension improved.

After six months, Luisa started addressing me in Italian when we were at the table. When it was about business, we still spoke to each other in English, but at the table or in the kitchen, or when we were relaxing after dinner, it became natural for us to switch to Italian. It was a miracle. Luisa enjoyed taking Maria shopping, fitting her out and updating her style, which included having Maria's hair bobbed and waved, just as Luisa had recently done to hers.

I watched them set off arm in arm, heads bent, conspiratorial laughter emanating from contented, smiling faces and marvelled at my blessed luck.

Business grows

The factory had been at full production for a good five years now. By the beginning of 1928, my investors had received their five-years' worth of a quarter of company profits each year and each of them chose to take up the option of retaining their investment by further injecting £1,000 pounds each into my business. If I wanted to increase production, I would have to upgrade my machinery in order to be able to accommodate greater volumes as well as increase the size of my refrigeration and delivery facilities.

Despite my many attempts to convince the government regulators to increase my quota for the production of margarine, easily my most profitable product, the powerful dairy lobby, fearful of the competition margarine represented for butter, held back margarine production across the country, even lobbying to have legislation enacted to make us dye margarine pink to clearly distinguish it from butter.

The ice business was holding its own, but with plenty of competition from other companies, and many larger establishments installing their own cooling facilities, I didn't think it was worth investing in more machinery for that section of the factory. Instead, the ice cream business was where I was looking to expand. There were a couple of new players on the market, but they had concentrated on creating novelty moulded frozen shapes on sticks which they sold mostly through small groceries and concession stands. Although they did make a small dent in my business, the taste for good quality ice cream only seemed to grow, so that I was able to keep producing for my home deliveries and commercial customers.

I added four more vans for deliveries, giving me a total of eight, allowing us to expand our service areas across the city and the new suburbs. I also continued to make use of the frozen freight railway network and my insulated boxes to ship further afield, as far as Port Pirie and Port Augusta.

Since the war, drinking in hotels had continued to be restricted to a closing time of six o'clock in the evenings, but in order to make a profit, more hotels had begun to offer dining services, and ice cream desserts were popular with young and old. I concentrated on producing vanilla-flavoured ice cream for most of the year, but I did add extra flavours at Christmas and Easter, with chocolate and strawberry being the best sellers.

When I was asked to give donations to charity events, I used the small cups system with tiny wooden paddles to make them easier to transport and serve. I never denied a request for a donation, especially when it was a school, orphanage or a reputable charity. Luisa and I attended many fundraisers organised by our local church, or other institutions. Now that Anthony had started school with the brothers on Wakefield Street, there were also many opportunities there to donate to fêtes and prize-giving nights. I recognised that I had been very lucky and was always keen to give back when I could.

There was much building activity in the city, with many companies investing in new premises so that the old ramshackle buildings were disappearing, and more elegant red-brick buildings were taking their place. The new Italian migrants often found their way into this growing building trade, facilitated by the Pomerino Construction, Stonework and Tiling Company, which had been established in Adelaide two generations ago by Gesualdo Pomerino and had grown into a sizeable and well-respected firm. The grandsons even went to Italy to recruit specialist stonemasons who were responsible for carving the stone facades of these new buildings with elegant marble columns adorned with ancient roman motifs.

The motor industry too had expanded rapidly with the Adelaide branch of the Holden company recently leaving the city to set up a manufacturing plant at Woodville, and they were now turning to engine manufacturing rather than just chassis building. This was welcome news for me, as more suburbs springing up around the western side of the city meant more potential clients for me. Our south-western corner of the city, in the streets behind our factory, was still jam-packed with tiny little cottages and small businesses, and our own street, South Terrace, was seeing many of the elegant mansions transformed into apartments or boarding houses. It seems no-one was interested in domestic service anymore, the old established families had long begun selling up and building themselves modern homes in the suburbs with up-to-date bathrooms, gas heating and electric light that didn't require servants to live-in.

The double storey sandstone mansion next door to us had been converted by the Fergusson sisters into six apartments over ten years ago. In the middle of the year, Luisa came home from visiting with them, telling me they were thinking of selling up and moving to be closer to family in Melbourne.

"What's the place like inside? Does it need a lot of refurbishing?"

"Why? Are you thinking of buying?" Luisa narrowed her eyes at me, a tiny grin forming at the edge of her lips.

"Not really, but since it's come up, we should at least consider it. For one," I continued holding up my forefinger, "it would get you away from the noise of the factory during the day. You've complained often enough about not being able to think over the noise. Secondly, it would give us more room for entertaining, and a lovely garden, now that Anthony is growing up and wants to have his friends come over. Thirdly, if we kept the apartments, it could make a wise investment."

Always up for a new challenge, Luisa didn't really need any convincing.

"I'll look at the books and find out what kind of price they are hoping for, shall I?"

I just shrugged my shoulders in reply, looking for that little sparkle in her eye that always came with a new project. There it was! I could leave the details in my wife's capable hands.

Within a couple of months, the deal was sealed. We took out a mortgage on the property, and following Antonio's usual sage advice, we put it into my wife's name so as to keep our personal and business assets separate. We moved into the larger apartment on the first floor that had three bedrooms, as we still had Maria with us, swapping with the tenant, a Mrs Jenkins, who was eager to stay on, but was fine with the smaller two-bedroom space downstairs, now that her son had married and moved to his own home.

We had five tenants, all middle-class widowed ladies, who each had two bedrooms, a dining room and parlour combined, a kitchen and a bathroom. There was a shared laundry facility downstairs and the original ballroom with adjacent kitchens had been retained, untouched, for use by all tenants if they wished to entertain. There were also two spare rooms and a bathroom downstairs, which we decided to turn into guest rooms, thinking that Luisa's parents and aunt and uncle in Gawler might be able to use them when in town. We made a few repairs and adjustments, changed the colour of the front door from black to a pale blue and painted the outside woodwork to match.

We spruced up the garden and had a tennis court installed out the back, for Anthony, though I thought I could probably use some exercise too. I had recently celebrated my thirty-seventh birthday and was starting to develop a noticeable fleshiness. Luisa's brother, Bart, promised he would teach us all how to play.

Luisa decided we needed to throw a party for all our family, friends, and tenants. I had a sign made up for above the front door: Cremona House as a nod to my origins. On the night of the party, the ballroom was resplendent, a three-piece orchestra had been hired and the doors at the end of the room opened to a tessellated tiled terrace and the garden beyond, which was hung with bunting and little candles in glass vases. As well as family, we had invited local friends and business acquaintances. Luisa and Maria, assisted by Elena, who had arrived a few days earlier, and her sister Beatrice as well as Luisa's friend Dot Sullivan who had brought her younger sister Selina, now all grown up, had all been busy cleaning, decorating, cooking, and serving a delicious buffet. Father Peter had been invited to come a little earlier so that he could bless the house and the delicate iron crucifix that Luisa had purchased for the occasion and was now hanging inside the front door. One of the guests was Mr. Barrow, who had asked if he could bring with him, his newly appointed assistant.

Margherita and Alessandro Pastore had recently arrived from

Melbourne. The gentleman, around thirty years of age, was a garrulous chap who flitted easily from group to group and encouraged dancing and singing. His wife Margherita was a most elegantly attired woman of remarkable poise and was carrying a very prettily turned out little two-year old girl called Angelina. As I pulled my wife for a spin around the dance floor, I couldn't help noticing that my sister had also been dancing with the same gentleman for a few numbers now.

"Who's that dancing with Maria?" I whispered into Luisa's ear.

"I've only just met him. He's the brother of Frances and Jeanie Braithwaite, the nurses who own the hospital down the street where I had Anthony."

"Is he a doctor?"

"No." Luisa giggled at my question. "Apparently he's in imports and exports; lives in Melbourne but stops in Adelaide for business trips."

"Is he married?" I asked as I peered to see if I could spot a wedding band on his finger as they came into our orbit.

"Don't know," Luisa answered as she placed a hand on my chin and turned me to face her again. "How about we just enjoy our evening, and you pay attention to your wife?"

I quickly corrected my bad manners and made sure my wife enjoyed herself. It didn't stop me from quizzing my sister at the end of the night.

"You had a very attentive dancing partner tonight," I said, trying to keep my tone and expression neutral.

"Yes, he was a very good dancer." That was all I got in return as she went off to her room.

My sister was twenty-eight years old. I knew I didn't have any right to interfere in her personal life, she had repaid me ten times over for any assistance I had previously provided her through the care and love she had showered upon us in the five years she had lived with us.

Nevertheless, I couldn't help wondering about this stranger who had turned up out of the blue.

On the Monday after our party, we received a most gracious note from Margherita Pastore, thanking us for welcoming them as guests and inviting us to come dine at their house at our earliest convenience. She supplied a telephone number and an address in Angas Street, southeast of the city square.

Further in the week, we received another four reciprocal invitations to another dinner, a Sunday lunch, a tennis party and a garden party. Each invitation was for the four of us, so Anthony and Maria were included.

The Braithwaite sisters sent us an invitation to a garden party-fundraising fête in a month's time. I had the habit of opening my mail in my office, after Anthony had gone to bed. If there was anything of interest to Luisa and Maria, I would leave it out on the dining table so they could see it for themselves the following morning. A mischievous smile crept across my face. I could just imagine Maria's face the next day as I gingerly propped the invitation up against the fruit bowl on the dining table.

Come Saturday, dressed in our most elegant suits, with the women sporting new cloche hats, fur trimmed collars and soft suede gloves, we hopped into my newly acquired silver Fiat Tourer with navy upholstery and drove the ten minutes to the eastern side of the city. The Pastores were renting one half of a newly built semi-detached two storey townhouse. At the front of the adjoining townhouse, we saw a shiny brass plaque announcing a medical doctor's practice. It turned out that the Swedish Doctor Nilssen used the bottom three rooms for his medical practice, and the family, comprising two small children and wife, lived upstairs. Like their neighbours, the Pastores had their family bedrooms and intimate day parlours upstairs and the front three rooms downstairs were a reception room with soft, elegant armchairs and loungers scattered around rich carpets and occasional tables. There was a dining room with a table large enough to host twelve diners, and a smaller room which was set up as an office. We had brought flowers with us and of course, a couple of 1-pint tubs of ice cream, which made Margherita's eyes sparkle. She winked at me.

"Wait till you see what I'm going to do with this."

Margherita had hired a male cook who would also act as waiter. We partook of an elegant French dinner with a consommé as a starter, a fish course, a meat course, a salad course, a cheese course and then a dessert. The dessert turned out to be a *Pêche Melba*, to honour our most famous Australian musical export, the operatic star, Nellie Melba and which incorporated our Imperial ice cream accompanied by vanilla scented poached peaches, a raspberry sauce and some delicately toasted almond flakes, a touching tribute.

I had occasionally dined on such fare when Zio Carlo entertained in London or Genova, but I was a very simple country boy and rather awed by it all. It seems Maria had been better-prepared. On the way home, Maria reminded me that she had been in service with a rich family in Cremona before the outbreak of war and had been schooled in appropriate dining manners by the Contessa, who spoke to her cook in French. The Pastores, who'd only been in Australia for around three years were delighted to be able to speak to us in Italian and complimented us on our linguistic skills, for which we gave full credit to my sister. After dinner, Alessandro played us some new music on his phonograph, some stirring patriotic songs with jaunty tunes and memorable, empowering lyrics. Margherita had her own contribution too, sharing Italian Ladies' Magazines with drawings and photos of daring Fascist Fashions, all sleek and black, with a militaristic bent, emphasised by little aviator caps and ties, and others of the Fascist Leader Benito Mussolini, looking most handsome and vigorous.

By the end of the evening, Sandro had rooted out my childhood nickname of Carlino and had invited himself over to practise my tennis the following Sunday, and also promised to bring Luisa sheet music copies of the new patriotic songs of the Fascist party for her to play. Equally, the women had been swapping child-rearing and shopping tips and planned to take the beautiful Rita to their favourite store run by friends, Mesdames Colley and Filleri, on the first floor of the Royal Exchange Building in King William Street, where the most exclusive hats and clothes were made to measure with pattern books, fabrics and trims flown in from Paris. This time, they would take Rita's fascist fashion samples to see if they could be replicated, giddy at the thought of starting a new fashion trend in conservative, old Adelaide.

I also learned the purpose for the couple's arrival in Adelaide. With the American border shut to Italian migration, there was a growing number of migrants from Italy choosing to come to Australia, and with those here requesting official documents so they could sponsor relatives, the workload had easily tripled for the kind Mr. Barrow, who was getting on in years and was keen to retire soon. Sandro had been sent by the Melbourne Consul, to learn the ropes from Mr. Barrow, with a view to taking over the Vice-Consul's role soon. Sandro had an accounting background, but it was his involvement in the nascent Fascist Party, including participation in the March on Rome in 1922 that had impressed the party's Immigration Consul in Melbourne, who had recruited him to this position, despite the fact that Sandro had no diplomatic service background.

As well as helping with all the necessary paperwork, Sandro

declared that he hoped he would be able to bring an authentic touch of Italy and pride in the fatherland to the Italians in the far-flung colony of Adelaide. Sandro had a very colourful, quite verbose, almost theatrical way of speaking, so I sometimes missed exactly what he was saying. However, since my business and civic associates were people of more puritan tendencies and a rather orthodox way of thinking and living, I was entranced to find someone who enjoyed a good glass of *vino* and a good table, and was a very attentive listener, keen to hear about how I had grown my business, how Luisa and I had met, how Maria had managed after losing her job when the uniform factory closed down, even how Anthony was getting on at school.

In return, he regaled us with stories of the brave and clear-sighted Mussolini, who was going to reclaim Italy's importance as a powerful, modern nation to rival Britain and France and who would no longer be overlooked in negotiations for land to grow her empire. He even delighted in describing Mussolini as the immigrant's friend, eager to protect us from injustice.

I had read brief snippets about Mussolini in our local papers, and sometimes, when I was able to access the Melbourne papers, there were more detailed reports, but in general, the reports were favourable, claiming Mussolini was doing a wonderful job of bringing order to Italy and thwarting the Communist menace which had previously had a firm grip on the nation, especially on its industry. Unlike here in Australia, in Italy, there were no more crippling strikes. Mussolini had banned the wheat imports and restored some of the lost agricultural sector, which in my opinion, being from a farming family, gave me some hope that the natural order of the world was returning. Most of my news from Italy had come from Maria, but now that she was here, we rarely discussed politics. The mail she received from friends spoke about mostly personal matters, and here in distant Adelaide, Italy was easily forgotten.

Our older brother Federico did write occasionally, but mostly about his work and his family, rarely about what was happening politically. My father-in-law Antonio, when he was running the grocery store in Port Adelaide, where many Italian lived, used to import some Italian newspapers and magazines, and even though they often arrived six-months late, at least they brought genuine news from Italy, but now that they had moved to Gawler, he no longer had customers for that source of news. I decided to keep an eye out for listings of ship arrivals, usually buried in the back pages of the newspaper, and next time I saw an Italian ship was due, I would head down to the port to see if I could have a chat with the captain.

In the meantime, I decided it was time to look into buying a wireless, so that we could receive the radio news. It was after all an Italian who had brought this enchantment to the world; it was time Mr. Marconi's invention graced our parlour too. We'd previously had no need for extra entertainment at home as Luisa still kept up her piano practice in the evenings, and Anthony was having violin lessons, so Luisa would act as accompanist when his tutor came to the house after school. If I had time, I would try to join them with my violin, as I enjoyed the practice too.

Once a fortnight, Luisa would have her aging uncles over for dinner mid-week, and they would always bring their violins, so I was able to have a little more sophisticated practice then too. I knew I was really quite rusty, but playing still brought me a sense of peace. Occasionally, Luisa's friend Dot, who had a fine soprano voice would come to sing whatever new aria she was learning, sometimes accompanied by her sister Selina, who preferred the more popular musical theatre numbers.

I missed my business and life chats with Antonio. For several years,

I'd had Armando as male company, though as he had been absent from Italy since the age of fifteen, he hadn't had much interest in Italian politics, or here for that matter. So, over the weeks, as I got to know Sandro better, and my tennis improved in order to ensure I was good competition for him, I was surprised at how much I enjoyed his company and was eager to help him achieve his ambitions.

Sandro made quick work of introducing himself around town, not only to the Italian traders, but to local and overseas government officials with whom he had dealings through his consulate work. He was surprised, he claimed, that we had not formed any Italian associations. He noticed that there were many Irish associations, there was even an association formed to encourage Irish migration to the city, and delegates who would go meet every incoming ship to ensure there was support for the new arrivals, including finding them a job.

"Does anyone do that for the Italians?" he asked.

I couldn't reply as I genuinely didn't know and had never thought to ask. The reality was that most of the Italian migrants who received permission to come out to Australia, were sponsored by a family member who had to guarantee them a place to live and a job, so a greeting committee didn't seem a necessity.

Sandro also suggested the possibility of forming a support group for Italian businesses to promote beneficial import and export links from Italy. I confessed I couldn't see how that would benefit my business. I certainly wasn't going to be exporting my delicate products, nor could I see myself needing to import products from Italy.

"What about equipment," he suggested. "Italian engineering is very progressive," he boasted.

As far as I was aware, there wasn't any equipment I needed that I couldn't obtain or have made right here in Adelaide, without having to pay for transport and importation fees. Sandro said he would make enquiries and obtain information about equipment for ice cream making. I was fine with that, no harm in looking at information. However, Sandro had more success with other traders who were looking for exclusive Italian products: silks and damasks, leather goods, olive oil, coffee roasters and grinders, pasta makers, bicycle and motor parts, and even just general goods like soap or kitchen and garden equipment. He convinced me to join an association he was planning to organise. He needed a venue to accommodate around twelve people, so I offered up the apartment above the factory, which was still furnished, but currently vacant.

I was intrigued by the people who turned up. They were mostly people I knew, either through my church activities or through visits to their businesses for my personal needs. Fiorentino Giaccio was the first to arrive. He was a quiet, unassuming gentleman who operated a tailor's shop on the corner of Currie and Grey Streets, and as I had previously ordered a couple of suits from him, I knew he already imported fine fabrics from Italy. He said he was keen to hear about the offers of better deals on imports touted by the assistant-consul. It turned out to be a very pleasant social evening as well. Maria had prepared an assortment of sweet biscuits and savoury morsels and had settled herself into the kitchen so that she could serve drinks and coffees as required. Sandro had insisted that we form a governing council and elect a president, vice-president and secretary. Constantino Verdi, who owned a well-frequented drapery business in Hindley Street became president, Giacomo Prinzi who ran the gun shop was vice-president, and Enrico Giglio, the owner of a Mica mine in Alice Springs but with a factory in Liverpool Street off the western end of Hindley St, was secretary. I agreed to allow the monthly meetings to be held at the factory.

I'm not sure if the meetings achieved Sandro's aims, but the gathering of members quickly grew to over twenty and had to be moved to our ballroom at Cremona House. The meetings became a perfect vehicle for me to bring up charitable causes, especially the support of the Red Cross which was dear to my heart. The president of the committee moved to appoint me as Treasurer of the charitable works sector. This allowed me to manage the first contributions from the committee and help me get started by hiring a hall, musicians, and caterers, as well as printing flyers and inserting newspaper announcements so that we could organise another gathering of local Italians for a fundraising ball.

The ball was a social and financial success, raising one hundred and fifty pounds. The president gave the first speech explaining the role of the committee, introducing the members of the governing council, and also thanking me for my organisational talents. Then Sandro gave a speech in his role as Vice-Consul, urging those present who needed help with paperwork regarding immigration or business matters not to hesitate to approach him, which was all regular and had been discussed in the previous meeting. Then he finished on an undiscussed topic where he praised Mussolini's efforts to unite the Italian people all over the world, using the natural intelligence and enterprise of her people as the guiding strength to create a modern Italian economy which would be able to stand proud on the world stage. He spoke so energetically of North Pole expedition leader Umberto Nobile, who was the first person to reach the pole in an airship and the recently signed Italo-Ethiopian Treaty, citing it as example of Italian military prowess. This did not elicit the response he had hoped for, as a group of young men started heckling him and were very quickly ushered out of the hall.

Loud verbal exchanges were followed by fisticuffs, but it was all over in a matter of minutes. After the fight was broken up, the objectors were given their ticket money back and told to leave. I recognised one of them as a young lad who had once come calling for my disappeared brother Nino, when he was still living with us. Apparently, he was a Francesco Ferrari, who worked as a barber, in a lane off Rundle Street. I decided I would need to speak to that young man, sooner rather than later.

I was not surprised to see a certain Mr. Braithwaite at our Spring Ball, unaccompanied by his sisters this time. I'd had a chance to talk to him alone at the Narma Hospital fête. I learnt that he had been a partner in a furniture importing business and, in the past, had made a couple of trips to Europe to source furniture, however, he did little of that these days, now that there were so many ships arriving in Australia and with the journey reduced to around four weeks, those who were able to afford European furniture, could afford to go to Europe themselves and choose their own furniture and ship it home themselves.

Instead, he had developed pattern books, which he showed to furniture retailers and then had orders made up in their Melbourne factory. I was sad to learn he had also endured a personal tragedy, having lost his wife to illness in 1923. He had a five-year-old lad who was cared for by his older sister.

He was tired of life as a travelling salesman and his sisters were encouraging him to set up his own business in Adelaide, now that his boy was ready for school, so that they could spend more time together. He'd also told me that he had not always been in the furniture business. His father had owned a fish shop at the Victoria Markets, and he had worked with him from the age of fourteen.

"Why did you give up the fish business?"

"My father passed away during the war, while I was fighting in France, and my mother didn't feel she could keep the business afloat, as I was the only son. She sold it and set the money aside for me, in the hope that I would return from the war and be able to start up another."

"But you didn't?"

"It wasn't for lack of trying, but I couldn't find premises that I could afford when prices skyrocketed after the war. Then one of my army mates suggested we pool our money and build something new. He had been brought up in his father's carpentry business, so he understood furniture. I'd always been able to draw, so I took charge of design and sales. We started selling other people's furniture, then my partner started building our own line of furniture. After the first year, I suggested branching out into importing. We've been quite successful, but I feel now that we're not doing the importing, my heart isn't really in it. I'm tired of always being on the road."

"Would you go back to the fish business?"

"Maybe, I'd be happy to do anything, as long as I could be my own boss. My partner, he's a great bloke but very pushy, likes to have his own way all the time."

"I have a brother like that," I commiserated, thinking of my time in Geelong with Beppe.

"Luckily, my sister's a completely different kettle of fish." I winked, as I led him over to a small group of ladies talking with Luisa and Maria at one of the stalls selling home-made cakes.

At the ball, I didn't get much of a chance to talk with Arnold Braithwaite, as there were so many other people eager to talk to me, most of them wanting to encourage me to make these Italian balls regular functions. When I came across Ronny Beltrini and his wife Emily, who ran a fresh fish shop in the Adelaide Central Markets, I pointed Arnold out to them, suggesting he could use Ronny's guidance.

Chatting the next day with Luisa's parents, who had come to Adelaide for the ball, we discussed the disturbance after Sandro's speech, and I brought up my suspicion that the leader of the dissenters was possibly a friend of Nino's. Maria piped up with: "Well, I'd be staying well away from him, if he's a friend of Nino's, he's bound to bring trouble."

Antonio had another opinion: "I'd be wondering why they were so angry at Sandro's words; it's not as if he said anything that controversial. He's the consular representative, of course he's going to be promoting the Italian government's aims."

Antonio suggested he and I take a little drive down to the Port after lunch, to visit our old haunts. It was a great idea, I got to call in on Bert and Frank and they filled me in on the gossip around the docks. Their saddlery business was still running, but the unemployment level in the port district was high and many employers were playing dirty tactics in an effort to decrease wages, or at least hold them stagnant. Port cargo traffic had also diminished by at least twenty-five percent over the last two years. In their opinion, migrants were made the scapegoat for the stand-offs between employers and trade unions. As the Italian migrants were the largest group of foreigners, they were the most visible, and were most often subjected to racist slurs and mistreatment. And there were some migrants, especially recently arrived ones, who weren't prepared to sit back and say nothing. They were prepared to agitate and start troubles, and mostly they were very anti-Mussolini whom they believed was a thug and a betrayer of the most monstrous sort.

I asked Bert to explain, but he thought these young men were mostly layabouts, who liked the sounds of their own voices. Most seemed to have been forced to leave Italy to avoid detention, which confirmed for Frank and Bert that they were the worst sort of Italian. After more news, including information that a group of young Italian men whose cart had broken down on the Port Road at Alberton, had been set upon by a group of other young men, while encouraged by the patrons of a hotel opposite, Antonio and I didn't venture any further into our old haunts and sped back home with trepidation along the same Port Road, which had finally been bituminised. In further discussions with Antonio, trying to make sense of the two sides we'd been presented with, we came to the conclusion that Sandro's group had plenty of supporters, prepared to do good for the local Italian community.

"Judging from the people I spoke to at the ball," reflected Antonio, "they seem to be upstanding, moral family men, whereas the agitators were young hotheads spouting anarchism, which won't help the Italians here to integrate."

I easily agreed with him.

A fortnight later, I managed to get away from the factory early and told the ladies I would pick up Anthony and take him for a haircut before his school concert that night. We found the barber in Twin Street and walked in as casually as possible. There were six barber's chairs lined up in a row with two already occupied and being tended to by two middle-aged barbers in short white jackets. I was mightily impressed by the elegance of this establishment.

A young lad showed us to our chairs, asked us what service we wanted, even offered me a coffee and a cool drink for Anthony, then he headed to the back of the store where we could hear people talking. Two barbers, also in short white jackets with soft leather tool belts slung across their hips from where an assortment of scissors and combs peeked, came out from behind the back entrance which was hidden by a dark red velvet curtain. One of the barbers looked at me oddly, then addressed me by my name.

"Signor Bodoni, and this must be your son, what brings you to this side of the city?"

He had addressed me in Italian. There was no need for me to say anything, as Anthony piped up immediately.

"My school's near here and we have to go back after my haircut, for our end of term concert tonight. I'm playing the violin."

The other barber wrapped a towel around Anthony's neck and started to engage him in conversation as Anthony sipped happily on his orange soda. I stared at the mirror in front of me, from where the young man's face appeared and asked him,

"How do you know my name?"

"I was at the Italian ball you organised a few weeks back."

"Did you have a good time?" I tossed back affably.

He hesitated, for quite a moment before replying.

"I was kicked out, remember?"

"Oh, sorry, I didn't recognise you," I answered as nonchalantly as I could.

Again, he hesitated, fixing me with a steely look through the mirror.

"It's rarely a good idea to lie to someone who can hold a razor to your throat."

This time I gawped and locked narrowed eyes with his reflection in the mirror, for what seemed an eternity. I broke the silent stare-down and furtively whispered:

"I know you were once a friend of my brother Nino. I haven't heard from him since he disappeared. I just want to know if he's alright."

Ferrari hesitated, but eventually answered is a soft, but still reluctant tone.

"He's doing fine."

"Where is he?" I replied.

"He's in Western Australia. That's all you need to know. If he wants to tell you something, he'll contact you. Sniffing around after him will not help him or you. Do you get my meaning?"

He couldn't have made himself any clearer. All I could do was nod. Ferrari snapped a towel in the air behind my ear, tucked it under my collar at the back and then proceeded to part my hair in order to trim it. We didn't say another word to each other. He retreated out to the back room before I had even finished saying thank you. I didn't tell anyone else about that incident, and Anthony had been too busy chatting to the friendly other barber to notice the tense stand-off.

I did question Sandro though, asking him why his speech at the ball would have caused such controversy. He handed me a couple of Italian newspapers.

"Read for yourself. It's the usual agitators who aren't happy unless everyone is miserable."

One newspaper had only high praise for Mussolini's ability to bring order to industry, restore jobs, create new opportunities, stand up to Britain, the USA and France in the peace negotiations etc. It went on to describe his prowess as a military leader, a genius even, and gave numerous examples of happy Italians, hard at work. Obviously, a party-funded publication, I concluded.

The next newspaper warned against the insidious erosion of democratic rights, but didn't elaborate why this was happening, making veiled comments only about the far-reaching ears of the Fascist Party.

The third newspaper denounced state control of industry as a foil for the dictator's grab for personal power, claiming that he was supporting the usual corrupt landowners and never had any intention of redressing the balance for the miserable poor, left starving in their hovels while the dictator drained the public purse in pursuit of ridiculous, self-aggrandising colonial ambitions instead of feeding his people.

I deliberated at some length on this one, seeing that the statements made could be supported by all I had previously read. And yet, the Australian newspapers, just last month had printed a full-page article written by a local academic, praising Mussolini's exemplary management of the nation which had been restored to law and order and flourishing industry. All were written in the most dramatic tones, it was difficult to discern which were truthful. The summer season was around the corner, and I had my hands full with my factory. Maybe Sandro was right, maybe they were just the usual grumblers. But my interaction with Nino's barber friend kept popping into my head. There was something I was missing.

Bombshell

In October, for the celebration of the anniversary of the Fascist March on Rome, which had occurred on the 27th of October 1922, Sandro had organised a dinner at the Convent Garden Restaurant in King William Street, where there were over a hundred signed up members of the newly formed Adelaide Italian Fascist Association, as well as at least another hundred curious onlookers.

The committee wore smart Fascist uniforms, carried the new Italian and Fascist standards and greeted the crowd with the dramatic fascist salute, of a right arm raised, with palms facing down and fingers held together, unearthed from ancient Roman customs.

Sandro had hired an Italian three-piece orchestra, so the night also began with stirring singing of the new Italian Fascist Anthem 'Giovinezza' and 'L'inno imperiale' and concluded with more rousing songs of Italy's peasant past like 'Bella Ciao', the rice worker's resistance song and some of the laments echoing the experience of migration. He welcomed everybody and began with a toast to 'Il Duce' and, in between courses, many other people gave rousing speeches, including one local gentleman, whom I had never met, describing his own involvement in the famous March on Rome.

It was a heady and exhilarating night, full of positive energy. One speaker had explained the system of clubs and support networks set up by Mussolini. They were there to benefit the education of the young and provide activities for healthy minds and bodies. He called on the men and women present to consider forming an organisation promoting healthy activities and the teaching of the Italian language to our young ones, imparting our precious culture before it was lost.

I thought of my son Anthony, whom I would love to see mixing with other young Italian boys. Luisa, Maria and I discussed being involved in such a venture, with Maria urging us to bring music to the club; we in turn encouraged her to offer her excellent teaching of the Italian language. The evening ended with another hearty rendition of the Italian Anthem as well as the Austrlian Anthem 'God save the King' and also the popular 'Song of Australia'.

The following year saw us become increasingly involved in these Balilla classes. First setting one up in Adelaide, then Glanville, where a large group of Italian fishermen and their families lived, and also in Port Adelaide. The classes were free for the children attending, but parents were required to be subscribers to the Fascist Organisation. Both adults and children were issued official Fascist Identification passports which included photographs organised by the ever-charming Rita Pastore.

Groups were run by volunteers. Sandro oversaw their setting up and organisation and worked tirelessly, communicating with the Minister for Overseas Affairs in Rome to request funds and teaching materials from Italy. He was very successful, even managing to secure a huge shipment of Balilla uniforms, including hats, socks and shoes. For some of the children, who lived in straightened circumstances and had never owned new clothes, the pleasure on their faces brought tears to our eyes, as well as those of their parents.

Luisa and the other female volunteers used classic Italian children's nursery songs and movement to teach rudimentary Italian to the very little ones, and Maria turned out to be a very patient teacher to the older children. I was so proud of both of them. Luisa had been born in Australia, had never set foot on Italian soil, yet here she was, singing and speaking fluently, engaging heartily in all things Italian.

I joined them in the organisation of a choir to which we taught traditional songs as well as some of the new Fascist songs. Our choir of approximately thirty children were often called upon to sing at the functions we organised like sporting competitions, dances, and picnics, and we were occasionally also asked to participate in other community events, including the Lady Governess' garden parties which were often dedicated to raising funds for the International Red Cross and other notable charities.

Other members organised sporting competitions, in particular, a European Football League, where we had many newly arrived British and other European migrants also form teams. We even had a journalist come to take a photo of us outside of Cremona House which was published in the Adelaide Chronicle in late May for an event we organised to celebrate the founding of Rome in 753 B.C. This was a pleasant surprise, as the Australian newspapers often only mentioned Italians when they reported the racist vomit which emanated from the former Prime Minister Mr. Hughes, who's vitriolic hate of foreigners was always repeated in the newspapers without censure.

Christmas 1929 arrived, and all the Gawler people came to us for Christmas lunch where we also entertained Maria's friend, Arnold, and his son, Harry, who had both moved permanently to Adelaide. His sisters Frances and Jeanie joined us, as did any of our Cremona House tenants who were on their own, and of course, we had Sandro and Rita and baby Angelina who also had no other family in Adelaide.

We set up a long trestle table under a run of shady trees in the back garden. Luisa and Maria had covered the tables in beautiful lace tablecloths, using softly scented boughs of pine trees and red paper lanterns for a little festive colour. I was very touched to see how kind my Anthony was, sharing his toys with Harry and Angie, and Zia Violetta's young children, Oscar and Mary, keeping them entertained while we adults discussed all manner of topics.

We invited the same people, plus Elena's sister Beatrice, her husband Jasper and daughter Anna to see in the New Year with us, as they had spent Christmas day with Jasper's family. I also invited my thirty employees and their families for an evening picnic in the park opposite the factory. The women organised games for the children, including some Chinese firecrackers, and the men organised food and drinks. I'd ordered in enough bread rolls for each adult and child to have three each, to be stuffed with pre-sliced cured meats and cheeses and plump salad tomatoes from the markets and a huge batch of Maria's *giardiniera*, a pickled vegetable concoction she had preserved in large glass jars six-months earlier. Arnold had brought along his trial batch of smoked fish – little local Tommy Ruffs which most of the men enjoyed immensely. There were candies preferred by the children and the whole range of Balfours' slab cakes, with ice cream and fruit, for dessert.

Camillo Ruggeri, one of the grocers from the Central Market who had been in my group of reservists, had given me a good deal on a case of pineapples, sent by rail from his brother Joe's plantation in northern New South Wales, where he had transferred to after the war. They wowed the crowd, as no-one, including myself, had ever eaten one before. I can report that, accompanied by vanilla ice cream and some mint leaves to balance out the sourness, they were a huge hit.

The sultry summer heat was difficult to work in, so we normally started work around 6.00 am and I sent the men home around 2.00 pm. On days when it wasn't as steamy, we worked an hour longer so as to build up our stocks. The first Saturday of the new year, 1930, was a blaster with the temperature reaching 109°F. The men had worked an extra hour every day that week so that we could all have the half-day Saturday off.

I had allowed myself some time off too and spent most of it under the dappled shade of an enormous plane tree at the end of the back garden where my dear ones occasionally came out to sit with me and brought me a drink or some delightful morsel. I mostly just snoozed the day away. In the evening, we listened to the wireless, played some music, and rejoiced at the light sea breeze which we could feel from our balcony.

Around 10.00 pm the house was quiet, but as I had slept most of the day, I was wide awake. I changed into comfortably loose cotton pyjamas and my slippers and took my bundle of newspapers to my study so I could read by the electric light on my desk.

About an hour later, I heard shouting from the street below. I ignored it at first, thinking it was just some people larking about in the park, but then I heard people running around the front of the factory. When I stood up to look out my study window, I saw a thick plume of black smoke coming from the back of the factory. I rushed to our bedroom, pulled the sheets and blankets off our bed, making sure Luisa was awake and yelled at her to call the fire brigade.

I sped down the stairs, out our front door, grabbing the keys to the factory side gates and rushed towards the back of the property where my vans were parked. I managed to drive six of them out, but the last one caught alight, and I couldn't reach the one next to it. I screeched at everyone to move away.

A great crowd had gathered with Luisa, Maria, Anthony, the tenants, and the neighbours from some of the smaller side streets behind the factory safely out of the way across the road in the park, except for Lucas Russell and his two sons from the scrap yard next door who had come armed with blankets and were helping me beat out any small loose fires. Frank Russell spotted leaking gasoline and dragged the three of us far enough away to be safe before the last van exploded.

"Stay back! Stay back! She's about to blow!"

The debris from the explosion projected onto the roof of my storage shed where I kept my wooden shipping crates and ice cream cartons. I heard the sirens of the fire truck approaching while Lucas' and Frank's strong grips on each of my arms, held me from rushing back in.

The fire brigade got into the action fairly quickly with four trucks and crews. The chief immediately took charge and managed to direct his crews to putting out the flames surrounding the remaining two vans. He also stationed some of his crew in the space between the storage shed and the factory, so they could prevent the flames spreading to the factory. It took an hour of pumping water, with each truck being sent for refills as soon as it was empty.

Once it was clear that the factory was safe, I promptly fainted, overcome by the smoke and also the exhaustion of the intensity of the battle. On the way down, I hit my head on the brick courtyard at the front of the factory. Maria had placed a call to Sandro who had brought his neighbour Dr. Nilssen to check everyone for the effects of fire or smoke inhalation, and his smelling salts helped me come around, but not without an egg-sized bump at the back of my head and my glasses sustaining a deep crack.

The police had arrived too and were wrangling the crowd, which had become enormous despite the late hour. They'd been attracted mostly by the sirens of the fire engines. I could hear a deep baritone voice repeating over and over:

"No more to see here, help the police do their job by heading back to your own homes folks."

After Dr Nilssen pronounced me capable of walking, I had a quick look around. Some of my tenants, Mrs Jenkins from number one and Mrs Paul from number three, had gone to the back kitchen of Cremona House and started brewing tea. Luisa, with Anthony, at least half her height now, called me over and pressed a very sweet, strong tea into my hand. I refused it at first, but she insisted holding the cup up to my lips.

"Drink, you need sugar for the shock."

When I was sure that there were no more spot fires, and the fire crews had been checked over by Dr. Nilssen for burns or breathing issues, and they'd had their tea, and were packing up to leave, I allowed Maria to lead me back to our apartment. Luisa and Sandro ensured the factory was properly locked up, once the police had looked over the charred wrecks of the two vans and worked out where the fire had started. They accompanied Luisa back up the stairs to see me and asked if I were well enough to answer some questions.

That was when I learnt that a couple of milk cans stuffed with newspaper and sticks had been set alight and hurled over the back wall that abutted onto Gilles Street near the primary school. The projectile had hit the rubber tyre of the furthest van in the south-west corner, which was where all the intense black smoke had come from. According to the fire chief, I'd done a super-human job of moving the other six vans in time. There was no evidence of forced entry anywhere.

Maria had offered the officers tea, and as they sat around the table with me, they asked me to think about who might have been responsible for this act of sabotage. I stared up in shock looking at Luisa, Maria, Anthony and Sandro in turn. Sabotage! But who would do that? I had no answers, I was just exhausted. They suggested I try to get some sleep and they would return the next day.

I was sure I wouldn't sleep, but as soon as I moved to the armchair, I was out, the emotional exhaustion getting the better of me. Luisa had suggested a bath as I stank of smoke, but all I had been able to muster was a change of pyjamas and to run my head under the bathroom sink tap.

The next day, the police returned late in the morning, accompanied by some photographers. They'd been investigating. The first thing they'd asked about was my involvement with the Fascist Club. In particular, if I had received any threats from opposing groups. I explained that we were a social club and did not engage with politics in any way. I also clarified that my involvement was as a volunteer with the children's choir and the organisation of social events and charity fundraisers. He didn't make any comments, just nodded, and wrote notes in his little book. But I was flummoxed when he asked me what I knew of a barber named Francesco Ferrari. Startled, I looked up immediately, but tried to keep my composure.

"Not much. He bought tickets for a charity dance I organised at the end of winter, two years ago."

"You were seen entering the premises where the man works in Twin Street on Friday, the 28th of September 1927 at 3.58pm and exiting at 4.26pm."

"*Madonna*!" I gulped silently, pretending to think.

"Oh, er … yes … I vaguely remember that. I think it was for my son's end of term concert. We stopped there because it was on the way to the laundry where we were due to pick up Anthony's other pressed uniform. He's not my regular barber, we just happened to be passing and I saw they had a couple of empty seats, so we went in. I'd been too busy that week to take my son to my own barber in Semaphore."

"So, are you saying that you had never met the man before?"

"Well not exactly, as I said, he came to the dance I organised, and had gotten into a bit of a scuffle with some of the other young lads who were all sent home. I recognised him, of course, when he came to cut my hair, he'd been in the back room you see, so I didn't know he worked there until he came up to my chair where the boy at the front counter had seated me."

"What did you discuss while you were having your hair cut?"

"Discuss? Oh ... nothing that I can recall ... probably the usual chit chat ... weather, sports, where we were from in Italy ... that kind of thing, I think."

I was telling the truth, though I knew it wasn't the whole truth, but there was no way I was risking my neck coming into contact with the young man's razor blade. The police seemed satisfied with my explanation and left shortly afterwards.

That evening, Arnold called past to check on us and brought me a copy of the afternoon newspaper where there was a long article about my business dealings and photos of my factory, the burnt-out milk cans and the charred remains of my vans and storage shed. No journalist had approached me, so I was puzzled at where they had gotten the information about my business history and when they had taken the photos. Combined with the police's surveillance of the barber shop, it made me feel very unsettled. I just couldn't fathom what was going on and what my role in this incident might have been. Arnold did point out one detail that the police had not pursued when they questioned me – my saboteurs had used a milk can stuffed with bits of wood and newspaper as a projectile. Where had that milk can come from? I had plenty of milk cans on my premises, but this milk can had possibly come from elsewhere, as there were no signs that anyone had climbed over my back fence.

I asked Luisa to organise a thankyou note and crate of beers to be delivered to the Russells next door. A couple of days later, Lucas came past, so I thanked him with a very sincere heart for all his efforts, telling him his son Frank probably saved my life, all our lives. I felt like crying but held myself together and poured us both a strong brandy instead.

"Have the police found the culprits?"

"Not yet. Still waiting to hear from them."

"Got insurance on the place?"

"Yes," I sighed with relief.

"Well, you'll be right then," he finished, raising his glass at me.

"Hope so," I replied as I knocked on the leg of a wrought iron planter near my armchair.

"*Tocca ferro*" I said, and turned to Lucas explaining, "Italians say 'touch iron' for good luck."

"Ah, we Brits say 'touch wood'. Seeing as I do that all day, I reckon I've got enough luck to see out me days," he guffawed, before gulping down the rest of his glass.

After a month, there was still no news from the police about any suspects. I had contacted my insurance company, requesting compensation for my van and the storage shed as well as the costs for the clean-up. The insurance company wouldn't pay me until the police released their report. When it arrived, I was incensed.

"*Mannagia la miseria!*" I screamed in utter despair, as I read the contents of the letter from the insurance company.

They had concluded that, in accordance with the police report, the fire was possible payback for my dealings with known political subversives, and on that premise, the insurance company cancelled my policy and refused to pay me compensation for my losses. My lawyer immediately suggested we sue the insurance company. Luisa advised that this was our only recourse, as without these funds, we would not be able to rebuild. I agreed but was disillusioned, reasoning that this action could take several years to resolve, and the only winner would probably be my lawyer.

I tried to apply for a new loan, based on my current assets in order to replace my equipment shed. Half of my vans were leased, and now I owed the leasing company money for two destroyed vans. Without insurance, no-one was prepared to lend me any money. I went to my investors, but their own businesses were struggling, with the economic recession beginning to bite. I chose to keep up production of the ice and shut down the ice cream and margarine lines until I was able to replace the containers. I was desperate, hoping not to be obliged to stand down any of my workers. So, I put them to work clearing the remains of the shed, erecting a basic new one with whatever material could be salvaged. I did not have the funds to replace my unique 1-pint and 1-quart tin-lined containers, so shipping to country towns was no longer feasible. However, a few weeks after the fire, I was able to secure a good deal on the new fashion of wax-lined cardboard boxes, holding 1-pint quantities of ice cream, which would fit into a tin-lined larger box and stay cold enough for shorter delivery routes. I was thrilled by this new discovery, and only needed to make minor tweaks to my production line to accommodate the new containers.

Despite my efforts, by Easter, things were beginning to unravel.

Already, with the steep downturn of the economy, some of my clients, especially the households, grocers, and smaller hotels, were feeling the pinch, and either reducing or cutting their ice cream orders completely. I had concentrated on getting the margarine production back up and running as soon as possible, but even there, many bakeries had reduced their lines and were concentrating on providing just basic bread and cheap biscuits. Luisa advised me not to deliver any more supplies to several city bakeries and hotels, as they had significant accounts left unpaid.

The cost of living had increased for the general population for all goods and services. Unemployment had increased; local parks became tent cities for evicted families. Soup kitchens were struggling to feed the masses that were turning up. Businesses throughout the state, and even government departments were shedding staff and reducing expenditure.

The Lord Mayor of the Adelaide City Council established a special fund for donations of food, clothes, and blankets now that winter was approaching. For my factory, the increased costs associated with electricity and water supplies, while relatively small, still had an impact on the running of my business. By July, the costs of my milk and cream had increased, and with less cattle taken to market, even the availability and cost of my fat supplies for the margarine production had increased.

In addition to my business worries, I was feeling desolate and afraid, with the notion of someone wanting to do me harm constantly terrorising my thoughts. What if the next time it wasn't the factory, but my family who were targeted? Luisa had decided that this was a random attack by vandals, and that she was going to put it out of her mind. I agreed to do the same, but whenever I left the premises, I always wondered if I would come home to find it still in one piece.

Every so often, without any particular cause, I would feel a rising sense of panic and my heart beats quicken, to the point where I had to stop what I was doing and take some slow deep breaths in order to recover. I tried to hide my attacks from Luisa as I didn't want to worry her, but Maria caught me out one day, as I was hiding in the stair well. She looked at me calmly and simply laid a hand on my back until my breathing returned to normal.

"I had the same reaction when mamma died, and I couldn't find another job, and Rico was pressuring me to get married. They stopped when I received your letter. These will pass too when you start to feel more in control of your business again."

"Are you sure?"

"Not really, I'm no doctor, but you know you can always count on me to support you."

"Don't say anything to Luisa, please."

"I can't promise that, but I won't say anything just yet."

My factory was still in production, but just hanging on. The company through whom I leased my vans withdrew access to my remaining four smaller vans when I was unable to pay for the damage to the other two, and was in arears in my lease payments, leaving me only with my two old lorries which I owned freehold.

I had no choice but to let go of all my drivers, it was the only reasonable thing I could do. I tried my best to find them other work through my acquaintances, but hardly anyone was hiring. Two of my factory workers were transferred to driving the lorries, and the youngest three on the factory floor also had to be terminated. I was mortified, but the workers remaining knew I was doing my best to keep afloat, and they were appreciative of still being able to retain their jobs, and for all of them, married men with families, it meant the difference between a real life and homelessness.

They had all agreed to a ten percent pay cut, as many other companies, including the giant B.H.P. were doing the same. Two years of droughts and poor harvests meant little surplus income from exports to inject into the economy, with a subsequent downturn in spending, both by consumers and governments who were desperately trying to repay international war loans. I had told my employees that if we could survive the winter, hopefully summer sales would see us pull through.

In September, I was still quite morose, so Sandro suggested a range of activities to take my mind off my troubles. The children's classes and the choir, which was called on to perform at various community events, kept me busy a couple of nights a week. Some members of the former Italian Traders Association had decided to split from any connections with the increasingly politicized nature of Sandro's organisation. They decided to set up some club rooms where any Italian and their friends, regardless of nationality, could attend, without the influence of politics or religion.

That gave Sandro the impetus to reorganise and to form a new and enlarged executive committee. I was appointed social events co-ordinator and head of the Youth Group. In early Spring, we organised a picnic gathering in Belair for the Italian community. I booked a train of several carriages, and at one of the committee meetings of the Fascio, we came up with the idea of selling raffle tickets, the proceeds of which could go towards subsidising train fares; a strategy that worked very well, as so many members who operated businesses generously offered a range of prizes for the raffle.

Again, Luisa and her friends organised games for the children. It was wonderful to see so many joyous faces as we all hopped on the train back to Adelaide. Sandro took the opportunity to hand out pamphlets on a huge range of topics which he had received from Italy, as well as small round metal lapel pins in the Italian colours and featuring the ancient roman symbol of banded sticks and an axe which the Fascist party had adopted as their logo. I briefly saw Maria and Luisa discussing with a group of other women over a pamphlet with recipes giving advice for frugal living, and another with tips for keeping the family healthy.

The other event I was involved in was a personal one, held on the first day of February 1930. Arnold Braithwaite had proposed marriage and Maria had accepted. Maria wanted a small, intimate wedding ceremony for just the closest family and a dinner in one of the small, private rooms at the Prince Albert Hotel in the street behind us, so no-one had to do any work. I asked her why she didn't want a bigger celebration.

"If mamma were still alive, then I would do it for her. Arnold has already had a traditional wedding; he doesn't need another one, and I don't like being the centre of attention. You should know that by now."

I acted as best man and Luisa as matron of honour and Anthony and Harry brought in the rings tied onto two little silk pillows and Arnold's sisters threw the flower petals at the exit.

Arnold had leased a shopfront with a small cottage behind and a decent rear yard, just around the corner from the Green Dragon Hotel. He had started a fish shop selling smoked, pickled, and fried fish, chips, and cold drinks. He had built a smoker in the back yard, expressly for this purpose and the smell from the smoker seemed to attract good custom.

Anthony and Harry were already at the same school, though in different grades, but Maria would continue to take them to school in the morning and shop for the day's supplies, and begin preparations for dinner, so Luisa had time to do her accounts. Then Maria would return home to give Arnold an afternoon break. Luisa would pick up the boys and drop little Harry off after school. At around 6.00 pm, after he'd had a couple of hours with his son, Arnold would go back out to the shop for the last two hours of the evening service.

Arnold had sensibly decided that he would trade Wednesday to Sunday, so they could have some time to themselves. He was a quietly spoken fellow, but a deep thinker, and I always enjoyed his company. He treated Maria with respect and was so grateful to her for taking him and his son under her wing.

There was no point inviting Beppe; he had sold his factory and all his worldly goods, and had returned to Italy at the end of 1928, when he turned forty, just as he'd always planned. He'd sold up everything and gone home to Cremona, where he invested his earnings in a newly built apartment block and happily settled back into the Italian lifestyle of a city gentleman, visiting his favourite bar every morning for espresso and gossip, moving on to a simple, home-style restaurant for lunch and fixing himself a soup or salad in the evenings after returning from his *aperitivo* with local friends. During the day, he walked or cycled all over the city, or took his motor car to the outlying villages.

Armando had set up a one-man ice cream factory from his home, but we rarely heard from them. There'd been no word from Nino in more than two years. I missed my brothers, but I had Sandro and Arnold, and the members of the Fascio, especially the executive committee, whom I'd started to socialize with more often, enjoying their perspective on business and life. And of course, I always had my Luisa and Anthony, my sister Maria and the whole extended Latorre and Nicoletti clan. I was indeed still a rich man, despite my business troubles.

After several months, I was bitterly disappointed that the police had refused to re-open the investigation into my factory fire but had taken my lawyer's advice and hired a private detective. Hopefully, we would get some answers soon.

Economic downturn

Regrettably, the summer season didn't save us. When I was unable to pay my creditors and had used up all the goodwill they were prepared to extend, I had to face facts. The only option was to go into voluntary receivership, hoping that specialised accountants could help with recovering monies owed to me and to liquidate superfluous assets while keeping my business running.

On the plus side, I owned the land, the factory building, and the equipment outright. I still had an extensive list of clients, even if the quantities they ordered had diminished. I operated through three licences, one for each product I manufactured. However, I also had two years of taxes owing on the land and arrears in my payments for the electricity, water, and sewerage services. And I no longer had the funds to buy my raw products.

The appointed Bailiff ran newspaper advertisements, offering to sell the surplus equipment I possessed, though that was minimal, as well as the ice and ice cream licences and the factory building (subject to a lease arrangement, so that I could continue operating the margarine business). The hope was that we could continue the manufacturing and the selling all three products if a sympathetic investor could be found.

Despite more than a month of advertisements through local daily newspapers and trade journals nationwide, no-one came forward. Our only recourse would be to sell via auction which was arranged for the afternoon of the 16th of May at the Megaw and Hogg's salesrooms in Grenfell Street. I was naturally distraught but didn't dare show my dismay with the family and my employees. They were all banking on me to find a solution.

The auction delivered me into the arms of a group of investors from Melbourne who agreed to my terms. I was joyfully able to announce to my employees that the investment group had agreed to keep the ice and ice cream manufactory going. My staff of ten were jubilant, as the unemployment level in the state had reached the thirty percent mark. There were many stories of women and children moving in with relatives and fathers and husbands sleeping rough in one of the many make-shift tent cities that had sprung up in the city parklands. At first, the police tried to move these men away, but their numbers grew such that the best they could do was manage them out of sight, in some corner of the parklands not frequented by the regular public.

The state government instituted a coupon system for basic food and sanitary goods, but in large, it was the church groups who managed the physical and moral deficit which had set in across the country. My greatest hope was that we could return to a decent sized production so that the men could retain their jobs.

But it was not to be. Within six months, I was forced to declare bankruptcy, which meant I could no longer operate as an independent ice and ice cream business for a minimum of seven years.

Both Luisa and I were distraught by the state of our affairs, but

Antonio and Elena rallied us on, getting us to focus on the fact that we still had each other and that the ebbs and flows of business were always unpredictable. They urged us to keep striving, keep believing that things would pick up.

I was still able to operate the margarine business which was listed under a different name and was now a partnership arrangement with my friend George Preston, one of my original investors and still the owner of several Samuel's Butchers franchises. My intention was that through the management of my receiver, the men's wages which were in arrears and my taxes would be paid off first, and then I could slowly pay my creditors and eventually be dismissed from bankruptcy.

My biggest creditor was the Milk Co-operative, who refused to provide me with any more milk. We both knew that they were hoping to force me out of business, as they had launched their own ice cream line two years earlier. They had invested an enormous amount of money in advertising, and I admit, it grated me to see their billboards all over the city. Unfortunately, they tried to cut corners, using inferior ingredients, so they couldn't beat the taste of my ice cream, especially for those customers who were more discerning, and still able to afford quality, which regardless of the economic mess the country faced, still existed in surprisingly good numbers, and had remained loyal to me, despite the glitches in production. While the Adelaide Margarine Company, operated under the same roof as my ice and ice cream manufactory, it was technically a separate Proprietary Company, so not affected by my declaration of bankruptcy.

We had retained our house next door, fortuitously in Luisa's name, and our tenants, mostly all senior-aged, middle-class women with secure investments, had continued to stay with us, and pay us their monthly rents, so that we could continue servicing the mortgage on the house. A few months after the sale of the ice and ice cream titles, I could quite cheerfully say that our lives had actually improved. The Melbourne investment group had appointed my loyal and dear friend Tino as the plant manager and someone else as an account and sales manager, a Mr. Solomon Crompton, who'd previously worked in shoe sales.

I continued to operate the margarine manufacturing for myself. The new ice cream company was able to secure new lorries for delivery, so that I could use my two old lorries for the Margarine Company. Margarine manufacturing still had strict government quotas imposed, but one of the other suppliers in the state, gave up their quota, so I was able to snap it up and double my production. I was limited to four main clients, but thankfully, they were consistent in their orders. I had just enough income coming in to keep us comfortably afloat.

This gave Luisa and I much more time to devote to our family and to our community involvement. I went back to practising my violin, and Luisa and I even found time to work on some new pieces together, which we happily performed at smaller Fascio gatherings, more often than not, held in the Cremona House Ballroom.

I renewed my efforts for fundraising for the Italian Red Cross, becoming its official representative in South Australia, and assisted Sandro in developing strategies to attract more people to sign up for the Adelaide Italian Fascist Association, or the Fascio, as we liked to call it. Unfortunately, a large percentage of the Italians in South Australia lived in very precarious financial circumstances, and even if they were sympathetic, could not afford the yearly membership fees of £5, which represented at least a week's wages for most.

The only people happy to keep paying were Italians with significant commercial enterprises who had been established in South Australia for at least twenty years; around forty key families. Sandro went to great efforts to curry favour with these more established Italians, visiting regularly, writing to them, encouraging them to donate prizes for our schools, youth group activities and balls. He had become very friendly with the owners of the Convent Garden Restaurant who eagerly held an Italian Ball on their premises, on the first Tuesday of each month. Sandro opened these balls up to everyone, provided they paid a modest entry fee.

Every so often, a young Communist tried to stir up trouble, mostly wanting to get in for free. Sandro laid on the charm and always managed to diffuse the situation. We did get the support of the Adelaide Police, who had been closely monitoring these subversives and would send a visible presence in the form of two constables to stand in view of the front entrance. Sandro's enthusiasm never seemed to waiver, despite many setbacks.

"The more signed-up members we have," explained Sandro, "the more money we can attract from the Italian government for our charitable causes and events."

Notwithstanding Sandro's efforts, the three Fascio groups we had currently organised, in the Adelaide Metropolitan area really consisted of only around fifty families in total. Our little Italian Saturday school expanded as the original children grew up and younger ones joined. We were able to recruit another volunteer teacher and assistant to take over the Glanville and Port Adelaide Schools.

In early January, we gathered the students from all three local schools as well as some students from the Fascio chapters in Port Wakefield and Port Pirie, to celebrate La Befana – the Italian Christmas witch who handed out small gifts and little lumps of coal made from sugar. The children came dressed up and performed in some self-composed theatrical numbers, games, and music.

At the end of the Italian academic year, in June, we also had a prize-giving ceremony to celebrate the work of our students, offering them certificates, books, pencils, fountain pens, slim leather or wooden pencil cases, medals and little trophies to commemorate their achievements. The many proud parents looking on, urged us to continue our work, declaring that through their children, they too were learning to read in Italian.

All of our efforts were regularly reported in the Italo-Australian newspaper produced in Sydney but distributed nationwide, as well as in the Adelaide Advertiser and the Southern Cross, the local Catholic newspaper. The positive tone of these reports were a welcome balance to the previous negativity.

In the family circle, we celebrated the safe arrival of my sister Maria's child, a girl she named Leonilda Giovanina, in honour of our deceased parents. She had Arnold's fair colouring with sandy curls and Maria's and my mother's distinctive sea-green eyes.

We also were surprised to be celebrating Bart's engagement to an equally fair girl from Gawler who shared all his sporting passions including horse-riding, golf, tennis, cycling and motor racing. She was Mary-Jane, a telephonist at the Gawler exchange. She came from a very well-known Irish family in the district, and they had met at a Catholic Carnival the year before. Bart, once he had finished his apprenticeship, had opened up his own Motor repair shop in Salisbury and was doing very well, as his passion for motor cars continued to grow. Elena couldn't understand a young woman who openly confessed preferring to spend time pursuing her sporting interests rather than mucking about in the kitchen but was secretly delighted she could still be the chief cook for her adored son.

In early 1934, Cremona House hosted a visiting Italian Tennis

Player, Giorgio de Stefani, and his mother. Luisa organised a most elegant reception for him with leading Italian businessmen and Adelaide sporting officials, and Sandro even invited many foreign embassy representatives here in Adelaide. Giorgio was a devoted tennis player, practising for two hours from 9 am to 11am when he retired for a bath and then would come to lunch around 1pm with his recently arisen mother, both of them attired in the most exquisite suits. My friend Fiorentino, the tailor, furtively sketched as many as he could, hoping to offer new ideas to his customers. Giorgio was also a consummate ladies' man, and I noticed he had Luisa and even reticent Maria blushing. He introduced us to the latest vogue in cocktails, of which he was very fond, without them seeming to have any effect on his stamina. His presence, which only lasted a few weeks during the lead up and beginning of the Davis Cup tournament, seemed to turn our lives upside down. It certainly inspired Anthony, Harry and their friends, who months later, were still hitting balls vigorously around our tennis court. We were often surprised by photographers and journalists on our doorstep, eager to catch a glimpse of the tanned, slick-haired super-man in our midst.

Later in the year, we had a world renown violist come to stay for the week that she was performing in Adelaide. The more sedate and regal Signorina Erica Morini, lived in Vienna where she played with the Royal Viennese Orchestra.

In Adelaide, she gave a number of recitals, which wowed our more affluent society members. I was ecstatic, firstly because she played my instrument of choice, but also because she stirred up long forgotten memories of my time at school with the brothers in Cremona and my first introduction to the violin. She praised Anthony's efforts and encouraged him to keep on practising, so that maybe he could come play with her orchestra in Vienna one day. The eleven-year-old boy's eyes lit up in wonder at the ethereal beauty who made such heavenly music.

In September, Luisa and I accompanied Sandro and Rita by boat, up the Spencer Gulf to Port Pirie for the *Festa della Madonna dei Martiri* which included a solemn mass followed by a procession where the statue of Our Lady, protector of Martyrs, an icon of the Molfettesi fishermen of the region, was paraded down the main street to the harbour for the blessing of the fleet.

The rest of the day was taken up with feasting, music, and dancing. There were a large number of Italian fishermen in Port Pirie and with Sandro's encouragement, they had already organised themselves into a very successful Fascist Association complete with a children's school, which proudly entertained us with songs, poetry recitals and thrilling running races.

We stayed overnight in Port Pirie and enjoyed a wonderful dinner put on by the women, in a local hall. We found ourselves eating specialities from the town of Molfetta, which was in the southern Italian region of Puglia. Luisa was delighted, as they served her famous *orecchiette*, but in a different style to the ones she had served to me when I first met her. This version featured sautéed, peppery *cime di rape*, the turnip tops my mother used to feed to our pigs, and was finished with fried breadcrumbs, making a delicate contrast between the garlicky, crispy crumbs, the pillowy soft *orecchiette* and the slight bitterness of the turnip tops.

After the main course, I went outside to have a chat with a group of men who all seemed to be local fishermen and was impressed to learn of their enterprising work in the fishing industry. Most of the men owned their own boats and some of them, more than one. They had the respect of the local council, in fact the mayor had made a very encouraging speech at the procession and had joined us for the dinner.

A gentleman in his forties approached me for a private word. We stood apart from the group and he asked me how well I knew the vice-consul.

Curious, I simply asked, "Why?"

"Did you know that the man refuses to endorse applications to bring out family members unless we agree to sign up to the Fascist Party first?"

"What do you mean?" I was genuinely surprised, but not particularly alarmed. Sandro had never hidden his ambition to increase membership. I wondered if he made membership a condition of filing immigration papers. This was the first time I had heard a complaint of this nature.

"I've been trying to bring out my wife and kids for three years now."

"Why do you have a problem with becoming a Fascist Party member?"

The man snickered and spat at my feet.

"You fool, don't you know what damage that idiot is doing to Italy?"

"According to what I've read, he seems to be doing the country some real good." I answered, moving quickly away, disgusted by the man's crude gesture.

I returned indoors to check on Luisa. She was standing at the piano, encouraging a young woman who was playing some of the Fascist songs we knew. I looked around me; everyone was jolly, there was much laughter and conversation, kids were running around, playing hide and seek under tables, there were even a couple of friendly card games on the go.

The next day, once we'd been back at sea for several hours, and Sandro and I were alone, I told him of my unexpected encounter.

"I only make a suggestion, to make the process smoother! I know the man by name, but I've never met him. He's the one who's the fool to think that Italy will accept his application while he is not a member of the Fascio. The Fascio is the officially elected government. I'm not the one who makes the rules. I put his application forward like everybody else. It's Italy that has rejected him."

I hadn't expected Sandro to become so vitriolic over a trivial matter.

"Is there something else going on Sandro? It's not like you to get so worked up," I said.

"Nothing with me, but Rita's had bad news about her mother," he confessed. "Rita has received a disturbing letter from her father with news of her mother's declining health. He has begged her to return to Italy while her mother can still recognise her."

Sadly, especially for Luisa and Maria, we put on a farewell party for Rita Pastore and her daughter Angelina. The little one was already five years old and had not met her grandparents. We were heartbroken for our dear and lively friend, knowing that a difficult time was ahead of her, and promised that we would take care of Sandro.

Luisa and I continued with our charity work as well as spending as much time as possible in Gawler, as Antonio, especially, was aging and found it harder to make the trip to Adelaide. It also gave us a chance to get to know Bart's fiancé Mary-Jane. Luisa and I often travelled up together in my aging Fiat Tourer, allowing Anthony to travel on the train with Zia Beatrice and her daughter Anna, and my sister Maria with Harry and baby Lea. Arnold was required to stay with his shop and quiet Jasper, Zia Beatrice's husband, who found the excitability of the extended Italian family a little confronting, remained to look after the boarding house.

Italia inches forward

The economic situation in the whole of the country did not improve and by the middle of 1935, my Melbourne investors had sacked Mr. Crompton and had put the ice and ice cream business up for sale once again. Luisa suggested selling the house to buy back the factory, but I wouldn't let her. Until the economy improved, it looked like ice cream manufacturing was not a good investment.

I'd been in contact with my cousin Bobby in Melbourne, who had complained of similar problems. They were staying afloat through Zio Roberto's wise real estate purchases, more than a decade earlier. It seems that my Melbourne investment group shared the same belief. To my horror, they sold their licences and their portion of the manufacturing to my enemies: the Adelaide Milk Co-operative.

Tino was made redundant, but I put him on in the place of one of my drivers, who had recently lost his wife and had decided to move to Port Augusta, so his wife's relatives could help look after his young children.

This time, I had to share my space with a Mr. Cecil Maxwell who had been employed at the Milk Cooperative for the last ten years. My employees were nervous for their jobs, but I explained that both the ice and ice cream businesses would still be operating. It turned out that Mr. Cecil Maxwell, had been a floor supervisor, in the packaging department, and had little real knowledge of the ice cream business and none whatsoever of the ice making trade.

Every so often, I would turn off his access to electricity and water, which he had no idea how to handle, causing pandemonium on the floor. The employees would make an enthusiastic show of tinkering with the machines, mostly clueless about how to resolve the problem. After about half an hour, I would turn everything back on again. It was hard to watch the man's despair and I felt guilty, but I rationalised, rightly or wrongly, now that I was back on my feet financially, if I had a decent chance at buying back the two businesses, preferably at a reduced rate, I had a good chance of keeping everyone employed and repossessing the business that Luisa and I had worked so hard to establish.

Eventually, it was my lawyer who came through for me. Not only did he win a protracted five-year battle with my insurance company who were required to honour our original agreement and pay me the sum of £4,000 that I had requested to repair my business after the fire, but also pay me a further £1,000 pounds for damages to my good name and my business. My lawyer argued that since the police had found no evidence on which to make their claims of sabotage, the insurance company had no right to withhold payment of my claim or to cancel my policy.

As I could now pay off my outstanding debts, my bankruptcy was unconditionally discharged, and I was able to begin trading again. My lawyer also approached the Milk Co-operative who agreed to sell the manufacturing licences.

With the money left over, I took Antonio's advice and invested in farming land outside of Gawler. It was a barley and wheat farm.

Despite the economic depression, both beer and bread were still being manufactured at constant rates. The farm already had a returned soldier who was managing the property and doing a good job of it, so I was happy to let him stay. I put the land in Anthony's name, so that he would have an asset to set him up in his adult life. He could choose what to do with it when he reached his maturity.

The purchase was an added incentive for us to go to Gawler, which now that the road had been fully bituminised, was a pleasant two-hour drive through lush farmlands with the soft violet peaks of the southern ranges keeping sentinel as we made our way north. Summer or winter, I never tired of the chance to drive out away from city traffic, relishing the change of scenery and the feeling of the wind whistling in my ears. It was the only time I felt like a young boy again, when I had been free of constraints, allowed to wander the fields around our *cascina* with my siblings and my cousins. When I had the odd moments to myself, I sometimes allowed myself to remember the little boy, so desperate to be a successful man, and wonder what he would make of me now. Hopefully, he would be impressed by my ingenuity and tenacity.

Finally, in October 1935, I was able to launch the Blue Label Ice Cream Company and take back activity of the whole factory without outside interference. This time I made it a public company, putting the company in Luisa's and her friend Dorothy Sullivan's names, and floating it with one thousand one pound shares from Luisa and an equal number of shares from Dot.

Dot had never married and had been working as a secretary for over twenty years for the managing director of Samuel's Butchers, living with her mother in Glenelg. She had wanted to invest in something to secure her own future. Luisa was delighted to have one more passion to share with her friend and our son's godmother. At the end of summer, in April 1936, we celebrated our successful take-back of the ice cream business. We had been able to finally get some insurance, and therefore, were able to lease vans again, which meant I could improve my delivery rates, the key element to growing my business.

The economy had begun to shift, and we were seeing small, but definite gains, as employment figures improved and both government and private enterprise spending on major works slowly brought the economy back into gear. There was a renewed sense of optimism as the state celebrated its Jubilee with parades, concerts, exhibitions, and competitions.

There had also been an unexpected win for Italy. Mussolini's forces had conquered the North-African nation of Abyssinia, merging with the other Italian held territories to become Italian East Africa. The long-held dream of an overseas empire for Italy, had finally been realised. I had been reading in our local newspaper about Italy's condemnation by the League of Nations and all the threats of reprisals and economic sanctions against Italy in the lead-up to her invasion, yet none of them were realised. The British and the French delegates to the League of Nations had made so many threats about blocking access to the Suez Canal and trade embargoes. The United States though, had ignored the international community and had continued to trade with Italy, especially supplying her with unlimited crude oil, vital to Italy's war ambitions. Similarly, Britain and France, whose delegates had organised the League of Nation's vote to place restrictions on coal and pig iron, were undercut by their own parliaments who refused to enforce them.

"Now that Italy has won the territories, the British will start sniffing out new trade opportunities for raw materials before the end of the month," suggested Camillo, my market trader friend.

Fiorentino, my tailor friend had feared having problems importing textiles from Italy, but his orders came through as expected.

However, in Australia, the perceived threat to British interests, had risen shackles. Sandro had spent a week trying to organise a venue for a special celebration of our Italian King, Vittorio Emanuele III being crowned Emperor, but had been blocked at every turn. The Trades Hall, which we had used before, many times, claimed their members would not be happy to lease to our organisation. The Cathedral Hall too rejected us, despite always supporting us and even hosting a mission by a Fascist priest just a few months prior. They claimed that they did not want to be exposed to any reprisals from the strong trade union movement.

Even though I knew I was risking my business again, Luisa and I decided that the gathering could take place in our recently refurbished shed.

Sandro organised a magnificent display with large, framed pictures of Mussolini and the King, festive bunting in red, white, and green and fresh flowers. News of the planned celebration spread like wildfire, and we had around eight hundred people turn up. Some had arrived on the back of trucks from country districts, from down south as far as Victor Harbour, from the Adelaide Hills, even from Port Wakefield. A boat with Fascio Committee members had even made it from Port Pirie. Many started turning up spontaneously in mid-afternoon, with ex-service men proudly wearing their uniforms, and committee members decked out in their Fascio black shirts and lapel pins. The police had been informed, and they had agreed to send constables on bicycles to patrol the area. We did not want any opposing groups to spoil this special day. There was spontaneous singing, an air of jubilation as people greeted each other with tears in their eyes.

Corrado Biagio, the Hindley Street wine merchant had supplied several dozen bottles of champagne for the initial toasts and Sandro had made sure plenty of beer, and cool drinks for the children, were also on hand. Women arrived laden with plates of sweet and savoury morsels. We quickly organised the children's choir members, most of whom were present, to gather at the top of the shed with some of our young musicians, including my son Anthony, to accompany them.

I began the proceedings welcoming everyone, young and old and asked them to join the choir in singing the national anthems of Italy and Australia and in saluting the flags. Then I introduced Sandro, who was a man enflamed with patriotic fervour as he stood on a couple of large crates which had been roped together to form a temporary stage. He read out one of Mussolini's speeches regarding the purpose of the Abyssinian campaign that had appeared in a newspaper sent from Italy a few months ago, imitating the Duce's emphatic way of speaking with his distinct hand gestures and the way he stopped mid-sentence to grab audience attention, giving the listener the pat phrases that were guaranteed to elicit cheers.

At the end of the performance, the crowd erupted with whistles, banging of pot lids, loud hurrahs, and long bouts of fevered clapping. Italy had finally taken her rightful place in the world again. There was jubilant singing, feasting, and drinking until the wee hours of the morning. We also rejoiced for ourselves, for all the racist slurs we had endured as a group, and individually. We felt we could finally hold our heads up high. We were worthy. No longer could anyone joke about Italy's poor military or economic performance. When the word Dago was slung at our faces, instead of slinking away, we finally had a rebuttal, we were the glories of Ancient Rome renewed, just as Mussolini had promised.

In the speech, given just before Christmas the previous year, il Duce, the Italian Prime Minister, appealing primarily to women, had asked them, as an act of faith, to hand over their wedding rings for the Fatherland. The wedding ring in Italy was called *la fede* which was also the Italian word for 'faith'.

Sandro made this his next mission. Over the course of the year, he made his rounds across the state taking his display of the Italian newspapers with pictures of the Queen of Italy reverently placing her own wedding ring on the recently completed grand monument in Rome, known as the altar to the Fatherland. He also showed later newspapers with women all over Italy doing the same thing, as well as Italian women in New York and even various countries in South America with significant Italian emigrant populations. It wasn't long before we caught the fever too. Sandro solemnly accepted donations from men, women, and children, some of them quite expensive, adding their names, a description of their donation of jewellery, money, or gold and silver items and their monetary worth to a ledger, and then also issuing the donors with a magnificent paper certificate, emblazoned with the Fascist Coat of Arms as well as that of United Italy, and the Prime Minister's signature. The certificate also described the donor's contribution and was counter-signed by Sandro in his role as Vice-Consul. He made sure to tell everyone that names and offers would be meticulously recorded and when the donations arrived in Italy, donors would be sent a letter of thanks from the Ministry of Foreign Affairs. In the end, approximately eighty people donated from around South Australia. Sandro had the names also published in the Italo-Australian newspaper, as of course, across the country, vice-consuls vied with each other to collect and publish the most donations.

It should have surprised me, but it didn't. I think I had guessed at

Sandro's declaration when I had seen the glint in his eye on the night of a Fascio Committee meeting when he described his efforts with the collection. Every time I spoke to him over the course of the following weeks, all he could talk about was how to get the gold to Italy. Finally, he admitted that the situation with Rita's mother had worsened, and she wouldn't be returning to Australia any time soon.

"I've spoken to the Consul in Melbourne. He's agreed that we simply can't ship the jewellery over, so I've volunteered myself to accompany him for this important task."

"Do you plan to come back?" was all I asked.

"I think so, once the situation with Rita's mother is resolved, but I have no idea how long that will take."

"What will you do there?"

"Oh, the Consul has promised to pull his connections to find me something in a ministry somewhere in Rome, so I can be with Rita and Angelina again."

"That will be good for you *amico mio*. I understand how much you've missed them. I wish you every success."

I opened my arms, and we gave each other a firm embrace. The Fascio committee would do the right thing and throw him a decent good-bye party, but I knew I had already lost him.

"What's going to happen with the vice-consulate here?" I almost forgot to ask.

"Oh, they'll find someone from the Melbourne consular team to replace me, I'm sure."

They did replace him, though it took almost a year for the young twenty-something diplomat to arrive. He was not the affable, bon vivant Sando had been. I was under no illusions, I knew Sandro had resorted to using standover tactics in order to increase his membership numbers, but apart from getting them to contribute to an initial one week's membership fee, he didn't force anybody's further involvement in the Fascio. Sandro had an easy charm and was able to talk to people, he could entice through his ability to get to know people, remembering little details about them, flattering them with his attention. Sandro was a purring cat who allows itself to be stroked in order to create connection.

The new Vice-Consul fancied himself a roaring lion. He thought people would jump to attention, merely through the force of his words, which incited division, hatred, and violence even.

I did the right thing, in Sandro's memory. I organised a welcome party, but beyond that, I left him to his own devices, concentrating only on the choir and the school. I barely even attended meetings, disliking their brusque self-congratulatory tone, without any pleasant banter with friends afterwards, which had once been my main purpose for attending.

The new vice-consul, Omero Spadafora, was always in a hurry. He visited boarding houses where the single men, often young, congregated, turning up in his black shirt military attire with a gun slung on his hip. Many of these men, only barely surviving with odd labouring jobs, daily victims of racist slurs, hoped he was to be their saviour. He certainly promised them the world.

Spadafora did not hesitate to show his disdain for our little Balilla schools, mocking the curriculum we had established of language, music, and culture classes. He took great pains to point out in a whole Fascio gathering that il Duce was not looking for intellectuals who could recite the glories of Rome, but foot soldiers to defend and grow the new Empire. He was very keen on sports and encouraged the football leagues, run by Leonard Santoni, a glamourous Gawler Place tailor with twenty staff, who was best known for being the first person in Australia to be married in an aeroplane flying over Adelaide, back in 1929. His marriage to the equally glamourous budding actress, Vera Chapman, had lasted less than three months before she had run off to England with a visiting theatrical troupe.

I resigned my position on the Fascio Executive Committee, not wanting to be associated with Spadafora's aggression.

It's a cruel world

By the end of 1937, I had more important problems on my mind. This time, it wasn't about my business, or the Fascio, but my family.

Just before Christmas in 1936, Antonio was harnessing his horse, ready for his day's activities. Elena had come to see him off with a list of supplies he needed to bring back for her confectionary business, and saw him crumple to the ground, clutching his chest. Bart had already left for his motor mechanic business in Salisbury, so Elena rushed to the fish shop next door to ring for the doctor.

With help from the neighbours, she managed to get Antonio inside and resting on the couch. He had re-animated, but his speech was slurred and his left cheek and eye droopy. When the doctor came, he was able to convince Elena to let her husband be transported to the hospital, where he could be monitored by nurses and rest more comfortably.

The neighbours called Luisa and she went into momentary shock. I saw her suddenly appear at the factory entrance, pale and trembling, barely able to speak. I had to give her a nip of brandy to revive her before she could tell me the full news. I called on Maria to come help Luisa pack, then I drove around to Zia Beatrice, who immediately said she wanted to come with us. Her daughter Anna had finished her schooling and was able to run the boarding house in her mother's absence.

Within the hour, with the factory left in Tino's capable hands, and Maria promising to look after Anthony, we were on the Main North Road to Gawler where we all gathered around Elena, including Bart, and Elena's sister Violetta and her family. After a few days, Antonio's condition improved, but he had lost the use of his right arm, and his right leg too was very unsteady. We had been able to bring him home in a wheeled wicker chair for Christmas, the following week, but he was very weak, sleeping most of the time.

Three weeks after the new year, there was another call, this time from Violetta, who informed us that Antonio had passed away in his sleep.

Antonio was seventy years old. Such was his popularity and importance that he had two funeral services. Elena was adamant that the Gawler undertaker was not going to get her business, as ten years earlier, he had led a small group of local councillors who had tried to get her shut down when they had first arrived in Gawler, citing the Cool Drinks Shop as the root of immoral influence on the town's youth.

However, a memorial service was organised in the Town Hall by the United Ancient Order of Druids of Gawler, of which Antonio had been a much-esteemed member. This community minded and hard-working secret society, who had evolved into a significant insurance and lending agency, even had a respectful obituary notice placed in both the Gawler Bunyip and the Adelaide Advertiser.

The actual funeral service was held at the Catholic Cathedral in Victoria Square, which was packed with both Antonio's and Elena's friends from the Port Area, Semaphore, Largs, Glenelg and Gawler, as well as our friends from the city. It was a very difficult day for all of us, especially Luisa and Anthony who wept inconsolably. Elena, who was fifty-seven years old, was gently cradled by a sister either side of her, all three in long black dresses with long black veils over their heads, kneeling stiff and erect for most of the service.

A horse drawn hearse and other horse drawn carriages, all decorated in black silk ribbons and glossy black feather plumes transported Antonio and his retinue to his final resting place in the Catholic section of the West Terrace Cemetery.

Elena came to stay with us after the funeral, and in the following week, there was an endless procession of visitors who came to pay their respects. They didn't stay long, just enough time to let Elena know that she was in their thoughts and would be happy to assist her in any way possible. Again, following tradition, no food or drink was served to these visitors. We worried about Elena's strength after the first few days, when it seemed the number of visitors did not dwindle. However, Elena remained steady, and mostly silent which was unusual for her, but her sister explained that she was doing this for Antonio's memory, and so that he knew he would be free to leave this mortal earth, knowing that she would be looked after. Some Italians believed that the dead were left roaming between earth and heaven until their loved ones were settled. I had been so young when I left my homeland, that I didn't really recall many of the reasons behind the traditional practices, but guessed that they were a source of comfort.

After taking a month to think about what her life would be like without Antonio, Elena decided that she would sell the Gawler shop and move to Adelaide. This meant she could settle some money on Bart, so that he could get married. Antonio had expressly asked his wife not to stand in the way of Bart's happiness with his fiancé. Mary-Jane's father was also quite unwell, and the young woman had been caring for him since she was sixteen years old, after her mother had passed away. Elena urged the young couple to make plans, while her father was still well enough to see his only daughter married. Luisa and I looked at each other, more than a little miffed. Elena had wanted us to wait a year when my father had died.

'It was different, you two were so young, you could afford to wait. Bart's already thirty-two and Mary-Jane is twenty-five. If they are going to start a family, they'll need to get cracking, explained Elena, pragmatic as always.

Six months later, the pair were married at St. Augustine's in Salisbury, where they had first met. They had decided to live in Mary-Jane's family home in Salisbury so that she could continue to care for her father. The only change in their circumstances was that Bart had decided to sell his one-man motor repair shop and had taken up a senior position in the engineering division of Holden's Motor Factory in Woodville. Bart had become a quietly confident man, someone who was sure of himself and did not need to brag about his achievements. While he was well-spoken and well-mannered, he tended to keep his opinions to himself. He was completely disinterested in joining me in any of my activities, telling me he preferred his own country-gentleman sporting pursuits. These days, he mostly played tennis in summer and golf in winter and had earned himself an impressive set of trophies and medals.

Mary-Jane was very quietly spoken too, joining him in his sporting pursuits, especially the cross-country horse races, and also involved in charitable works within her parish. Zia Violetta informed us that her fruit cakes and scones were highly sought after at local fundraising bake sales. The wedding was quite large, as Mary-Jane had three older brothers who were married with children, as well as numerous aunts, uncles, and cousins on both her mother's and father's side, since her family had been established in the Salisbury area for several generations.

On the day of the wedding, all the adult members of the extended Latorre family were still wearing black in respect for Antonio's passing, never a flattering colour on my Luisa. She had not been sleeping well, getting very hot and sweaty at night, even though we were still in winter. She had caught a cold in July and was still coughing. She looked pale and had lost some weight. While we were sitting at lunch, Zia Violetta noticed that Luisa barely ate anything and asked her whether she had seen a doctor.

"Dr Nilssen has given me a cough tincture, but it hasn't made much difference," she explained forlornly.

Zia Violetta turned to me, alarm registered in the firm set of her jaw:

"Make sure she gets a warm lemon and honey drink in the morning, and before she goes to bed at night. It will loosen the congestion in her chest and soothe her throat. Add a dash of brandy in the night-time one, to help her sleep and some Ferro-Chino in the morning one as a pick me up to stimulate her appetite."

It was the remedy my grandmother had always prescribed for me if I came down with a cold when I was younger, so I vigorously agreed to make sure Luisa looked after herself, despite knowing how much she hated the bitter aftertaste of the dark amber Ferro-Chino herbal tonic.

It had been a tiring few months, with Luisa helping her mother to put the Gawler business on the market and pack all her things. However, Elena hadn't wanted to live with us, and had decided to buy a house a few doors down from her sister Beatrice, on West Terrace, which was already operating as a boarding house for fellow Italians, mostly newly arrived young men. Despite our implorations to take some time to rest, she simply declared,

"I'm only fifty-seven. I'll have plenty of time to rest when I'm dead."

Luisa was only consoled by the fact that her mother was less than a ten-minute walk away from us.

A few weeks after Bart's wedding, Luisa woke me up one night with a hacking cough that wouldn't stop. When I put my hand on her back, I could feel her nightgown was soaked through and she was shivering. I jumped up and found her a fresh nightgown, helped her to get into it, and then wrung out a flannel in cool water to wipe down her feverish limbs.

I tried to get her to lie down, but that made her nauseous, and her cough worsen. It was too late to call the doctor, but I knew there would be someone at the Braithwaite's Hospital, I could at least ask them what I could do to ease her suffering. Jeanie picked up the telephone and said she could leave the matron in charge and come down to see us. It took a good half hour for Jeanie to arrive, by that time, Luisa was coughing up blood.

Jeanie's expert eye quickly surmised the situation. She hadn't seen Luisa since Antonio's funeral and noticed immediately that she had lost a significant amount of weight. She pulled out some opium tincture and put a few drops into a small glass of water which she slowly encouraged Luisa to drink. The drops had the effect of calming her coughing and sending Luisa to sleep. I started to explain about Luisa's cold, but Jeanie stopped me, looking me straight in the eye.

"This is not a cold Charlie. She's lost weight, her chest is aching and sounds very congested on one side only, she has a fever and night sweats and now she's coughing up blood."

I continued to search her face, not sure what she was trying to tell me.

"They are the classic symptoms of Tuberculosis."

I sank immediately into a nearby chair, staring wildly at her.

"You mean ... consumption?"

Jeanie nodded gravely as I dragged my hands through my hair and let out a loud wail, drawing a terrified Anthony peering into the room. Jeanie encouraged a dozy Anthony back to his room and then returned to me.

"Pull yourself together," she scolded harshly. "Tuberculosis is a notifiable disease, and the patient is required to be isolated as soon as possible. With rest and the correct cure, many recover these days. She's young and strong, we must do everything we can for her."

I nodded mutely, not knowing what to do with myself, such was the fear which had gripped me. My lungs seemed to be caught in a vice and I could barely breathe. I could feel the rising panic flood my body and my breathing become shallower and more rapid.

Jeanie grabbed my skull and forced my head between my knees, urging me to breathe slowly to the rhythm of her steady count, until I regained control of my lungs.

"I'm going to call for our ambulance and I'll have someone come to remove the bedding and disinfect the apartment. The disease is highly contagious, and you and Anthony and other family members are at high risk of having already caught it. We'll have to administer the sputum test to determine whether you are safe."

I just continued to stare at her dumbly, unable to comprehend what was happening. Eventually, Luisa, while still asleep under the effects of the opium, was wrapped in a warm nightrobe, socks and a cap and carried out on a stretcher by two sturdy masked porters and taken to hospital, while I was sent to Anthony to explain what was going on.

We dressed quickly, throwing on winter coats and hats, as the August early morning air was very crisp. I drove us the one block to the private hospital, and we sat shivering and unsure in a small waiting room, where the window to the outside had been opened wide. Jeanie explained that good air circulation was vital and that we were to please wait till the doctor arrived.

"Under no circumstances are either of you allowed to wander through the hospital, potentially infecting others. When you've seen the doctor, you'll be allowed to see Luisa who has been put into a special single room, designed for tubercular cases."

In the meantime, Frances had been charged to strip all the bedding and soft furniture and remove the rugs from the apartment and the office. All the linens and blankets would need to be washed in carbolic acid and aired in strong sunlight in order to disinfect them. She would see that floors and all surfaces were cleaned, and phenol mist sprayed to disinfect them.

Once a suitable hour had arrived, she would need to inform all the tenants of Cremona House and also our factory workers. She would arrange for all of them to undergo the sputum test over the next couple of days. She suggested I write letters to Anthony's school and all the people we had been in contact with over the last six months.

"Just let people know that they may have come in contact with a person who may have been tubercular in the last six-months, and they are urged to have themselves tested, whether or not they have any symptoms."

Anthony and I met with the doctor, took a sputum test, by spitting into a little glass vial which was sealed before being sent off for analysis. We were told we would not know the results for a few days as the culture needed to grow in a laboratory and be examined under a microscope. We were issued with linen face masks and advised to go home but to keep to separate rooms, and away from other people. We were also told to keep the windows of our apartment open to allow for air circulation.

It was the end of the week before we could call in on Luisa, but were asked to stay behind a glass window, so we couldn't really speak to her, just make signs, and reassure her of our love. She was quite heavily sedated still.

A nurse from the Infectious Disease Hospital at Northfield came to see us and was satisfied with the precautions taken. The nurse also explained the treatment options available to us. She noted that we were living in comfortable circumstances and suggested that Luisa be sent to the Nunyara Sanatorium in Belair, where the most up-to-date cures for the body and mind were available to tubercular patients.

When Jeanie telephoned to report on Luisa's condition, I mentioned the Sanatorium and she urged me to make enquiries. Fresh air and opportunities for supervised diet and exercise were the best-known methods for ridding someone of the disease, the curse of city dwellers. Thank goodness for the telephone we had installed almost ten years ago. There was a place for Luisa, and she could be transferred there tomorrow. Anthony and I would be allowed to come to see her, as often as we wanted to, as they kept their patients in the open air, under wide verandas, to encourage the lungs to heal, and supervised the weaning away from strong pain medication as the patient improved, so she would be more alert and able to partake in salubrious walks to rebuild her lung and muscle strength.

Anthony and I tested negative to the Tuberculosis bacterium, as did our close family and our tenants. However, there were a couple of cases on the factory floor, and they were encouraged to get treatment via the

Infectious Diseases Hospital, who sent out visiting nurses to inform close family about how to support the patient, how to prevent cross-contamination, and how to disinfect their premises and keep themselves safe. The biggest problems were the handkerchiefs into which patients coughed phlegm or blood. These had to be handled with extreme care, preferably burned, and the person dealing with them was encouraged to wash their hands in carbolic soap, as well as change and disinfect aprons worn over clothing.

I made sure to send Tino around to the families of the affected men with an extra week's wages, which was the best I could do. Anthony had returned to school but had been unable to focus. He begged me to be allowed to stay home so that he could visit his mother.

I would start early on the factory floor and then head out to Belair in the early afternoon. Dot, our friend of many years and Anthony's godmother, came to help us after work. Her office was situated near the Central Market, so while Anthony and I were visiting with Luisa, she would come in and sort my accounts. Elena had her hands full with her boarders, but she came in the late mornings to check on Anthony and make sure he was at least out of bed and doing some of his schoolwork. She usually left us something to eat for lunch and dinner, often too much, as neither of us had any real appetite. Maria too dropped in around the same time and got some of the housework sorted and sent out our laundry, though a few days a week, she would take the train to go and visit with Luisa. Bart would drive to town after work on Tuesdays and Fridays, have an early dinner with his mother and then drive them both to Belair to spend some time with Luisa, occasionally also taking Elena's two sisters and his cousin Anna.

By November, Luisa was looking much better. She had been deemed a good candidate for Collapse Therapy which involved something terrifying called 'artificial pneumothorax' a surgical treatment which temporarily removed air from the pleural cavity giving it an artificial rest, denying the tubercular bacterium the means for developing further. Eventually, the lung cavity would fill up with air again and the surgery had to be repeated.

After more than six months and two surgeries, the night sweats had begun to diminish and the coughing had eased, certainly there was no more blood being ejected. Luisa had started to put on some of the weight she had lost, she was in less pain and had even begun walking around a little to rebuild her muscular strength.

One Sunday, Anthony and I were allowed to take her for a short drive. We headed to the seaside, to Glenelg, where she had spent her early years in South Australia. Watching the waves while taking in the sea air soothed and calmed her. But she was still so, so fragile. My little bundle of energy and enthusiasm seemed to have completely disappeared. Not even Anthony playing her one of his exam pieces on the violin was able to elicit much interest from her. She was vague and far away, locked inside her pain.

A few months after her third surgery, it was clear that her improvements had stopped, her face wearing a permanent mask of hardship. We were told that her other lung was sounding congested. There was no other remedy except prayer. Zia Beatrice came to me and spoke about a herbalist who practised in Sturt Street. He was extremely popular, with locals praising both his kindness and his knowledge. He was a middle eastern fellow and knew ancient uses of plant medicine. She encouraged me to go to see him. He wouldn't come to the sanatorium, but he said if I got her home, he would visit. The sanatorium decided that there was little point in keeping her there, as the cure was no longer working. They agreed that she would be more comfortable at home, under her own doctor's supervision, provided we continued to take every precaution for our own safety.

Luisa came home, where all her loved ones could dote on her. The herbalist did come to see her, gave her some strengthening herbs which we were to brew in a tea, but the tea made Luisa so nauseous, she couldn't keep it down, so we didn't continue with the treatment, preferring to give her softened ice cream, whose sweetness and creaminess were easier to tolerate. I couldn't help smirking, as I was feeding her with small spoonfuls. I reminded her of our competitor's slogan:

"It's a health food not a fad!" She snorted so loudly, I laughed heartily too; it was a rare sign of the old irreverent Luisa.

Fourteen-year-old Anthony was a nightmare, refusing to go to school, yet unable to spend more than ten-minutes with his mother without breaking down, distressing her even more. I tried being gentle with him, tried to help him understand what he could do to ease her pain.

"Read to her, play her some soft, sweet music, just hold her hand and talk to her, tell her what's going on with your friends, your aunts and uncles and your cousins."

But when he couldn't do even these simple tasks, I became stern with him, forbidding him to break down in front of his mother.

"It's just pure selfishness, you're only thinking of yourself. It's time to grow up."

That only led to more histrionics, and he began absenting himself, leaving me worried for his safety. Mostly, he went to his grandmother's or Maria's place to be with Harry. Both women urged me to be gentle with him. He was losing his mother, after all. But overwhelmed by my own distress, I was unable to be of any real use to my son.

In March, Luisa turned forty years old. She was in too much pain to care. Those of us who loved her, were overwhelmed by the cruelty of her pain. She had lost so much weight; her face was unrecognisable. Her skin was constantly sallow and covered in a permanent sticky sheen. She often convulsed into excruciating spasms, and the hacking cough had well and truly returned, leaving her breathless and unable to speak. We were forced to administer the opium drops which meant she spent her days in a fog. Her eyes were permanently glazed, and while she attempted to smile when she saw us, she couldn't focus for long, not even find the strength to squeeze our hands.

For four weeks after her birthday, I sat by her side every minute I could spare and watched her slip away. At times, I prayed for God to take her quickly, to remove her from the barbarous pain. At other times, I prayed for God to save her, to bring back my Luisa of the last twenty years, the young coquette, the passionate musician, the new wife, the mother, the businesswoman, the organiser, the leader.

And I prayed for myself on days when I couldn't accept the inevitable. I prayed for guidance and the strength to bear God's plan, even though I raged against it. I spent many hours just lightly holding her hand, staring at the beautiful face, ravaged by misery, reminiscing about our years together, especially replaying the first time we met, remembering the sensation of having felt like the gates of heaven had opened.

And I also asked, why? Why my lovely and kind Luisa? What could she have possibly done to deserve this bitter end.

I let Elena and her sisters organise the funeral.

Anthony had been living with my sister for the last month. He was better off there; I had no words to comfort him. I was escorted to the front row of the Cathedral with Anthony between myself and Arnold and Maria. Elena and the other family members were on the other side of the aisle and the coffin had been placed between us. The usual Latin verses were recited, and the priest spoke at length in English and

Italian, detailing Luisa's life story, her connections, her good works. It just all sounded like a swarm of bees above my head. I heard piano music, some familiar hymns. I didn't know if it was in my imagination, or someone was really playing. I think I saw Dot and her sister come to the altar to sing something, I couldn't be sure. I looked to Anthony. My brother-in-law, Arnold, had his arm around him, and my son had his teary face buried in his shoulder. I could see my son trembling. I tentatively touched his elbow, but he shook me off.

Finally, we were outside. The coffin had been loaded into the back of a black hearse. Someone shepherded me into another car. It was my own silver Fiat tourer, with black ribbons forming a V-shape as they rose from the tip of the radiator to the edges of the front window. Tino was driving. I sat up front with him. My son, my sister, her husband, and her children slipped into the back seats, and we made our way slowly from Wakefield Street, across Victoria Square, down Grote Street and across West Terrace to the cemetery where Luisa would be laid to rest next to her father.

As we turned into West Terrace, I caught a glimpse of the twenty or so cars behind us and the long line of mourners on foot behind them. Maria suggested that there were at least a thousand people. I looked quizzically at her; I hadn't really understood what she said. She put a hand on my shoulder and quietly whispered,

"She's out of pain now."

I nodded. Those were the only words that had been echoing around my head for the past few days. After her coffin was lowered, the funeral director arranged me, Elena, Bart, and Anthony in a row at the end of the plot and asked only close friends and family to come past to express their condolences. I dutifully shook hands, accepted kisses, or hugs, unaware of who was passing in front of me.

Finally, we were driven home. I went to our bedroom, closed the door, removed my shoes, then lay on the stripped bed, an indescribable exhaustion forcing my body down into its depths. Apart from using the old chamber pot, I barely moved for three days. Someone had come in and covered me in a blanket and left a glass and a pitcher of water with a beaded doily cover by my bedside.

When I eventually arose, it was mid-afternoon. There was no-one in the apartment. Through the kitchen window, I looked across at the factory, there were no signs of activity there either. I could smell myself though, the rancid sweat revolting me. I went to the bathroom, filled the tub, stripped off and sat in the steaming water until well after it turned cold, just watching the light filtering through some tree branches as it swam through the high window. I dressed and tiptoed down the back stairs, into the garden. The air was cool and some of the trees were showing their autumn finery. I sat in my wooden chaise longue, not really thinking, just observing – a bird swooping, a leaf falling, a spider web slowly disintegrating, until one of my tenants, Mrs Jenkins, brought me some tea and sandwiches and helped me find my voice again.

The factory had been closed since the funeral, nearly five days. Dot and Maria had conferred with Tino, and they had decided it was the right thing to do, as a sign of respect for Luisa. The men were as devastated as we were and needed some time to recover. When Mrs Jenkins telephoned her, Maria had immediately come around and suggested I drive out to see Tino, who still lived in Port Adelaide. It was good to see him, and good to be able to sort through the jumble of words in my head. On the way home, I stopped in on Elena. She had aged considerably since Antonio's death. Her faded red hair of the last few years was now completely white and the long locks she had always kept in a braided knot at her neck had been bluntly cut to reach her chin. She didn't say much, just gave me one of her big hugs and on a sigh, whispered,

"We'll get through this, but we'll never be the same again."

Then, she cut a piece of cake, wrapped it in some brown paper, thrust it into my hands, motioning to the door urging, "go get your son, he needs you."

Elena was wrong. Anthony was stiff and formal with me, not able to look me in the eye. I felt the same. I knew I had failed him, but I didn't know how to get him back. Maria and Arnold both said to just give it time, which is what I did. I asked him to come back to the apartment, which is where he came to sleep, but he spent most of his time with Maria, who had at least encouraged him to keep preparing for his Music examinations. We really only met up in the evenings. After Dot had helped me put my accounts in order, especially keeping an eye on my mortgage repayments, my bills and the collection of monies owed me, I would go to Maria's for dinner, but I spent most of the time in the shop doorway, talking to Arnold. When Anthony had finished his meal and had packed up his things, we walked back around the corner and about a block down South Terrace to Cremona House and readied for bed. With Luisa's energy gone, everything felt cold and miserable.

In July, Maria came to me, concerned for Anthony. He couldn't concentrate on any of his studies, and his music tutor had let her know that he didn't think Anthony would be ready for his exams.

"What do I do with him, Maria?"

"I've had a letter from Beppe, suggesting Anthony come to him. He says that a new International Violin School opened up last year in the town centre and he knows the director. The new term starts in September, and as soon as you give your permission, he'll enrol him."

"What does Anthony think?"

"I haven't spoken to him yet. He's a very emotional young man, he can't seem to concentrate on much and loses patience easily. Arnold thinks it's a good idea to get him away from the sadness here, and maybe give him some focus again. He also suggested that I go with him and stay for a few months, make sure he's settled. It will also give me a chance to go and see Rico and Nicola as well as catch up with Beppe."

"How will Arnold manage without you?"

"I'll take Lea with me. Harry's fourteen and should be preparing for his Public Service Exam in November. Arnold is capable of looking after the house and meals. He can send their clothes and linens to the Chinese Laundry down the street. It will only be for around three months. I'll be back by early December."

"Can I trust Beppe? He wasn't a great influence on me when I was in Geelong. I don't want a gambling, drinking, womanising son returned to me," I fretted.

Maria smirked.

"Apparently, he's quite the squire about town and is following more erudite pursuits now that he's mixing with the town elites. He's been called in by the school to act as interpreter for the British and American students."

"*Va bene*, I'll talk to Anthony to see what he says. And Maria, *grazie*, to you and to Arnold. This is very generous of you both."

"No need to thank me, I'm only following your lead. You've done so much for our family, let us support you this time. You don't need this worry now, while you're trying to put your own head in order. Let me take care of Anthony for you. What do you say?"

Maria gathered me in her arms for a firm hug, then with a kiss on the check, she whispered, "mamma was so proud of you and papà too would have been proud."

Anthony's eyes, round and deep brown, like his mother's sparkled with interest for the first time in a year. He vowed he'd do his best to make me proud of him again.

"I'm already proud of you son, I just want you to be happy and to find some direction in your life. You know your mother and I hoped you'd be able to use your musical talents to find a place in a reputable orchestra. She would have been ecstatic to be able to give you this opportunity to study music at an international level."

"*Si, papà*, I know. I'll give it my all, I promise."

I organized the tickets and travelling papers at the Shipping office for Anthony, Maria, and Lea, who was now six years old. Then I wrote a long letter to Beppe, confessing how difficult my relationship with Anthony had become and asking for his help as a mentor to my son. They left a couple of weeks later, so that they could be in Italy by early August, in time to get Anthony settled and comfortable before the start of the academic year. Luckily, he already had his Fascio identity card as a member of the Youth Guild, as without these, he could not be enrolled. He would need to make himself known to the Cremona counterparts, but I was happy that this would give him a chance to meet young people his age too and improve his Italian.

With Anthony gone, I concentrated on my businesses. The economy was picking up speed again and I'd even been able to increase my margarine quota. With my butcher friend George as an equal partner in this business, I was now able to receive better quality tallow and in greater quantity too from the Samuel's private abattoir, which was in Thebarton, so I could send my own drivers out there to collect my raw material.

The ice cream business, since I had been forced to update my packaging, was now bringing in more profits too. The trucks I leased had been upgraded, using railcar technology to improve their refrigeration and freezing capacities. This helped enormously, both in the deliveries of ice and ice cream, which had blessedly increased, since employment had improved and more people were frequenting places of entertainment like dance halls and restaurants, where ice cream desserts were de rigeur.

Dot stopped by several evenings a week, bringing a couple of chops, some mince, or the occasional steaks. I quickly sautéed them in the pan, accompanying them with vegetables from the plot Maria had established in my garden, while Dot took care of my accounts, making sure I knew what bills were due that week and what monies were owed me. Larger companies tended to pay me with bank drafts sent by their accountants, but smaller groceries and households preferred to pay cash on a weekly or fortnightly basis which they gave to my drivers, whom we had equipped with a system of carbon copy receipt books so we could tally the money they brought back.

Dot ferreted out one driver who was pocketing way too many tips and wrote him an official letter of warning, but when, in the next fortnight, he hadn't mended his ways, she sent him a letter firing him, as she reasoned that I would be too soft, worried about his family. She was brutally blunt.

"The man knows right from wrong; he's been given a chance to mend his ways, now he has to face the consequences. It's the right thing to do, and it also warns the other men that you are in control of your business and won't be trifled with."

She was right, I knew it, but I missed Luisa's compassion even more. I knew she would have done the same thing, but with more thought to the man's family, and she would have allowed him to save face in front of his peers. Still, I was grateful for Dot's help, as since Luisa had taken

over my books when I was twenty-seven, I had not really kept my hand
in with the complexities of double entry bookkeeping. I offered to hire
an external bookkeeper to assist me, but Dot rebutted with:

"No-one has the stake in the business that I have, and no-one has
more incentive to see it do well."

I couldn't disagree.

I had given up my involvement with the Fascio children's choir and
it had immediately been disbanded. Other members had taken over the
Saturday schools, but without Luisa's and Maria's enthusiastic musical
and language support, even they were floundering.

The new vice-consul was concentrating his efforts on starting *Dopo-
lavori*, after-work clubs, held in small halls, dotted around the city and
suburbs, where young men could practise their boxing skills and sword
play, and discuss politics. He particularly encouraged a morbid fear
of the Communist element, and there were an increased number of
violent clashes between both groups, on one occasion, even involving
a gunfight and knife slashings, resulting in arrests and a much larger
police scrutiny.

In the newspapers, and on the radio news, there was much talk
of a German Chancellor named Hitler, who it seemed, had fashioned
himself after Mussolini, rallying the German people around the notion
of expanding their territories and taking their rightful place among the
leading nations of Europe. The Germans had colonies in China, but
they were also looking for territory in Europe and Africa. They made no
secret of wanting to reclaim the territories between France and Germany,
the coal rich Ruhr region, which had been transferred to France through
the Treaty of Versailles after the Great War.

Arnold and I went to see the newsreels at the Cinema in the Regent
Arcade, and were alarmed by the feverish, almost slavish devotion to

Hitler portrayed in images of Germany. We even saw one where Hitler toured Italy, sitting at the head of a motorcade alongside Mussolini, both leaders exclaiming their great friendship and admiration for each other while visiting the massive accumulation of military might. I confess, my heart tightened at this image, not in admiration of Mussolini as I should have done, but in fear of all the armaments I saw in the background, vividly seeing flash before my eyes, the thousands of mutilated men who had come through my hospital in Vicenza.

Arnold and I discussed at length what would happen in case of another war, rumours of which were circulating at ever increasing speed. We were both forty-eight years old, technically still of an age to be called up as reservists. Though, now that I was a naturalized British Subject, that could possibly mean fighting for Britain. The thought of it horrified me. I could understand fighting for Australia, but why would I fight for Britain? Arnold, who was the third generation of his family to have been born here, also felt the same, especially after having experienced the madness of the Western Front.

At night, I found falling asleep difficult, my mind wondering what our leaders were thinking contemplating military action when party after party, all over the world had promised to use diplomatic solutions to international stand-offs after the end of the last war. What worried me the most, was the vitriol against the Jews in Germany. What if the same thing started to happen here? And what if after the Jews, the Italians were next? In the newspapers, we were already the scapegoat for unfair work practices and unemployment, diluting of the white race, destruction of British culture, disease, crime and rape, the list ever-increasing, published across the country, without a anyone defending us. There had been the most awful cartoons published, both from Germany and from Britain against the Jews, whose faces were rendered ugly and distinctly Mediterranean in countenance. It was obvious that whipping up public hysteria didn't seem too hard to do.

I worried about Anthony. He wrote me a couple of lovely long letters about his activities. It seemed his social life was going very well, but he didn't say much about his musical studies. I didn't want Anthony to be caught up in Italy if war were declared. I wrote to both him and Beppe, urging them to keep an eye on the political situation and begging them to make sure they both return to the relative safety of Australia before shipping channels closed. By the end of August 1939, I had lost faith in the British Prime Minister, Neville Chamberlain to have any real control over Hitler, now that Japan was looking like it would join Hitler. Mussolini had been playing cat and mouse with Hitler for a couple of years, but everyone speculated that he too was going to sign a military pact with Hitler. I feared for my country and my countrymen, in Italy and all around the world. I wired Anthony with the details of the passage I had booked for him, choosing to have him leave from Napoli, rather than Genova which was too close to Germany for my liking. I also re-iterated my invitation to Beppe, but he was fifty-one years old now, and preferred to take his chances in Cremona. I wired Rico and Nicola, prepared to pay their passages to Australia, telling them I would arrange travelling papers as soon as I heard from them. I received no reply, not knowing if they hadn't received my wire, or were not interested in my offer. I didn't dare write again in case my letters had been intercepted and might land my brothers in trouble with the Italian authorities.

My anxiety for the fate of my family prevented me from sleeping and I found myself getting testy on the factory floor over minor incidences, something I had never done before, even during Luisa's illness.

Anthony returned to me, unharmed. He was tanned and physically fit with a smile back in his eyes. His light brown curls were gone in favour of a sleeker look, and he had grown a couple of inches. He had turned sixteen in May. He was no longer a boy but was still trying to get away with a cheeky grin to gain favour. I asked him to be honest with me and tell me what he had done in Italy and what he wanted to do now.

"I enjoyed the first six-months at the Music Academy, but when Professore Antonioni wanted me to try out for the Milanese Orchestra, things became so serious. He expected me to have lessons every day and practise for hours on end in between. He forced me into having private classes, so I didn't even have the company of another student, just a sour old professor who was never satisfied. Seriously, Pa, I promise I gave it a real good go, but it was all so boring! Unfortunately," he grimaced, "the trials were in November. You recalled me too early papà."

"Do you actually want to continue with your music?" I asked, clenching my stomach, terrified to hear the answer I knew was coming.

"Honestly, pa, I don't think I can hack it anymore. I'm happy to keep playing my violin for fun, but I don't think a professional musician's life is for me."

"So, what is it you actually want to do?"

"Don't really know," he answered, hunching his shoulders flippantly and throwing himself into the low armchair, legs crossed with the top one swinging wildly up and down and a huge sheepish smile covering his face. I controlled myself even though I felt like throwing a brick at this pampered pooch. Where did he come from? Surely not from Luisa and me? Was this Beppe's influence? No, I had to accept that Anthony had always been like this, giving up as soon as a task was too difficult and always looking to blame others or unfortunate circumstances for his failures. Maybe it was being an only child, used to having everything come to him so easily? There was no point contemplating what had been. It was time to set him on a better path, one that I could supervise directly.

"Well, I guess you'll be taking over my business soon enough. It may be time you come to work with me and learn the ropes from the bottom up?"

"Great pa, that sounds fantastic." He jumped up, without even asking any more details and sauntered off, waving at the door, telling me he was off to see Harry.

I sighed, every bone aching. What wrongs had I committed that these penances had been thrust upon me? Yes, I had been proud of my achievements, but hadn't I always looked out for my family and community too? Luisa's cruel death, Anthony's indifference – did I really deserve them?

Chaos Again

The declaration of war against Germany by the United Kingdom and subsequently, Australia's mimic of such declaration by Prime Minister Menzies had occurred in September last year. I had been a naturalized British subject for nearly two decades yet had no idea what this would mean for me as a portly, fifty-year-old, with a nineteen-year-old son. In the last war, moves to make conscription compulsory had been defeated twice, yet I had still been forcibly evicted, in a deal the Australian government had made with its Allies so that it could meet its quotas for enlisted men required by the British.

I was sitting in Maria and Arnold's parlour after they had closed up shop one Saturday night, talking about the impending war. Anthony and Harry had gone out to meet with friends. Harry was still only seventeen, but he'd been taking a keen interest in political affairs, and much to their despair, Maria said she was sure Harry would jump at the chance to volunteer as soon as he could, as he'd always dreamed of becoming a pilot.

I wasn't so sure about Anthony. My son was mostly just interested in a good time. True to his promise, he was pulling his weight at the factory, learning how to operate and troubleshoot the machines. He had been made welcome by the other men, mostly because he was friendly and amusing, a good raconteur, and a keen observer of other people's foibles, which gave him plenty of material with which to regale the men. Too much like my brother Nino, I felt, who had been easily distracted and always looking for attention. While Anthony was dutiful on the factory floor, he'd shown no real interest in the actual running of the business. I kept telling myself that it had only been a short time since his return from Italy. Normally, this wouldn't have concerned me too much, but I reasoned that the outbreak of war could easily shut me down again, especially in the manufacture of ice and ice cream. I knew I had little time to shore up my interests in order to create a buffer against another economic downturn.

These were the thoughts that ricocheted through my head as I took my leave from Maria and Arnold and walked back to the factory, thankful for the cooler air on my face after a particularly warm November day. One of the precautions I had already taken was to move out of Cremona House and rent out our apartment to a new tenant. This decision was taken mostly because the burden of the memories of my life there with Luisa, especially those of her last days, were difficult. Mrs Jenkins, who had been a tenant for several decades, agreed to act as concierge and to oversee the maintenance of the whole property for me, for a reduction in her rent. We still had our cosy apartment above the factory, which had mostly been used for storage over the last ten years. I had organised a clean-up and set up bedrooms for myself and Anthony, so his room had been ready upon his return from Italy.

As I moved past the tall brick fence separating Cremona House and the factory, I looked up to the windows on the first floor and realised one of the dining room windows was slightly ajar with the heavier curtains drawn back and a light on. I assumed it was probably Anthony and Harry who had come home early, so wasn't overly concerned when I opened the locked front door and made my way up the stairs. However, I was not expecting to encounter two policemen in their distinctive blue serge on my landing.

"Mr. Bodoni?"

"That's me officers. These are my private quarters. I didn't think the police were in the habit of trespassing," I accused, my arms crossed, and my hat cocked back on my head, waiting for an explanation.

"We were doing our rounds and noticed a window open," declared the taller one.

"Surely that's not unusual on a summer evening?"

I knew I sounded irate, but these were not the fresh-faced new recruits usually sent out on bicycle rounds. Firstly, they weren't wearing the bicycle brigade's distinctive dark blue round cap. Secondly, they were definitely older with several stripes on their shoulders. No, these one's had definitely come looking for something.

"Did you find what you were looking for?" I stole a glance at my office door, which was wide open, when I knew I had made a deliberate choice to close it behind me as we were leaving.

Clearly uncomfortable at being caught out, the officers made feeble excuses and stepped gingerly around me, bolting noisily down the stairs. I positioned myself at one of the front windows but stayed back so they wouldn't see me looking. They walked down the street and got into a car, confirming my suspicions. I went into my office and carefully looked around.

"What the devil were they after?"

I spent a good hour looking through the files on my desk and in my drawers and cabinet. Nothing seemed missing or even out of place, which made me all the more worried. In my apartment, the same fear rose in me. Nothing seemed touched or missing. I wasn't sure about the dining room window or the lamp. I could possibly have left both open before I went to Maria and Arnold's, I couldn't be sure. However, I was absolutely sure about my office door.

The following morning, there was no sign that Anthony had slept in his own bed, so I assumed he'd stayed at Maria's. I put on my regular widower's black suit with white shirt and black tie, topped with my black fedora and walked the couple of blocks to St. Patrick's at Grote St. for the 7.00 am mass. Maria and my niece Lea, Elena and her sister Beatrice and daughter Anna were already in their usual pew. I slipped in beside them, quickly checking that Anthony was indeed at Maria's.

On the steps of the church, after the service, I nodded my hellos and shook hands with a number of regulars but didn't linger. The family service I had usually attended with Luisa was at 9.30 am, so there were few of the people we normally mixed with. I preferred it this way, as I was tired of the sympathetic looks and enquiries after my state of mind. Such encounters were awkward all around. I was just trying to get along, as best I could, day by day, without thinking too much about anything really.

Elena suggested we go back to her place for coffee, and I was happy to accompany the ladies, just around the corner on West Terrace, to sit in Elena's small backyard with a cigarette and an espresso, and some of Elena's homemade aniseed biscuits. I didn't say much here either, just happy to listen to them chatter about plans for the week ahead. Later, I accompanied Maria and Lea home and told her about the encounter with the two policemen the night before.

"Are you sure you don't know what they were looking for?"

"No idea, I've been awake most of the night trying to come up with an answer."

"Did they go into your apartment?"

"They may have, I don't normally lock the door, but I think they must have heard me come in and got out to the landing just as I was coming up the stairs."

"But you lock the front door to the building, and the factory gates are always locked after everyone leaves, so how did they get in?"

"That's what puzzles me. The only thing I can think is that they climbed over the gates or over the wall at the back of the factory, or even through the upstairs open window, but that would have required quite a bit of effort as they were no spring chickens."

"Be careful Carlo, it's probably to see if you have information on Italy. Things are not going to go well for us once Italy enters this madness, and if Mussolini ends up siding with Hitler, life is going to become very difficult. After you left last night, Arnold and I kept discussing all possible scenarios. I've decided to apply for a Hawker's licence, so if Arnold is required to leave for military service, at least I'll be able to keep the shop going."

"Good idea Maria. I'm still thinking about whether I should just shut the factory down now and cut my losses."

We were only at the beginning of summer, so I decided to see out the summer season and then I would make a decision. The federal parliament had passed the National Security Act last September, declaring sovereignty over all industrial efforts, allowing the government to direct both men and women towards industries essential to the war effort only. Already tailors and the popular shirt-making factories on my doorstep had been converted to the manufacture of uniforms, and other industries would soon follow. In the afternoon, I called George, my margarine manufacturing partner, to hopefully talk over our options. He was frazzled by the new rationing rules applied to butchers, and suggested I would soon face similar restrictions, if not more severe ones, especially for the ice cream. I knew he was right and hoped only that I would be able to hold out till Easter, the end of the summer season.

By early March, with my encouragement, over half my staff had already gone to take advantage of better pay at the factories that had been rededicated to the war effort, making weapons or other necessities for the fighting men. This allowed me to shut down both the ice cream and ice making machinery with a clear conscience.

Luckily, margarine had been requisitioned by the military, so my quotas had finally improved, in fact doubled again. This meant George and I were making up the loss of income from our other productions, reasonably well. I also cancelled the leases on my vans and retained only the two older lorries, and my aging, but still beloved, 1925 Fiat touring car. Anthony, myself and Tino, now a thirty-nine-year-old father of two, were the only ones left. As Tino was Australian born, he assumed he'd be co-opted into the newly formed Civilian Labour Corps, but he promised he would try to stay with me for as long as needed.

On the afternoon of the last Sunday in April, the second anniversary of Luisa's death, I finally had her headstone installed at the Catholic Cemetery, where I had invited a very select group of our closest friends and family to join myself, Anthony and Father Peter, for a small prayer service. I had come to terms with her loss, but still felt quite empty inside, lacking any real enthusiasm for my work or other causes. I was infinitely grateful to the people around me this morning, who hadn't given up on me, and I expressed my thanks to them for the efforts they had made in Luisa's memory.

We went back to Elena's boarding house and of course we talked about Luisa, which was good for Anthony, as he was really still a child when Luisa became ill, but it pained me even more, to realise how much my life had changed from the one I had dreamed of, the day I met Luisa and her family.

Anthony and I were outside in the garden having a smoke with my long-time friends, Tersiglio and Giacomo, whose wives had been close friends of Luisa's, helping her with the Saturday schools and other charitable causes. They had also withdrawn their involvement from the Fascio in 1936, when the new consul had dramatically changed direction.

Giacomo was the owner of a sports store and stocked rifles along with other hunting equipment. He'd been visited by two policemen, late one afternoon, before Christmas, just as he was closing. They had been quite menacing, insisting he produce his trading licenses, but also asking for the ledgers of the clients who had purchased guns, and he felt that they were targeting the Italian ones, taking down their addresses. I thought back to the night of the visit I'd had, but my clients were so varied. I didn't have a client list per se, though Luisa had set up an alphabetised card index with names and addresses. I hadn't noticed any missing in the following weeks, but I would go back and check again.

Tersiglio, who'd arrived in Australia when he was just two years old and had taken over his father's grocery store which had always stocked many of the foods the Italian migrants craved, sourcing them from all over Australia, as well as in Italy, had had the same experience and knew that some of his clients had also had these visits around the same time.

"Deliberately menacing they were! I found them in my side yard where I keep my delivery trucks. They asked for my papers for the trucks, without giving me a reason as to why they needed them, even though I did demand to see them. I wouldn't hand anything over until I saw some form of identification. They were dressed as policemen, but they were both detectives, and not from the Hindley Street Station, but probably from the Police Headquarters in King William Street. I commented that it was unusual to see detectives in uniform, but that made them more insistent. They were quite rude, almost disdainful, I'd say. They didn't call me 'dago' to my face, but their looks spoke for themselves. I was shocked because I normally get on quite well with the Hindley Street bobbies. They look out for my shop at night or when I'm not there, and if there's any information they need about some shady dealing, I look out for them if I can."

"Wait, so you think they were deliberately disguising themselves?" squealed Anthony, who was becoming quite agitated, pacing nervously up and down the path from the back door to the vegetable patch.

"Ssh," I insisted with a finger to my lips. "The boarders upstairs," I whispered, as I pointed to the upstairs windows. "We need to be very careful." Tersiglio and Giacomo nodded vigorously in agreement.

"I heard on the radio news earlier this week that the British have begun rounding up the Germans and putting them into Internment Camps," revealed Giacomo in hushed tones. The rest of us looked at him with increasing anxiety.

"That's it then," said Tersiglio, "we're done for. The government here will for sure plan on doing the same thing, like they did in the last war, but this time, if Mussolini enters the war alongside Hitler, we'll be classed as Enemy Aliens too. I was just a lad, living in Port Adelaide during the last war, and I saw the miserable conditions they kept the Germans in on Torrens Island. Living in tents, sleeping, cooking, and eating in the mud they were."

There was no reply to Tersiglio's prediction. Anthony was still vigorously pacing. The three of us didn't need to say anything, we just looked into each other's eyes, nodding in resignation before re-entering Elena's dining room. Their cars were parked outside, but Anthony and I had walked, so we started back to the factory together after the others had gone. Anthony began babbling about going to see a friend, but I grabbed his arm.

"This is no time for playing, I need you now Anthony. I need you to take over the business. You'll be alright if you keep your mouth shut and your head down, but I'm sure they'll come for me."

"What are you saying pa?" Anthony's eyes began blinking furiously. He was continuously clutching and releasing the rim of the cap he was carrying.

"I'm saying that it's time to grow up! Your mother and I made so many sacrifices to save this business, so that we could provide for you. You've had an easy, spoiled life so far. If you want to honour your mother's memory, then you also have to honour her legacy and keep the business going."

I'd been talking very fast, my head down to avoid obstacles, still in hushed tones as we strode purposefully around the corner into South Terrace. Anthony stopped at the corner. His face had blanched except for two red spots on his cheeks. He looked like he was about to cry.

In a reedy, trembling voice he faced me:

"I can't do it pa. I'm not good at making decisions, anything too complicated just confuses me and makes me nervous, and then I can't think, and I end up doing stupid things in my confusion."

I looked at him in astonishment. Not because he had refused, but because he had spoken the truth, which I had stubbornly refused to see before this, imagining that mine and Luisa's progeny would have automatically inherited our intuitiveness for business and commerce. I nodded my head.

"Yes Anthony, I know, but you are all we have. I've already shut down the ice and ice cream machines. You'll have George Preston and your Aunty Dot, they'll help you with the accounts side, you just have to keep production running for the margarine company. You know how to do that."

I looked into my son's warm brown eyes, with their pupils slowly returning to normal; saw the furrowed brow ease slightly. He nodded a faraway yes, but neither he nor I were convinced. I had to try, nevertheless, I had no other option.

A few days later, when there was a vigorous pounding at the door one evening, I braced myself for the police. I calmly rolled down my sleeves, put my jacket on and refastened my tie, hesitating about whether I should take my hat. I'd already packed a small suitcase which was sitting to the side of the apartment door. As I went downstairs though, I heard a familiar voice calling out my name. It was George Preston who rushed inside as soon as I opened the door.

"We need to talk," he gushed, breathlessly.

"Calm down George, let's go upstairs."

I poured us a brandy as he took a seat at the dining room table, his eyes were furtively looking about, his fingers drumming the table, and his right knee furiously bobbing up and down.

"What's happened," I asked as calmy as I could, handing him his brandy, and downing mine in a quick gulp.

"The police came to my home. They insisted I go to the station. I was there for over three hours; they've only just released me."

His voice was shrill and his face red and blotchy.

"What did they want from you?" I asked, confused.

"They questioned me about you, about our business dealings. They had a record of all the times I'd attended parties at your place or gone to one of your events in the last ten years."

"Ten years!" I repeated, sinking into my seat. "They've been spying on me for ten years?"

"They know everything! Remember that time you had the party for victory in Abyssinia? They knew how much wine and beer had been delivered, how many people were there. They even knew what Sandro had said to everyone. You know what that means Charlie? They planted spies in the gathering! Spies everywhere! They're building up evidence against you!"

I didn't respond, too stunned by what I was hearing. I just stared at George as he continued to babble hysterically. I narrowed my eyes as the lightning bolt struck, trying to connect with his suspiciously roving eyes.

"They sent you here, didn't they?"

George lowered his eyes, just for a brief second and continued babbling, repeating what he'd just told me, trying to impress upon me that he was just trying to warn me and that I needed to leave for my own safety. His erratic blinking gave him away. I shut the conversation down, assuring him I would reflect on his advice. In a few minutes, I suggested he had better leave, reminding him that we were probably being watched. I also recommended that he refrain from returning here. I ushered him down the stairs and smiled ruefully as I watched the relief flood his face. As soon as I shut the door behind him, I rushed upstairs. From the small study window, I saw him walk briskly and get into the back of a black Ford parked a short distance down the street.

"So, the police want me to run. For what possible reason?"

About a year ago, the smallest of newspaper articles had warned that all Enemy Aliens were required to be registered with their local police station. The Italian Consulate had been required to disseminate the information in Italian, to let everyone know that they were to remain within fifty miles of the police station at which they were registered. I was a Naturalized British Subject, so this notice had not applied to me. but this was of no use to me, I was now considered an Enemy Alien. I wondered whether they hoped I would run, so that they had free access to my papers or my factory, or whether that was George Preston's invention? Maybe I had disturbed them that evening in early January? Whatever the answer, I knew that my time was limited. When Dot arrived the next afternoon, I told her what was going on.

"Well, they obviously have nothing on you, otherwise they would have arrested you already. If anyone wants you to run, it's probably George so he can get his greedy hands on the factory," she continued, confirming my suspicions.

"I'm sure you're right," I replied.

Anthony was taking a bath, so I set about cooking dinner for the three of us while Dot was in the office, sorting out the paperwork. Once we were at the table. I clearly impressed upon both Dot and Anthony, that if what George said was even only half true, then the Police had been watching my movements for a long time. I warned them to be wary of George Preston. He was clearly hoping to gain from my disappearance, possibly taking over the Margarine License in his own name if I were out of the picture. Both of them were solemn and worried, but Dot reached out to cover my hand:

"Don't worry Carlo, you can count on us, can't he Anthony?"

Anthony couldn't speak. He gave his godmother a weak grin, looking over at me with puppy dog eyes. He looked like he was four years old again.

The wheels turn

Once I heard that Mussolini had declared Italy at war against the Allies on June 10th 1941, I knew it would be a matter of days. I stayed put, not visiting anyone, just writing to the extended family, to warn them of my suspicions and to remind them how much I was thankful for all their support over the years. I begged them not to get involved, to do everything to keep themselves out of trouble, but if possible, to watch out for Anthony as he was terrified, and easily panicked.

First came the letter from the Minister for State of Defence Coordination, requiring me to shut down my ice and ice cream manufacturing as they were deemed non-essential industries, but allowing the margarine manufacturing to continue. Then a few days later, a Monday morning, three Police cars rolled up advising me that they were here to arrest me as an Enemy Alien, according to some kind of Federal legislation. As I ducked to enter the backseat of one of the police cars, with my hat and my case, I saw Anthony gesticulating at one of the policemen, with Tino trying to calm him down, and then Tino being separated from him and directed to another waiting car.

My heart was pounding so heavily, I could only hear its irregular rhythm in my ear. I was trembling uncontrollably, terrified especially for Anthony and Tino. I didn't know if I would ever see them again. I was ordered to sit, and a Constable slid in on the other side of me and placed me in handcuffs which were wrapped around a horizontal steel rod inserted behind the front seats. Before we could drive off, the car stopped to give way to my two lorries, being driven off my lot by other policemen. I turned my head to look through the back window to check on Anthony and saw another policeman come out the front door holding my radio. As we headed east along South Terrace, an alarmed Mrs Jenkins, in a dressing gown, stared at me forlornly from the barely opened door of Cremona House.

I could taste the acid bile rising to my mouth as the nausea caused by the stale air in the car began to overcome me. With my hands locked behind the front passenger seat, I had to hunch over to bring my collar close enough to my hands so I could loosen my tie, but in doing so, I couldn't help vomiting the contents of my stomach all over my shoes. There were groans of disgust from my seat companion and the driver.

"Could have waited, mate. We'll be there in a jiffy."

I said nothing, lost in the depths of terror. Within moments, we pulled up into a courtyard around the back of the three-storey Police Headquarters building on King William Street, south of Victoria Square. My handcuffs were released so that I could get out of the car. The driver passed me his handkerchief, but the other policeman just laughed at the both of us. He was the one who took me into the building and put me in a private cell in the basement. The doors were locked, but a hatch opened in the top half of the door, and a pitcher of water was passed to me.

In the left-hand corner of the cell, behind the door, there was a metal washstand bolted to the wall, with a white enamelled metal bowl, matching cup and painted white metal lidded slops bucket. I poured some of the water into the cup, rinsing out my mouth and spitting it into the slops bucket. Then I poured some of the water into the bowl and used the handkerchief to wipe myself and my shoes down as best I could, again throwing the water out into the slops bucket followed by the handkerchief. I was repulsed by the realisation that I would probably need to defecate in that bucket too, should the need arise. There was a long narrow wooden bench attached to the right-hand wall with a thin blanket on it, and higher up the wall was a system of iron bolts and chains, fixed to the wall, presumably to secure a prisoner there.

I sat down on the edge of the bench, wondering how long I would be there. As my heart eventually stilled, I became more acutely aware of the noises around me. Fresh air was coming from a narrow, barred window, in the wall high above the head of the wooden bench, which seemed to lead to an outside yard, as I occasionally saw shiny black boots clip past and could also hear the noise of engines. Not car engines though, these sounded like motorbikes. I knew I must have drifted off to sleep as I woke up with long, darker shadows on the wall opposite the window and the bench.

I was strangely at peace, as I'd dreamt I was a lad again, snuggled into my cubby hole on board ship. As I tried to readjust to my surroundings, a voice behind the door called out my surname as the hatch opened and a mottled older face told me to stand facing the wall opposite the door, with my arms up. When I had complied with the request, the cell door opened out into the corridor and two other policemen entered, positioning my arms behind my back, attaching handcuffs, and marching me out of the cell, up two flights of stairs into another room where two plain clothes men, presumably detectives, were waiting for me.

I was informed that I was being held as a National Security Risk in accordance with the National Securities (Aliens Control) Act passed by the Commonwealth on September 8th 1939. I was to be held in the Adelaide Police Headquarters for as long as it took to compile a statement from me, and then I would be transferred to the military authorities, initially at Keswick Barracks, then wherever they saw fit.

After that, I would face a military tribunal who would determine my sentence, and I also had the right to appeal the sentence. The detective's face was inscrutable. He spoke in a dispassionate manner, never looking at me, just reading from his notes. There was a younger officer sitting next to him with a stenographer's pad, and I could see the strange squiggle of his notes as we spoke.

They began by asking me my full name, date and place of birth, place of residence, marital status, children, occupation. Then they asked me to recount my journey to Australia. As I spoke, the older detective occasionally glanced at his notes, to confirm whether I was telling the truth, as he was able to remind me of the name of the ship and the exact date I had arrived in Melbourne in 1912. I must have given him a surprised look. He simply said: "It's on your application for Naturalisation."

They asked me about my military service in Italy and questioned me at length about my political leanings. I could tell them the honest truth. I had left Italy as a fourteen-year-old boy, by economic necessity. I had no experience beyond the local affairs of my small town. I had no interest in politics. After my forced repatriation to Italy in 1918, I had worked alongside the Americans and had spent my spare time learning about motor cars. The only communication I had with Italy was with my immediate family to whom I sent letters and money. I had no intention of returning to Italy, but of course, it was my childhood home, so naturally, I regarded my fatherland with fondness.

Next, they moved on to my activities in Adelaide. They had detailed notes about my in-laws and questioned me about Bart, focussing stupidly on why he went by the name Bart when his real name was Bartolomeo.

"It's just a short version of the name, surely that's obvious," I answered, quite perturbed by the fleeting look of glee on the detective's face when he thought he had asked that perceptive question.

They also wanted to know about Bart's work, why he'd closed down his motor shop to work at Holden's. I proudly said that Bart had an unparalleled engineering background and was looking for a better opportunity for his talents. They asked me to describe what he did at Holden's. I confessed I didn't know much about the particulars of his position, just that he was very happy there, in the Engineering Department. They asked me to confirm notes about his wedding, and details about Mary-Jane's family. Again, while I had met them all, I didn't socialise with them as they mostly all lived in the Salisbury-Gawler area.

They also asked me questions about Elena's boarders, to which I again explained that I took no interest in her business. If I were visiting my mother-in-law, I might bump into them and I would engage in general chit chat, but otherwise I couldn't even tell the police their names.

Finally, they spent a good hour asking me detailed questions about my activities with the Fascio. I told them that I had initially helped to form the Italian Trader's Association, as an opportunity to get to know others, and in the hope of forming a mutual aid society, but after a short time, the needs of the group changed, and I had followed the new vice-consul who had formed the Adelaide Italian Fascist Association while others had peeled off to form the Italian Sports and Social Club on Carrington Street.

"When did you meet the vice-consul?" they asked.

"I met Mr. Barrow, the previous vice-consul in 1917 when I sought his help to contact my brother in Mexico, and then after the war, he helped me with the paperwork needed to sponsor my brother and sister to come to Adelaide. I invited him to a house-warming party when we first purchased Cremona House, the house next door to my factory. As he was close to retirement, he'd been sent an assistant by the Italian Consulate in Melbourne and had asked if he could bring his replacement to the party. Alessandro Pastore was relatively new to Australia. Our wives got along well, and we became personal friends. As one does with friends, one tries to help them out.

Alessandro's father -in-law was a descendant of a very important family in Rome and were ambitious for him and had encouraged him to move to Australia in the hope that he would have a better chance of securing a position in diplomatic circles. He was following the Italian Department of Overseas Affairs directives to establish Fascist Clubs in Australia so that migrants and their families could retain their culture."

"Did you not see that as disloyal to Australia, since in your Naturalisation request, you swore allegiance to our King?"

"I was never disloyal to Australia. I became involved because I wanted other Italian Australians, and especially their children to remember the rich culture they had inherited."

"But you sang the Italian anthem and saluted the flag at your ceremonies and events."

"We also saluted the British flag and sang God save the King and Song of Australia at the same events."

I reminded them that the choir had performed at other, non-exclusively Italian events, including some events attended by the Governor and Lord Mayor of Adelaide, but the detective just continued to glare at me. My heart sank, fearing that whatever I said in my defence would just be ignored. The detective continued with his accusations.

"You are wearing a black suit today, as you have been observed to do every day. Isn't black the Fascist colour?"

I sat there with my mouth open, quite incredulous.

"You know I am a recent widower! Even in British society, black is worn to denote mourning."

I was disgusted by this line of questioning. I had answered most of their enquiries as dispassionately as I could, knowing that it was important that I keep my temper under control, that I give them no extra reasons for charging me, but this one threatened to be my undoing. I broke out into a furious sweat, the heat engulfing my face. My hands began shaking so much, I was forced to tuck them under my thighs.

Still the questions continued, having me recount all the events I had organised and their purpose. When I forgot one, I was reminded of it, confirming that I had been under close observation for at least ten years. Then came the realisation as to why I had been arrested and was being questioned at such great length. The detective ferreted in his folder and produced our Fascio documents, mine, Luisa's and Anthony's. That's what they'd been looking for in my office, I suddenly realised. They were a type of Identity Document, little cardboard folders with our photos and official stamps. This time, the dour detective waited till I locked eyes with him.

"Do you admit, that having organised all these events, you are seen by your fellow countrymen as the chief Fascist in this state?"

"Chief Fascist!" I couldn't help throwing my head back in laughter.

"I organised the Saturday schools and ran the choir. I was never the president of the Fascists, nor even on its executive board after Vice-Consul Pastore left in 1936. My wife and I participated in the events, organised some of them, even held many at our own home and factory, but our intentions were purely social. I never had any interest in the political nature of the party. In fact, you can check with Vice-Consul Spadafora, who was glad to get rid of me from the executive committee precisely because he felt I had no political inclinations."

"Your vice-consul ran from his dwellings in the middle of the night and is apparently on a ship heading to Japan, as we speak. He did us a huge favour, leaving his office files completely open, and you are listed as the number one Fascist subscriber."

"So, I'm to be your scapegoat, based on a list of names?"

I let my chin fall to my chest and my arms flop to my side. Slowly, I looked up and tried to catch his eyes.

"Really, it's come to this false accusation?"

"Your actions speak for themselves."

After my questioning, night had fallen and I was returned to my cell, given a meal, and to my dismay, forced to defecate in the slop bucket which had not been emptied during my absence. I asked if I could communicate with my son but was told that it would be up to the military authorities. As I lay shivering under the open window, huddling into the corner of the bench as best I could to protect my back from the winter wind, I ruminated over the proceedings I had just endured. As far as I could understand, I was destined for imprisonment by the military authorities, no matter what I said. It was clear though, that it was my testimony which would determine how long I would be staying locked up. Unless I was able to appeal the evidence brought against me, I would be imprisoned for the duration of the war.

The last war had lasted four years. How long would this second war last? I panicked at the thought that it might last a decade, given all the new technologies on land, sea and air which had developed in the intervening years. What if they transferred me interstate? Would I see Anthony and my family and friends ever again?

The terror that gripped me rendered me unable to think, unable to sleep, even unable to swallow as I left all of the boiled cabbage and grey strings of what smelled horribly like boiled mutton on my plate on the open hutch.

The next afternoon, I was returned to the interview room, where my statement which had been typed up was read to me, and I was asked to sign it. It was a document of a solid twenty or more pages. I was too tired to retain, or even understand what they were reading out to me, too tired to think of any rebuttals. My head ached and my stomach, though empty of food, threatened to spill more accumulated bile.

I was photographed and fingerprinted. My hat and suitcase were returned to me, then two men in military uniform shepherded me towards the back of a large, canvas covered truck. If the situation hadn't been so serious, we could have had a party. Here were my Italian friends of the last ten to twenty years. Selected men from the Adelaide Fascist Association, mostly those with businesses in Hindley Street as well as those from the Port Adelaide and Glanville Associations.

Some extended a hand to me, which I gratefully shook, some just glared at me in disbelief. The Port Adelaide and Glanville men, mostly fishermen and dock workers, described their shock at being pulled from their beds by a pre-dawn Military Police raid and thrown into trucks, without any notice. They'd left their wives and children in nightgowns, wailing at their front doors. They were asking me all sorts of questions I could not answer, the more poignant one being "who will feed my family?"

At Keswick, we were placed in alphabetical order and numbered off in groups of six. It was military service all over again. We were given a tent, some blankets, thin canvas sacks to be filled with straw to use as mattresses and ordered to put up the tents in a ring on the oval. By the end of the week, there were about a hundred of us. Latrines, shower blocks and a mess hall were made available to us. I was able to have a shower and clean my vomit and perspiration smelling suit.

A week later, we were required to pack up and were told we were leaving as internees for an Army camp in Tatura in north-eastern Victoria. Before we left, we were supplied with postcards made available through the Red Cross, who would ensure they were delivered to their intended destinations, however, we were allowed to use only twenty-five words or less in English. I wrote to Anthony:

"I'm fine, being sent to Victoria. Stay out of trouble. Do your best with factory. Remember how important you are to me. Love papà."

I did my best to help those who could not write, or speak English, to complete theirs while the guards watched on suspiciously, but did nothing to stop the older ladies from the Adelaide Red Cross Society complete their mission. Despite my own involvement with the International Red Cross, I did not recognise any of these kind volunteers. I discreetly asked if they would pass on a verbal message to their leader Mrs Carr, but they just showed alarm, letting me know that this would compromise their future work. One lady did look at the address I had written on the card and noticed the surname. She lifted an eyebrow and whispered "Bodoni" and nodded. I didn't know how that would help me, but it gave me just enough hope to allow me to get some much-needed sleep that night.

The next day, we were marched to the Keswick railway station, where we were met with many anxious faces of family members eager to get in a few last words with their male relatives. I saw Dot, Elena, and Maria in the distance.

"Anthony," I yelled in their direction.

They nodded wearily. Maria was tapping her hand against her heart, and I understood that to mean her to be communicating her love. There were also less-friendly members of the public, yelling and spitting at us. Some even dared to throw stones gathered from the sidings, without being stopped by any of our guards.

The three-day journey by train to Tatura Internment Camp was punishing. We were packed tightly into old rail carts which bumped and rattled day and night, all the way to Melbourne and then 112 miles north to Tatura Township and finally marched the short distance to the camp. Along the way, more and more intended internees were picked up: Italians and Germans and the occasional Japanese. Whenever the train stopped for any length of time, there was a repeat of the scenes we experienced at Keswick. Only once, were we fed. Plain bread, an apple and some black tea. Rudimentary latrines were available at the ends of each cabin so that we could relieve ourselves.

When we finally stepped down outside the Tatura perimeter fence, late in the afternoon, I was confronted with equidistantly arranged, long rectangular wood and corrugated iron huts, as far as the eye could see, with enormous watch towers positioned at the corners of the two compounds facing each other. The whole area was surrounded by double rows of barbed wire fencing. It looked like the drawings of ancient Roman military instalments from my schoolbooks.

The Italians were directed to one side of the double compound, the Germans and the Japanese shuffled off to the other side. I was assigned to the eighth hut from the entrance, along with twenty-seven others. We were sorted into alphabetical order, and I saw a few familiar Adelaide faces in my hut, but not people I knew well.

First, we were assigned a wooden bed with a thin hessian sack stuffed with straw to serve as a mattress. The legs of the bed were quite low to the ground, with only just enough room to store a small suitcase underneath. It was separated from the next bed by a canvas curtain, which could be drawn the length of the bed to give the illusion of privacy from our neighbours. The place smelt of disinfectant and certainly had a hospital sense of order any matron would have proudly claimed. We were commanded to deposit our belongings at our specified bed number and immediately line-up outside again.

The air was cool, much colder than I had expected it to be, and many of us were noticeably shivering as we waited outside our hut for the next order. We were taken to a large mess hall where, a small group at a time, assisted by a guard, we were allowed to sort through a pile of dark red, dyed woollen coats, which I later learned were army cast offs from the last war. Most of us put these coat on immediately, grateful for the warmth. Our guards also handed out thick socks, in the same colour, which were equally appreciated.

Next, we were taken to another mess with a servery at one end and tables covering the rest of the area. Guards explained that we were to line up on the left of the middle corridor and when we reached the servery, we were to collect a tray, plate, cup, and utensils, then we would file past the servery windows where six of us at a time would be served the meal of the day. Tonight's meal was a single small scoop of mashed potatoes, a tablespoon of tinned green peas and about half a cup of what we were told was a lamb stew, which had more turnips than lamb, accompanied by a slice of bread, all to be washed down by a mug of pale tea. I was desperate for a glass of water but didn't see any on offer and didn't want to draw attention to myself by asking a question.

When we were marched back to our huts in single file, some of us were assigned a task for the following day and told that we would be collected by a guard and escorted to our chores at the appropriate time. A guard informed us that it would be lights out in an hour's time at 9.00 pm and reveille would sound at 6.00 am, after which we were to be lined up in three neat rows outside our huts by the end of the second bugle call at 7.20 am. Then, we would be escorted to breakfast which was available from 7.30 to 8.00 am.

"Do we need to be fully dressed for roll call and breakfast?" called out one young brave internee.

"Not for roll call," was the short, curt answer given in reply.

Subdued, we retired to our hut. In murmurs, we introduced ourselves to our immediate neighbours. Some grouped themselves on one bed and began talking, always in quiet whispers. I didn't have the energy to socialise. With a thumping headache, I made my bed up with the sheets and blanket supplied. I politely asked my neighbours on either side if I could draw the curtains, changed into a set of pyjamas and climbed in. There were no pillows, so I neatly folded the clothes I was wearing and stuffed them under my head and draped the coat over the blanket. I desperately wanted to drown out the noise of the hut and just go to sleep, but the isolation made the noises more acute and menacing. Finally, around an hour after lights out, the talkers had worn themselves out and the hut became still, except for the rhythmic noise of the snorers, to which I involuntarily contributed, I was sure.

The following morning, after reveille, those on kitchen duty were given fifteen minutes to get ready before they were escorted to their first tasks. The rest of us were told that the bathrooms and latrines were available till 9.00 am after which, those on bathroom duties, would be collected. We were to ensure that our mattresses were rolled to the foot end of the bed, our bedding was to be neatly folded and placed alongside the mattress, our personal effects neatly arranged in our luggage which was also to be placed on top of the bed. Two people were picked out from the line-up and put in charge of sweeping and washing the floors. All of us, including those who had been assigned cooking or cleaning tasks, were to be back in front of our huts in our neat three rows by 9.30 am for inspection. Many of the men grumbled, it was easy to see those of us who had experienced military service before, as we simply got on with what we had to do, without questioning the value of the exercise. Most of us were over thirty years of age but it was actually quite hilarious to watch some of the men struggle to fold a sheet or blanket. I observed, laughing internally, but did not dare comment out loud. I had immediately understood that if I was to get out of this situation, I would need to keep my head down. I would wait and see how the next few days panned out in the hope I could apply for an appeal to my sentence relatively soon. I knew instinctively that I had to make sure I passed as an ordinary, non-consequential internee if I was to shake off the No. 1 Fascist tag with which I had been triumphantly branded by the Adelaide Police.

At 9.30 am, the Camp Commander, a retired Major from the Great War, arrived with his officers who inspected our huts. The Commander explained how our daily lives would be regulated, what we were allowed and not allowed to do, especially regarding movement around the compound, our responsibilities towards maintenance of the facilities and our rights according to the Geneva Convention. The most important thing I heard in a long lecture while we were forced to stand outdoors in the chilly July wind, was that we would be allowed to write to our loved ones twice a week and receive unlimited letters and small packages. However, we were warned that all mail would be censored, and anything not written in English would be confiscated. He told us that over the next few days, we would be gathered to elect a camp leader, a deputy and quartermaster who would be responsible for the distribution of provisions. These men would be elected for a four-week term. We would also need to elect a supervisor for the maintenance of each hut, as well as a works supervisor and kitchen supervisor, roles which would also be rotated. I did my best to remain anonymous, not volunteering and shaking my head "no" when others nominated me for a role. Some of the men who knew me asked me why I was being so quiet.

"I'm tired," was all I gave in reply.

We were advised that for our own safety, any monies which we carried upon ourselves should be deposited in the camp bank, and we could draw on our own money, or money we earnt by voluntarily participating in the camp production teams, to spend on personal items at the canteen like cigarettes, matches, extra razors, soap, writing paper, pencils and stamps and even a selection of tinned foods and fresh fruits when available. I had taken the precaution of sliding ten One Pound notes in a hidden space in the heels of each of my shoes. I only had one pair of shoes, which I wore all the time, and at night, tucked around my waist with the laces tied together. I wasn't sure what to do, I would wait and see what the others did.

I had no chores allocated to me that day, so I went for a wander around the camp. I met up with several others from Adelaide and we explored our confines together, talking in frenetic whispers, trying to make sense of our new reality. We found the workshops where all manner of production was taking place, most of it destined for use by the Australian military authorities. With the few friends I was walking with, we argued over the dilemma of assisting the Australian Government in its war effort, especially since all four of us, Naturalised British Subjects of twenty or more years, decent citizens who had significantly contributed to the economic development of our state, had not been deemed Australian enough to avoid internment.

Over the next few days, we received our allocation of paper and pencils, donated by the Red Cross. I learnt that many other religious and secular support groups also sent spare clothes, books, and materials to help us in our confinement. We were only allowed to send two letters a week. I decided to write to my sister Maria first, as I knew she would be better able to spread the news within the family. I assured her I was physically and mentally fine. I explained where I was and my situation, in the broadest of terms, so as not to attract censorship. I asked for news about Anthony, the rest of the family, Tino and my factory. My letter was only half a page, but I hoped it was enough to reassure them. I had no idea how long it would take to get a reply. I also sent a warmer letter of encouragement to my son, reminding him of my love and encouraging him to seek the help of Maria, Elena, and Dot before making any rash decisions. I offered to write letters for the men who might not have the skills to write to their own families, a gesture which was appreciated by many.

After two weeks of detention, now the end of July, I had not one, but three replies and a package to be collected from the little building near the entrance which served as a rudimentary post office. I had just returned from my shift on lunch-time kitchen duties where I had peeled, boiled and mashed potatoes. There was no butter, margarine, cream, or milk to add any flavour to them.

"Aren't we in the middle of dairy country here?" I asked one of the guards, who was a local.

He was an older chap, probably around ten years older than me, he just shrugged. I didn't know if the shrug was because he didn't know, didn't want to tell me, or that he was simply hard of hearing. I didn't want to repeat myself, so just mixed in a little warm cooking water and salt, as I had been instructed.

My hut supervisor greeted me with my three letters. He was one of the fellows from Glanville and had attended many Fascio events. I shook his hand and asked, "and you, anything for you?"

He pulled a wad out of his jacket pocket where I saw a neat page of handwriting and a child's drawing on the back. I placed my hand on his shoulder, "how are they?"

"They're fine, but the landlord kicked them out. They've moved in with my parents and my older brother's wife. It's a bit crowded, with eight of them in a two-bedroom house, but Loretta's found some laundry work, so hopefully they won't go hungry."

"I'm glad for you, Patrizio" I said, as I tapped his shoulder a few times and then drew the curtains around my bed, to read my letters in peace.

He lingered at the foot of my bed:

"My older brother's been working at the Mica mine in Alice Springs with Giglio's mob. Don't know if they'll round him up too, but it's hard to get news to him in normal circumstances. Do you think I should try to write to him, or would that just alert these bastards, and risk his detention too?"

"I'd wait and see for the moment; we don't know what we're dealing with here. Best not to alert the authorities of his whereabouts, I'd say."

Patrizio sighed as he wandered off, hands in pockets and back hunched.

I read Maria's letter first. As I knew she would, she had advised the rest of the family, provided me with a succinct summary of everyone's state of being and reassured me that Dot and Anthony were doing their best to keep the margarine factory in production. Tino had been questioned by the police, but then released. He was still at the factory, though he'd been informed that he should expect to hear from Manpower soon. She wished me well and asked if I could be sent any packages, and if so, to let her know what would be most practical to send.

The second letter I opened was from Dot. She confirmed what Maria had said about the factory and let me know that George Preston had immediately come sniffing around, as I had guessed he would. She wrote that she had used her most flowery Irish sentiments to warn him off, claiming she would report his actions to her boss, the head of the Samuel's Butchers Franchise. In the meantime, she had asked her boss to see if he could look into the allegations made against me but had not received any news. She too finished with a request to let her know if there was something she could send me.

Finally, I opened the letter from my son. It was short, but sweet. He assured me he was doing his best to fulfill his promise to me. He was also keeping an eye on his Nonna Elena. He was staying with Zia Maria, as he did not like to be at the factory site alone at night and hoped that was alright by me. He talked about the orders and how he was taking guidance from Tino, learning more about packaging and shipment. He ended with the hope that I was being treated well.

When I finally made it to the Camp's Post Office, I retrieved a package from Elena, with ground coffee beans and a copper *Napolitana* coffee brewing pot. It was quite battered, but I recognised it as the one she had given me for my first factory. It brought tears to my eyes, soon to be replaced by a heart leap of joy when I saw she had also included a couple of packets of cigarettes and some matches as well as a dozen of her famous aniseed biscuits. As soon as I got back to my hut, I wrapped my treasure in my pyjamas and wrapped those in my blanket. I didn't want to risk losing my gifts to another hut mate or in one of the random searches made by the guards without warning, where precious things seemed to be confiscated for spurious reasons. I left the hut whistling with my mug, saying I was going off in search of some hot water.

I had been arrested on the 15th of June 1940, had spent a few days in custody at Adelaide Police headquarters, had been held at Keswick Barracks for around a week and then transferred to Tatura, arriving on the 28th of June. While at Tatura, my case had been reviewed by the Alien's Review Board and I had been recommended for internment. I was also informed that I could appeal this sentence and that I would be advised of the procedures by correspondence.

Instead of my mood improving as the weather improved, I became ever more anxious awaiting the arrival of this information. I made lists of reasons why I shouldn't be interned. I decided that my main argument should be that my extensive experience with machinery and motors would be found useful for the war effort, and therefore, I was wasted in internment. I would have to convince the panel that my involvement with the Fascio had been exclusively a social one. I listed names of people who could be approached to vouch for my activities with the Fascio. I contacted people that I had worked with on the Finance Committee of the church, Father Peter of my local parish, Sister Assumpta of the Largs Bay Orphanage, Mrs Carr of the Red Cross, even the principal of Anthony's school in the hope that they would vouch for my good character and philanthropy.

On the 18th of September, I was granted a transfer back to Keswick to prepare my defence and to await my scheduled appeal date, which took a whole three months. I had only three of the people I had contacted write submissions in my defence, and even those statements were vague. But the Military prosecutor presented statements from double that number of people, accusing me of harassing them to join the Fascio. Some of these names I had never heard of before. I was not appointed a defence lawyer but was given the opportunity to face the committee myself. I did my best to prove that these allegations were falsities elicited in revenge or fear.

The panel did not want to hear the real truth, that is that the local Police had some hidden motive for wanting to get rid of me and had made up, or deliberately misinterpreted most of the evidence against me. Two weeks later, I learned that the Board of Appeal had chosen to ignore my protestations. So, rather than be released by Christmas as I had hoped, I was being returned to internment, not even to Tatura, but to Hay, in country New South Wales, as the Tatura site had become too crowded.

While I had been in Adelaide, I had been allowed to have brief visits from my family, and to continue to send my two letter a week quota. By the time I had returned to Hay, my desperation was compounded by family news that included information that Harry had joined the RAAF as soon as he had turned eighteen, and that both my son and my brother-in-law had been summoned by the Allied Works Council into the Civilian Army Corps.

Arnold was sent to a cannery in Port Adelaide, while Anthony was going into Civilian Army training and was to be confined to barracks at Woodside for at least three months, which meant that he could no longer keep my factory going. Tino had also met the same fate, drafted into a boot factory. I wondered how much George Preston had been to blame for that.

Bart, much to his wife and his mother's distress had lost his job and was being sent as a technician to Navy Headquarters in Canberra. While he was in an industry deemed absolutely necessary for the war effort, as the Holden's Woodville plant were producing aviation engine parts, he learned that because of his association with me, his employers had been ordered to stand him down. I wrote Bart a letter expressing my sorrow at the turn of events, but I never received a reply. This was when the reality of my destiny finally hit me. I saw a long, lonely road ahead in isolation, my every movement to be regulated and monitored.

I fell into a deep depression, going through the motions, complying with my captors as needed, but spending the rest of my time on my bed, not talking, not thinking, not engaging. Just sleeping, locked in my dreams of the early years of my marriage with Luisa, the happiest times of my life.

Others did try to reach out to me, even the camp doctor came to visit me on the request of the camp Catholic priest. Nothing could rouse me. There was a deep well of infinite tiredness in my bones. My head was incapable of holding a thought. When I was required to do a task, I worked mechanically, not making eye contact with anyone, not talking to anyone. I couldn't even be bothered eating. I preferred the feeling of emptiness in my belly as I drifted away on my narrow wooden bed.

In early June 1941, a year after my arrest, I found I would be returning to South Australia, to a newly established internment camp called Loveday, outside Barmera on the Murray River. Annoyed at having to move again, I wanted to be left alone to expire away so that I could join my Luisa. I replayed all the major incidences in my life, examining them for their value at the time, and the consequences they had delivered. I especially re-examined my relationship with Sandro. I admitted, that in the light of what I knew now, I had been naïve to become so enthusiastically involved with the Fascio. Yet, I also recalled my joy, and my pride, when I remembered the young teen Anthony and his friends playing the violin and other instruments, with Luisa's accompaniment, and the young boys and girls of the choir lined up to sing. How my heart had swelled when we were received with grateful applause at all the events to which we were invited to perform.

I recalled all those faces of people who had congratulated me, yet who had failed to turn up in my defence. The bitterness at my treatment ate away at me. I couldn't understand, or forget, the way in which I had been betrayed.

My other constant thoughts revolved around the people I had failed, my own son Anthony in particular. I felt I had neglected him in his formative teen years, too busy with worrying about the business and mucking around being the big man about town with the events I thought were philanthropic. I had been emotionally absent, at a time when I should have shown interest in his intellectual and moral development. When I was fourteen, I had my Zio Carlo to guide me, to show me what was right and wrong, to talk to me about my future. I found it difficult to recall times when I had done that for Anthony. Certainly, I had provided for his physical needs, but I'd rarely spent time just chatting to him about his thoughts and dreams. Was I the only one to blame? Why was Anthony so disinterested in taking over the business? Had I displaced my own musical ambitions onto him, assuming that he wanted what Luisa and I had yearned for, and not given him a chance to form his own desires? It was all too late now, nothing would ever be the same again, I shuddered as I rolled over to my other side.

On the train to Loveday, I found myself sitting with some of the Adelaide men, the recently appointed new members of the Fascio committee. I did not know these men well on a personal level, most of them having been relatively new arrivals from Italy, despite Mussolini's ban on emigration. Most had come from small villages, families with numerous children and little means. They had been allowed to emigrate because their relatives in Adelaide had been able to guarantee them a job and accommodation and the fifty pound security they were required to have. Most of these young men had worked in construction or retail in and around the city.

I had a chance to ask them why they had joined the Fascio. The consensus seemed to be that they had grown up with Mussolini as Prime Minister. They had been involved in the Balilla classes as infants and the Giovani Fascisti movements as teenagers. At school, their teachers and even their textbooks held Mussolini up as saviour and supreme being. They were just continuing with what they knew, and it was a good way of staying connected with people their age. Of the six I was talking to, four of them readily admitted that they had hoped to meet a good Italian girl, from a good family through their involvement. I asked them how they felt now. One of them, Renato, simply uttered:

"Sooner or later, they'll round up all the Italians. The whole of Australia is screaming for our blood. An individual's politics won't matter, we'll all be locked up. Might as well get used to it and make the most of it."

Renato had been locked up as long as I had, as he too had been clearly identified amongst Vice-Consul Omero Spadafora's papers as an Adelaide Fascist Association Executive Committee member. Renato had come from a small village outside of Naples. His father and grandfather were cucumber farmers and he had been sponsored by his uncle to help tend his crops situated in Campbelltown. Since his internment, he proudly announced:

"I've been having English lessons, so that I can read the newspapers for myself and write my own letters."

Lorenzo, who'd attended one of my balls, at which he had met his fiancée, asked me why I had stopped running the choir and the Red Cross balls. I explained the circumstances of Luisa's death and my dislike of the new vice-consul's manner. I also told them what I had learned in my police interview regarding the vice-consul's furtive exit from the country. They were shocked at his disgraceful act of self-preservation. Renato confirmed that none of the committee were aware of the impending danger and had not even received a phone call from the vice-consul, or had the luxury I had been afforded, of Police visits, as a warning.

"*Sporco vigliacco*," muttered Lorenzo, the Italian condemnation for cowards. The others quickly formed the sign of the horns, with the index and pinkie pointing forward, and the other fingers closed into the palm. Unanimously pointing their hands to the floor, they made the sign reflexively, intending to keep the evil spirits of Spadafora's double-crossing from further maligning them.

I pondered on Renato's words. Maybe he was right, maybe we were all to be rounded up. I hadn't made any effort to read newspapers regarding Australia's involvement in the war, but they were available to us, and after my conversations with these young men, I decided to learn more about the attitude to Italians that would make the government liable to intern us all. I promised myself, once I reached this new camp, I would make more of an effort to keep up to date with what was going on.

Loveday

When the train finally stopped, we were marched to the Loveday Internment Camps, around four miles away. Loveday turned out to be a group of three camps in the middle of a vast, empty plain. We arrived in winter, after a week of rain, and the whole area was a mud bowl. From the front entrance, the usual tall watch towers guarded infinite rows of barbed wire, the Italians were allocated to Camp 9, an elongated diamond-shaped arrangement with over thirty corrugated iron huts, four mess halls and kitchens to service them, a small hospital and workshop, two latrine and ablutions areas and some other small buildings which became the canteen, the quartermaster's store, the camp leader's office and the post office. In the distance, I could see electricity poles and flat grassy areas, even a tennis court. My loss of appetite, and the child-like portions we were allocated, had served a useful purpose; I'd lost my distinctive paunch and was feeling lighter on my feet. Sandro's laughing face as we played tennis together in my back garden, flashed before me, though I doubt I had any flexibility in me left after sleeping on hard wooden planks every day for the last year.

The dormitories were similar to those at Tatura, with thirty men per hut. We were gathered in the open air again, to meet with the Commander, a Lieutenant - Colonel, a gentleman in his sixties, who spoke in an eloquent and comforting way, encouraging us to make the effort to co-exist harmoniously with each other and the men assigned to guard us, as well as welcoming us to make the spaces our own by decorating in and around our huts. He told us we would find the necessary equipment in the Hobby shed, and through our elected representatives, we could make requests for other materials.

We were reminded that under the terms of the Geneva Convention, we could not be forced to work, but those of us willing to relieve the boredom of long days could join in the agricultural production of the complex and would be paid one shilling per day for our efforts. Once again, we were called out in alphabetical order and numbered off to our assigned dormitory. It was the same arrangement of straw-filled sacks on narrow wooden benches, but there were also little one-drawer nightstands attached to the right-hand side of each bed, but no curtains between the beds. I found myself in a dormitory of mixed ages, with Italians from all over Australia.

As the days progressed, we soon learnt that our captors had not bothered to understand, that while we were all of Italian heritage, we all spoke our different dialects and our political leanings started with the distinctly indifferent, the fascist and anti-fascist, and even the confirmed communist. Mixing us all together in the dormitories did not make for easy sleeping.

However, we spent most of our time in the mess halls, where we naturally gravitated towards our fellow sympathisers. I wondered what had happened to my brother Nino and his barber friend Ferrari. There were many Queenslanders here in my compound, but no-one seemed to have heard of my brother Armando from Brisbane, as most of them seemed to be cane farmers from further north of the state. I hoped that meant that he had escaped this doom.

We had been urged to elect a camp leader and other functionaries to represent us. Again, I stayed away from taking up any position that might brand me as a leader. If I had any chance of getting out of here, I reasoned, I would have to remain as meek and mild and as anonymous as possible. My one consolation was that I had been reunited with some of my friends from Adelaide, in particular Fiorentino, Giacomo, Enrico and Tersiglio. All in our early fifties, we formed a little group, spending our free time in the mess, playing cards or reading newspapers and books that had been supplied.

I'd never been a reader for pleasure, but I developed a taste for the escapism it afforded, especially with Moby Dick. When the Apostolic Delegate visited, we also received some classic books in Italian and I had the chance to finally plough my way through the famous *I Promessi Sposi* (the Betrothed), by Manzoni, set in my home region of Lombardy in the 17th Century during the Spanish Occupation of Italy. I fumed at the injustices portrayed and cursed the circumstances that had befallen the mostly ignorant and powerless peasants, a situation which was still happening two centuries later, despite Italy's valiant fight for independence.

On days when the weather was reasonable, we walked around our compound, played *bocce* and watched the younger men play tennis or *calcio* or engage in boxing matches. An orchestra had been formed and instruments provided by the YMCA. Despite often sitting in on their rehearsals and their concerts, I couldn't bring myself to join. My music-making had been so much tied to Luisa, just the thought of playing without her opened too many painful wounds.

Fiorentino's tailoring skills were in constant demand, as men asked him to adjust clothes or sew names onto them. I sometimes joined him, resurrecting the basic skills I had learned aboard ship in my youth. I also resurrected some of my whittling skills, using the copious amounts of Mulga roots which had been dug up from the surrounding fields by some of the younger internees, eager to make the shilling a day offered for their labour. After a few practice ones, I was able to make decent plain recorders which the orchestra added to their repertoire. I had packed a photo of Luisa and I in our garden with Anthony as a young six-year-old and fearful of creasing it further, I fashioned myself a wooden frame for it.

Giacomo, who, like my brother had enjoyed going out hunting, had the experience to be able to fashion a little wood stove from a couple of discarded fruit tins, so that we could use my *Napoletana* to make coffee, which both Elena and Maria generously kept sending, along with tins of hard savoury biscuits they made, usually aniseed flavoured *taralli*, made without eggs or sugar. I shared these with my friends and my hut mates when I could or used them as payment when I lost at cards.

The guards allowed us to prepare the coffee, provided we did so outside and only during daylight hours. We received weekly coupons, which allowed us to purchase items from the store. I used mine to buy writing paper, soap, toilet paper, cigarettes and matches, however, there were often shortages, and despite not being worried about money, I did suffer from lack of tobacco.

I had not been a smoker while Luisa was alive, but after her demise, it was something I had picked up to pass the lonely evening hours and also keep me away from the lingering call for oblivion, which the temptations of alcohol provided. About once per month, a film was shown in one of the messes. The newsreels beforehand only spoke of the battles the Allies were involved in.

Much to our distress, by Easter 1942, our access to daily newspapers had vanished. Now, only selected clippings were posted up on a wall in one of the messes. Instead of being allowed to peruse the newspapers ourselves, a reader was elected, who read out the English and simultaneously translated each sentence into Italian. A retired law professor, he did a good job, but it was tedious, especially when men interrupted or heckled each other, so I often left to read my own choices from the makeshift library.

A visit by the Swiss Consul resulted in the distribution of Red Cross lettergrams, which we could write to our relatives in Italy. My friends and I debated the wisdom of this, wondering if it was wise to let Italian authorities, now overrun by the Germans, to single out our relatives as people with connections to the British Empire. We decided we would not send lettergrams, as none of us had wives or children there. However, we chose to allow the International Red Cross to take down our incarceration details, in case letters were able to get through to us from relatives in Italy.

In May 1942, rumours went around the camp that the Japanese had landed in Australia after intense bombings which had wiped out Sydney. Some of the die-hard Fascists in our midst did a celebratory lap of the compound but, given that there had been no corresponding flurry of activity by the guards, none of us believed the news, assuming it was rumours and just shook our heads at the naivety of the revellers.

It turned out that the false news had come from Camp 14A, where there were other Italians held, mostly from Queensland. That night, I sought out one of my hut mates, Sebastiano, a fellow I knew was from Brisbane and asked him if he ever communicated with anyone from camp 14A. He said he had a cousin there, and they occasionally exchanged letters. I asked him if he would mind asking after my brother Armando. For the favour, I gave him my government allocated half-ounce pouch of tobacco that I had kept in case I ran out of cigarettes.

It took several weeks, but I was overjoyed when I received a letter in my brother's hand. It had been more than six years since we had last communicated. His message was short and terse. He described how he had gone to the jetty in Brisbane to greet an Italian ship hoping to take advantage of the festive crowd to sell his ice cream and had been accused of making the Fascist salute, a complete fabrication.

He had been interned at Stanthorpe Camp in Queensland then transferred to Loveday since the 16th of June 1941, just four days after my own arrival in Loveday. I was astonished. I'd already written my two allocated letters, so I gave another hut mate some of my canteen coupons, in order to borrow his name and number to reply to Armando. I simply said I was sorry for any action I may have committed that brought distress to him, but that he was always my brother and I had great affection for him. I described that I was in camp with many Adelaide fellows that he would know too, and were it possible, would he be interested in joining us? I had no idea if this were possible, but I would do my best to make it work. His reply came through a letter received from Sebastiano's cousin. I was overjoyed, as he had replied he was keen to come across. In that brief reply, the grey cloud of oppression which seemed to have accompanied me since Luisa's passing, began to lift, and I felt the tiniest little ray of sunshine penetrate through the fog.

The next day, I went to see our Camp Leader, who had been elected as our representative. I didn't know him personally, but we all felt he was doing a good job of keeping everyone happy, and of negotiating small comforts for us from our captors, including a takeover of the kitchen by some Italian chefs amongst us, so that at last we had food with flavour, even if it was the same old cabbage and potatoes which we endured, knowing there would be some handmade pasta on Sundays.

Prince Bertoldo Del Prato was a man in his late fifties, who had been living in Sydney. He was apparently related to the Italian Royal Family and a committed Fascist, though he was very careful to treat everyone in camp equally, which meant we mostly all got along well and there had been few altercations amongst groups. Every request or favour in camp was done through friendship or barter. I chose to bring along an unopened packet of coffee grounds which turned out to be a good choice. We had a nice chat, exchanging our stories. He was surprised when I gave my name, and he said he remembered reading Luisa's substantial obituary in the Italian-Australian newspaper. When I explained my request, he said he regretted that it was unlikely to be fulfilled unless there were extenuating circumstances.

However, a few days later, he sought me out in the mess hall. In a few days' time, after lights out, I was to put on the performance of my life. In my bunk, I was to writhe around in agony and one of my friends would go to talk to the guards to tell them that I needed a doctor. The doctor, an Italian internee himself and one of our sympathisers, would have me admitted to the small hospital from where my request to have my brother transferred would be made on compassionate grounds. Apparently, the Army doctor allocated to the hospital would be on leave and it was the ideal time to make this request. I understood the dangerous nature of this deception, the theatrical part I would need to play, and that the doctor would expect some recompense for endangering his reputation, all of which I undertook to give.

Over the next few days, I ruminated on how I would be able to convince that guard that I was sick enough to be transferred to the hospital. I decided on Luisa as my inspiration, knowing that her mischievous sense of fun would surely have approved of my tactics. After light's out. I fumbled under my mattress for a dampened shirt I had hidden there. I changed quietly and began moaning and coughing. As previously arranged, after a few minutes of my theatrics, long enough to wake the people alongside me, Fiorentino crossed the hut to come to my side, pretending to wake me and then whispering as loudly as he could, letting anyone still awake hear that I was soaked through from perspiration and hot from fever. Then Giacomo would don his shoes and coat, come over to check me and then rush out to call for a guard to fetch the doctor. Meanwhile, I was to slowly intensify the moaning and coughing, until the doctor arrived, and I was safely stashed in a hospital bed.

A month later, I was declared safe from malaria, and I had Armando in the bunk next to me. He'd been doing it tough on his own. His wife, Agnes, was still in Brisbane, living quite precariously with her mother. She had found some work as a bar maid to keep them afloat, but there was little spare money she could send him.

Armando had always been a lean but muscular fellow. Now he was skinny rather than lean, and even his cheek muscles had drooped, out of condition with very little to smile about. He said he had volunteered to do some wood cutting, but he was not strong enough for that. He'd only hoped to earn a little extra money to keep himself supplied with cigarettes. However, he had noticed that there were a lot of tall grasses and he'd asked if he could collect them to fashion into thin rope which he braided together to make belts. There was another fellow in the compound who polished pieces of discarded tin cans to make belt buckles and they shared the profits, with even the guards prepared to barter for them.

Another hut mate, Angiolo, who had been a sailor for thirty years and had jumped ship in Fremantle, spent his time patiently building replica ships in bottles. He took orders from the internees and the guards, detailing each one with something symbolic to the purchaser. Enrico had asked Angiolo to include three interwoven hearts in his bottle, on which he asked to have the name of his wife, his little girl Teresina, and his own, so that he could have something special to send to them for Christmas.

I had no patience with the workshop, but I did continue to write letters for the internees who needed my help. They tried to pay me, but I rarely took anything, except a cigarette or a couple of matches if Armando or I were out of them. I was heartbroken for a man called Pippo, who'd been rounded up and interned only a week after his wife had arrived from Italy with their six-year-old daughter and ten-year-old son. They spoke no English and he hadn't heard from them, despite having written several letters to his former boarding address. He was terrified that they were homeless or had met an even worse fate.

I wrote immediately to Elena, giving her their last known address in Port Adelaide, hoping she might be able to find them through her connections. It took a few weeks, but Elena did not let me down. A group of about ten women and their children were all living on a celery farm at Lockleys with Mrs Rossi, whose husband had been interned. They were banding together, sharing their rations to make ends meet and working on the celery farm that the Rossi's had been contracting to work for the last ten years. Elena was able to give Pippo's wife Francesca, the news that her husband was safe and had tried to contact her. She encouraged Pippo to write again as Mrs Rossi would be able to read and translate the letter for his wife.

By the beginning of summer 1942, the area around Camp 9 was a flourishing garden. Thanks to the vision and the agricultural know-how of our Lieutenant-Colonel, the wasteland that greeted us when we first arrived was now a well-irrigated and extremely productive zone producing many fruits and vegetables that found their way to our kitchens as well as into seed banks to be sent around Australia, where agricultural production was desperately encouraged in order to alleviate the food shortages of the first years of the war. He had also had the foresight to plant pyrethrum to create insecticides, and opium poppies to create morphine for pain relief and anaesthesia for surgery.

The internees were allowed seedlings to produce their own vegetable and flower gardens in the spare spaces around our huts. This had the added advantage of minimising the mud after rains or the sandstorms we had experienced during our first Easter. One of my hut mates had managed to snare a little finch who'd come to investigate our garden plot and someone else had built a stick cage for it. The bird had been nicknamed Fortunato, for the good fortune he had of enduring his captivity with us.

Despite having Armando and my friends around me, the relentless and monotonous repetition of the days, which we had no option but to endure, played with our psyches, turning us all into despondent, nervous wrecks, quick to flare up in defence of the most minor insult or altercation. Our only change in routine was on Sundays, when the priest came early to say Mass and we had sports competitions, theatre, and musical recitals. One Sunday afternoon, just before Christmas 1943, Armando and I were called to the little office by the main compound gates. We looked at each other anxiously on our way there, unsure of what to expect. To our delight, we found Dot. She had tried to get permission for Maria to come too, but it had been denied, as she too, had been classed as an Enemy Alien and had restrictions placed on her travel. Dot had managed to get on a train to Barmera, then had been able to hire a bicycle from the local postmistress to come out to Camp 9. She had brought a package with her, and very astutely, had brought a homemade fruitcake for the guard, who had done his duty by searching our package for weapons, but had not touched the cool cotton shirts, straw hats, coffee, packaged biscuits, and candies that she had placed in a canvas bag. Out of sight of the guard, she had also passed us each a small roll of one pound notes, she'd tucked into a false bottom in her handbag.

I was desperate for news, but it was not good. Anthony had been very distressed and had started mouthing off, complaining that he was being discriminated against in the Army, as he felt he had worked hard to prove himself, but had been denied promotions, while other less worthy lads around him had all moved up the ranks. His hullabaloo had resulted in his being hauled in for an interview by the military police, which had frightened the living daylights out of him, as they had suggested he could be sent to an internment camp for his disloyal words. Apparently, he had naively said he would happily fight the Japanese and the Germans, but he could not fight the Italians.

No-one had received a letter from Anthony in six months and we'd been fretting he had been sent off-shore. While I was annoyed by his stupidity, I was relieved that this meant he was likely to remain in Australia, safe from danger. Even if he was bored to tears with the menial jobs he was required to do, at least he was free and able to enjoy the occasional days off, rather than being stuck behind barbed wire.

Dot regretted that she'd been obliged to allow George Preston to run the margarine manufacturing a couple of days a week. As she was not an owner, she had been unable to be allocated the manpower needed to keep up production. She had cleaned out my office and securely stowed all of my affairs and furniture into the now disused storage shed, as she did not want to risk my things being ransacked while no one was on the premises. She was the first to inform us about severe food shortages, food stamps and fuel rationing. Thankfully, Elena and her sisters and my sister Maria were still doing well, managing to eke out a living in their own respective ways, though not immune from racist attitudes, especially Maria who still had a pronounced Italian accent though she spoke impeccable English.

Dot herself was still working as a secretary at Samuel's Head Office but many of the other secretarial staff had either chosen to move or been forced to move to industries supporting the war effort, so found she was run off her feet. We asked her what news she had, of any of the Italians back in Adelaide or at war, but she said the newspapers reported little, except for the capture and internment of Italian Prisoners of War, some even being transferred here from British camps. However, she was able to confirm that the Japanese had managed to bomb Darwin back in February 1941, though none had landed ashore. The only invasion she could report on was the American GIs, some of whom had taken up residence at Elena's boarding house, relishing the homemade pasta and the tomato sauce they called gravy, reminiscent of the one made by their own Italian grannies back in the US. I smiled at the thought of Elena charming her way into a young man's heart through her cooking.

We were only allowed half an hour with Dot, so she hastily passed on messages from Armando's wife whom she'd been able to contact. Dot had sent Agnes several packages of her mother's old clothes, which Agnes had been able to sell quite profitably on the black market. That news cheered Armando up immensely.

We returned to our hut, with lighter steps after seeing a familiar face, deciding to keep our package untouched till Christmas Eve, where we could wear our new shirts and share our goodies with our friends.

They were eager to hear about any news of the outside world and were as gobsmacked as we were, to hear that Churchill had openly denied our Prime Minister military assistance, and we decided that John Curtin had done the right thing siding with America. When they heard about my mother-in-law feeding the GIs of Italian descent, they were quite surprised and wondered if the fathers and grandfathers of these boys were locked up like we were? I hadn't thought to ask that question, though I'd heard that there were some men locked up with us, despite having sons who had volunteered for the Australian Armed Forces and who had shipped out, before their male relatives had been rounded up. I wondered how they were feeling.

I set out to write to Anthony immediately, just reminding him that the only thing I needed from him was that he remain safe. The letter I received in reply was full of rancour about our loss of the factory, his endurance of racist jabs, the lack of respect shown for his efforts. It frightened me.

"Bah!" I shouted, throwing down the letter on Armando's lap. "Still unable to see the world except through his own selfish eyes! He's going to get himself into so much trouble if he thinks the military authorities care one iota about his idiotic attitude."

As I had predicted, and secretly relished, Anthony had been transferred to an Army Staging Camp in Terowie, outside of Peterborough in South Australia, which according to some of my more geographically knowledgeable inmates, was a major rail distribution hub. In my mind, he was tucked out of the way and hopefully, out of danger.

In the last year, Armando, sick of just sitting around, had volunteered to go out to the field camps, helping with the grape and fruit harvests in summer, bringing in the wheat and barley in autumn, planting in the spring. He quickly regained his muscular strength and was much cheerier. Physical activity wasn't what I needed. I decided I would volunteer with the English classes which were held in the afternoons and evenings, helping with basic reading and conversations, reciting and correcting dictations. This way, other more competent teachers could focus on grammar classes for the more advanced. I enjoyed flicking through the simpler books, looking for 100-word passages I could transcribe into my own exercise book for dictations. I was taken-aback at how my work was appreciated by my fellow inmates, who often asked me to recount my story. After three years in captivity, I was better able to control my emotions, and finally able to look back with pride at my achievements since leaving Italy over thirty years ago.

No end in sight

Out of the blue, in July 1943, we were informed that Mussolini was no longer Prime Minister and that the new Badoglio Government had withdrawn from the war and allowed the Allies to land in Sicily to repel the Germans. Most of us didn't believe the announcement, we asked our representative to ask for proof. We were granted the installation of a radio so that we could hear the news announcements for ourselves. Since we were no longer at war, we assumed that we were to be released and we celebrated our good fortune. A week later though, our hopes were dashed. Some of us were to be released, not to our homes, but to Manpower, the governing authority which controlled civilian production during the war. Of course, Australia was still at war with the Germans and Japanese. Quite a number of the Italian internees were released, but they had to go to work where the Government sent them, mainly in back breaking work in road construction or mining, so it was mostly the younger ones who were released. Armando and I, and my friends, all applied for release, but only Armando was accepted, probably due to the fact that he had volunteered to do extra work around the camp.

He left in late September and was sent to the Mile End Railway yards where he dealt with the large amount of freight being moved around the country. As he wasn't far out of the city, Maria was able to walk to see him some Sunday afternoons at the Army Barracks at Keswick. Severe fuel rationing meant there was no public transport anymore.

Every week, more and more Italians were released from Camp 9, until by Christmas, we were informed that the rest of us would be transferred to Camp 14D, around twelve miles away, but still in the same region. Giacomo and I were the only two left of our little Adelaide friendship group to see in New Year's Day 1944 together, but by July, our commanders had taken steps to be rid of us too. Giacomo, a city boy all his life, was being sent to a dairy farm in Myponga, while I was being sent to the Salt Works at Port Price on the Yorke Peninsula.

I was fifty-five years old, expected to engage in hard, manual labour in full sun. I took myself to the camp doctor, unfortunately, the Italian one who'd helped me bring Armando over to Camp 9, had gone. But this time, there was no need for artifice. I very simply explained my situation to the doctor and described my ailment to him, asking whether he thought I was physically fit to do the job to which I was being allocated, since the camp's own doctors had declared I had a ventral hernia, back in 1940, when I had first been interned. The doctor rifled through my papers to the bottom of my file to confirm that my attestation was correct. He then thumbed his way more carefully through my subsequent six-monthly medical reports and noted that the more recent reports did not mention anything about a hernia. He looked at me for a long moment, then asked me to disrobe so that he could check for himself. I knew that the bulge, which had been there since my early thirties, never really disappeared, and since I had lost considerable weight, it was actually more pronounced, so that he didn't even need to feel around for it. When I put my shirt back on, he asked me what kind of activities I had done in camp.

"I did all the camp management tasks asked of me in the kitchen and ablutions without a fuss," I started. "I also participated in giving the men English classes," I continued. "I wasn't able to volunteer for physical work outdoors, as I also suffer from heat stroke easily, but I did help my hut mates by watering the small garden plots around our hut."

"Did you ever play football or participate in the wrestling matches?"

I tried hard not to laugh, grateful this time that the good doctor thought we all had the intelligence of four-year-olds.

"Of course not, doctor, I'm in my fifties, those are sports for young men. I stuck to playing cards."

The next time I was called into the Commander's Office, it was simply to sign the papers for my transfer to Wolseley, near Bordertown, where I would be assisting a busy grocer.

Arriving at my new post, I was astounded to find it was the location of one of Australia's inland aircraft fuel depots, constructed to safeguard Australia's fuel assets in case of external attack or invasion. Not only was the grocer's a busy place with constant comings and goings, built to service the railway station on the Melbourne line, but the work proved physically light, interesting, and varied.

My supervisor, Jim, a Cornishman, was my age and, due to his short sightedness, had spent part of the Great War as an orderly in an American Field Hospital in France. We spent many a pleasant evening on the verandah of the grocery shop, regaling each other with stories from our respective wards. He had spent the intervening years working in his father's hardware store in Mosman, a Sydney suburb. He had been married but had also lost his wife, just as war had been declared.

"I was just grateful that my daughters were grown, and both married before we lost our Alice."

After hearing about my internment experiences, he showed great sympathy. We were two, lonely and broken men, stuck, not knowing how to move forward. All we could do was garner comfort from our shared misery, and hope that the war would end soon. He restored my faith in human nature.

On the 15th of August 1945, Jim and I, and a few other people who had come into the shop, stood quietly around the radio as Prime Minister, Ben Chiffley, officially announced the end of the war. We celebrated with the few sly beers Jim had squirreled away, and hearty cheers, all of us looking forward to finally going back to our own homes.

It turned out that I would be required to remain in Wolseley until well after the war in Europe and the Pacific was over, not allowed to return to Adelaide until May 1946. Even then, I had restrictions placed on me. It seems my initial report by the police in Adelaide followed me everywhere. My movements were to be heavily regulated; I was to report to the local constabulary once per week, and I was not allowed to meet up with my former Italian Fascist associates. And no end date was provided for this restriction.

Once censoring and restrictions to personal mail had been dropped, I spent most of my evenings either writing a letter or reading one. Arnold, Maria, and Lea had been able to remain living together throughout the war, and now Arnold had been released from his job at the cannery and had returned to working in the fish shop with Maria. Thirteen-year-old Lea was still in school, helping her mother in her free time. There had been no news of her half-brother Harry for a long time, except that he had been fighting in the Pacific, until September 1945, when they had received news to say that Harry had been shot down with his plane in New Guinea. Maria and Lea were shocked to see how rapidly Arnold aged at the news. He was barely able to speak, with no energy to move. He spent his days just staring vacantly at the photo of eighteen-year-old Harry in his RAAF uniform, so proud of himself, so young. Maria had thought to arrange a chair at the entrance to the family quarters, so he could see the comings and goings of the shop, but that had not had any effect on Arnold's listlessness, instead, he had frightened the customers.

I could not imagine my dear friend in such a state. I wrote to him, expressing my sorrow for the loss of his son, my own son's best friend for so many years, recalling how close we had all been. I begged him to write back to me, instead I received a letter from Lea, describing both Maria's distress and her father's failing health. Doctor Nilssen had told them to prepare for the worst, as he did not believe Arnold's heart would hold out much longer. I wrote to Manpower, attaching a letter from Dr. Nilssen, begging for some leave to visit, but was refused, as he was not a blood relative.

It was Dot who wrote to tell me of the simple funeral which had been held. I could only write to her in return, express my gratitude at her continued support and beg her to do what she could for Maria.

Once I'd left Loveday, I'd stopped receiving packages from Elena, and she had never been a consistent letter-writer, but in mid-August, I did receive one letter regarding Anthony's imminent dispatch by ship to Port Moresby. He had been given two days recreation leave in Adelaide and had come to stay with her. She said he was fit and well, had calmed down considerably, and seemed restored to the happy-go-lucky young man he had once been. He had been surprised by the latest transfer but was looking forward to it. It seems he was to join a contingent of Australians being sent to rebuild the port facilities after their bombing. I was so relieved to hear Elena's news of his improved attitude and hoped I would be released before he came home again.

Elena also informed me about her son Bart. It seems he had been trained as a Dental Technician and had very much enjoyed the work. After his training, he had been transferred to Melbourne, still working for the Navy, making dentures and other necessary fittings for recruits, who could not be shipped off with poor dental hygiene, as this posed a risk to their whole unit. Mary-Jane, freed from looking after her father after his passing, had applied to be transferred to be near her husband and had been granted permission to do so. She had been sharing a flat with some other girls, working in a munitions factory while Bart had been living on base, but now that war had ended, Bart had decided to stay on in Melbourne and had already been offered a job with a Dental prosthetics firm. Both Bart and Mary had been deeply shocked by the level of suspicion and harassment directed at them, in a community where they had once been seen as popular, leading members. This had been a significant contributor to their decision to remain in Victoria, making the choice to live as quietly and as anonymously as possible.

News of Zia Beatrice and her daughter Anna came via her own letter. Anna, now in her mid-twenties, had become engaged to a Stan Belmonte, a serviceman of Italian origin, but who had been born in Broken Hill, and had joined up with the Australian Army in 1939, as soon as war had broken out. Stan had found himself billeted to Zia Beatrice's boarding house when his unit had been recalled from North Africa to defend Australia after the fall of Singapore in early 1942. Quite soon after the war in the pacific had been declared won, Stan had made it safely back to Adelaide and had proposed immediately to the girl whose photo and rare letters had sustained him during his participation in the battles against the Japanese in the New Guinea jungle. Stan was one of three brothers, sons of a well-known construction pioneer in Broken Hill. He wanted Anna to come live with him. Her mother, now widowed herself, was contemplating a move to Broken Hill too.

Elena's youngest sister Violetta, still in Gawler, had survived the war reasonably comfortably. Born in Melbourne, with an English husband, she had been left alone by the authorities. She had seen her son Oscar go off to war, but he had returned safe to his wife Jennifer and baby son Bill. Her daughter Mary, in her early twenties, was also recently engaged and still living in Gawler. They had been sheltered for much of the war. With many of the German-origin local farmers interned, there was plenty of work for any able-bodied person in the Barossa districts, where the fertile lands had been devoted to food production of every sort and most of the clerical and retail work upheld by women. Violetta and Richard had turned their vast garden into a productive fruit and vegetable orchard, and to their chickens and goats, had added an annual pig to be raised for cured ham which had also enabled Violetta to keep sisters Elena and Beatrice, and my sister Maria well supplied, though petrol rationing, and restricted train movements, had sometimes made shipping the goods to Adelaide an interesting endeavour.

Violetta and Philip had also kindly looked after my own property, which had continued to be well-managed and produce good wheat and barley crops most years. She assured me that the profits had been set aside for Anthony upon his return. I was so relieved and grateful and wrote to thank her immediately, expressing how much her custodianship had meant to me and how much she had honoured Luisa's memory through her kindness. I also confessed that without the resourcefulness of the three Nicoletti sisters, I would never have been able to make a success of my businesses and would never have survived these last harsh and bewildering six years in captivity.

My sister Maria though, was not faring well. She had been so stoic during the war, carrying on the fish shop started by her husband, enduring many cruel comments, even by people she had known for many years. I was desolate that I could not be by her side in her hour of need. She had her sisters-in-law, the indomitable, but ageing Braithwaite sisters who continued to support her, and Dot, Elena and Beatrice always kept an eye out for her, with Dot even organising for one of the market traders she knew well to deliver fish and other goods directly to the shop, so that Maria didn't have to go out unnecessarily.

I wrote to Maria every day, just to remind her that she was always in my thoughts. I could do so little from so far away. I had again attempted to obtain permission to visit my sister, declaring she needed my help to sort out her affairs after the death of her husband, but again my requests were denied. I knew if Maria could hear from our brothers in Italy, that would bolster her spirits, so I wrote to my cousin Bobby in Melbourne to see if he could obtain news through any ships sailing to Europe carrying mail. Unlike the Italians in South Australia and Queensland, the Victorian Italians had been well protected by their Catholic Bishop who had vehemently opposed large-scale internment and had managed to keep ordinary Italians gainfully employed in their small businesses and farms. While I was happy for them, I railed against the indiscriminate injustice of the whole saga. Bobby had quit the ice cream business but had bought a bakery and supplied his stalls in the Victoria Markets with fresh, traditional loaves, every day. His brother Frank now owned a flourishing café in the city centre. They had been very fortunate.

Bobby's reply turned my world upside down. Not only had our families in Melbourne fared well during the war years, but they had been joined by my younger brother Nino, who had even married and settled down. Jim heard me scream in disbelief and saw me standing on the verandah violently shaking my head. He rushed out worried for me.

"Bad news?"

"Not at all, the bloody best news I've had in a long time. *Alleluia!*" I yelled as I broke out into a feeble dance.

Reconnecting

When he'd scuttled out of Adelaide back in 1928, Nino had made his way to Perth with the Filleri troupe, staying on in Fremantle, when the famous prize-fighter moved up the coast. Finding occasional work on the docks, he took up with the local Communist sympathisers, reconnecting with acquaintances from Milano.

The Fremantle Docks proved a very volatile area, with little work available to Italians and fierce altercations between Italians and Unionists. The local anti-fascists had shunned them, lumping all Italians in as one lot, to be feared and kept away from all but the most degrading work.

One night, a group of Nino's friends had infiltrated a cinema and had planted themselves in pairs in various locations around the room. When Mussolini appeared on screen, they had shouted insults and jeers, yelling out loud that he was a traitor and a murderer. Before management could be called, the newsreel had ended and they had sat down again, cheering enthusiastically for the next clip which showed King George and Queen Mary at the launch of a new ship, so that management could not find the perpetrators without disrupting the film. However, at the end of the show, when he and his friends were reunited on the street, they had been set upon by other Italians and in the scuffle, he had been stabbed several times and thrown to the footpath where he had cracked his head. The violent altercation had resulted in both he and another friend being transported to the hospital with severe wounds.

Nino did not remember much of what had happened as he'd sustained enough injuries to keep him in the hospital for over a month. When he was released, he'd discovered that his friends had left Fremantle under the threat of murder. Signora Camara, the woman who ran the boarding house in which he and his friends had been living, advised him that he had been lucky to have recovered and to have been separated from his idiotic friends.

"It's time for you to think seriously about your own life and to start fresh, away from your useless political games! You'll end up either deported, or dead," she'd admonished.

Despite the month in hospital, he was still suffering from violent headaches and couldn't support himself. He had thought about contacting me, but knew that our personalities were destined to clash, so thought he'd go back to Geelong, to Beppe. He negotiated a steamer passage to Geelong by working as a kitchen hand for the cook. He'd taken heed of Signora Camara's advice and kept his political opinions to himself and stayed away from the other crew. When he got to Geelong, the cook had been very pleased with his work and had suggested Nino stay on. Tired and miserable still, Nino had enjoyed the quite calm of the older man, and the methodical and relatively straightforward work of the kitchen, so decided to take up the opportunity, without stopping to see Beppe, as he didn't want to be dissuaded from his decision.

He'd worked on the steamer for a good five years. By 1933, he was thirty years old and had quite some money saved. He felt it was time he returned to some semblance of civilisation. One day, on a return trip from Brisbane, Nino, with his usual easy charm, engaged in some chat with a young man called Cristofero and his father, Gregorio Martino, a journalist, and owner of an Italian newspaper in Melbourne. The gentlemen were attending a newspaper editors convention in Brisbane. They arranged to meet for drinks and Nino was charmed by the sophisticated duo who were eager to hear about Nino's teenage experiences in post-war Milano and the scuffle between left-and right-wing extremists in the economic and political chaos that had ensued.

By talking through his experiences, Nino had seen for himself how his own political opinion had been formed by his peers and by the circumstances in which he'd lived, and how fifteen years later, those ideals barely mattered to him anymore, and certainly seemed out of place in Australia. The fight had gone out of him. He was just looking for a calm, secure life. He'd only known father and son for a week, but they'd made a strong impression on him. He'd admired their elegance and poise and their cultivated minds. He'd looked down at his rough, worn hands, his grubby apron and the smell of onion that wafted permanently around him. He was tired of being a peasant he decided. He stayed till the end of the summer, and then told the captain he was heading to Melbourne. During his time onboard, he'd had the opportunity to improve his English and was determined now to improve himself, in his presentation and his mannerisms.

Once in Melbourne, dressed in a new navy pin-striped suit and two-tone brogues, he approached several Italian restaurants, eventually stumbling across our cousin Frank, who now owned his own restaurant establishment in the basement one of the city's leading hotels. In his interview, when the topic of their Italian origins surfaced and Ossolaro was mentioned, Frank realised that Nino was the son of his father's cousin, and mine and Beppe's brother. That was how Nino fell back into the family fold.

He'd been astute enough to understand that Frank had cultivated some interesting associates, including selected members of the police, but Nino stayed clear, concentrating on his work, and paying careful attention to the mannerisms and speech of the more elite clientele. After a year, he'd managed to secure a job in the hotel proper, as part of the front of house team, where thanks to Cousin Frank's useful contacts, he'd worked his way up to the position of concierge.

It was through his acquaintance with Frank's brother Bobby, that Nino had found his niche. Not only had he been introduced to the Italian Club in Melbourne, but he had carved himself out a role as the gracious and amusing compere for the monthly balls and entertainment evenings. He'd even managed to find some friends to put together some comedy skits he had written, which had been well-received.

By 1938, when war seemed imminent, Nino had taken Bobby's advice and had paid the eight pounds needed to become a Naturalised British Subject. He'd also met Josephine, the recently widowed wife of Bobby's maternal cousin Peter. Josephine had grown up in Carlton, her parents establishing themselves as pastry chefs. Peter and Josephine had married in 1935 and two years later, had been blessed with a daughter, Grace, a pretty dark-haired, porcelain-skinned doll with the deep brown eyes and the heart-shaped face of her mother. By the time her daughter was two, Josephine had lost her husband to a particularly virulent bout of pneumonia. Having grown up in the pastry shop, Josephine decided to return there and run it for her aging parents, in order to support herself and her daughter. She had always been close to Bobby's wife Carla, as they had been at school together as girls.

After having been widowed for nearly three years, Carla had insisted Josephine join the family table at the Italian club one Saturday evening.

Nino had been immediately smitten, though Josephine had still been quite wary of male attention. Nino had bided his time, and after befriending Josephine and showing her the utmost deference for more than a year, he had finally taken Carla's advice and proposed marriage, so becoming husband and father to two women who adored him.

I was overjoyed to hear Nino's news, though saddened he had not been in touch with us sooner, especially for Maria's sake, who'd been a second mother to him most of his young life.

Towards the end of 1946, administration of the Wolseley facility was being transferred to the Air Force and Jim and I were granted permission to return to our respective home cities. Anthony and I were finally reunited. He was a grown man now, taller, and broader shouldered than me, the physical work he had been performing had shaped him into a handsome twenty-five-year-old. We both ended up in Elena's boarding house, where my mother-in-law continued to dote on Anthony's every whim, as if he were still a child.

It was time to see for myself what had happened to my business. Despite Dot's careful surveillance, the margarine equipment had been stolen from the factory premises. I could immediately see that it had not been ripped out by vandals but had been neatly dismantled. There was no need to wonder who the culprit had been. Before paying a visit to George Preston, I decided to visit the bank, where I learned that as I had failed to keep up my payments for the factory site, the bank had foreclosed on the mortgage I had taken out in order to recover my business. My property was now owned by the bank, who were planning to sell it to recover my debts now that the war was over, and there were returning servicemen eager for new opportunities. My other main source of income, Cremona House, which I had had the foresight to transfer to Anthony's name after Luisa's death, was still earning money. Blessed Dot had continued collecting the rent and had squirrelled it away into an account under her name, safe from the prying eyes of the bank. She had proudly handed over the bank book, explaining all the entries and the few exits, which she had used to sustain me, Armando and his wife, and my sister Maria. I folded her into my arms, weeping openly, in gratitude for this amazing woman who had been a true friend through this protracted and overwhelming ordeal.

Together, we went to see a lawyer who investigated George Preston's activities to find he had indeed stolen the equipment of the Southern Margarine Company and removed them to a building in his name in Sturt Street. According to the company's tax schedules of the last six years, he had continued to make a sizeable profit thanks to consistent orders from the military.

My name though, had been conveniently removed from the title of ownership, with a person unknown to me, called Frederic Crafter, having fraudulently been sold my fifty-percent shares. The lawyer suggested we sue for theft. Dot was fired up at the news and suggested I go to the police. I wasn't going anywhere near a police station ever again.

I decided to hold on, waiting to see how the bank's sale of the factory panned out and to see what moves George Preston would make once he heard about my release. The news of George Preston's success at my expense ate away at me, and in the first few months after my return, I found it difficult to re-immerse myself into a regular life, spending my time holed up in Elena's kitchen. Once Maria returned from a brief visit to Melbourne, she slowly coaxed me into taking regular walks and eventually re-connecting with family and the few friends who weren't worried about being associated with me, as I was still being monitored by the police.

I spent a lot of time wondering what to do with myself. If I were honest, I decided, I should admit that my work at the grocer's in Wolseley had actually been quite enjoyable. Not having ultimate responsibility for anything, just enjoying the small interactions and the regular routine, had actually been quite pleasant. I had to question whether I even wanted to go into business again.

Anthony, transformed into a self-confident young man, had quickly found work as a barman at our old neighbours at the Green Dragon Hotel where he'd been engaged as bar manager. He enjoyed the sociability of the job, as well as having some responsibility, though not too much as to be stifling. By Christmas the following year, he'd even become engaged to Linda, a bubbly girl who worked at one of the department stores in town.

Eventually, at Dot's insistence, I had my lawyer send a letter for reparation to George Preston, who eager to keep his operation running and out of the courts, made me an offer of six thousand pounds. It was not an overly generous offer, but a substantial one which would at least allow me to recover financially. I decided to take it and settle some of it on Anthony, so he could put down a deposit on a house for himself and his new wife. The wedding, in May 1948, was a small intimate affair, as Linda's mother was a widow too.

My factory site had eventually been sold to the private school two doors down, who also made me an offer on Cremona House, so that they could expand their premises. When I had inspected Cremona House on my return, I had found an overgrown garden, and apartments in a desperate state. I didn't have enough funds to complete all the necessary repairs, especially to the bathrooms that had been hastily tacked on to the outside of the building by the previous owners. One of these bathrooms had even been boarded up, as there was so much water damage to the floor, it threatened to topple into the garden below any day.

I had a last look around, particularly in our bedroom on the top floor where Luisa had expired her last breath, and I spent some time in the ballroom downstairs, where we'd had so many glamorous parties and fun Fascio gatherings. Those days were definitely over; crowds made me nervous.

Just when I was feeling like I could begin to breathe again, more devastating news arrived. We had finally received word from Federico, who let us know that Beppe had died in 1945, just before the end of the war. He had died in a hospital in Cremona, suffering from stomach cancer. Federico had included a letter from Beppe's lawyers, who had instructions on how his estate was to be distributed. Beppe had left Maria his apartment building in Cremona. For Federico, our youngest brother, Nicola, Armando, Nino and myself, he had left equal amounts of money in American investment bonds, which he had purchased ten years before the beginning of the war. The only stipulation in his will was that we had to return to Cremona within ten years of his death in order to receive our allocation. I did laugh at that fool of my brother and his romantic notions. I wondered if he had hoped to have us all re-united around his gravestone. We weren't told how much the bonds were worth, and I grimly suggested to Maria that I wouldn't put it past him and his warped sense of humour, to have us go to Italy and find they were worth a token dollar. However, Maria had stayed with Beppe when she had accompanied Anthony to Europe and told us his apartment building was in an excellent location and provided it had not been bombed or had fallen into disrepair during the war and Beppe's illness, it could be a considerable asset.

To my dismay, this substantial financial windfall led Maria to making the decision to return to Italy with her daughter Lea. She wrote to Rico, asking him to find her a small *pensione* in Milano. Rico had assured her that with their knowledge of English, they might find work with the Americans who were now swarming Europe with their massive rebuilding plan designed by General Marshall. I knew the depths of Maria's sadness, understood intimately the legacy of her loss of Arnold and her adopted son Harry, as well as the toll of the worry for me and Anthony during the war years. Influencing her decision most of all though, was the sting of the racism she and Lea had experienced. She felt she would never be able to trust anyone ever again.

"Lea and I both need a fresh start, somewhere we don't need to keep looking over our shoulder."

"But you've been in Australia over twenty-years, and with Italy bombed to smithereens, it won't be the same place you left." I implored her to reconsider.

"It will take some time to arrange our passage, but already Italian ships have started bringing out more Italian migrants, so I'll be able to find something on a returning ship hopefully. Nino is going to make enquiries for me. I think I'll have more chances if I leave from Melbourne."

I was left shattered. We were all living in Elena's boarding house as Zia Beatrice had finally sold hers and had moved to Broken Hill to be with her daughter Anna. Within a month, the bulldozers had already torn down the walls, ready for a more modern building to be erected. My previous life was very rapidly being dismantled.

Maria was right too. No sooner had the war ended, that the stream of European refugees had begun. Europe was vomiting them out as fast as it could, and from every nation people were desperate to start over.

Immigration Minister Arthur Calwell had made the emphatic call for Australia to populate or perish, and suddenly, the Australian population that had prided itself on its pure British roots, was now being urged to accept people from all over the world, regardless of race or creed. The power of propaganda! How stupid we all were to put our faith in these marionettes, ready to pivot whichever way they needed to, just to stay in power, hammering down anyone who didn't fit with their plans.

I was at the kitchen table the morning after Maria's announcement, having my morning coffee with Elena. I hadn't slept well and was only half dressed, in my trousers and singlet, no shirt and still barefoot, unable to gather any enthusiasm.

"At least you're still here Elena," I sighed as I stirred in some sugar.

"Not for long, Carlo."

I looked at her, puzzled. She was barely five feet in height, sixty-eight years old and still strong and determined. As well as running the boarding house during the war, she had also worked in the kitchens at the Grosvenor Hotel opposite the Adelaide Railway Station.

"Are you ill?" I stood up in alarm.

"Relax, I'm not ill. I'm just tired. I've worked non-stop since I was twelve, looking after my mother during her illness, and my father and my sisters after my mother died. Then looking after my own children and my grandson, and anyone else that crossed my path. It's time for me to retire."

"Are you going to sell up then? What are you thinking?"

"Yes, I'm going to sell up and I'm moving back to Melbourne."

"Melbourne? Why?"

"Bart's asked me to come to live with him and Mary-Jane. They've just bought a new house."

"But what about me," I couldn't help wailing. It felt like a bomb had exploded in the room and everything before me was swaying in and out of my field of sight.

"What you're going to do, you silly man, is marry that girl who has devoted the last ten years to looking after you. Then you're going to accompany your sister to Italy, make sure she's set up right, then you can come back here and enjoy your grandchildren."

"Marry? Grandchildren? Marry … Do you mean Dot," realisation dawning.

"Of course I mean Dot, and you'd better get that sorted before I move to Melbourne, because I'm not coming back once I've gone. And as for grandchildren, if I'm not mistaken, there's already one on the way." She finished her sentence with a wink and a hearty slap on my back.

It had the effect of finally waking me from my trance. When Maria came down for her morning coffee a few minutes later, I looked up at her sheepishly.

"Dot and I are coming to Italy with you," I blurted.

"Have you actually asked her yet," replied Maria, laughing at me, and winking at Elena.

"No!" I looked down at myself, in my dishevelled state. "I need a bath and I need to get ready."

The light wooden chair with its much-repaired straw seat fell back with a heavier thud than I had expected. I picked it up, gripped its top rung firmly, looking deeply into the eyes of Elena and Maria in turn. They were smiling back at me.

"*Ma … sul serio*, are you both sure? Should I really ask Dot to marry me? What if she says no?"

There wasn't the fluttering heart like when I'd met Luisa, but I knew in my core that I also had a love and respect for the woman who'd been so faithful to me, pulling me through the blackness of the last ten years.

"Anthony has his own life, Maria and Elena are leaving. I need to think of myself now, to forge a new path," I told myself. "I've started over many times before, I know I can do it again. I don't want to be a burden to Dot, hopefully, she'll see I still have a few good years in me yet."

It was a surer-footed, almost sprightly fifty-seven-year-old who wandered up the stairs and then came tripping down an hour later, hat firmly covering my still full head of hair, though grey at the temples. In my pocket was a ring box with a signet ring that Luisa had bought me for my fortieth birthday. It seemed appropriate that Luisa's last gift to me, unite us.

Renewed

"Delivery for Bo-Bodon-eye."

"Thanks lad, into the storeroom. This way please."

The second shipment of floor polishers we ordered from Italy has arrived and, thanks to Anthony's diligence, most of them are already spoken for. I'm minding the shop this morning while Dot's gone to have her hair set. We're attending Giacomo's daughter's wedding tomorrow and I'm looking forward to catching up with some of my old pals, all of whom eventually have moved on with their lives, despite the confiscation of property and the loss of liberties during our internment.

Anthony's out on his sales calls. His gift of the gab and his good looks are serving him well with his door-to-door demonstrations. His idea of offering lay-by terms is working well. He loves being out on the road, meeting new people. He would never have lasted in the factory but I'm very proud of the man he's become. Baby Christopher is doing well, looking so much like Anthony at that age, and we've just been told that there's another on the way – Linda will have her hands full.

I saw these floor polishers in a shop in Milano when Dot and I accompanied Maria and Lea back to Italy. We stayed long enough to see them settled and help Maria with the sale of Beppe's apartment building, so that she could buy her own place in Milano, close to our brothers Rico and Nicola. Her letter last week brought me added satisfaction, as she let me know Lea had secured a job in the Australian Consulate in Milano as an interpreter, to cater to the huge surge in demand for all the Italians hoping to emigrate here.

Most houses in Italy have tiled floors, so the polishers are popular there, and although I know Australians prefer carpet floor coverings, I have a hunch that things might change with the influx of new migrants from Europe and the corresponding upsurge in house construction now that the restrictions on building materials have eased. It helps that newspapers and magazines continue to advertise the new fad of wall-to-wall linoleum and waxed floors have become the latest trend.

There's been quite a bit of interest from the local housewives here in our little shop on the Jetty Road in Glenelg that Dot and I manage. I'm pleased that my eye for a business opportunity has not failed me yet. Maria is acting as our agent in Italy, and I'm sure that by the end of the month, I'll be wiring her for another shipment.

We had a lovely Christmas with Dot's brother and sister and their families, and Anthony, Linda and her mother Silvia, and Christopher, of course. Though, on these special days, I can't help remembering my old life with Luisa. In the evening, we had a phone call from Elena, and I did get to speak to Bart too, which made me very happy. We've managed to put the disappointment of the war years behind us and are back to being friends.

I called Armando and Agnes who chose to go back to Brisbane after the war. Armando has joined up with Agnes' brother, who took over the bicycle shop from their father. He does the repairs out the back. It's a modest life, but he's happy. I suggested I could lend him some money if he wanted to get his own business, but he said his heart wasn't in it. He was happy with the bonds Beppe had left him, which he has used to pay off his mortgage, so that they are living quite comfortably.

I called Nino in Melbourne too. He hasn't changed – still making wise cracks, but he's relishing his role as husband and step-father and being managing director of the Italian club. He wants Dot and I to come visit for Easter as he's organised a huge swing band extravaganza at the club. I think I'll take him up on his offer. It will give me a chance to check on Elena and Bart too.

Violetta and Phillip celebrated Christmas with their children and grandchildren in Gawler but came down to visit us the next day and we're planning to go there for New Year's lunch. I showed Phillip the six Ligurian olive tree saplings we brought back with us and asked him to look into what would be the best soil conditions for planting them out. I've been talking to them every day, making sure they thrive. I think that instead of importing rancid olive oil from Italy, we should start some plantations here. You know what I'm like, my mind always turning. Last year, on the ship on our way home from Italy, I met a couple of Sicilian brothers whose family have been olive oil producers for generations. We discussed the plans of the mechanised olive presses I had sketched in Cremona at length. I'm determined to build one here in Adelaide once I can source some good olives, apparently there are some mature trees in the Adelaide Hills behind the home of an old Italian family orchard.

Zia Beatrice is coming down from Broken Hill to spend the summer with her daughter and grandchildren in Semaphore. There's a whole contingent of Broken Hill Italians all coming down together, so yesterday, I went to air out Elena and Antonio's old house which a few families will use for the month they are here. Elena's last tenants left over a year ago and the place is in desperate need of repairs, but Stan, Anna's husband, has volunteered to sort everything out, since he's in the building trade.

Every morning, around 8.30 am, I stop at Gino's Fruit Shop on the corner. His daughter Amelia watches the front counter while we go out the back for an *espresso*, then I amble down to open up our shop. I close up again around midday and enjoy the short walk back to our home, in time for a simple lunch with Dot. Then she comes back with me to sort out our paperwork. If she's still there at closing time, around 5.00 pm, we'll take a detour along the seafront, and maybe stop for a drink at one of the hotels, before heading home.

Tino, my most trusted employee from my ice cream factory days has been surprised by the slow rhythm of my new life. He can't correlate the younger dynamic man, always rushing around, wanting to do and be everything to everyone, with this older one, happily sitting in the window of this one room little shop, watching the world go by. I always address his or others' concerns in the same way.

"It's in the silence that the most important things in your life are revealed to you, there's no need to rush about trying to find them."

Born in Belgium, of Italian parents, Laura migrated to Adelaide as a child. She pursued post-secondary studies in Italian, French, English and History, which she would go on to teach at various schools around Adelaide for forty years.

While preparing a unit of work for her Year Nine History students in 2014, to mark the Centenary of World War One, Laura came across an unusual photo in the Archives of the State Library of South Australia when searching for information about local War Memorials from the Great War.

The black and white photo was taken in front of the Semaphore Jetty where a temporary memorial had been erected and featured a well-heeled, large crowd celebrating Empire Day in May 1917. Among the thick crowd was a small horse-drawn covered ice cream truck with a distinctly Italian surname emblazoned on the canvas covering.

So began the search for the story behind this picture, the fruit of which is presented to you in this debut novel. This is a work of fiction, but faithfully and deliberately based, as much as possible, on the real history of the early Italian migrants to Adelaide and the history of the Italian diaspora of the late 19th century and early 20th century.

To protect the privacy of the families involved, the names have been changed, but the story is largely based on the variety of experiences of these early migrants whose numbers were few compared to the post-WWII emigrations, and therefore, whose stories are often overlooked.

Lest we forget, our early pioneers, from every nation they came.

Acknowledgements

To all those who know me personally, who've put up with my obsession with this story for almost ten years. Thanks for listening!

To my editor and beta readers, whose invaluable encouragement and critiques helped shaped my ideas and my writing.

To my parents, who fostered my love of reading and encouraged my sisters and I to always think outside of the box.

To Cav. Professor Desmond O'Connor, (Flinders University, College of Humanities, Arts and Social Sciences) whose seminal research and publications fuelled my curiosity for the story behind the facts.

To fellow Italo-Australian authors, Zoe Boccabella and Debbie Terranova; your publications gave me the confidence to believe there was an audience out there, somewhere.

To my sister Claudia Callisto *aka* "The good Italian Girl" – you've always been the trailblazer – I'm proud to follow in your footsteps!

Recommended Reading

FICTION

Boccabella, Zoe, 2022. *The Proxy Bride*. Sydney: HQ Fiction.

Terranova, Debbie, 2018. *Enemies within these shores*. St. Lucia, Queensland: Terranova Publications.

REFERENCE

Broomhill, Raymond Charles, 1978. *Unemployed Workers: A Social History of the Great Depression in Adelaide*. St. Lucia, Queensland: University of Queensland Press.

Cresciani, Gianfranco, 1980. *Fascism, Anti-Fascism, and Italians in Australia: 1922-1945*. Canberra, National University Press.

Cresciani, Gianfranco, 2003. *The Italians in Australia*. New York: Cambridge University Press.

Martinuzzi-O'Brian, Ilma (editor), 2013. *The Internment Diaries of Mario Sardi*. Alphington, Victoria: Lucerne Press.

Monteath, Peter, 2018. *Captured Lives: Australia's Wartime Internment Camps*. Canberra:NLA Publishing.

O'Connor, Desmond, 1996. *No need to be afraid: Italian Settlers in South Australia between 1839 and the Second World War*. Adelaide: Wakefield Press.

Paganoni, Antonio and O'Connor, Desmond, 1999. *Se la processione va bene: Reliogisità popolare italiana nel Sud Australia*. Roma: Centro Studi Emigrazione.

Press, Margaret, M. RSJ, 1991. *Colour and Shadow:South Australian Catholics 1906-1962*. Adelaide: Archdiosese of Adelaide.

Spizzica, Mia, (editor), 2018. *Hidden Lives: War, Internment and Australia's Italians*. Brisbane: Glasshouse Books.

For a behind the scenes look into the inspiration for this book and some of the stories that didn't make it into the final edit, connect with me on my website or my socials by going to:
https://linktr.ee/lauradimartino